TEMPT A LADY

Rayne felt her gown slip farther down her arms. "Mr. O'Malley, I do wish you would—"

"Make love to me," he finished for her.

Yes, yes, she wanted to say.

"Say it. Tell me that you want me," he whispered against her skin. "Tell me that you want me to love you, and that you won't regret it later."

She would never regret it no matter what her fate. Rayne laid her hand on his cheek. "You steal my breath," she told him.

"I'll steal your virtue unless you come to your senses and leave me."

"Will you steal my heart, too?"

"Are you offering it?"

TEMPT A LADY

SUSAN WELDON

AVON BOOKS ◆ NEW YORK

TEMPT A LADY is an original publication of Avon Books. This work has never before appeared in book form. This work is a novel. Any similarity to actual persons or events is purely coincidental.

AVON BOOKS
A division of
The Hearst Corporation
1350 Avenue of the Americas
New York, New York 10019

Copyright © 1994 by Susan Carey Weldon
Inside cover author photo by Jon Thomas
Published by arrangement with the author
Library of Congress Catalog Card Number: 94–94324
ISBN: 0–380–77738–X

First Avon Books Printing: October 1994

AVON TRADEMARK REG. U.S. PAT. OFF. AND IN OTHER COUNTRIES, MARCA REGISTRADA, HECHO EN U.S.A.

Printed in the U.S.A.

RA 10 9 8 7 6 5 4 3 2 1

To Helen Carey, who first told me I should write, and who listens patiently when I ramble on endlessly about my characters as if they're real people. I love you, Mom.

Acknowledgments

To my critique group, Terri Wilhelm, Carol Quinto, and Ruth Owen, true friends and wonderful writers.

Special thanks to my cousin, Carol Hanson of Reno, Nevada, who introduced me to Virginia City and acted as my researcher.

Deepest appreciation to Joyce Flaherty, Ellen Edwards, and Christine Zika for having faith in me and knowing my characters better than I did.

Especially, I want to thank my husband, Sam. Now, do you know where all that paper went?

Chapter 1

Nevada Territory, 1863

Johnny Harkins hurried into the C Street entrance of Virginia City's International Hotel. Passing through the dimly lit lobby, he slowed his pace to tip his slouch hat. "Evenin', Winn. O'Malley in his room?"

Behind a long counter, the hotel keeper peered over his spectacles. "He's got company. You hear me, Johnny? I wouldn't bother him if I was you."

Johnny disappeared around a corner and took the stairs two at a time to the third floor. He dashed to the door marked Two and pounded with his fist. "O'Malley! You gotta come quick." Pressing his ear against the wood, he gulped in harsh breaths. "You in there, Case?"

Seconds passed. He raised his fist to knock again, but the door burst open. Case O'Malley's large body filled the entrance.

Furious green eyes caught yellow sparks from the glow of gas lamps in the hall. "What the *hell* do you want?"

Seeing that O'Malley wore only half-buttoned gray striped trousers, Johnny swallowed hard and squeaked, "It's your partner."

1

"What's he done?"

Johnny snatched off his hat, stammering, "Jasper's givin' over his mining stock."

Suddenly a large hand hooked around the back of Johnny's neck and yanked him into the room. Johnny watched O'Malley stride to a table beneath the window and return with a bottle of whiskey and glasses. Licking his lips, Johnny rubbed his damp palms over his blue woolen shirt.

O'Malley poured two drinks. "Explain. And it had better be damn good."

Glancing past his disgruntled host, Johnny stared openmouthed at the double bed. There, a woman with bright red hair and blue eyes reclined seductively among the tangled sheets. She winked at him. The reason for O'Malley's anger registered. Johnny gulped down his drink and hopped back.

"Not so fast. You've already ruined my mood." Frowning, O'Malley raked his fingers through his tousled, black hair. "What has Jasper done now?"

"He's playin' cards over at the Virginia Saloon." Sneaking another glimpse of the woman, Johnny flashed a set of crooked, tobacco-stained teeth. "It's a high-stake game, Case. Jasper's losin' bad."

O'Malley emptied his glass and grabbed his shirt. "Jasper's wagering mine stock?"

"He's playin' with that new fella, Devereau, who got into town yesterday. I think Jasper might be gettin' fleeced." Offering a dismal excuse for a smile, he sidestepped and set his glass on a small table. "Sorry, Case. Figured you'd wanna know."

O'Malley stuffed his shirt into his pants. Hand-ing over a twenty-dollar gold piece, he said, "Thanks. See me when that runs out."

Johnny inched out the door, the gold piece hidden in his fisted hand. "You're an ace. You get there right quick, you can win back Jasper's stock. Everyone knows you're the best gambler in the Comstock."

O'Malley swore under his breath and closed the door. He collected his boots and sat on the edge of the bed to tug them on. A shameless grin slid over his mouth as he turned to his companion and burrowed his hand under the sheet to caress her shapely thigh. "Wait for me?"

"Honey, I'd wait all night . . . for you." The woman allowed her fingers to lazily drift over his shirt toward the front opening of his pants. "Hurry back."

Case heaved a heavy sigh and caught her wrist. Groaning in exasperation, he twisted around to accept a scorching kiss.

Three hours later in the Virginia Saloon, Case O'Malley sat with two men at a round table piled high with handsomely engraved stock certificates to the O'Malley-North Mine. Behind him, a woman in a green taffeta dress grazed her nails across his back. A crowd of spectators pressed close.

"Call or fold, O'Malley?"

Case popped an imported cigar into his mouth and struck a light on the table. Clamping the cigar between his teeth, he held the match and puffed. From inside a cloud of smoke he declared, "I'm calling, Devereau."

Case withdrew a brown leather pouch and

threw a bundle of stock down with the rest. Hearing his partner make a choking sound, he clapped Jasper between his shoulders. "Turn over my cards and see what a winning hand looks like."

Jasper North blanched. His hand shook as he flipped over the cards one by one. He grinned, then crowed, "Top four kings, Devereau. I told you you'd never beat O'Malley."

Under the table, Case kicked the older man's foot. "Pipe down."

Case nodded at the other player, an attractive man in a dark suit with ruffles at his throat and wrists, and watched his face grow hot and flustered as he revealed a losing hand of a full house. Case raked in his winnings. "Enjoyed the play, Devereau. If I ever catch you trying to fleece my partner—"

The boisterous establishment went abruptly silent.

Devereau's chair toppled back as he shot to his feet. "You calling me a cheat?"

The spectators promptly dispersed, retreating into a wide circle around the two men. The barkeeper plunked down a shotgun, the resounding thump a dire warning.

Case stacked his winnings into a neat pile. He blew a smoke ring and looked up. "Nope. You're awfully touchy, though."

Their gazes locked for a long, tense moment before Devereau turned and shoved his way through the anxious crowd. Gradually, the raucous activity in the saloon returned to normal. The piano player shook his head and hammered out a rousing tune.

The woman who continued to stand behind

Case leaned over and whispered in his ear. Her perfume hung heavy in the smoky, stale air.

Case rose and pocketed his profits. "I'm already engaged for the remainder of the evening, darlin'." Leisurely kissing her hand, he whispered, "Maybe another time. If you'll excuse me, I'll have a word with Jasper."

Jasper sidled close. "Not here."

"All right. Let's go in back."

They walked together into a stuffy, crate-filled supply room behind the saloon. Case lit a lamp.

"Thank God you came," Jasper said. "I was about to lose all my shares in the mine."

Case braced his shoulder against a wall. "I've told you time and again you shouldn't drink when you gamble."

"I'm just not as good a player as you. Hell, no one is." He shifted his weight from foot to foot, his eyes lowered. "You gonna keep all my shares?"

"If I give them back, you'll probably lose them again, or hand them out on the streets, like last time. I think they'll be safer with me, but nothing's changed. We're still partners."

"You mean it? You won't cut me out?"

"You found the gold. It's only fair."

"You're damn decent."

Case threw back his head and laughed. "Well, don't brag about it. I'd rather be known as a scoundrel."

"We wouldn't have a plug nickel without your know-how on how to tunnel and have them square riggings built."

Case squeezed Jasper's shoulders. "We have a deal, remember? You dig and I tell you how. But from now on, I'll guard your money too."

His head hung low, Jasper groaned. "I have another problem."

"The stock or the gold, they're both yours. Whenever you need either, ask."

"It's not that." When Jasper looked up, his craggy face reflected an inner torment. "My daughter's coming. You gotta help me."

Case stepped back, a dark eyebrow lifting. "I didn't know you had a daughter."

"I had a fine woman once and she gave me a darlin' little girl. Rayne's been in one of those ladies' finishing schools these past years." Jasper slicked his gray mustache with a finger.

Good God, Case thought. *A lady, coming here.* "When's she arriving?"

"She might be in Carson City now." In a lower voice, he added, "Think I made a mistake about the day she was supposed to get there, though."

Case's shoulders sagged as he released a weary sigh. "Why the devil is she in Carson City when Wells Fargo runs a dozen stages in and out of here every day?"

"I figured it'd be safer for her. Her telegram said a small detachment of soldiers joining the Territorial Cavalry Volunteers at Gold Hill were riding along most of the way, but I didn't want Rayne coming into Virginia City alone."

Drawing on his cigar, Case nodded.

Jasper grabbed Case's arm. "It's been five years since she's seen me. She's eighteen now." He glanced down at his soiled, brown frock coat and wrinkled trousers. "Will you go get her for me tomorrow and escort her here in style? I can't have her seeing me looking like this."

Case felt a moment's sympathy for his partner

but pulled free. "I have plans. She's *your* daughter. You go get her."

"Rayne's a real lady. I can't expect her to live in a walk-up over the livery. I have to find her a better place. She's real pretty, like her mother. She was a beautiful baby, all pink and sweet with big brown eyes."

"What kind of a father are you, asking me to escort your daughter? You know my reputation."

"I know you get along with the ladies real good, but you leave the decent girls alone. I know you wouldn't take advantage of my Rayne."

Case puffed hard on the nub of his cigar. From between his teeth, he said, "Damn right I leave decent girls alone. I'm not looking for a wife, or *any* woman. I have all the females I want. I go where I please, play cards or drink all night, and no one tells me I can't. I damn well like it that way."

"I wonder if Rayne has her mother's curves by now," mused Jasper in a low voice. "Mary was the loveliest angel. The first second I laid eyes on her, I had to have her. Lost my senses, that's for sure."

"What happened?"

"Got her with Rayne and her folks disowned her."

Case snapped his gaze back to Jasper.

"But I did the honorable thing and married her. I shouldn't have done it to an angel like her, but I couldn't help myself. I was head over heels for her."

A cynical grin played over Case's mouth. He had been wise to steer clear of innocent women, but his partner's confession bothered him. "I gather you left this woman and your child?"

Jasper studied the floor. "Mary was better off without me, Case. Her parents hated me from the first, always insulting me and making Mary feel bad. They knew I wasn't good enough for their girl. It turned out they were right. Chicago's a hard town for a nobody like me. I always figured to send for her and Rayne when I struck it rich, though."

"We've been together for three years, and the last year and a half we've made a pretty penny. You just now sent word of your good fortune?"

"I never had anything till we hooked up. It's been so long and ... Reckon I was ashamed of what I did. Mary probably hates me." He met Case's gaze. "Case, I have another problem."

Crushing his cigar under his boot, Case gritted his teeth. "Spit it out. I'm going back to my room in one second. I had to leave a satisfying diversion in order to rescue you this time."

"You know that magnificent house you've built and were gonna move into this week?"

Case squinted at the older man. "What about it?"

Jasper stole toward the door. "Seeing as it's finished now, and you still have the room at the hotel, I figured you'd let me—"

"I think I know where this is leading."

"Now, don't get riled. Rayne won't stay long once she sees how rowdy Virginia City is."

"Dammit, Jasper, you'll give me gray hair before I'm thirty."

"You *are* thirty. It won't inconvenience you much since you're all settled in the hotel already.

You'll just move in your house a little later." Jasper touched Case's arm. "You'll do it for me, won't you? I want her to be proud of her old man and think I'm respectable."

"You'd be rich if you didn't always throw your money away."

Case shoved his hands in his pockets. Telling himself he was a fool for not strangling his partner, he mumbled a string of clipped oaths. He remembered his refined, domineering mother and how she had made his poor father's life miserable until the day the house had burned down and taken them both. He'd seen firsthand the way a woman with proper notions could humble a man. His father had been proud of the improvements he'd made on their Missouri farm, but his mother had always nagged that he had not prospered enough, that they weren't accepted into the more elite social circles. That his father was not as good as other men. Case wouldn't wish a *lady* on his worst enemy.

"All right! I'll go get your daughter, and you can use my house while she's here."

"You won't be sorry. Just wait until you see what a woman's touch is gonna do."

Case shoved past Jasper and threw open the door. "I got everything I want or need. If she changes one thing in my house, *one* goddamn thing, you're both out. And don't tell everyone in town I'm holding your shares. Let them think I own them now. Maybe they won't be so tempted to clean you out again."

Jasper released a long, relieved sigh. Then, whistling merrily, he followed Case from the back room.

He waited until Case had departed the saloon before he headed for the elaborate mahogany bar.

"A round of drinks on Case O'Malley!"

The following morning Rayne North stood in the center of Carson City's main thoroughfare. A continuous train of freight wagons wended its way through the plaza, which boasted a lone liberty pole. The thunderous noise pounded her ears as powdery alkali dust rose in great clouds and coated everything in sight, including, to her annoyance, her. On the planked sidewalk in front of a row of closely built white frame stores, she cursed a man she'd never met.

After a long, grueling journey, she'd thought her father would want to personally welcome her to the Nevada Territory. She hadn't anticipated a grand welcome, but to be left waiting in a strange town rankled. She retrieved her father's telegram from her reticule and swiftly scanned it. She wasn't mistaken. Case O'Malley, her father's esteemed partner, was supposed to escort her the rest of the way to Virginia City.

Esteemed partner, indeed! The man hadn't even bothered to show up.

The noon stage to Virginia City had just left, stranding her. She was beginning to believe that her mother was right, that Jasper North's fervent reports of his redemption and newfound riches were probably more lies.

All of her life Rayne had excused her father's behavior because, despite his shortcomings, she loved him. But she should have listened to her mother, who'd spoken from experience: Never love a rogue unless you want to spend your life alone with a broken heart. Her father was rogue, and no doubt his partner was just like him. From the shocking stories she'd been told about Case O'Malley by the woman who kept the rooming house, he had even fewer morals than Jasper North.

According to Mrs. O'Flannigan, her father's associate spent an inordinate amount of time in saloons, swilling whiskey, gambling, and, worst of all, sharing his affections with women of questionable reputation. Rayne hoped O'Malley didn't show up after all. The thought of traveling alone with such a reckless man terrified her.

She must do something soon, or else wait for the next stage. She'd stayed the night in Carson City and stood in the sun for three hours as a courtesy to her father and his partner. Hot, tired, and dusty now, she felt uncommonly irritable and refused to wait any longer. If Case O'Malley did show up, she would not travel with him. She looked up and down the street one last time. Other than a tall, striking man clad in a black, long-tailed frock coat, she saw no one who wasn't engaged in some sort of bustling activity.

The man in black, who had just left the hotel directly across from her, stood out from the others in the street and left her curious. Noticing the brilliant pin on his lapel, his shiny stump-toed boots, and a stylish black hat tipped rakishly over his right eye, she wondered about his occupation. He appeared very self-confident. Stepping back, he flashed a smile and tipped his hat to a woman and the small girl she was holding by the hand. After the blushing females passed him, he scanned a knot of people standing to his right. Evidently he was looking for someone in particular.

An awful premonition took root in Rayne's mind. Good heavens, this handsome charmer could not possibly be Case O'Malley!

A sudden bump against her leg diverted Rayne's attention to a large dog at her side. His scruffy, dust-covered fur stuck out in all directions. Woeful, brown eyes sought hers as he lifted a paw and whined pitifully. Instinct warned her not to encourage the animal.

The whine repeated, lower, longer. Tilting his head to the side, the animal gave another heart-wrenching whimper. She dropped to one knee and patted the furry head. Instantly she regretted her deed. Not only did her glove come away soiled, it gave off an odor similar to something long dead. The dog sniffed her reticule, nearly toppling her over in his enthusiasm. Understanding brought Rayne to her feet.

Earlier, she had saved bacon left over from her breakfast in a napkin rolled up in her reticule. It wasn't her affection the dog craved, but the hidden food. She hugged her purse to her waist and looked away, but it was no use. She felt the animal's soulful eyes bore into her, heard his panting breath, and saw his pathetic form in her mind. Without looking down, she surrendered the bacon. A loud crunch told her he had devoured his treat in one bite. She dared not look at him again. She was in no position to adopt a stray, no matter how he tugged at her heart.

Another brush against her skirt changed her mind. If she kept him, at least she'd have one friend in this strange place, but she turned to find the dog a short distance away. Her fickle friend sat outside a restaurant, his tail wagging, his whining refrain gaining him yet another benefactor. Here was a true scoundrel. He'd stolen her heart and gone his merry way without so much as a by-your-leave.

She removed her soiled gloves and tucked them into her reticule. Once again, she gazed up and down the busy street. The striking man in the black frock coat appeared to be watching her. He touched the brim of his hat. Her heart fluttered. He looked so dashing, so handsome—so very respectable. She was certain he couldn't be her father's partner, whose face would surely show signs of his excesses.

The captivating man smiled at her, and a warm feeling settled in her stomach. Without thinking, she smiled back. Immediately he stepped from the sidewalk into the congested street, heading directly toward her. His response to her innocent gesture caused her heart to lurch. Merciful heavens! What had possessed her to behave in such a forward manner? He must have taken her action as some sort of invitation. Panic robbed her breath as she considered the conveyances clogging the thoroughfare.

She chose the first available person, a kind-looking driver unloading a freight wagon nearby, and hurried to his side. "Sir, would you be going on to Virginia City?"

The short, bald man scratched his gray whiskers. "That I am."

"I'll be most grateful if you'll take me with you." She twisted her fingers together, afraid to learn the whereabouts of the man in the black frock coat. "I'm in *dire* need of transportation."

"You don't wanna ride in this bumpy wagon, miss."

"Sir, my father's expecting me. Do you know Jasper North? He'll generously reward you for your trouble."

"Sure, I know Jasper. He's Case O'Malley's partner." He stopped and looked her over before he agreed. "Hop aboard. That your baggage over there on the walk?"

"Yes. Sir? . . ." Rayne hesitated, gathering enough courage to speak her mind. "A woman can't be too careful, so I hope you aren't offended if I ask you a question. Are you a respectable person, or will I have need of a weapon to defend my honor?"

The man's blue eyes twinkled with amusement as he withdrew a gun from under the front seat of his wagon. "You take this here pistol, ma'am. If I even look at you the wrong way, you just shoot me dead."

"Thank you, no. You've answered my question."

Case O'Malley strode confidently toward Harley Atkins's wagon. He didn't know why he'd agreed to collect Jasper's daughter, except that he must be the biggest fool in the Comstock for always coming to his partner's rescue. With so many people on the street, he hadn't been sure of her identity at first. When he'd finally spotted her from the description given to him by the hotel proprietor, the episode with the dog had held his interest. To his amazement, he had been pleasantly moved when she'd allowed herself to be victimized by the mangy beggar.

As Case navigated the busy street, he watched

her converse with Harley. Thin, with a prideful bearing, she wore the silliest hat he'd ever seen. Case grinned. An ostrich feather protruded from the side and jiggled with every movement of her head. Her gray dress looked matronly and not of the best quality, but as Jasper had guessed, she did have womanly curves.

While Harley loaded her baggage on the back of the freight wagon, Case approached her. He removed his hat and asked, "Miss North?"

She turned slowly, biting her bottom lip. "Yes."

Judging by her hesitant response, he had the distinct impression she dreaded meeting him. Hat in hand, he swept her a gallant bow. "Case O'Malley at your service. You needn't resort to crude transportation, Miss North. I'll see you safely into your father's waiting arms."

As he met her alarmed gaze, Case remembered Jasper's description. In the future he would never believe a word his partner said. Her eyes were not brown but a vivid hazel framed by generous, dark lashes. When she tilted her head, her eyes changed color in the sun. Seductive, mesmerizing, they intrigued him.

Capturing her hand, he gently turned it over and pressed his lips to her warm palm. He felt a tremble pass up her arm and smiled. Either the lady was as aware of him as he was of her, or he frightened her. "Considering Jasper's neglectful memory and tendency to omit facts, you probably aren't even aware that I'm your father's business partner."

After a brief hesitation, she pulled free. Her fingers curled as she pressed her hand against her stomach. "My father wrote me. I just . . . You aren't what . . ." She took a deep breath and added quickly, "Mr. O'Malley, I apologize for any inconvenience my father has put you through, but this kind gentleman has already agreed to provide me with transportation. I hope you don't mind."

"But I *do* mind. Your father has entrusted your welfare into *my* care."

Interesting, he thought. She wasn't beautiful, but she appealed to him. Her nose was narrow and fine, her cheekbones tapered, and her full lips tilted up at the corners. Her hair, parted down the middle and drawn severely into a knot behind her head, appeared ordinary—plain brown.

"You will be much more comfortable traveling with me, my dear."

"Oh, I rather doubt that, sir." Smoothing her gown, she met his gaze. "I've already given you my answer."

"Then you leave me no choice but to insist," he countered, his barbed tone conveying his impatience.

She retreated a step, inhaling sharply. Case sighed with exasperation. She was going to be a nuisance, after all. Although he found her reticence refreshing, he wasn't used to rejection, especially from women. Irritation needled him. Normally women fawned over him, sought his favors. If he wasn't mistaken, Jasper's daughter seemed determined not to travel with him.

He leaned close, saying in a low voice, "Rest assured, Miss North, I have no designs on your virtue."

Her eyes opened very wide, her lips parting. He

had meant to reassure her, but he'd shocked her instead. It was a perfect example of why a man couldn't be himself around a proper lady. At all times he had to mind his manners so that he did not offend a lady's delicate sensibilities. This lady was not only proper, but she also appeared too naive for her own good. Harley Atkins was a stranger to her, too, yet she readily trusted *him*. Harley was a decent sort, but Miss North had no way of knowing that.

She recovered quickly, to his surprise. Holding her head high, she spoke so low that he had to strain to hear her words.

"Mr. O'Malley, you leave *me* no choice but to speak bluntly. My father has his good points, but his judgment is, unfortunately, sometimes remiss. I prefer not to trust my welfare to a man of notorious fame." She inched closer to the freight wagon and held out her hand for the driver's assistance. "If you will be so kind, please give Mr. Atkins directions to my father's residence."

Anger surged through Case. Damn woman, dismissing him like a dog underfoot. What right had she to unfairly rebuff him? He was guilty of many things, but he'd never force his attentions on an ingenuous woman. He just might make an exception in her case.

Cramming his hat on his head, Case felt a muscle tick along his jaw. He'd come all the way to Carson City on Jasper's behalf, and he damn well wasn't about to return empty-handed!

"Atkins," he snapped. "The lady's baggage goes to the new house on B Street."

His mouth twisting into a wicked grin, Case swept Jasper's daughter off the wagon seat and, ignoring her squeals of outrage, strode off down the sidewalk with her in his arms.

An hour later, Rayne sat stiffly on the single, padded seat of the buggy where Case O'Malley had deposited her. She folded her hands in her lap and tried to concentrate on the distant snow-covered mountains surrounding them. If she must travel with a man of dubious reputation, she could at least enjoy the view. She found it bewitching. The absence of trees in this locale fascinated her. Sagebrush and greasewood painted the landscape gray.

She hadn't spoken to her father's partner since he'd so shockingly picked her up and carried her through the street to his waiting buggy. His occasional penetrating gazes unnerved her. His eyes, a most sinful shade of green, caused a quivery feeling to invade her stomach. She found the way he looked at her positively indecent, as if he saw right through her clothes.

No respectable man would have behaved in such a manner. She should have slapped him. When he'd held her in his arms, bewildering sensations had coursed through her body, leaving her breathless. Unable to utter a complaint at the time, she wished now that she'd somehow found the courage. He had smelled of tobacco and a fragrance reminiscent of a lush forest. He'd carried her effortlessly, his strong arms strangely comforting. The uncomfortable memory heated her cheeks. Any decent woman in her place would have slapped him. To her eternal shame, she hadn't wanted to.

He hadn't done or said anything untoward since

then, but the possibility remained that he might. The woman at the rooming house probably had no reason to lie about his defects of character. Rayne wished with all her heart she possessed the know-how to deal with a man of his scandalous reputation. Clearly he posed a danger to a virtuous woman, especially one with little experience of men in general.

It wasn't fair. He didn't look at all like he should, not depraved and displeasing. His black frock coat fitted his shoulders splendidly. Despite her abhorrence of his forward manner, she could not deny his handsomeness. She had to admit, his dark, wavy hair and those mischievous green eyes lent him a raffish charm. Such good looks were wasted on a man with little or no morals.

Grazing her thumb over her palm, she remembered her shock when he'd pressed his lips to her skin. Prickles of pleasure had skipped up her arm. The distressing sensation remained with her still, worrying her to distraction. She mustn't be normal to feel this way—particularly when the cause of her unease was a man who indulged in pleasures beyond her wildest imagination.

"Was your journey agreeable?" he asked.

Rayne remained silent, determined to ignore him and the wicked effect he had on her. Soon, though, she relented and replied carefully, "*That* part of my travel was agreeable enough, if somewhat bumpy."

Out of the corner of her eye, she saw him grin before he said, "I hope your stay in Carson City allowed your . . . you to mend."

Cautioning herself not to rub her bruised bottom, she focused her vision on a distant mountain. Even *he* would not be bold enough to refer to an unmentionable part of her anatomy, albeit indirectly. "Because I wasn't met, as my father's telegram stated," she remarked with slight inflection, "I stayed the night at a rooming house."

"Were the accommodations acceptable?"

"My lodging on the lower floor suited me adequately."

"You must not have had much privacy, though, if they are still using sheets of cotton domestic as room dividers."

Rayne gasped, then slapped a hand over her mouth. Case O'Malley was indeed a scoundrel to mention the *inadequate* room and remind her of how embarrassed she had been when the lit lamp silhouetted her figure against the flimsy dividers, for all the guests to see. Slowly lowering her hand, she arranged a fold in her skirt, then frowned when the end flopped over his leg. She snatched the material back, accidentally brushing her palm over his thigh. Seeing the slight tilt of his head, she felt her face burn. Good Lord, he probably thought she'd meant to touch him there.

Never in her life had a man made her feel so strange. Her stomach felt as if she'd swallowed a wagonload of feathers. She wished she had the courage, or daring, to ask him to deny the allegations made by the woman at the rooming house. For all *she* knew, the woman might have lied. If only that was true. If O'Malley turned out to be a person of good character, she would feel much more comfortable in his presence.

Cautiously she forced out the words. "I met a

Mrs. O'Flannigan at the rooming house. Do you know her?"

"You bet," he returned without hesitation. "Bridget has a wealth of knowledge about most everyone in the Comstock. She's also a very *close* friend of Governor Nye."

Since he appeared untroubled by her remark, Rayne continued, "She spoke of you, Mr. O'Malley."

The corners of his mouth lifted briefly as he calmly gazed ahead, his attention focused on handling the two horses.

"I hope this doesn't upset you. Normally I hesitate to reveal information given to me in confidence, but inasmuch as you're my father's partner, I feel I should tell you what this woman is saying about you."

Featherlike lines at the corners of his eyes deepened as he aimed an unprincipled grin at her. "I gather you are willing to make an exception in my case and pass on a delicate bit of gossip. To what do I owe this favor, Miss North?"

He stared at her intently, looking much too confident. She wondered how many women had lost their purity because of his stirring, green eyes. She didn't know why, but the thought disturbed her.

"You were about to recite Bridget's *glowing* accounting of my virtues."

Heat crawled up her neck. "I should never have mentioned the conversation."

His lips puckered, then aligned briefly. "I presume Bridget told you I'm a womanizer? Yes, I can tell by your pink cheeks that she did. Did she also mention that I indulge in other sinful pastimes as well?"

Rayne straightened. She swatted her hand on her skirt and it released a cloud of yellow dust. Praying her voice sounded unconcerned, she asked, "Are you admitting to Mrs. O'Flannigan's charges?"

"I enjoy diverse pleasures in life. I am, after all, unattached and accountable only to myself."

"You needn't apologize, Mr. O'Malley. I assure you, it is of little consequence to me."

"I see no need to apologize for a way of life that satisfies me, a way of life I have no intention of forgoing. I do, however, hope that you are no longer afraid of me."

"Afraid of you? If you are referring to my preference to travel with that kind Mr. Atkins, you are mistaken," Rayne lied smoothly. "After waiting for three hours, I was tired and anxious to reach my destination. When you first approached me, I had no idea who you were."

Stealing a glimpse of his striking profile, Rayne felt her limbs grow weak. O'Malley wore a devilish smile. The man upset her, churned her insides, and turned her mind to mush. She shouldn't have spoken to him at all. Seated this close to him, she felt the heat of his body, smelled the intoxicating scent of bay rum. He was entirely too masculine a man for a woman to retain her senses in his presence.

Drawing on the reins, he abruptly halted the buggy. A wheel on his side skidded into a rut, causing them to tip at a precarious angle. He reached out and wrapped an arm around her before she could pitch forward. Rayne's breath lodged in her throat as her chest smacked against his.

One dark eyebrow slanting upward, he inclined his head. "Sorry. I wasn't watching the road as I should have. Are you all right?"

She couldn't speak. Blood rushed through her veins. Her heart thumped. Dizzy from the intimate contact, she shook her head, then squeaked out, "You may let go of me now, Mr. O'Malley."

Hearing him chuckle, she realized his arms remained around her, but it was *she* who held on to him. Abruptly she uncurled her fingers from the lapels of his coat. Straightening her hat, she averted her gaze. But she could not dispel the image of his green eyes lingering on her face, or the shiver of excitement darting down her spine.

"I don't mind if a pretty woman holds on to me."

Her eyes opened wide. "Surely you don't think I did so intentionally."

Devilment sparkled in his green gaze. "My dear Miss North, women claim they enjoy being in my arms. My reputation attests to it."

Speechless, Rayne fumbled for a reply. If only he would stop staring at her mouth.

"Have you ever been kissed?" he asked in a low, intimate tone.

"Certainly," she stammered.

"Who kissed you?"

She was so flustered that rational thought escaped her. His finger grazed her jaw, sending a delicious shiver down her spine. "I . . . I don't recall his name at the moment."

A slow, knowing grin crept over his mouth. "If you'd been kissed by me, my dear, I'd wager you wouldn't soon forget my name."

Rayne was shocked into silence by his arrogant statement.

"What? No argument? You disappoint me, Miss North."

She pushed his hand away. Taking a deep breath, she said softly, "You must be incredibly strong to carry around such a monstrous ego."

Sporting a broad grin, he stared at her mouth again. She opened her lips to insist he stop taunting her, but her intention flew from her mind. He caught her against his broad chest and slanted his mouth over hers.

She had dreamed of her first kiss, of the dashing man who would lay claim to her heart, but her dreams had been those of a child. Case O'Malley had not figured into them. He kissed like a real man, a man who had learned his lessons well. His unexpected action caught her so off guard, she couldn't breathe, or move. Then, just as quickly, the kiss was over. He left her dazed, her head spinning.

"Mr. O'Malley!" She shoved trembling hands against his chest. "I ... you ... you ..."

He released her instantly and, as if nothing had happened, turned and whipped the reins, righting the wheel and sending them hurrying along the road. A contented expression played over his face as he said, "Forgive me, Miss North. I forgot myself."

He didn't look the least bit remorseful. Her lips tingled and a butterfly fluttered in the vicinity of her heart. Only a devil could make her feel this way. Only a devil would then deny her the opportunity to give him the chastisement he deserved.

His kiss had been quick but earth-shattering. Without a doubt, she'd be doomed to the everlasting fires of hell if Case O'Malley ever kissed her with all the passion that she was convinced dwelled in his unholy soul.

Chapter 2

Perched halfway up the steep side of Mount Davidson, more than seven thousand feet above sea level, Virginia City never ceased to amaze Case. The streets had been cut into the mountainside every forty or fifty feet, like steps, and the tops of the buildings appeared level with the streets above them. Below the city, beyond craggy hills, lay a pale desert fringed with trees. Snowy mountains bulged beyond a fiery lake before they faded into a hazy background. The spectacular vista appeared endless.

As they climbed higher, Miss North's breathing became more labored. The thinner atmosphere accounted for some of her distress, but Case suspected he was partly responsible. He glanced at her and hid a smile. She looked so damn proper, her back as straight as a timber, her hands folded in her lap, her elegant nose stuck in the air. Not even the sprinkling of yellow dust on her clothes threatened her dignity.

He had surrendered to a moment of weakness, not expecting that something as simple as a kiss would affect her so deeply. His motive had been a rather perverse desire to convince her that Bridget O'Flannigan had told the truth. He cursed silently, unable to deny that he had also enjoyed kissing her, holding her in his arms. The sooner he rid himself of Jasper's daughter, the better.

He hoped Jasper had followed his orders and opened the house. By now the crates should have been unpacked and the Chinese house servant hired. If his partner had not fulfilled his end of their bargain, he might very well drop Jasper down a shaft and let him rot.

Case usually slept until midmorning and then went to his office to oversee his mining operation. At night he gambled and divided his time between his friends and his women. No one suspected he was anything but a scoundrel and good-natured gambler, and that suited him fine.

A year ago, government officials had approached him to enlist his aid and he had since been a secret supplier of gold to the Union effort. His work was dangerous enough what with southern sympathizers around, that he didn't need anyone suspecting that he was anything other than what he appeared to be.

Thinking of the shipment scheduled to go out to New York in a week, Case scowled. He didn't trust his partner's loose tongue, and he certainly didn't need the added distraction of Miss North.

Upon entering the city, Case put his thoughts aside and noticed Rayne's attention riveted on the multitude of men and the variety of vehicles crowding the narrow main thoroughfare. She probably hadn't expected Virginia City to be so lively. Quartz wagons, freight teams, and buggies followed one another in an endless procession past saloons, brick stores with iron shutters, hotels, express offices, and houses four to six stories high.

Speculators stood conversing in groups on corners or on shaded balconied, boardwalks. Here, too, as in Carson City, the air was thick with alkali dust, giving man and beast alike a ghostly appearance.

"Good heavens!" she exclaimed, turning to stare at a marching band parading down the center of the business district. The group of men was quite a spectacle in flaming red flannel shirts and fire helmets, with shiny, black leather belts and boots.

Suddenly a rumbling explosion from deep in the earth rattled the buggy and spooked the horses. Case spoke in a soothing voice that calmed the animals. He glanced at Miss North, about to explain the sudden noise, when another loud boom shook the ground, causing her to bounce on the seat. Pressing her hand over her heart, she gasped. "What was *that?*"

"Blasting in a tunnel."

"Do they dig beneath the town?"

"Night and day," he explained. "The Comstock silver lode runs for two miles hundreds of feet under Virginia City and Gold Hill. The main vein's as wide as a New York city street."

"You've been in it?"

Seeing her amazed look, Case confided, "I designed the interlocking timbers supporting the walls. Without them, the tunnels would cave in."

"I'm impressed. You must be very talented. Why haven't you tried your hand at engineering?"

"I have." Until three years ago, when he'd met Jasper in a Denver saloon. They'd discovered they made a perfect team. Jasper had a talent for finding gold and silver, and Case had the skills to mine it. Being a wealthy mine owner in a rowdy town also provided access to women, spirits, and gambling, and he was well satisfied with his life. "Now I've found an easier way to make my fortune," he finished.

The clogged street suddenly opened and Case drove the buggy forward. Out of the corner of his eye, he saw Miss North grab her hat with such haste that the ostrich feather snapped in half.

"I've broken my plume," she said, sounding forlorn as he stopped the buggy beside the planked sidewalk in front of the row houses.

Hoping to bring a smile to her face, he said, "Looks better without it, if you want my opinion."

Someone called his name and Case tensed. A yellow-haired woman in a flashy red dress strutted toward them. With a lascivious grin, she draped her arm over his knee.

"Case, darlin', what are you doin' out at this hour?"

An upstairs window of a nearby establishment slid open and a well-endowed woman poured into a tight-fitting, low-cut dress leaned out, called his name, and waved. Case waved back, then cursed his stupidity in unconsciously stopping in front of his favorite place of business with a lady present. There was little help for it now. "Bessie, this is Jasper's daughter, Rayne North, come to visit. I fetched her from Carson City."

Bessie nodded. "How do?"

Rayne smiled sweetly, her wide hazel eyes taking in every aspect of Bessie's flamboyant dress. To Case's astonishment, she offered her hand in friendship. He found himself gazing at her with admiration.

"You drop by and visit with me later, you hear, Case? I've been lonesome for ya."

He patted Bessie's hand and removed her arm from his leg. "Later," he returned, hoping Jasper's daughter was as naive as he thought. For some inexplicable reason, he didn't want her to know his plans for the evening.

Beside him, Rayne looked away, her cheeks flushed at her sudden realization.

Heat spread from Case's neck to his forehead, and he cursed. There was no call for embarrassment. He had long-standing friendships with many women, and he wasn't ashamed of it. Before another disaster could strike, he drove the buggy up a steep side street. "We'll be there soon. Hold on, Miss North."

"Breathing is difficult," she said after a moment. "Do you think it's from the height?"

"The air is rarefied. I suggest you limit your activity until you get used to it."

"Perhaps it would be wise if you took your own advice, Mr. O'Malley."

Case choked as he stopped the buggy in front of his recently completed home. The two-story brick house clearly delighted Miss North. She stared in awe at the white columns supporting the wraparound porch, and admired the huge windows with white shutters.

"Is this my father's residence?"

Until I throw him out, Case thought irritably. "The last time I was here, it wasn't ready. I hope Jasper has it in order."

He climbed from the buggy and studied the house. He saw no signs that Jasper had attended to the chores assigned him. Fishing a key from his pocket, Case stalked toward the front door.

"Mr. O'Malley."

Case turned. Bracing his hands on his hips inside his frock coat, he raised his eyebrows.

She looked hesitant as she balanced herself on the narrow rung of the buggy, her reticule clutched to her chest. "A gentleman usually helps a lady from a conveyance."

He strolled toward her. "My pleasure, Miss North," he replied, a devilish gleam in his eyes.

Indecision crossed her face as her fingers tightened on her reticule.

"Change your mind, my dear?"

Lifting her chin, she returned, "I forgot, Mr. O'Malley, that I am not with a gentleman.

Case's brows shot up. The lady had spirit, and he admired women who didn't cling to a man. He gave her a mocking smile, and laughed aloud when she suddenly hopped down without his assistance.

He followed behind her, watching with interest. Her hips swayed engagingly as she walked. He wondered if the narrow circle of delicate lace at the throat of her dress hinted at a preference for lace on her underclothes, too. Hearing the rustle of her petticoats, he stared at the house to ward off the sensual images the sound brought to his mind.

He unlocked the door and ushered her inside, removed his hat and left it to dangle from the round newel on the banister at the bottom of the staircase. Beyond the hallway, in the parlor, crates lined the room, sawdust littered the floor, and no help was at hand. Damn Jasper's hide. He would kill him as soon as he got his hands around his scruffy little neck.

"My father assured me his home was ready for

my arrival," she said, her voice heavy with disappointment. "I thought he'd be here to greet me."

So, Case thought, Jasper had told his daughter the house was his before he'd even asked permission to borrow it. "Your father's minding the office until I get back," he replied. "I'll see that you are settled and send some men to clean."

"Thank you, but all I need are my clothes. So long as the bedroom is in order, and I can have a hot bath and something decent to eat, I'll manage."

She peered into the parlor and shook her head. "Just look at where someone has placed that beautiful table. The side chairs are all wrong, too."

Case bristled. "They look fine to me."

"They just need rearranging. The table should be here, in the middle. It needs a nice lace doily and a lamp." With a finger on her chin, she eyed the rest of the room. "It will be magnificent if all of the furnishings are as nice as these. I love mahogany don't you? The wallpaper is hand-flocked, but I'm amazed my father chose that deep rose color."

Straightening, Case watched her place her reticule and her ruined hat on a marble-topped table. "What's wrong with the wallpaper?" he asked.

"Why, nothing, Mr. O'Malley. I meant it's very tasteful. I would've chosen it myself." She looked around again. "How fortunate I arrived in time to take charge of the house."

"I'm not sure Jasper will approve if you change things." *My* things, Case thought with disgust. "There are some very expensive, imported objects in those crates."

"How on earth did my father procure such luxuries in a town built into a mountain?"

Case heaved a breath, controlling his temper. "From San Francisco. Freight wagons continuously cross the Sierras day and night, supplying the town. Anything is to be had if one has the wealth to buy it."

"I hadn't imagined such a thing."

"Miss North, you haven't mentioned how long you plan to visit your father."

"I'm not sure. For as long as it takes, I presume," she said as she moved toward the door to the main room. "I'm certain my father will be pleased to have my help. After all, what does a man know about dressing a house? It's lovely, but if he leans towards those pretentious candelabra on the mantel, everything in those crates will have to go."

"I happen to like the candelabra," Case declared. The excitement dancing in her eyes frightened the hell out of him. It was just like a woman to want to change things. He, not Jasper, had chosen all the furnishings, and even if he did say so himself, he had excellent taste. "The candelabra were made in Italy from solid silver taken from our mine. And what do you mean, they'll have to go?"

She slipped past him and headed down the hall, toward the kitchen.

Case followed close on her heels. "Wait just a damn minute. If you think—"

She whirled around, giving him a reproachful look.

Hell. He shouldn't have spoken so rashly. He'd give away their deception if he wasn't careful. He heard the creak and groan of wooden wheels grinding to a halt in front of the house. Before he could speak, she darted past him.

"It's that kind man with my baggage. Hurry, Mr. O'Malley. Mr. Atkins's wagon is blocking the street."

Unable to control his indignation at being ordered about, he glared at her.

"I beg your pardon," she said contritely. "Will you please see to my belongings? They are heavy, and I . . ."

Case paused in the doorway, wishing Jasper to the devil. Although he was eager to be about his own business, it wasn't in him to refuse a lady. He bowed low. "Your obedient servant, Miss North."

While O'Malley deposited her possessions in a room on the second floor, Rayne waited below. She fortified herself with a deep breath. He had proved as troubling as his scandalous reputation, leaving her emotions in a state of turmoil.

Hearing several loud thumps, she reluctantly went up the stairs. It might not be seemly to enter a bedroom with a man present, but surely these circumstances were unique. O'Malley seemed in a temper, and she worried he might damage her father's house. She found him in a large room, struggling with a magnificent bedpost.

"I'm surprised the bed is not set up," she said, observing the mattress leaning against the wall.

When she received no answer, she refrained from making any further comments. Most likely her father slept on the floor. Knowing his disreputable past, she surmised he wasn't used to such prosperous surroundings. What puzzled her was

O'Malley's strange mood. She saw his lips move and wondered what she'd done to incur his anger.

She folded her arms over her chest and watched him move a heavy walnut headboard. His strength surprised her at first, until his coat stretched tight across his broad back, indicating heavy muscles in his arms and shoulders. When he bent down to adjust the side rails, his trousers hugged the contours of his long legs, displaying the lean strength there as well. He turned slightly. His blue, flowered vest emphasized his flat stomach.

Rayne swallowed. God had used a masterful hand when He made this man.

She pretended to study the mirrored dresser, but her eyes returned to Case time and again. He raked his fingers through his hair. The unruly waves lent him a roguish air, which suited him all too well. His profile was another divine creation; his square jaw, straight nose, green eyes, and white, even teeth made her breath catch in her throat. She understood why women would find this handsome devil difficult to resist.

He dropped the mattress onto the finished bed frame and dusted his hands, then crossed the room to bend over another crate and easily pry it open. Rayne watched with fascination, remembering the thrill of being held in his arms. The unbidden thought brought a fiery blush to her cheeks. Case O'Malley was definitely not the sort of man she wanted in her life.

Having witnessed her mother's misery, Rayne had learned her lesson well. Men were unreliable creatures concerned only with appeasing their own lusty appetites. Still, her father had changed, and so could O'Malley, if he wanted to.

"The linen and curtains are here, Miss North," he said before disappearing into the hallway. Curious, she followed him into another, smaller room. "You may bathe in here," he informed her in a businesslike tone. "As you can see, the tub has been enclosed in the finest mahogany wood, both behind and below. There's enough room on the sides to place a dish for soap or whatever. The black, oddly shaped object with the thick pipe extending up and into the wall is a stove. Use the copper kettle to heat the water, unless you prefer it cold."

"It's very nice," she returned hesitantly, disturbed that this rogue was explaining bathing procedures to her. She wished he'd leave now, before the conversation became more embarrassing.

"Do you need instruction in its use?"

Rayne shook her head. She and her mother had been poor most of their lives. She had learned at an early age how to fuel and light a stove, as well as the heavier labor required to run a household.

"If I pump on the wood handle, I presume water pours from the spout."

"Very astute. Because this floor is higher, it does take a while longer than the one in the kitchen."

He flashed her a dazzling smile, and she followed him into another bedroom. "I've been remiss in my manners," she said. "I haven't properly thanked you for your kind assistance today."

"You are quite welcome, Miss North. Your father will be here presently. It's unlikely a female servant can be found, but Hung Lee will provide adequate service."

Her eyes wary, Rayne stared at his broad back. "What is a Hung Lee?"

Glancing over his shoulder, he looked surprised and amused. "A person, Miss North. Hung Lee is Chinese. His cooking is excellent and he does washing, too. Your father was to have hired him, but I suspect he has forgotten. I will personally see to the matter when I leave."

Abruptly he threw open the window and plucked a cigar from his inside pocket. She watched in dismay as he bit off the end, struck a match, and puffed heartily. Fragrant smoke curled around his head, floating over to where she stood. Taking out her lace-trimmed handkerchief, she covered her nose and cleared her throat.

He squinted at her through the smoky haze, and then, dumbfounding her, a distressed look came over his face. Holding out the cigar, he searched the room. She found his predicament amusing. He obviously hadn't considered the ramifications of lighting the cigar and now suffered the dilemma of what to do with it.

She crossed the room and gingerly took possession of the smoking object. Nose crinkled, and eyes watering from the noxious fumes, she held her breath, stuck her arm out the window, and dropped the cigar.

His wry smile conveyed his relief and abashment.

Casting about for a harmless topic of conversation she said, "I admire the house's construction and spacious rooms. Even the windows are large and allow adequate light. My father did an admirable job of designing it."

O'Malley looked down his fine nose at her, a

disgruntled expression on his face. "Your father did *not* design the house." Not allowing her an opportunity to question him further, he continued, "There's another bedroom across the hall. When the furniture's in place, you'll be even more impressed."

A sudden, dismaying thought came to her. Rayne raised a hand to her throat.

He studied her intently. "Something troubling you, my dear?"

"You seem very familiar with my father's home. You ... do you ... that is ... will you be living here, too?"

"I designed the house, if you must know." He moved closer. Her fingers tightened on her throat. "You seem awfully upset to think of me in the same house with you." Anger flashed in his eyes.

Fearing he'd taken her inquiry in the wrong way, she stammered, "I ... no. I mean ... if my father has invited you, I can have no objection. You've proved yourself trustworthy thus far, except for—"

The gleam in his eyes intensified, unnerving her. Dear God, did he know she'd almost mentioned their kiss? She stepped back and met the solid resistance of the wall.

Bracing a hand on either side of her shoulders, he held her captive. She didn't flinch or bat an eyelash. The effort not to do so required extreme concentration. Nervously she wet her lips, unable to tear her gaze from his.

"We're alone, Miss North. Are you afraid? Remember, I'm a womanizer of the worst sort. Why, I probably don't have any conscience at all. You, my dear, are completely at my mercy."

Rayne exerted every ounce of willpower she possessed to maintain a semblance of calm. He stood closer to her than any man she ever knew, so near she felt his body heat. A strange knotting sensation tightened in her stomach and sent shivers up her arms. She stared into his green eyes. Would he stand this close to that woman Bessie?

Closer?

Would he kiss Bessie tonight? She swallowed, torn between envy and fear.

"Lost your tongue, Miss North? Relax, I won't hurt you."

He lowered his head until his mouth hovered just above hers. "Unless you want me to kiss you," he murmured, his voice low and seductive. "Is that why your lips are parted and inviting? I always oblige a lady." He inched closer. "If she asks."

A tremble quaked through Rayne as she pressed her body against the wall. Using her hands for support, because her knees had gone limp, she stared at his mouth. She didn't want him to kiss her again. She refused to compromise her honor with a man like him, no matter how handsome she found him. Clearly she'd underestimated his power, the skill he possessed to render a woman senseless.

"Let me go, Mr. O'Malley," she demanded weakly.

Rayne nearly collapsed with relief when, with a fierce scowl, he turned away. "If this is an example of the way you mean to behave—" She broke off when he swung around and grabbed her wrist. His action propelled her into his arms.

He kissed her long and passionately. She trembled violently, too shocked to fight his impetuous attack. Her heart faltered and missed a beat. Blood ran hot in her veins, warming her skin. She went still with wonder when his lips gentled on hers, moving in a slower, more sensuous rhythm. She became aware of his masculine scent, the hardness of his chest, the slight scrape of his rough cheek against hers, the pressure of his fingers on her spine.

He released her abruptly and returned to the window. Staring out at the sky, he tugged at his collar and breathed deeply, jamming a hand through his hair. His voice sounded pained as he said, "I apologize, Miss North. I'm not generally in the habit of attacking innocent young women."

She still felt slightly dizzy and missed the warmth of his body. The thought shamed her. She had never dreamed a man could make her feel this way. Humiliation drained the color from her cheeks. She should not have allowed herself to respond in such a manner. He appeared remorseful, but even when he detoured around her and strode out the door she could not look at him or utter a single word.

Chapter 3

Rayne flattened herself against the closed front door. It had taken an effort of will to retain a semblance of composure as she saw Mr. O'Malley out.

When her breathing grew more even, she sat on the bottom step of the stairs and considered her reaction to him. She'd never imagined a man could turn her bones to butter and her mind to mush. Maybe she wasn't as proper as she thought. She suspected a true lady wouldn't allow herself to be overwhelmed by a man's kiss. She should have tried harder to resist him. Instead, she had reveled in the strength of his arms, the masterful way he'd moved his mouth over hers.

Was she wanton? Would she behave so brazenly with *any* man? She groaned, dismayed by the absolute certainty of the answer. Only Case O'Malley could inspire such reckless excitement in her.

And *he* was an unscrupulous womanizer!

That was it, of course. The man had most likely spent years learning to be an expert in lovemaking, so she need not feel ashamed of her behavior. But from this moment on, she must take care never to be alone with him, and *never, ever* allow him to kiss her.

* * *

In Case's room at the hotel, Jasper shot up out of the tub of water, sputtering. "You tryin' to drown me?"

"Give me one good reason why I shouldn't." Case dunked Jasper's head in the water again before he released him. "Do you have *any* idea of what I've been through today?"

Jasper dashed a hand over his face and shook his head. Droplets of water flew in all directions. "Rayne get here all right?"

"No thanks to you." Case pitched Jasper a bar of soap. Watching his partner lather his skinny, hairless chest, he added, "She's in your hands now."

"Is she as pretty as I remember?"

"She'll do." Case grabbed a whiskey bottle and flopped onto his bed. He took a hearty swallow. "But you're going to have to behave yourself."

Jasper froze. "What do you mean?"

"You guessed right." Case bit back a grin. "She's a proper lady."

"Said so, didn't I?" Jasper finished bathing and quickly rinsed. "Throw me a towel."

Case stretched out an arm, caught the edge of a towel on a table, and sent it flying. Taking another swig from his bottle, he settled back with his arm behind his head.

Jasper stood and wrapped his dripping body, shivering. Glancing at Jasper's spindly legs, Case grinned. "You'll have to mend your ways, you know. You can't spend your evenings in a saloon while she's here."

Jasper went white. Stepping from the tub, holding the towel against his waist with one hand, he shoved his fingers through his hair.

"Yessir, your daughter's a fair judge of character. Even if she hadn't heard of my reputation beforehand, she would've seen past my pretense."

"God Almighty." Jasper fell on a chair, his shoulders slumped. "You got to help me. I can't stay home every night."

"No, sir, I did my part. I delivered her for you and even settled her in *my* house." He swung his legs over the side of the bed and sat up. "I sent Hung Lee over. He should be there by now, and I've hired some men to clean up the mess you were supposed to have taken care of today."

"I meant to, Case. I just got busy at the mine and forgot. I don't know what to say to her."

"Just tell her you're glad to see her, and sorry for the past. And find out how long she's staying. You didn't invite her to live here permanently, did you?"

"I didn't actually invite her. I wrote and sent Mary some money, but I never thought Rayne would come all the way out here. I want to see her, but—"

"Get dressed," Case ordered, having heard enough to satisfy his curiosity. "I bought you new clothes. You'll want to look like a prosperous mine owner."

Jasper groaned, "I can't face her, not after the way I've treated her and her mother."

"If you value your life, you will. You'll get dressed and haul your cantankerous ass over there and impress your daughter with what a fine gentleman you are."

"Damn, Case, you're a hard man."

"And another thing. I left orders where everything's to go. If you want to keep on living, you'll see that she doesn't touch any of my belongings."

Jasper opened his mouth to protest, but Case's frown silenced him. He rose and hastily began to dress.

Case laid his arm over his brow. The motion shut out the light, but it couldn't keep thoughts of Rayne North from his mind. He recalled the way she'd looked when she'd petted that mangy dog, her hazel eyes tender with compassion. Then when she found out who he was, she'd looked at him as if he were Satan's spawn. Maybe she had been right to fear him. He had lost control in the buggy and in the house, dragged her into his embrace like a two-bit whore, and kissed her against her will. He'd enjoyed every second of it and would wager she had, too. With a little practice— Christ, what was he thinking?

Rayne was his partner's daughter. If that weren't bad enough, she was innocent and naive to boot. Start messing around with a girl like that, and she'd be talking marriage and babies, and inviting the preacher to call. It would be best to steer a wide path around Miss North. He valued his freedom too much to get caught in a marriage trap.

"You know, you could come with me, Case. I mean, seeing as you've met Rayne."

"She's more trouble than you are. If you didn't have such a good nose for sniffing out ore, I sure as hell *would* drown you." Case lifted his arm from his face. "Go meet your blasted daughter and leave me in peace. I'm planning on getting drunk as a lord and finding solace in a warm, willing woman."

* * *

Rayne stood in the bedroom and sighed. She longed to sleep in a soft, clean bed, and restore her vitality after her long days of travel, but she knew it was impossible with so much to be done. She set to work unpacking the crate O'Malley had pried open, and selecting a washcloth and towel from the linen supply, she headed for the washroom. A long, luxurious bath would rejuvenate her.

Afterwards she inspected the tall walnut wardrobe, pronounced it clean enough to house her clothes, and unpacked her few dresses, wishing, absurdly, that they weren't all so plain. She changed into a slightly wrinkled but serviceable brown woolen dress. Removing the pins from her hair, she shook her head. The long waves fell about her shoulders. Her movements deliberately slow, she brushed her hair, closing her eyes to relish the soothing strokes. A vision of Case O'Malley strayed into her mind, intensifying her enjoyment. She grew warm all over as tingles of pleasure skipped over her skin. The wayward, unwanted image drove her back to reality and the chores facing her.

She decided to put the bedroom in order first. Once she knew a large feather mattress with fresh linen awaited her, she could then devote herself to an afternoon of hard work. As she fitted white sheets on the bed, she noticed the fine quality of the fabric. Her father must have employed someone with taste and refinement to choose the appointments she'd seen so far in his house.

After Rayne had pulled, tucked, and smoothed the bedsheets until they were so tight that a coin could bounce on them, she turned her attention to the bare windows. But, she didn't know how to hang the burgundy draperies and sheer lace panels without help. The tops of the windows were higher than she could reach. She was considering the problem when a commotion downstairs drew her attention and she hurried down to investigate.

From the bottom step, she saw four ragtag men prying open crates in the parlor. A short, slight fellow was sweeping the floor just inside the room. He wore an odd combination of leather sandals, baggy dark pants that ended several inches above his ankles, and a short white tunic under a brown, sleeveless outer garment. A black pigtail hung past his knees, and his eyes were slanted up at the corners. She had never seen a more curious-looking individual. True to his word, O'Malley had sent men to put the house in order.

Not wanting to disturb the men, Rayne watched for a moment before she tiptoed down the hall toward the kitchen. She found this room untidy too. Her stomach gave an unladylike growl, reminding her that she hadn't eaten since early that morning. She only hoped her father had food and cooking utensils in the house. She searched the white-painted cupboards and eventually discovered an assortment of pots and pans. Congratulating herself, she turned around to hunt for something edible and nearly fell over the strange little man with slanted eyes.

"Pardon me, sir. I didn't hear you enter."

She considered his bewildered expression and decided he must not speak English. She introduced herself, twice, and waited patiently for a reply. The answer she received wasn't what she expected.

"What you doing in Hung Lee's kitchen, Missy North?"

Startled, she retreated a step. "I beg your pardon. I didn't realize who you were."

"Hung Lee cookee belly good."

"Mr. O'Malley praised your skills. Mr. Lee." She glanced toward the front of the house. "I saw you were busy, and I didn't want to trouble you."

"Hung Lee washee belly good, too."

She felt the beginnings of a smile on her lips. Quickly she checked it. "He said that also."

"You like poke and licee? Hung Lee fix."

Rayne stared stupidly at the Chinaman, not wanting to offend the man for not understanding his speech. Her stomach rumbled. "Yes, I like it very much," she said.

Hung Lee bowed, then stood with arms folded in front of him. Rayne concluded she wasn't wanted or allowed in *his* kitchen. She smiled, gave him a brief nod of encouragement, and headed for the parlor.

There, three of the men unpacked and placed objects according to instructions the other man read aloud from a long list. She watched silently for several seconds. Although she agreed with the arrangement of most of the furnishings, a few were not displayed advantageously. She moved forward, about to offer a comment, but someone touched her arm and she turned.

"Papa!" She recognized him instantly. Jasper North's dark hair and mustache were now gray, and he was thinner than five years ago. His clothes were different, too. He looked so dignified in his dark gray coat, trousers, and vest from which a silver pocket watch dangled. Cut from the finest cloth, his suit testified to his wealth.

With a catch in her voice, Rayne said, "I've looked forward to seeing you. My, you do look grand." She held out her hands and Jasper clasped them both.

"You're the spitting image of your ma when I first laid eyes on her. You find everything okay?"

"Yes, Papa."

"I hope your travel wasn't too great a hardship."

Rayne smiled at him, her eyes sparkling. "I saw such wonderfully peculiar things."

"And Mary. Is she well?"

Wanting to avoid the subject of her mother for a little while, she told him, "I was just about to see to the placement of the furnishings."

Jasper's smile faded, replaced by dismay. "You mustn't rearrange anything. Each item must be in its proper spot."

"I don't remember you being so particular." She moved beside him. "You'll see. Your house will be perfect when I finish. I must compliment you on your judicious selections. You've chosen some lovely things. Except for the candelabra. As I told Mr. O'Malley, they're a bit pretentious."

Jasper twitched and cleared his throat. "You told Case they were *what*?"

"Pretentious. Gaudy," she said, flushing. "I must say, I was surprised you sent a man of O'Malley's character to meet me, even if he is your business partner."

"Don't go looking down your nose at Case. He's very respected here. He's generous to a fault and smart, too," Jasper insisted. "I owe him more than I can ever repay."

"It isn't his generosity or intelligence I question." Leaning forward, she confided in a lower voice, "It's his morals." The memory of his sparkling green eyes flashed through her mind, interrupting her train of thought. "He . . . Some people, more than others, easily fall prey to a beguiling man, but you're a prosperous gentleman now. Look at the difference in you. You've invested wisely in a beautiful home and furnishings, whereas Mr. O'Malley—"

"What I've got is thanks to Case." Jasper walked Rayne into the hallway. "You're welcome to your opinion, but don't bandy it about in town. He has more friends than enemies. Some might not take it kindly if you talk against Case."

"Why, I would never speak ill of him to anyone else," she declared, hurt that her own father felt it necessary to chide her. Not wanting to sour the moment with an argument over O'Malley, she said, "I'm so pleased by your reformation. Mother was beside herself when you finally sent money. I always knew you'd make amends when you had the means."

What she didn't tell Jasper was that she'd come to Virginia City on her mother's behalf. Her mother's welfare depended on her, yet she still loved her father, despite the difficult life he'd thrust upon them. Quickly, without emotion, she recited the words she'd practiced so often. "The reason I've come is to make sure you continue to fulfill your obligations to my mother."

Jasper licked his dry lips and looked down as if ashamed.

"For myself, I ask nothing," she continued. Conflicting emotions coursed through her; the love she bore him warred with the resentment she'd felt when he'd abandoned her and her sweet mother to endure the penny-scraping hardship of poverty. "Just seeing you after so long is enough for me, but Mama needs your help."

Jasper patted Rayne's hand. "Rayne, honey, I'll help you all I can, but at the moment my money's not my own."

Her eyes widened. "I find that incredibly hard to believe. Why, this magnificent house attests to great wealth." Rayne glanced around, shaking her head. "I didn't notice earlier, but the knobs on your doors, even the keyholes, are solid silver."

"But the house isn't—"

"I may not have seen it often, but I do recognize silver."

"It's from our mine," Jasper explained. "Didn't cost me anything."

Pain coiled around Rayne's heart. All her life she had made excuses for her father, prayed he'd turn his life around and accept his responsibilities. "Mother could have made good use of all that *free* silver," she said, tears welling in her eyes.

Jasper paled and lowered his gaze. "I'm sorry, sweetheart. I always meant to send her a little something. I'll make it up to her, I promise."

Rayne's heart sank. Beneath his fine clothes he was still the same man who'd put his own desires ahead of home and family, she realized. Her mother had been right to send her to Virginia City. If she hadn't come, Mama would never have seen another penny of his newfound wealth. In the past, her father had not kept his promises, and

Rayne was going to make sure that he did keep them now.

She gazed at him, her eyes still moist. "I've missed you terribly, Papa. I don't know why I've ruined our first minutes together. Let's discuss this later."

"What is that smell coming from the back of the house?" Jasper said.

"There's a peculiar little man named Hung Lee in the kitchen." She inhaled the tantalizing aroma and her mouth watered. "What's poke and licee?"

"Pork and rice," he told her with a smile. "You'll get used to the way Hung Lee talks."

Rayne sighed with relief. "I confess I was uneasy when he told me what he planned to cook, but it smells delicious." She turned toward the stairs. "Now that you're here, I think we should put your room in order. Won't it be wonderful to live together again after all these years?"

Jasper touched her cheek. "It will at that."

That evening in the Virginia Saloon, Case tilted back his chair and sighed with pleasure. He'd enjoyed a satisfying afternoon of undisturbed sleep, soaked in a relaxing tub of hot water, eaten a delicious meal, and smoked as many cigars as he'd wanted. Although he wondered how Jasper had made out with his daughter, he stopped himself from dwelling on it, reasoning it was not his affair. *She* was not his affair.

Since he'd wasted the better part of the day, he decided to spend most of tomorrow tending to business. He knew Jasper would show up at the mine early since it was unlikely he'd be able to go out at night under Rayne's watchful eyes. Case felt a moment's pity for his partner. In some ways, Rayne reminded Case of his own dictatorial mother.

Winking at Annie, a dark-haired, curvaceous beauty, Case looked forward to a night of shameful amusement. In answer to his unspoken invitation, Annie smiled seductively and strutted across the room. When she reached him, she propped her hip against the edge of the table and bent forward. He breathed in her sweet perfume and admired the abundant breasts spilling over the low neckline of her cherry red dress.

Catlike, Annie slid a leg between his legs and rubbed her knee along his thigh. She leaned closer and brushed her lips across his forehead. He felt her breasts under his chin, her arms around his shoulders. Annie was wild, wicked, and sinful— exactly the kind of woman he wanted. Annie always stirred his senses and set his blood pumping. A touch of her fingers and the feel of her sensual tongue on his skin was all it took to arouse him. He'd tumbled her on the floor occasionally because they couldn't wait to get to bed.

An inviting smile playing over his mouth, he caught her waist and pulled her onto his lap. Her fingers grazed his cheek before settling on his neck. He felt her knee press intimately between his legs, and rose to the occasion.

"Want more privacy?"

"Let's go to your room," he said in a low, seductive voice.

"I'll get a bottle. You wait right here."

"You bet."

Case watched Annie walk to the bar, the calculated swing of her hips deliberately provocative.

An image of Rayne North flashed in his mind. She moved with an unconscious sensuality he found all the more enticing because she was unaware of its effect. When he realized his thoughts had turned to Rayne again, he let out a growl of exasperation. He had to be crazy. Annie was hot and available. Only a fool would deny himself the pleasure of her body.

He glanced around the saloon. He felt at home here with the smoke, blaring noise, and gay atmosphere. Inlaid with brass and ivory, the bar ran the length of the room, the mahogany indicating the saloon's substantial profits. Magnificent murals decorated the walls. At a corner table, a dealer slid cards from a sterling silver honest box decorated with abalone-shell inlays. Music from a tinny piano came from behind him, making him want to tap his foot. Everyone was drinking, gambling, and speculating around him.

Times were flush in Virginia City. He loved every second of it.

He sat up straight. He could've sworn he'd spotted Jasper's gray head across the saloon. Case stood, leaned to his right to confirm his suspicion. His partner had accomplished the inconceivable. He'd dodged his proper daughter. Case pushed his way through the crowd of patrons.

Clamping his hand on Jasper's shoulder, Case swung him around. "Up to your usual tricks? How'd you get out?"

The older man shook with relief. "I thought it was Rayne. You scared the stuffing clean outta me."

"How did you escape?"

"Climbed out the window."

Case roared with laughter. "I would've given anything to see how you dropped to the ground without breaking your neck."

"Near 'bout did."

"You get along with your daughter all right? She settled?"

"I suppose so. Those men you sent were there earlier, unpacking your crates. Hung Lee showed up and cooked a scrumptious meal. Rayne tired herself out today." Jasper loosened his shirt. "She'll probably sleep late and not even miss me."

"Don't count on it. She's the type who's up at dawn."

Jasper slumped on a nearby chair. "I just wanted to watch the card games awhile, Case."

"Your daughter hasn't gotten it in her head to start moving my things, has she?"

Jasper gave Case a pleading expression. "I tried. Honest I did. She didn't rearrange much, and you can change everything back later."

Case watched Annie weave her way through the crowd toward him. She pressed her body against him, whispering an indecent suggestion in his ear to which he responded by slipping his arm around her waist and holding her close. But his attention returned to his partner. "What about my candelabra?"

Jasper moaned.

"Well? Where did she put them? In the parlor? Upstairs?"

His voice barely audible, Jasper confessed, "She gave 'em to Hung Lee."

"She *what?*" Case bellowed.

"You had to be there, Case. There was nothing I could do. I told her to put them where she liked, figuring, you know, we could move 'em later. I didn't know she'd give 'em to that Chinaman."

Imagining Hung Lee with the silver, branched candlesticks in his shanty on the lower side of Virginia City, Case hid the beginnings of a grin and warned, "Don't let her touch anything else."

Moving away, he guided his companion between the tables and glanced over his shoulder. "I'll expect you at the office at a decent hour tomorrow. We have a shipment of ore to get out to the mill."

A short time later in Annie's room, Case tried to keep his mind on the wicked delights she was bestowing upon his body. "How 'bout another drink. I've had a tryin' day."

"Sure, Case."

Annie was always agreeable. He watched her parade naked to the bureau to refill his glass. She had a beautiful body, lush and creamy white. When she returned, he gulped down the liquor and rolled her under him. She squealed, wrapped her legs around his hips, and arched up against him.

He kissed her the way she liked, his tongue ravishing her mouth. Annie didn't want tenderness, she craved a hot, satisfying coupling. Moments later, she twisted and burned beneath him, her ardent moans muffled by his mouth. How the devil could his mind keep returning to another woman?

Feeling compassion for Annie, and disgust that he kept remembering Jasper's daughter, he brought her to completion without entering her. He held her tight, felt her stiffen, then go limp. Maybe he'd drunk too much.

Excuses. He was old enough to know how to hold his liquor.

The truth cut through his mind with a razor sharpness. It shredded his defenses and shocked him.

Rayne North was the woman he wanted in his bed. He imagined her with her tangled hair spread across his pillow, her body pressed into the mattress beneath his.

No. He was drunk. He had to be.

Within the hour, Case returned to the Virginia Saloon. Several patrons turned to look at him with surprise. Perhaps he should've gone to his hotel room instead of announcing to the world that his evening with Annie had ended so soon. He walked forward and braced his elbow on the bar, his dark expression daring anyone to taunt him. He stared ahead, seeing nothing, his thoughts gloomy.

He had been knocked for a loop by Jasper's innocent daughter.

"Jasper's in his cups."

Case glanced around the saloon, then at the man who'd spoken. "Where is he?"

"Left a few minutes ago," the man answered. "I wanted to lead him home, but he insisted he could make it alone."

Case shut his eyes. "I'll take care of it. Thanks."

Case finally spotted Jasper walking down the street, using the wall of a building for a guide as he wove his way up an incline. When he reached his partner, Case flung Jasper's arm over his shoulder and encircled his waist to hold him upright, which wasn't easy since he didn't feel sober himself. Together they plodded up the steep path, occasionally taking two steps backward and having to retrace their way. Case knew he treated Jasper harshly at times, but he had assumed a sort of guardianship over the hapless man. If he didn't take charge of Jasper, who would?

The older man could never sneak into the house without awakening his daughter. Case didn't look forward to the undertaking himself. But dammit, it was *his* house. He reserved the right to enter it whenever he pleased, and if he disturbed Miss North in the process, too bad. After the pleasure she'd robbed him of this evening, he'd feel little remorse.

He managed to unlock the front door without undue commotion despite Jasper's mumbling incoherent phrases, which luckily came out too low to be heard. Case hauled his burden to the stairs and glanced up. A dark void loomed ahead. He considered removing their boots but quickly dismissed the idea—if he released his grip on Jasper, he might never hoist him upright again. Slowly, cautiously, he climbed the stairs with Jasper in tow. Occasionally Jasper's boots thudded against the steps, but Case kept the noise to a minimum. Case congratulated himself; even in his inebriated state, he made an excellent sneak thief. Unfortunately, Jasper chose that moment to revive and struggle violently.

Clamping a hand over his partner's mouth, Case shook him and whispered fiercely, "Quiet! Wanna wake your daughter?"

Jasper plucked at Case's hand, lost his balance, and reeled backward—taking Case with him. They toppled. They thumped down several steps, their grunts and groans echoing. When they were sprawled on their backs, their heads below their feet on the stairs, Case released a string of vile oaths.

Momentarily stunned, Case counted the bruises he felt on his body. Jasper's arms and legs flailed, his agitated movements confirming he'd suffered no serious damage. Grasping at one another, they regained their footing.

Light from above splashed into the hall and grew brighter. Case looked up and saw that the noise had indeed awakened Jasper's daughter. She stood on the landing, clad in a modest white cotton nightdress with long sleeves and a collared neckline. Holding a lamp high over her head, she appeared only half-awake.

Case swallowed around the lump in his throat. His initial assessment had been wrong. Her hair wasn't plain brown at all. Tangled from sleep, the magnificent mane flowed over her shoulders and shimmered with red sparks. The transformation astounded him. She looked ravishing. The glow from the lamp cast half of her face in shadow, but lent her gown transparency above her waist. Unable to help himself, he stared long and hard at her unbound, voluptuous breasts. Heat licked his insides.

She moved the lamp, angling it so that light fell over their faces. "Has my father been hurt?"

Unable to furnish an adequate defense, Case lifted Jasper up the stairs. He prayed she didn't smell the strong odor of liquor until after he'd left. Case's forehead creased with the effort of dragging Jasper onto the landing. Ignoring her disheveled appearance and the torching effect it had on his body, he stumbled past her. Out of the corner of one eye, he saw her cover her nose with her hand.

"Is that spirits I smell?"

Case froze. To protect Jasper, he purposely reminded her of his reputation. "You needn't blame your father. I'm responsible."

"Are you saying you encouraged my father to drink?"

Damn. Did she have to pursue the matter? Make him feel guilty? The only other woman who had ever made him feel like a recalcitrant child was his mother. He just wanted to get the hell out as soon as possible. When Rayne moved forward, he said with a growl, "I'll take care of him."

Case continued down the hall and deposited Jasper in his bed, then he returned to the landing. Rayne stood where he'd left her, her shoulders sagging. Her lips curled into a doleful frown. Suddenly he became aware of her uncertainty, her vulnerability. He didn't need this. But his eyes roamed over her face. An electric current passed between them. He channeled all his efforts into standing erect, appearing sober, but he sidestepped to steady himself.

She lifted her chin, attempting to convey her displeasure with a sorry imitation of a haughty rebuke, but this only heightened his awareness of her. He sensed she felt it, too. A slow, wicked smile formed on his mouth.

Twisting her fingers into a fold in her nightgown, she declared, "You smell of perfume, Mr. O'Malley."

Impertinent, astute baggage. He had hoped she wouldn't mention it. He wondered if the thought of him with another woman bothered her. Thanks to Jasper, Rayne probably considered him a graceless inebriate.

"You may show yourself out, Mr. O'Malley. I must tend to my father." She paused briefly, lowering her eyes. "Thank you for at least seeing him home."

Here was the sort of woman he strictly avoided. Case gripped the banister, descended the steps without another mishap, and stalked out of his house.

Chapter 4

He had been turned out of his own home.

No matter how sweet Miss North's voice had sounded, that's what it amounted to. He had been *dismissed*. Case headed for the hotel, silently cursing the woman with each step. He felt completely sober now, thanks to her. It was impossible to believe he'd felt desire for Jasper's daughter. And she'd been wearing a prudish nightdress, too.

For the first time in his life he was unable to put a woman out of his mind—a woman he didn't even want. Sure, he could win her if he made the effort, but a woman like Rayne would be nothing but trouble. Rounding a corner, he nearly stumbled over yet another female. He grabbed the woman's arms and steadied her.

Bessie Magovern's hands stroked his chest as she visibly wilted. "Case, darlin', I was waitin' for ya." She flattened herself against him, her hands snaking over his shoulders. Her fingers tangled in his hair. "Come home with me."

"That's a temptin' offer, Bess."

Bessie's full breasts crushed against his chest, but Rayne North's shapely body filled his mind.

Bessie pouted and played with a button on his

coat. "Jasper's daughter sure is pretty," she said coquettishly.

"Yeah. Pretty damn frightening."

"Don't ya like her?"

He heard the hopefulness in her voice and gently rubbed her shoulder. "She's too innocent and proper for the likes of me."

"Oh!" Bessie beamed. She licked her lips with the tip of her tongue "Guess there's no cause to worry, after all."

"What's that supposed to mean?"

"Why, nothing, Case." She pressed against him and whispered, "Forget about her."

He captured her wrists, "You think I'm not good enough for her, don't you?"

"You got enough women to worry about." Her mouth turned down. "You ain't got time for me now."

Suddenly ashamed at his outburst, he locked arms with her and led her down the street. "I'll see you home, Bessie. Buy you a drink, too. How's that?"

"Ain't exactly what I had in mind, but I guess it'll do."

Case glanced at Bessie, studying her painted face in the gaslight. She was sweet and obliging, a good friend. He had a good mind to go back to her room with her, and Rayne North be damned. But the thought of Rayne immediately cooled his impulse. "I have an early day tomorrow, sweetheart," he said. "I've neglected the mine too much lately."

She squeezed his arm. "I'll miss ya, darlin'. Johnny Harkins has been wantin' to see me special. Maybe I'll give him a chance."

Johnny Harkins!

It had been a miserable day all around, Case thought. He'd been set on his heels by Jasper's daughter, and now, if it was to be believed, Bessie was replacing him with Harkins. Throwing back his head, he laughed at the irony and squired Bessie into the nearest saloon.

Rayne visited her father's room before she returned to hers. Setting the lamp on a small table next to his bed she considered his sprawled body. She tugged off his boots and dropped them on the floor. Neither her action nor the fall of his boots disturbed him. The room reeked with the smell of stale whiskey. With her hands on her hips and sadness in her eyes, she listened to him snore.

She carefully covered him with a blanket. "Good night, Papa," she whispered. Then she picked up the lamp and quietly left.

She walked down the hall, thinking of Case O'Malley. He had admitted his responsibility for her father's fall from grace, but at least he had had the decency to bring him home. Lord only knew what would've become of Jasper if he'd been left to find his own way. What power did O'Malley hold over her? He was utterly unsuitable, a scoundrel through and through. No decent woman in her right mind would pay him any heed.

Why then, did the mere thought of him make heat pool in her stomach?

As Rayne placed the lamp on the bureau and cupped her hand to blow out the flame, she caught a reflection of herself in the mirror. Mr. O'Malley had stared at her with a strange expression on his face. Straightening, she stood on her toes and observed herself. She sucked in a slow, horrified breath. Through the thin material of her nightgown, her breasts were plainly visible.

Merciful heavens!

Her cheeks flamed. She grabbed the lamp and held it the same way she had in the hall, praying her suspicion proved false. With a sinking feeling she realized that even more of her body showed through the gown. In one swift movement, she blew out the lamp, returned it to the bureau, and dove into bed, jerking the covers up to her chin.

She'd never be able to look O'Malley in the face again.

Early the following morning, Rayne once again stood beside her father's bed. Because of him and his disturbing, disreputable partner, she hadn't gotten enough sleep. Nudging her father's foot, she amended her opinion. Case O'Malley alone had ruined her rest and caused her to toss and turn the entire night. No matter how hard she'd tried not to think of him, whenever she'd drifted toward sleep, the image of his arresting face and green eyes had tormented her.

The one time she had managed to doze, she had dreamed of him kissing her, his mouth tasting her lips with practiced ease, and she helpless and unwilling to let him to. She had woken up frantic and thrown off her covers. Surely he'd been sent by Satan to lure her.

A bath that morning had cooled her amorous yearnings. There was no place in her life for a man like him. Just as soon as she was certain her father would fulfill his obligations to her mother, she'd leave Virginia City and return home.

Rayne nudged Jasper's foot again and received an agonized groan in response. "Wake up, Papa. The day's wasting."

Another louder, more agonized groan came from the bed. Rayne pulled back the covers and turned his face toward her. He looked dreadful. Despite her disgust with his behavior the previous night, she couldn't help feeling compassion for his misery. "After you've eaten, you'll feel much better. Let me help you."

Jasper opened one bloodshot eye but quickly shut it again. "Ah, Rayne, let me sleep some more."

Clearly clemency served no purpose with her rascal of a father. She poked his arm with a finger. "You must get up. Mr. O'Malley will be expecting you."

"Just let me die in peace." Jasper rubbed his hip. "Did we fall down the stairs?"

"From the commotion you made, I believe you did." She leaned over him. "Are you hurt?"

"Even my eyelashes hurt. Rayne, honey, I think I should rest today."

Rayne tapped her foot. "Surely you should be at work by this hour."

"Case'll take care of things until I get there. He always does."

A ghost of a smile played over her mouth. "Better than he cared for you last night, I hope." Then, turning serious, she warned, "He's a bad influence on you."

Jasper mumbled something indistinguishable and rolled over to search for the covers.

"If you insist upon associating with a man like

Case O'Malley, the least you could do is refrain from drinking with him."

"Wasn't with Case."

Not with Case? Papa must be delirious, Rayne thought. She filled a glass from the pitcher of water on the bureau. "Here, drink this and explain."

He pushed himself up on one elbow. "Did you thank Case for bringing me home? He didn't have to, you know."

She stared at her father. "What did you mean, you weren't with him?"

Jasper swung his legs over the side of the bed and groaned again. He clamped his hands over his head.

"Please," she coaxed, "tell me who you were with last night. It's very important."

"Wasn't with anyone," he returned, groaning again. "Case just happened along and helped me home. Did he say different?"

She held out the water. "Yes, he did. Apparently he was trying to protect you."

"Damn," he groused, grabbing the glass. "Wish you'd told me that straight off. I wouldn't have bothered to confess."

Rayne crossed her arms over her chest, annoyed more by her own lack of insight than her father's remark. Disappointment coursed through her, but she reminded herself she must make allowances for her father.

"Papa, I realize it must be hard to refashion your life without stumbling once, especially in a city so full of enticement. Why, with all the liquor and gambling, it's amazing that everyone doesn't lose their money overnight. Come eat your breakfast and you'll feel better. Then we can go wire

Mama some money. She's managed without you for years but you're in a position to help her now."

Jasper drained the glass. "I know, and I'm sorry about that. Have to check with Case first, though."

"Whatever for?"

He rubbed his temples and made a smacking sound with his lips. "My tongue tastes like I ate my socks."

She shook her head as she refilled his glass. It seemed drinking was a vice that claimed its own retribution.

"Now, tell me what Mr. O'Malley has to do with this."

"He's holding my shares of stock."

Shocked and suspicious, she sat beside him on the bed. "Why?"

Jasper scraped his fingers over his day's growth of whiskers. "Case won them in a card game. He owns everything."

Her heart plummeted. It couldn't be true. Yet her father sounded convincing, and she saw no reason for him to lie. She didn't understand why, until now, he had defended his partner. "Mr. O'Malley cheated you out of your money? I wouldn't have believed it of him."

"Case don't cheat. He's just holding my stocks for me."

Rayne jumped to her feet. "Are you really that naive?"

"Rayne, honey, Case—"

"Is apparently unscrupulous," she finished. She paced across the room, then swung around. "You must make him return your stock."

"Case is doing me a favor."

"A *favor*?" Folding her arms over her chest,

Rayne sank into a chair. "Papa, the man has beguiled you." *He has beguiled both of us,* she thought dejectedly. "Does everyone in town know of this?"

"He made me promise I wouldn't tell anyone he's keeping my shares."

"Oh!" She leapt to her feet again. Her outraged heart thumped in her chest. "You must insist he give back your stock. If you won't speak to him, I shall."

Rayne prayed her father would show some backbone. She didn't want to face Case O'Malley, particularly not regarding this delicate matter. Rightfully the burden should fall on her father's shoulders.

Jasper's already wrinkled brow furrowed more deeply. "Rayne, honey, you mustn't go upsetting Case."

She shouldn't upset *him*. "Why, pray tell? Why are you protecting him? You are his unfortunate victim. He has grievously taken advantage of you."

"I told you, Case is respected around town. And he's my partner. Without him, I'd have nothing."

"You found the mine. You told me so in your letter."

"Yes, but Case tells me how to tunnel for the ore. We're a team."

Some team, she thought. Her father did all the work and O'Malley reaped all the rewards. "Papa, please, promise me you'll speak to Mr. O'Malley about returning your stock."

"No need to," Jasper said, shaking his head. "I told you, Case is my friend. He's only protecting me. What's wrong with your thinking, girl?"

She laid her hand on his shoulder. Deep inside,

she'd always known her father was weak, but she hadn't realized he could be hoodwinked so easily. Surely their mine produced more than enough silver and gold to support even O'Malley's dissipated life. But Case O'Malley was a rake and a scoundrel; he could charm the birds from the trees if he wanted to, and he'd certainly had no trouble charming a harmless old man.

Friend, she thought, her eyes narrowing darkly at the word. The serpent in the Garden of Eden was more of a friend to Adam. Mr. O'Malley must be made aware that his cunning tactics would no longer be tolerated. She only wished the burden hadn't fallen on her. Rayne made certain her father ate part of the delicious breakfast Hung Lee had cooked before she dressed and prepared to find Case O'Malley. It was not a task to which she looked forward. Her cheeks flamed at the thought of seeing him again.

By the time Rayne reached C Street, however, her mood had improved. It was a beautiful day, if she discounted the occasional gusts of wind and swirls of dust. She caught wisps of conversation from the people who swarmed on the boardwalks, discussing the war raging in the East. Mule trains and pack wagons jammed the main thoroughfare, impeding traffic, and somewhere in the distance a band played a funeral dirge.

There were too many sights and sounds to enjoy to dwell on Mr. O'Malley's defects of character. Besides, if she waited a while longer to confront him, her temper would cool.

On his way to the office, Case strode down the street, pausing often to speak with acquaintances,

especially the women. His notoriety afforded him
a standing in this city; being rich, eligible, and the
best gambler in town earned him a certain respect.
Despite the bruises to his ego and his body from
the night before, he felt especially blessed this
morning. Those restless hours had fortified his
goal: He would avoid Jasper's daughter at all cost.
And if he did encounter her, he swore he wouldn't
allow her to get under his skin again.

Case reached into his inside pocket and discovered it empty. He dashed between moving traffic
and headed for an establishment across the street.
When he reached the walk, he frowned. Two
buildings away, Rayne North strolled toward him.
Case quickly ducked into the cigar store. Although
he felt foolish, he knew the action would insure
his sanity.

He replenished his supply of cigars before reluctantly turning his attention back outside. From the
dark interior of the store, he saw Rayne stroll past
the smudged window. He watched her pause to
examine the gaudily painted wooden Indian,
Pocahontas, which held a handful of fine Hava-
nas. Looking around to make sure no one saw her,
Rayne touched the wooden figure and laughed.

Case was fascinated. In her new bonnet, which
covered her hair and framed her face, she looked
sweet and desirable. She backed away, still staring
at the Indian. He would never have believed Jasper's proper daughter could show such delight
over a cheap cigar store display. Curiosity drove
him to trail behind her when she moved on.

She admired the wide balconies that enclosed
galleries on the second floors of the buildings that
lined the street. She smiled at the iron stands of

red geraniums, and hanging baskets of flaming nasturtiums, cascading through the black railings.

Farther along, she haggled with a Chinese fruit vendor and purchased several items from his basket. The antics of an organ grinder's monkey made her giggle. Under the pretext of fidgeting with her bonnet, she even peeked into a saloon.

Case grinned.

Next she gawked at a bawdy poster on a wall. Her hand covered her mouth. Realizing the poster was one of his favorites, he laughed at her shocked expression and pink cheeks. Called the *Wild Horse of Tartary*, the billboard illustrated a naked woman strapped to the back of a black stallion lunging up a dark mountain.

While she pondered an advertisement promoting pills, tonics, and syrups, Case paused to light a cigar. When he looked again, she was observing a Wells Fargo Express employee distributing letters, packages, and papers.

A horrendous tremor from the mine rattled the boardwalk. Case barely noticed the explosions anymore, but Rayne stood deathly still, staring at the ground as though it might collapse beneath her feet. Case resisted the urge to walk over and reassure her. The tremor passed and she walked on hesitantly.

He followed her awhile longer, intrigued by her captivation with everything around her. Contrary to Jasper's expectations, Virginia City seemed to bewitch her. When she took a stick of candy from her reticule and gazed longingly at it, Case smiled. He wondered if she would give in to wicked temptation and actually eat in public. To his delight, she did indeed break off an end and, glanc-

ing furtively around, pop the sweet into her
mouth.

When Rayne became caught in a fast-moving
crowd of men, Case stepped forward. With relief,
he discovered it wasn't necessary to betray his
presence. Samuel Clemens handed her to safety.
Highly respected as the editor of the *Territorial Enterprise*, Sam knew everyone in town. Case felt
confident Rayne was in good hands. He watched
them converse for several minutes before Clemens
pointed in the direction of the O'Malley-North
Mine.

Gradually Miss North's destination became obvious to Case. He didn't know why she was seeking him out, but he didn't like it. Dodging vehicles
in the street, he quickly slipped away to his office.

Rayne said good-bye to Samuel Clemens and
observed the boisterous activity filling the streets
and sidewalks, aware that she was on her own for
the first time in her life, free to make her own decisions. Virginia City thrilled her.

Reluctantly she admitted she wanted to delay
her meeting with Case O'Malley. She had planned
exactly what she'd say to him, but she would need
to lead into it gradually. She couldn't just walk in
and attack him.

A group of men passed her, all four tipping
their hats. Rayne smiled and nodded. She met the
gaze of an attractive man with light brown hair
and eyes. He doffed his hat and executed a gallant
bow. Then, evading the small gatherings of speculators jamming the walk, he strolled toward her.

The man stopped in front of her, turning his

fashionable hat in his fingers. "You appear lost," he said. "Might I be of assistance?"

"Thank you, but Mr. Clemens kindly gave me directions to my destination."

"Perhaps I might offer my escort then. It isn't safe for a lady to walk this street alone. Where I come from, a gentleman always offers his protection."

Intrigued by his southern drawl, Rayne studied his gray, single-breasted cutaway coat, the edges of which were finished in darker gray braid. The black waistcoat fit him superbly. A wide striped silk neckcloth tied in a bow lent him a sophisticated air. Compared with flamboyant Case O'Malley, this man's attire gave the impression of understated elegance.

Rayne smiled with approval. "You are very gracious, sir."

"My name is Paul Devereau. It would give me great pleasure to escort you, Miss . . . ?"

"North. Rayne North. Thank you, but I am nearly at my destination." She admired his dark brown mustache and friendly smile, noting the way his hair curled over his ears. "Perhaps another time, Mr. Devereau."

"Please, call me Paul. Manners are informal in this part of the country. Difficult to accept, but one tries to adjust."

She found him attractive. Unlike O'Malley, she couldn't imagine Paul Devereau ever taking advantage of a woman's virtue. "Thank you, Paul."

"I hope you won't think me forward, Miss North, if I ask you to join me for lunch later at that restaurant across the way. I realize we haven't been properly introduced." He gave her an engaging grin. "I hope you will say yes. You will, won't you?"

Feeling a trifle daring, and persuaded by his charming manners, she replied, "Yes, I shall be delighted to join you. Say, in an hour?"

"You won't regret your decision." Leaning forward while maintaining a discreet distance between them, Devereau gestured toward the International Hotel. "I shall meet you there and count the seconds until then, Miss North."

Rayne set a straight path to the mine office. The sooner she faced Case O'Malley, the better.

For the third time in ten minutes, Case glanced at the door. He was certain Rayne had been headed for his office. Not that he wanted to see her. She made him feel like something that had crawled out from under a rock.

Why, then, are you disappointed she hasn't come? a nagging inner voice taunted.

At last Jasper had finally shown his haggard face. Case had sent him to the mill to see about a shipment of ore. Worry creased Case's forehead. Jasper had looked like death warmed over, and Case wondered if he himself would look the same in a few more years. Distracted by the disturbing thought, he gazed blindly at the papers on his desk.

Minutes later a soft rap on his office door announced Rayne's arrival. Feeling contrary and annoyed at his anticipation, he remained seated and called, "It's open."

He didn't bother to look up when she entered. Imagining how her emerald green dress would contrast with her hazel eyes, he figured it was the safest course. He already knew she would look scrumptious, even if the garment buttoned to her throat and covered her arms. She needn't expose her body to appear feminine. She was slim and elegant. The thought that he was probably the only man to ever have seen her in her nightdress gratified him.

"Good morning, Mr. O'Malley. Since I found myself in the vicinity, I thought I'd pay you a call."

Her cheerful greeting surprised him. After their run-in last night, he'd expected a tongue-lashing. He raised a brow. "Isn't this a rather forward move for a woman of your refined breeding, Miss North?"

She stepped in front of him, laying her reticule and a small collection of fruit on his desk. "I understand that propriety is viewed differently here than in other parts of the country."

"Women *are* free to express themselves in Virginia City without being condemned for their actions, if that's what you mean."

He felt the heat of her gaze and wondered how she'd taken his remark. There had been an unintentional insinuation in his words, if one was sophisticated enough to recognize it. Miss North, of course, wouldn't make the connection. He looked down and scribbled notes alongside a drawing of timbers for the mine.

"I owe you an apology, Mr. O'Malley."

Case's head jerked up. "I believe my hearing isn't functioning today. Would you mind repeating that?"

"Judging from something my father said, I fear

I should apologize," she said as she fumbled with the ribbons of her hat.

Case noted the slight quake of her hands when she placed her bonnet on the desk with her other belongings. "Interesting choice of words. Why do you fear making amends?"

"A regretful choice on my part." She drew figures in the dust on his desk. "I apologize for dismissing you from my father's house last night."

So Jasper had confessed the truth for once. It was the only possible reason for her apology. "I appreciate your generosity, Miss North, but I accept some of the blame for misleading you."

She waved her hand, giving a dainty cough.

Case frowned. Although he already suspected the reason for her watery eyes, he asked, "Have you caught a cold?"

"How do you breathe this foul air?"

With an exaggerated flourish, Case puffed on his cigar and exhaled a thick cloud of smoke. Opening the window behind him, he flicked out his half-finished Havana.

An attractive shade of pink stained her cheeks. "You needn't have done that," she said.

Like hell, he thought. Ladies always found a man's simple pleasures offensive. He grunted and returned to his paperwork.

"You seem unusually well today."

He tilted his head and gave her a rueful smile. "Were you hoping you'd find me hugging a chamber pot?"

Her eyes opened very wide. "Most certainly not. It would be uncharitable to wish illness on anyone."

"Even me?"

Case found himself suddenly wishing she'd worn her hair down today, so he could see it again. Although it appeared softer, drawn loosely back and wound in a large roll at her nape, he remembered how the rich chestnut waves had looked last night tumbling over her shoulders. Heat surged in his veins.

"May I sit?" she asked.

Prompted by her gentle reminder, Case left his seat and came around the desk. He slid a chair close and held out his hand. "Please, allow me to assist you."

She considered a moment, then reluctantly offered her arm and let him clasp her elbow.

Piqued by her manner, he gave in to a wicked temptation and remarked, "I'm delighted you came to see me, my dear. I admit I thought you uninterested."

She sat down stiffly and carefully arranged her skirt to hide her ankles. Case propped his hip on the corner of the desk and crossed his arms over his chest.

"I don't know what you mean to imply, but the reason for my visit has nothing to do with you . . . Well, in a way it does, but . . ." She took a deep, unsteady breath.

"If you want me to kiss you again, all you have to do is ask."

"I most certainly do not!"

"You didn't enjoy my kisses? Come now, Miss North, I know better. Look at how soon you've sought me out."

Briskly she fanned her flaming face with a hand. Feeling a twinge of guilt for taunting her, he smiled sweetly and said, "What do you want from me, Miss North?"

She avoided his gaze. "I want nothing from you for myself. I must ask you about something else my father said."

He wasn't sure he wanted to know the real reason for her visit just yet, so he stood and offered his arm. "Sounds serious. Let me show you around first, and we'll discuss what's on your mind afterward."

"I'm not sure I should."

"Trust me. Your virtue is safe."

"I rather doubt that," she mumbled, refraining from taking his arm. "But I suppose a few minutes won't matter."

Her reticence challenged him, but must she behave as if he had smallpox? Masking his annoyance with a polite smile, he led her into an enormous building with ceilings forty feet high. Steam hissed through square openings in the floor and rose to the rafters. She looked horrified to see men enter and depart through the columns of steam.

"Special clothing protects the miners from harm. The mouth of the shaft is over there."

"This is fascinating."

Her unfeigned enthusiasm pleased him so much that he made an effort to explain the construction. "Partitions divide the shaft into four smaller sections, three of which house metal cages used to hoist men, supplies, or ore."

She pointed at an iron pipe, a foot or more in diameter, beside a pole. "And what does that do?"

"It's used for pumping. The rod drives up water from below and keeps the tunnels from flooding."

"Very impressive, Mr. O'Malley."

Case stepped behind her. She tensed. A sensuous fragrance floated all around him. With a start, he realized it came from her. Too soon, she recovered her composure and walked around. He followed, explaining, "Carpenters, blacksmiths, and machinists work in the other wings. At the end of the building is an engineer."

"There's more involved in digging for ore than I realized."

Case stopped several inches behind her again. She turned her head and raised her eyebrows. He understood now. Miss North hadn't been treating him with disdain. His nearness bothered her just as hers did him.

Pleased with his discovery yet not wanting to spoil the momentary peace between them, he said, "We won't disturb the engineer. He must keep constant watch on the dial showing the location of the cage he monitors. The lives of the men are his concern. Any distraction may prove fatal."

So could his attraction to Jasper's daughter, Case thought.

Chapter 5

C ase O'Malley rattled Rayne more than she would have believed possible. Once again, he stood close behind her, much too close. His actions were deliberate, she knew, yet his behavior did strange things to her stomach. It wasn't fair. He was not only devastatingly handsome, he looked superb in his tailored black coat and trousers and he smelled wonderful. If a woman could somehow resist his dashing appearance, she'd surely surrender to his sense-shattering scent. This man had robbed her father, she reminded herself. If she wasn't careful, she would end up a victim, too.

She stepped a few paces away, hoping her motive in wanting to move away from him wasn't too obvious, then turned and faced him. "The special clothing you mentioned." Deploring her quavering voice, which betrayed her strain, she asked, "Does everyone who goes into the mine wear these garments?"

"I'll show you." He set off in the opposite direction. "This way, Miss North." A hint of a smile played over his mouth as he waited by a door. "I've scheduled a meeting this afternoon. Please hurry."

"If you're pressed for time, Mr. O'Malley, I won't keep you from your obligations." Adopting a regal posture, she swept past him. "I have an engagement of sorts myself."

"I didn't realize you knew anyone else in Virginia City."

"Just this morning I met a *charming* man," Rayne replied. "He invited me to luncheon with him. What room is this?"

"A changing room. The clothes hanging over there are worn into the mine. In the sweltering temperatures below, they not only protect the men but also insure they are dry when later they go outside into the cool air."

Crossing the area, she noticed the woolen shirts were all gray or blue. There were caps and narrow-brimmed felt hats, and either blue cotton or thin woolen overalls. "If I went into the shaft, would I have to wear garments like these?"

"Yes, indeed, Miss North. Not the latest style, but I wager you'd look fetching—even more fetching than you do in that dress."

Knowing his gaze raked her body, Rayne stood still. If she turned and looked, would she find the same expression on his face as last night? Dear God, she'd forgotten he had seen her body through the nightgown. "I really must speak to you about my father."

"Won't you be late for your luncheon with *charming* Mr. Clemens?"

Rayne blinked. "How did you know I met him?"

"I know a lot of things, my dear."

She whipped around. "You saw me this morning, didn't you? If you knew I was searching for you, why didn't you make your presence known?"

"I haven't yet developed the ability to read minds. I did notice you, but you were being entertained by Clemens. It would have been uncivil of me to intrude."

Rayne cursed her inexperience. He was staring at her in that intimate manner of his. His eyes had darkened to a much deeper shade of green. Was he imagining her body unclothed? The uneasiness she experienced every time he came near her stabbed her stomach.

"I am not meeting Mr. Clemens," she finally said, thankful her voice remained steady.

"Oh? Did you meet yet another charming man?"

Self-conscious, Rayne folded her arms over her chest. "That, sir, is none of your business."

"Being a man of such *notorious fame*, as I believe you referred to me, chances are that if you've met someone of equally unsavory character, I will likely know him."

"The main bull in the pasture usually does recognize his competition," she remarked quietly.

"Bravo, Miss North. I do admire spirit in a woman, amongst other things."

"It seems to amuse you to unnerve me."

He gave her a devastating smile. "Perhaps. You haven't told me the name of your most recent conquest."

"Paul Devereau."

O'Malley closed the distance between them and, resting his hands on her arms, caressed her. His smile slipped into a sardonic grin. "Will you kiss him as passionately as you did me?"

Fury and excitement raced through Rayne. His hands felt hot on her skin, even through her dress. Surely he couldn't be jealous. Yet it was the only explanation she could fathom for his interest in her affairs. The idea so thrilled her that she boldly retorted, "I doubt he would behave as forwardly as you, but I'll consider your suggestion."

He arched a brow, clearly amused. "You think to compare him with me?"

Unwilling to further engage in a war of words she could not win, Rayne took a step toward the door. But he wrapped his arms around her and pulled her against him. "Unhand me this instant, you unmannerly oaf!"

"I think not. So ... I'm an unmannerly oaf now?"

She attempted to twist free.

"Stand still, or I'll bruise you. I don't want to— ouch! You kicked me, you vicious little hellcat."

Rayne pushed hard against his chest, twisting again. It was tempting to remain in his arms. He was so large, his chest so broad. Pretending to take a calming breath, she closed her eyes and breathed in his heady scent. She mustn't let him weaken her defenses. Already she felt faint. "Please, let me go," she implored.

"Relax. Don't move against me that way."

She obeyed. She had little choice at present, and the sensations brought about by her struggles were not altogether unpleasant. If she escaped from him unscathed, she would never allow herself to be caught in a similar situation—alone with an unconscionable man. She took a deep, shuddering breath.

"Admit the truth," he said, his tone low and seductive. "You like being held in my arms. Back at the house you were purring like a kitten."

Actually, she thought, it was rather nice now that she'd stopped fighting him. O'Malley's body felt warm and comforting. *Too warm, too comforting.* She glanced up at him. She stared at his firm, attractive mouth. Against her will, she wondered what would happen if he kissed her.

When his head lowered, she held her breath. She thought she didn't want him to kiss her. He was dangerous, a man bent on self-destruction. His mouth hovered over hers, his breath caressing her lips. Her heart thumped, her stomach pitched. Her lips parted on a sigh.

At the last second, his mouth veered left and slid over her cheek. He nibbled the tender area below her ear. "You have a passionate nature, one I'd dearly love to explore," he said provocatively. "But now's not the time."

She fell against him, breathless, trembling, and, to her shame, a bit disappointed. "Mr. O'Malley," she whispered.

Abruptly he released her and stalked toward the one small window.

Rayne immediately felt the loss of his embrace and crossed her arms over her heaving chest. She attempted to steady her wobbly legs. The man was a devil.

"Forgive me *again*, Miss North. I'm not myself. You may slap if you wish."

She hastened toward a chair against the wall and, sitting, touched the spot where his lips had grazed her skin. She felt both hot and cold all over. "I won't strike you. It would be rather pointless."

He poked a finger inside his collar. "You mean

I'm forgiven because I'm inclined to brash behavior?"

"Precisely." She puffed out her lower lip and blew air upward, over her face. "More's the pity."

"You're right on all counts. Fortunately, I'm beyond redemption."

Rayne stood. Something in the tone of his voice made her think she'd hurt him.

"Wait in my office, please. I'll be with you presently."

She had been dismissed. Perplexed by his brusque turnabout, she lingered in the doorway, watching him. He braced his hands on either side of the window frame and hung his head. She had the impression he sought to hide something from her. But what? She doubted she'd ever figure out her father's complex partner. Her spirits sagging, she went to wait for him in his office.

Minutes passed before she heard his boots on the wood floor. Although she was sure he'd made her wait on purpose, she vowed to maintain a semblance of decorum in his presence and master her unseemly awareness of him.

When he entered, his dignified air drew her attention. No visible signs of their recent tussle showed in his distant manner or aloof expression. But to her chagrin, the unruly yearning he'd awakened in her body plagued her still.

Standing behind his desk, his hands in his pockets, he said, "Tell me why you came. And come to the point this time, Miss North."

"I spoke with my father this morning," she returned in a rush, anxious to be done with the matter. "He informed me that you hold his mining stocks."

He stiffened, his eyes narrowing. "And?"

"If you have any regard for decency, you must return them," she said in one quick breath, before her courage could desert her.

O'Malley's dark eyebrows shot up and his jaw visibly tensed. *How dare he act innocent of his crime?* Rayne railed silently. "Surely even you will admit it's reprehensible to take advantage of your partner."

He aimed her a lethal glare. "Are you implying that I defrauded your father?"

Rayne summoned her courage and held her steady gaze on him. He looked ready to strangle her, his eyes reminding her of green ice. She tried to swallow, but her throat had gone dry.

"Accusing a man of being a cardsharp is a sure way to meet your Maker in these parts." He pulled his hands from his pockets, leaned forward, and splayed his fingers on his desk. "You should be thankful you're a woman, Miss North. I've shot men for less."

Rayne instantly regretted her allegation. O'Malley appeared deceptively calm, yet there had been a noticeable edge to his voice. Remembering his reputation, and her father's inability to see past Case's charm, she steeled herself to stand firm. "If you are truly innocent, then all you need do is return my father's stock."

"And you, my dear, seem unduly concerned about your father's finances. I wonder why."

The sarcastic tone of his voice dismayed her. "I don't know what you mean to imply, Mr. O'Malley, but I am only concerned with my father's welfare."

"You wasted little time in getting here. I've found a fly usually heads straight for the honey."

"I assure you I have no designs on my father's wealth."

He laughed, but it was a grating sound. "Just as well. If real money is your goal, you should have been a little friendlier to me. I can be very generous."

Rayne straightened and rounded the desk. "You are wrong. I spurned your advances because I've been brought up to protect my virtue. And I have no designs on my father's money, or yours. I only want my father to provide for my mother."

Case crammed his hands in his pockets again. "You lie so easily, I warrant I'll take anything you say in the future with a grain of salt."

Her action was reflexive, fueled by her wrath. The sharp crack of her open palm against his face echoed in the silent room. Staring at the flaming imprint on his cheek, Rayne felt as shocked as he looked. Her hand stung something awful. She shuddered. "A *gentleman* would never call a lady a liar."

"A *lady* should never call a gentleman a cheat," he shot back.

"Prove your innocence, Mr. O'Malley, and I'll gladly apologize. I want to believe there was a reason for your actions."

Raking his furious green gaze over her, he laid his hand over his red face. "If you think I'm guilty, prove it."

Rayne attempted to gain control of her raging emotions by sucking in a ragged breath. His affronted manner warned her that she had committed a grievous trespass. His features seemed carved of granite. Consumed with anguish, she lowered her gaze. She shouldn't blame him. His actions were a natural result of his decadent way of life.

"Sit down, Miss North."

She glanced up to see him gesture toward the chair behind his desk. Although she questioned his intention, she felt too drained to offer an argument. Seated, she noticed his drawings for the mine and admired his bold script. Every precise detail spoke of his talent, not only in sketching but in engineering. If he wanted to, he could turn his life around.

Sliding paper in front of her, he dipped his pen in ink and put it in her hand. "Write your mother's name and address. I presume she still lives in Chicago?"

She looked up again, her eyes wide with surprise.

"Yes, Miss North, I will personally wire funds to your mother. You needn't worry on her account again."

Although relieved, Rayne felt weighted down by his refusal to defend himself. "Mr. O'Malley, I truly wish you'd deny outright that you took advantage of my father."

"Don't tell me you'd believe the word of a cardsharp." He clasped his hands behind his back, a cynical twist to his mouth. "Write quickly, before I change my mind—unless you really don't want the money sent to your mother."

Insufferable man. Despite the violent quake of her hand, Rayne scribbled out the information.

"You may leave now, Miss North."

Rayne almost laughed. She'd ungraciously

turned him out of her father's house last night. Now he was throwing her out of his office. It was just the sort of behavior she'd come to expect from him. With as much dignity as the circumstances allowed, she rose, collected her belongings, and departed.

From the window, Case watched Miss North's alluring stride. He shouldn't allow her to traipse about without an escort, but he wasn't her guardian. The aggravating woman needed a keeper, someone stronger-willed than Jasper North. Then again, he mused, he pitied the unfortunate man who might accost her. She may be innocent, but she had enough spirit to frighten twenty years from a man's life.

With a sour expression, he returned to his desk. He had more important things to do than worry about her, especially after she'd accused him of swindling Jasper. That bothered him more than he liked to admit. He had numerous faults, and he readily admitted them, but his integrity was above reproach. She might have had a little faith in him, but he supposed her conclusion wasn't unreasonable, given his reputation.

He couldn't change his ways now even if he wanted to. Not only did the Union depend on him, but the miner who acted as his accomplice was also to be considered. The Union had picked Case because it was unlikely anyone would suspect him of any secret government activities. Hell, most of the townspeople looked up to him *because* of his exploits. Except Miss North. She was the only person who'd ever rebuked him. He hadn't minded her assessment of his manners. In fact, he'd found baiting her quite enjoyable. But implying he'd duped Jasper had been an insult. Furious, Case scowled.

Damn irritating woman.

His face still smarted like hell. Perversely, he cherished that slap. In the course of two days, he'd discovered a fiery temperament beneath Miss North's proper, innocent countenance. He would have thought less of her had she calmly accepted his accusation. He'd willingly wager a shipment of his own gold that she truly had no designs on her father's wealth.

Remembering her mention of the gambler who'd tried to fleece Jasper, Case recalled Devereau saying he'd just come from Sacramento. He made a mental note to check up on the man.

Lord save him from an ingenuous, desirable woman and her impact on a lusty man. Earlier, in the changing room, he'd been unable to turn around, afraid he'd shock her into a swoon. Even she couldn't have missed the bulge in his pants. She should be hanged for a witch, he thought with a sneer. He'd behaved badly, again, but he hadn't been able to resist taking her into his arms. In the future, even if it meant he must bind his hands, he wouldn't touch her again.

A lazy grin spread across his mouth. Sooner or later she'd learn the truth about Jasper's stock shares and she'd feel contrite. He imagined her chagrin when it came time to apologize.

Yes indeed, he thought. He planned to savor the moment for a long, long time.

As Rayne continued up Union Street, toward the commercial district, she pushed thoughts of Case

O'Malley from her mind. Instead, she concentrated on her laborious climb up the mountainside. Descending the streets earlier had been much easier than this return trip. She steadied her vision on the sagebrush and stunted pines that dotted the landscape above Virginia City and finally reached her destination breathless.

She found Paul Devereau waiting for her in front of the International Hotel. Together they entered the elegant dining room. Her recent altercation with Case O'Malley made her appreciate Paul Devereau's genteel manners all the more. He moved with grace, complimented her often, and lavished attendance on her until she felt like a queen.

Yet she couldn't help wishing he were a little less polished, a little rougher around the edges, just like . . .

Checking her wayward thoughts, she listened to Paul describe his ruined plantation in Louisiana. Since she abhorred the institution of slavery, she cautiously avoided offering a comment on that controversial topic. He had lost everything. She felt sorry for the loss of his home and life as he'd known it.

After her encounter with Case O'Malley, Rayne felt ravenous. They dined on fresh, imported oysters, loin of veal, boiled potatoes, green corn, and finished with mince pie.

"What will you do now?" she asked, curious about Paul's plans.

A look of determination came over his features. He set his crystal water glass on the white linen cloth and smoothed the lace-trimmed edge with his elegant fingers. "I've ventured to this godforsaken territory to seek my fortune. When I accumulate enough capital, I intend to restore my home to its former grandeur. Unfortunately," he added with a dispirited sigh, "my abilities seem limited to governing a plantation."

She folded her hands on her lap and searched his attractive face. "You are an educated, refined gentleman, Mr. Devereau. I'm sure you'll find a way to fulfill your dream."

"Recently I came upon a windfall, even more money than I needed to reconstruct Deverwood. But just as quickly, I lost it."

Rayne waited patiently, hoping he would elaborate. Finally, although she knew it wasn't polite to question a man about his private dealings, curiosity made her ask bluntly, "What happened?"

"I was enjoying a pleasant game of chance the other night with an inexperienced but interesting man who boasted he owned half of one of the best-producing mines in the Comstock. Naturally I doubted his claim. You can imagine my incredulity when not only did he unwisely wager his shares but also admitted he had them on him.

"I merely engaged in the play for amusement, you understand. I was so astounded when I won, but gratified by my good fortune, I allowed another man to join the game. He deftly outfoxed me. To my chagrin, I later discovered I had been outsmarted by a seasoned gambler. The man was so good, I'm not altogether sure I wasn't cheated. It was a humiliating experience, and I swear I shan't play again."

Suddenly alert, Rayne leaned forward. "I don't believe you mentioned the gambler's name."

"O'Malley. Case O'Malley."

A cough worked its way up her throat and she covered her mouth with a napkin.

"You seem distressed, Miss North." He fell silent, his eyes round with dread. "My profound apologies. It was unforgivable of me not to make the connection. Jasper North is a relation to you."

She cautiously sipped from her water glass. Meeting his gaze, she revealed, "He's my father."

"I sincerely hope you will not hold this breach of conduct against me. That fellow, O'Malley, had the audacity to imply that I fleeced your father. I swear, I had no such intention. Why, a man would have to be an accomplished cardsharp to attempt such a maneuver. I have, however, learned a valuable lesson." He hooked his thumbs around his lapels and smiled. "I will never indulge in such a sinful sport again."

"Mr. Devereau, rest assured, I have no intention of reproving you for gambling. I know you meant my father no injury and were only engaging in what you deemed a harmless amusement."

He looked so relieved, Rayne knew she'd been right to believe him. His confession, however, led her to a stark conclusion.

Case O'Malley was innocent. Dear God, he had actually won back her father's mining stock from Devereau!

Chapter 6

Four days later, heading for his office, Case detoured around one of several huge mounds of earth heaped near the mine building. As he did every day, he glanced at the windowsill. Foreboding filled him when he saw the rock perched there.

It was a signal that his fellow operative, posing as a miner, wanted to meet. Face-to-face encounters were dangerous, requested only in the event of a dire emergency. In two days the shipment of Union gold was due to go out, and in order for the bullion to be included on the wagon train headed for New York, the ore must reach the U.S. Treasury in Sacramento on time. Sentiment in Virginia City was mostly pro-Union, but there existed a small, secret society of pro-Confederate sympathizers known as the Knights of the Golden Circle. Case scowled. They were a thorn in his side.

To meet his fellow spy, he'd have to go down over a thousand feet into a mine shaft. He shuddered at the thought. It was an ordeal he suffered only for the good of his country: for no other reason would he enter the earth's steamy bowels.

He hid his affliction well. A mine owner shouldn't feel trapped and short of breath in closed places. Jasper knew of his adversity to the tunnels, and thankfully, kept Case's secret.

Case entered his office, went straight to his desk, and threw open a bottom drawer. He took a swallow from the bottle of whiskey stashed there, and felt a little better. He glanced at his pocket watch, noting the time. With an hour until his rendezvous, he figured he might as well relax. He tilted back his chair and propped his feet on his desk.

His patience neared the breaking point. Since his clash days ago with Jasper's daughter, she hadn't yet apologized for accusing him of swindling Jasper. She'd sent verbal messages by way of her father requesting that he visit, but Case felt justified in denying her appeals. He would not be summoned like a pet to his master.

Did she actually believe he hadn't heard she'd been keeping company with Paul Devereau? With a wicked grin he imagined her reaction when the man failed to make another assignation. Remembering Devereau's fearful expression the evening past, when Case had given him a dire warning to cease his pursuit of Rayne, he laughed. Miss North had just been relieved of her suitor.

He excused his behavior entirely. He wasn't jealous of Devereau. It was just too much of a coincidence that the same southerner who had tried to win Jasper's mining stock now courted his daughter. The investigation into Devereau's character, begun yesterday at Case's request, would soon provide answers.

Case heard the door open, and hid the liquor on the floor. Normally he abstained until evening, unless he had to bury himself in a cramped, suffocating tunnel; he didn't even dare think of the rats. He closed his eyes as a tremor strong enough to rattle his bones shook him.

"I got another message for you from Rayne," said Jasper as he flopped his dusty hat on the desk. "She feels real bad for thinkin' you cheated me. She wants you to come to supper tonight."

"No, thanks, I'd rather face a slew of rats than crawl to any woman, especially your daughter. You sure you weren't the one who told her the truth about me?"

"I kept my mouth shut, just like you said. Case, she's beside herself, acting as crazy as you. Can't even sneak out of the house without her catching me."

Case crossed his arms over his chest, his mouth set in an obstinate line.

"If you ask me," Jasper complained, "you two ought to pair off."

"Like hell. I don't want my life changed." Case capped the bottle, put it away, and locked the drawer. "If your daughter wants to atone for her slur on my honor, she can damn well haul herself over here."

Jasper groaned. "Rayne was only concerned for me, Case. Why are you being so damned stubborn?"

Case ignored the older man's question. "I have to go down below to make sure my instructions are being carried out correctly. If they don't set the timbers close enough to the walls, we might have another cave-in."

"I check every day, Case."

"I know you do. It's not that I don't trust you.

I just feel it's my obligation to show my face every so often."

Together they strode toward the changing room. "You're gonna get sick again."

Case spun around. "I didn't get sick the last time," he said indignantly. "The cage comes back up so damn fast, it makes me dizzy, is all."

"That damn contraption makes my head feel like it'll pop," Jasper said.

Sympathizing with his partner's plight and recalling, too, how his own mother had harried his frail father, Case gripped Jasper's shoulder. "Take today off. I'll mind the office and see that the shipment of ore gets to the mill."

"Rayne won't like it."

Case gave Jasper a shameless grin. "A woman like Rayne isn't happy unless she's reforming a man. Tell her you have my permission. That should stoke her fire."

"I don't deserve a good girl like her," Jasper mused out loud on his way to the door. "You two want to fight, leave me out of it."

From the second Case stepped into the iron-framed cage with open sides, anxiety gripped him. He placed his feet wide apart on the solid floor to brace for the rapid drop. His respect for his partner always rose a notch when he went into the tunnels. Jasper had to be part mole to be able to go down there every day.

His body swayed as the walls of the shaft flew past, and his breath lodged in his lungs. He flashed by a large room, catching a glimpse of men standing about, holding candles and lanterns; their voices and the clang of machinery faded away as he continued to descend. The cage finally jarred to a stop at fifteen hundred feet. Case expelled a ragged breath. After he offered a prayer of thanks that he'd survived the harrowing plunge, he quickly left the cage and entered the main drift.

The one-hundred-degree heat hit him immediately. He practically tore off his woolen shirt as he followed the narrow-gauge tracks used by cars to haul out ore. Coming upon a miner wearing only a breechcloth, he was tempted to strip to his own underwear.

He turned in to the east-to-west crosscut and paused next to several men who chipped with picks at a ravaged wall of crumbly ore. Wiping his face with his handkerchief, he nodded at a man who, using a candle stub for light, sat on a timber to work a lower portion of the wall. Case spent several minutes speaking with the miners in this section before he accepted a chunk of ice from the constant supply sent down from above. Then he wandered into another short shaft.

He sucked the ice and waited. Within five minutes, his associate arrived.

"Don't know how you stand it down here, John," Case said, pressing cold, dripping fingers to his fevered brow. "Hell's fire can't possibly blaze any hotter."

John rubbed the back of his neck. "So far, I've lost twenty pounds, Case. If the war ain't over soon, I'll be nothin' but a scarecrow." He glanced over his shoulder before he confided, "Got some news for you."

Case sidled close, his eyes steady on the tunnel opening.

"Heard talk your next shipment might be diverted south. Best be on the lookout," the miner whispered. "Maybe you ought to send out your regular shipments to San Francisco on Wells Fargo, like the rest of the mine owners."

"Thanks for the warning, but I prefer to freight my gold personally. Wells Fargo's best guard is in my employ, and I trust him. I'll not risk the Union's gold, though. I'll think of something."

They shook hands, then Case left the miner and retraced his steps, returning aboveground. He couldn't escape the sweltering tomb fast enough.

Late that evening, Rayne thoughtfully paced the parlor. Case O'Malley had to be the most stubborn man alive. After what had transpired between them in the mine office, she'd concluded that she mustn't spend time alone with him again. She didn't trust him, or herself. Every time he touched her, her blood raced through her veins, muddling her mind and rendering her susceptible to his power.

But the obstinate man refused to cooperate.

She'd thought a quiet dinner would provide a safe environment in which to apologize. With Papa and Hung Lee present, O'Malley wouldn't have an opportunity to arouse or confuse her further.

Brushing her fingers over the spot under her ear where he had pressed his lips, Rayne shivered. Whenever he came near her, she felt like a small, defenseless creature about to be snared by a hungry wolf. No matter which way she turned, he blocked her path, waiting to devour her. There was only one problem with her analogy: Case

O'Malley didn't resemble a ferocious wolf. Far from it. Each time she saw him, he appealed to her more strongly.

She almost wished he *had* taken advantage of her father in that card game, instead of winning back her father's shares from Paul Devereau.

Sitting on a side chair by the window, Rayne sighed. She had just spent four miserable days grieving over her wrongful treatment of Case O'Malley. If his refusal to allow her to make amends was his way of getting revenge, he was even more insufferable than she'd first thought.

A noise from the front of the house snapped her out of her reverie. She parted the Brussels lace curtains and peeked out. It was her father. She scurried to the front hall and opened the door.

"Papa, you're late this evening." She took his hat, looped her arm through his, and guided him toward the stairs. "Have you eaten?"

Jasper nodded. "You shouldn't have waited up for me, Rayne."

"I wanted to. I missed you. Did you deliver my message to Mr. O'Malley?"

"Case won't listen. The way he's actin' you would think he'd been insulted by the queen of England herself."

"Did you tell him I wanted to apologize?"

Jasper followed Rayne upstairs, into his room. "He's not himself lately. But he'll come around. A man like him doesn't like having his honor questioned."

Rayne's face heated with distress.

Jasper patted her hand. "Don't worry so much. You thought you were doin' right. It's my fault for not making myself clear. You shouldn't have taken up for me after all the hardship I've caused you and your mother. I'm sorry, Rayne. Do you think she'll ever forgive me?"

"Yes, Papa, but only if you're truly reformed. Our lives weren't easy after you left."

"Rayne, it's hard, and I . . ." Sitting on the edge of the bed, he yawned and began to remove his shoes. "It's been a long day, honey, and Case wants me at the office early tomorrow."

Rayne extinguished the lamp before she left her father's room, then she returned to the parlor. Standing in the center of the room, she kneaded the back of her neck. Papa seemed remorseful for his neglect of her and her mother, and he appeared to have stopped wasting his time on hedonistic pursuits. But without proper supervision, he could slip at any moment; already he'd almost lost everything on a turn of the cards. No wonder her gentle, sweet mother had failed to change him.

Her thoughts turned to Case O'Malley. She rested her hand on the Italian marble fireplace and frowned. Glancing across the room to a gold-leaf mirror from France, she once again wondered who had chosen the furnishings for her father's home. O'Malley might have, but immediately she dismissed the thought. Only a person of refined tastes could have selected the Persian carpets and rich window hangings, the dainty porcelains, and quality linen and flatware.

The image fit Paul Devereau, a cultured man, a man who appreciated the value of fine possessions. Well, someone in Virginia City must have excellent perception to have chosen these objects. Except for the garish candelabra, which she'd given to Hung Lee. Considering the room again,

Rayne sighed heavily. Although she was happy for her father's good fortune, she felt sad that her mother had never owned one precious object. Housemaids like her mother owned little of value and spent their lives toiling for others, especially if they had been abandoned by their husbands and left with a child to support. Well, her weak father was now rich and in a position to finally do his duty to his family.

For years she and her mother had lived in a small room behind the kitchen of her mother's wealthy employer. By saving every penny, her mother had ensured that her daughter would be well educated, even if it meant occasionally tutoring Rayne herself. They had been poor in material things, but rich in love, in direct contrast to the family who provided them shelter.

They were fortunate that Mr. Kingston was a fair employer and a generous man. He treated her mother respectfully and paid her a decent wage. But Rayne had always felt sorry for him. Overindulged, his intemperate wife and unmannerly children never appreciated the kindnesses he bestowed upon them. The son and daughter had been horrid to Rayne, calling her names, snubbing her and her mother at every opportunity.

Her mother's wealthy family had disowned Mary for marrying Jasper; but they could not change her connection to their prestigious name. Rayne smiled, remembering her mother's unabashed laughter when she'd gotten her daughter into a fine finishing school for proper young ladies.

Rayne shook her head, dispelling the memories. Thanks to her father's newfound riches, her

mother would not suffer Mrs. Kingston's demands
and high-handedness for much longer. But she
could not deny that she owed a debt of gratitude
to Case O'Malley as well. He had saved her father
from losing his mine stocks in a reckless card
game, and now Jasper could fulfill his obligations
to his family.

And Rayne would find a way to repay her debt
to Case.

Two days later, Case halted his team on a small,
grassy verge on the Geiger Grade Road, about
four miles north of Virginia City. He searched the
area. Ahead lay a way station in a narrow canyon
at the base of a dangerous curve called Deadman's Bend. There, he expected the attack his operative had warned him about.

The shotgun guard sitting beside him on the
wagon nodded to a passing teamster.

"We'll rest the horses a minute," Case said. He
brought out two cigars from his inside pocket and
handed one to the guard. "Imported from Ger-
many." As they shared a light, he shifted his
weight on the hard seat.

"Worried about the curve, boss?"

Case expelled a cloud of smoke, clamped the cigar between his teeth, and tapped the reins. "First
sign of trouble, jump off. No use you getting killed
over a little gold."

Hefting his double-barreled shotgun tighter
under his arm, the guard returned a sly grin. "You
mean the rock in the strongbox?"

Case stared ahead, silently cursing the man's astute guess. "Heard a rumor bandits plan to stop

one of my shipments. Figured I'd test the information before I sent out the real ore."

"Thought so. When word gets out of how you drove the wagon yourself, instead of risking others, you'll be a hero."

Case's face darkened at the possibility. Fame of that sort would bring him undue attention. Some of the miners sympathized with the South. As it was, he and the other mine owners had been sneaking out ore at a rapid rate, dispatching it from dawn to dusk via caravans over the Sierras to California. His was just one of several enormously rich mines: the Gould & Curry, Ophir, and Savage rivaled the O'Malley-North.

"I'll make you a deal, Rogers. If I die, you can spread the story of what a hero I am. Hell, you can raise a statue to my memory, for all I care. But if I survive this daft undertaking, you keep it under your hat."

"You ask a lot, boss. You got any more of these imported cigars?"

Case grinned. "You bet."

"You got yourself a deal."

Case saw Deadman's Bend up ahead. An auspicious name, he thought as he contemplated the precipitous curve. One look at the rugged canyon below caused him to question his sanity. His daring feat might likely get him killed. His mood grim, he wondered if Jasper's daughter would grieve for him when she heard of his death.

Holding the horses to a walk, he drove the wagon cautiously around the bend. He felt Rogers stiffen beside him and glanced up in time to see a flash of light.

Instinct drove him. A curse on his lips, Case shoved the guard from his seat.

A rifle shot rang out. The sudden blast echoed in Case's ears, the percussion and the grazing bullet causing a split-second of pain to tear through his head. The jolt unseated him, and then he was falling over the side of the wagon, down a sheer incline. The sky, the ground, jagged rocks, sped past. Still he fell. He slammed against a ridge and heard something crack. The impact forced the air from his lungs. When finally he came to rest on a flat ledge, a paralyzing pain gripped his leg. Dirt and loose rock rained over him. He froze, afraid to move. Above him, the sounds of gunfire drifted down the canyon.

Then there was silence.

"I'm comin', boss. Cover your eyes."

Slowly Case moved his left arm. A searing pain lanced his chest. He sucked in a careful breath, then wiggled his fingers, wrist, and finally his entire right arm. Flopping that arm over his eyes, he waited.

Then he imagined he saw her. Standing in a hazy mist, Rayne North wore a prim black dress and clutched a prayer book in her hands. On her mourning hat, a black ostrich feather danced in the wind to the accompaniment of a thundering funeral dirge.

In the middle of writing a letter to her mother, Rayne paused to turn up the lamp. The long, lonely hours stretched on endlessly.

An abrupt banging from the hallway startled her. Her letter forgotten, she ran toward the front door, but the banging began again before she got there, and fearing the door might split under the severe abuse, she quickened her pace. The ungodly commotion could wake the dead. She opened the door to a dust-covered man trying to catch his breath.

The man whipped off his filthy hat and announced, "Jasper sent me to warn you."

She motioned him inside. "Is something wrong?"

He fumbled with his hat and strove to control his breathing. "O'Malley's been hurt in a fall. Jasper's having him brought here."

"Here?" Rayne's hand went to her throat. "How did he . . . He won't die, will he?"

"The doc don't think so, but he can't be sure till he checks him over." He glanced out the door, up the street. "They were right behind me." Turning back to Rayne, he said, "You best decide where you want him."

Rayne couldn't think straight. O'Malley had been hurt. Of course Jasper would want to care for him, but everything was happening so fast, she didn't know what to do. "Upstairs, to the right," she stammered, sure her father wouldn't mind if she moved him to the small room adjoining hers so she could give his bedroom, located a safe distance down the hallway, to his partner.

"Need help getting it ready?"

Prompted by the man's question, she assured him no and hastened to the second floor. She changed the linen on her father's bed with shaky hands, lit all the lamps, and then did the same in the room adjacent to hers. Then she rushed downstairs, where she asked Hung Lee to prepare clean strips of cloth and hot water.

Still the men didn't arrive.

As her stomach clenched, she strove for calm. She barely knew Case O'Malley. Why did the thought of him injured and in pain disturb her so deeply?

While the man who had delivered the news paced and twisted his hat, Rayne counted the seconds. The clop of horses' hooves, followed by the screech of a wagon brake, finally announced the arrival of the rescue party. Rayne's stomach pitched again. She wanted to run down the walk to see for herself how badly Case had been hurt, but she knew it was best to remain inside, out of the way.

Loud voices came to her, some concerned, others shouting orders, and her anxiety increased. Finally they entered the house. Six men, three on either side, bore a makeshift stretcher of narrow logs and canvas on which lay a barely recognizable man. She clapped a hand over her mouth to hold back a cry of alarm.

Grit and blood covered one side of O'Malley's handsome face. The other was red and swollen with angry scrapes. His left leg lay twisted in an unnatural manner.

When the men bearing the stretcher reached the second floor, Rayne took the pile of cloth bandages Hung Lee held out and led him up the stairs after the others. On the landing, she halted and looked back. The kind-looking man tromping up the stairs must be the doctor. They exchanged brief introductions and she hurried to catch up with the others, dismayed to see they had brought O'Malley to the wrong room!

O'Malley's howl of pain, when the men gently

lifted and placed him on the bed, forced her to accept the situation. If she pointed out now that they had mistakenly put him in an inappropriate room, and insisted they move him again, it would cause him additional suffering. Apparently no one thought anything of this arrangement. And even though this room had a connecting door to her own room, O'Malley wouldn't be able to offer any trouble, at least not until he regained his health.

She laid the bandages on the bureau and moved to take a closer look.

The doctor pulled off his brown coat and rolled up his shirtsleeves, then firmly ordered the other men out the door. They filed out solemnly, and Rayne heard their heavy boots tramp down the stairs.

O'Malley stirred and groaned miserably, and the sound pinched Rayne's heart. She leaned over him. "Mr. O'Malley, can you hear me?"

She thought she detected a brief flicker of one eyelid, but before she could investigate further, she realized the doctor was standing over his patient, holding a wickedly long, sharp knife in his hand!

"What are you going to do with that?" she demanded, ready to jump to Case's defense.

"Why, I'm going to cut off his pants, miss."

Rayne expelled a relieved sigh and retreated a step.

"I have to strip him naked to have a proper look at him." The doctor's blue eyes bore into hers. "I suggest you wait outside. This is no place for a lady. I'll call you when he's decent."

"Oh!" Heat suffused her cheeks. "Yes, yes, you're right."

Rayne stepped out into the hall and leaned heavily against the closed door. What a dolt she'd been to think the doctor had meant to cut off Case's leg! She had been prepared to wrestle the man to the ground to stop him. But naturally the ruined clothes must be removed. How silly she'd been not to realize that!

During the next half hour, while Rayne waited in a hall chair, Hung Lee came and went from Case's room. The doctor never summoned Rayne. Curt expletives broke the silence several times, always followed by savage howls. Rayne pitied the unfortunate doctor. She feared Case O'Malley would be a troublesome patient, both now and in the days ahead.

Jasper touched her arm, jolting her from her thoughts. She hadn't heard him enter the house or climb the stairs. Her father's haggard appearance reflected his concern for Case. For the first time she noticed how much he'd aged in the five years since he'd left her and her mother.

"How is he?" Jasper asked.

"He's being cared for."

Jasper lowered his head and shuffled his feet. "Don't know what I'd do without Case. He treats me like a father."

"He'll get well soon enough, if I'm any judge. He's too obstinate to die."

Jasper's mustache lifted as he smiled. "Case didn't want me to have him brought here, you know. He threatened to seal me off in a tunnel."

"I don't understand," she said. "Who can take better care of him than us? Not that I look forward to the prospect. I suspect he will not take to convalescence easily."

"Rayne, honey, Case doesn't want to be around *you*."

Her mouth turned down. "I suppose he has justification for wanting to avoid me. I treated him abominably. But he'll be unable to avoid me now." Her eyes twinkled as she considered the possibilities offered by his confinement. "Whether or not Mr. O'Malley agrees, he'll have no choice. He must accept my help and allow me to make amends."

"So long as you don't waste your time trying to reform him. Case is set in his ways. I owe him and I aim to repay him now."

"As do I, Papa. Believe me, I'll do everything in my power to alleviate Mr. O'Malley's suffering and aid in his recovery."

Chapter 7

S natches of conversation penetrated Case's drugged mind. He had wanted to remain alert, but pain had made that impossible. He'd given in and swallowed the laudanum the determined doctor had forced down his throat. Despite this languid sense of drifting on clouds, if he put forth enough effort, he could concentrate long enough to grasp what was going on around him.

She was here; he knew that much. She loomed above him, an expression of profound worry on her face. Then again, maybe he was dreaming. Surely the real Miss North would never show such concern for him.

"Are you quite sure he's unconscious?" Case heard her ask.

"I gave him as little laudanum as I could. If he complains of pain later, you may administer more, but watch him closely. Too large a dose could prove fatal."

Good God! thought Case. *My life has been entrusted to the one woman in Virginia City who hates me.*

"Will I hurt him if I wash the dirt from his face, neck, and hands?"

"Not if you're gentle," the doctor replied. "I've

bound his ribs and set his leg. The wound on his forehead is merely a scratch, but he's likely to suffer headaches for a while. He incurred many bruises. He should heal nicely, though, provided he receives plenty of rest and care. The most important thing is that he remain in bed."

Sensing two pairs of eyes watching him, Case continued to feign unconsciousness.

"Are you sure you're able to manage?" the doctor continued. "Case strenuously objected to being brought here."

"It's my belief that Mr. O'Malley is incapable of deciding what's best for his own welfare at present. Papa and I will dutifully care for him."

As hard as he tried, Case couldn't prevent the moan that escaped his throat. This was a terrible predicament! Trussed tighter than a hog ready for slaughter, he lay at the mercy of Jasper's daughter. Hell, she probably anticipated stuffing an apple in his mouth and roasting him over a low fire.

"I trust you implicitly, Miss North. I've left a salve on the bureau for his scratches. I'll stop by tomorrow to check on him."

"Good-bye, Doctor," said Rayne. "Thank you for coming so quickly."

Hearing the door close, Case relaxed. Alone at last. He surrendered to the drug, which worked its wiles and took away all his troubles.

Rayne stood silently beside the bed, her gaze lingering on Case O'Malley. He looked so vulnerable, so different from his usual cocky self. The narrow bandage circling his head dipped lower on one side. Above the sheet, which the doctor had draped midway down his chest, the top edge of another, tighter bandage showed.

She studied his long length stretched beneath the covers and winced. The brace the doctor had fashioned for his lower left leg ruined the symmetry of his unconscious body. Never in her life had she been alone in a room with a man who wore only his underclothes.

What was she supposed to do now?

If she had personally led the men upstairs, O'Malley would now be in the room down the hall instead of in the room that connected to hers. She wouldn't be faced with the problem of caring for a handsome rogue who shattered her senses each and every time they came in contact.

Rayne cautiously inched closer to the bed. In order to properly tend him, she must learn the extent of his injuries. She suspected the kind physician might have withheld information to ease her mind. Tomorrow she'd send her father to the hotel to obtain a nightshirt, and either he or Hung Lee would dress O'Malley.

Rayne warily observed her patient as she grasped the edge of the sheet. The doctor had assured her that Case was unconscious. Encouraged by his even breathing, she lifted the cover and flicked her eyes over him. Her heart leapt to her throat. Immediately she dropped the sheet, slapped her hand over her mouth, and retreated a step. She closed her eyes in an attempt to erase the sight of his magnificent, naked body from her mind. The vision, however, had been scorched into her memory. His flat stomach, muscular thighs, the dark hair tunneling from beneath the bandage in a straight line all the way down to—

Merciful heavens! She hadn't meant to look at *that* part of him.

Now she wished she'd remained calm and not dropped the sheet as if it were on fire. Although she wouldn't have admitted it to herself before, she'd always wondered about the differences between men and women.

When Rayne's heart finally started to beat normally, she crossed to the bureau, where she dampened a washcloth, picked up the salve the doctor had left, and returned to the bed. Fate had thrust Case O'Malley into her life. Although she'd been allowed no say in the matter, his well-being was now in her hands. Given these circumstances and her attraction to this man, her best course would be to hold her emotions at bay and not dwell on his impressive attributes.

After a quick study of his scrapes and bruises, she tenderly dabbed at the specks of dirt along his jaw. Her ministrations wouldn't help him heal faster, but she would feel better if she knew she'd tended him in some way.

She considered how his stubborn jaw said so much about his personality. And his mouth certainly betrayed his lusty nature. But the small cut above his upper lip softened her heart toward him. Although he angered her at times, she regretted his injuries. She cleaned a spot on his forehead and noted how his dark, thick eyebrows slanted at a rakish angle. It was a perfect attribute for a devil.

When she grazed the cloth over his eyelids, they flickered. Holding her breath, she waited, afraid she had awakened him. She relished this moment of secret discovery and she wanted this private time to last a little longer. Touching him without his knowledge *was* pleasurable, she mused. She returned to her chore with a smile. Down the bridge of his nose, over the other cheek, she slid the cloth, her gaze steady on the damp skin. Her attention returned to the small cut above his lip.

She turned his face with a finger and swept the rag up and down his neck, enticed by the spot beneath his collarbone where dark curls began. His broad shoulders and arms were free of dirt. Relief and disappointment coursed through her. She longed to skim her fingers across his skin. She imagined the sensations that action would bring her. Even unconscious, Case O'Malley was able to make strange demons stir in her stomach.

Tipping his head, she glanced at his eyes and found them tightly closed. Again the injury above his lip drew her. He had such a fine mouth, sensuous and firm. It reminded her of how his kisses inflamed her ... Her thoughts were definitely not proper. *Concentrate on another part of his body,* she lectured herself.

She slipped her fingers under his wrist and stretched her hand beneath his. The difference in size and texture between his hand and hers amazed her. She saw how small her own looked compared with his. His palm felt hot against hers.

Enough!

She dragged a chair close to the bed, sat, and opened the jar of salve. She began with his face, smearing a small amount on each scrape, all but one of which were located on his left side. As she dabbed the ointment on his chin, she felt the friction of a day's growth of heavy whiskers. She roamed her eyes over his abused features, thinking how handsome he looked despite the injuries.

Her fingers splayed on his cheek, she contemplated the tiny cut on his mouth. She understood now why it drew her. She wanted to kiss it. To defy convention and indulge her fantasy. O'Malley would never know, a little voice told her. She slid closer, moving from the edge of the chair onto the bed. No one would come into the room; father and Hung Lee had both retired for the night.

Rayne bent forward, her head directly above his. Case O'Malley defied convention whenever he wanted. He'd certainly disturbed her peace of mind with his brash behavior. Now it was her turn. Before she lost her courage, she pressed her lips to his wound and drew back. Luckily, he hadn't awakened. And then another temptation took root in her mind.

She grinned as she stroked a finger across his mouth. When he'd embraced her, he hadn't given her a sweet, tender kiss. He probably never would. Slowly, fixing her gaze on her target, she angled her head and brushed her lips over his. Running her tongue over her tingling mouth, she sat back and tucked the sheet neatly across his chest.

Rayne glanced toward the door that separated this room from hers. Tonight she needn't worry. He would probably be incapacitated for weeks, unable to put weight on his leg. Resting her hand on his chest, she thought ahead to the coming days. Managing two rascals wouldn't be easy.

She returned the salve and washcloth to the bureau, but she left the chair next to the bed. Then she picked his clothes up off the floor and piled them for Hung Lee to launder.

Ready to retire for the evening, Rayne stopped by the bed one last time to assure herself that Case still slept comfortably. She became aware of a raised area in the sheet. The bulge hadn't been there before. And because it centered in a private area, she debated several seconds before curiosity drove her closer. She couldn't bear the suspense of not knowing the cause of the protrusion, but she had no one to ask. Finally, beset by inquisitiveness and concern, she laid her hand over the raised area.

Good God! The poor man had swollen out of all proportion!

She lurched away, then shrank back farther, questioning if this swelling was a natural occurrence or a result of his injuries. She was sure of only one thing—she'd never ask any *man* about it, especially not Case O'Malley.

When her back came up against the door, Rayne whipped around and fled to the safety of her own bedroom.

Peeking through a slitted eyelid, Case made sure Miss North was gone. He wouldn't make the same mistake twice. He moved his head in a quick scan of the room and was rewarded by blinding pain and a wave of dizziness. Focusing his eyes took greater effort than he had expected, and objects around him looked obscure. He hoped his affliction was an aftermath of the laudanum, not a permanent consequence of his accident.

The next time he opened his eyes, he saw more clearly. He wondered how long he'd dozed. The drug limited his periods of attention, made him

flit in and out of consciousness. Physical stimulation, however, brought him to reality, as he'd discovered when Miss North had ministered to his
wounds. If it hadn't been a dream, that is.

If her tender care *had* been a dream, he hoped
the wondrous episode happened again. He could
have opened his eyes and learned the truth easily
enough, but he'd remained motionless, submitting
to the luscious torture. Never before had a woman
lavished him with such loving touches. Had he
been fully conscious, he still wouldn't have betrayed himself. Surprised by her gentleness, he regarded her inspection as innocent and born of
natural curiosity. His feigned unawareness had
protected her. She would not have touched him so
intimately otherwise. He could well imagine her
embarrassment if she'd known of his cognizance
through most of her ministrations.

But she had played hell with his battered body.
He doubted any other woman would have af-
fected him as acutely. The thought unnerved him.
He'd give a month's gold and silver from his mine
to have seen the expression on her face when
she'd lifted the sheet and discovered his naked
state. He'd forfeit six month's profits to have witnessed her reaction when she'd seen his erection
and boldly touched it through the sheet.

Miss North had even kissed him.

It had taken great restraint not to respond to
her lips pressed against his. The achingly sweet
sensation lingered still to torment him. Rayne
would likely kill him with kindness and sexual
frustration before he healed enough to escape. If
he hadn't been so damned stubborn, he would

have allowed her to apologize days ago and thus saved himself a hell of a lot of misery now.

The drug was wearing thin, he realized. His leg throbbed. And when he attempted to move, another, worse pain stabbed his chest. He took a deep breath, then groaned. The damn doctor had bound him so tightly, the bandages restricted his lungs. Breathing shallowly, he forced himself to relax . . .

Case opened his eyes again. He must have dozed briefly, because someone had turned down the lamp. He guessed it must be the middle of the night. Glancing toward the other room, he saw that the door was ajar. A brighter light shone beyond the opening. He heard a soft rustle. Then he saw her reflection in the mirror above the bureau. The vision brought him fully awake. Clad in her nightdress, Rayne was brushing her hair. The long, leisurely strokes held him spellbound. With her head tilted to one side, her dreamy expression brought an excruciating tightness to his chest, exaggerated by his cracked ribs.

She tilted her head the other way and drew the brush from her scalp to the ends of her waist-length tresses. He watched her, enchanted, imagining himself performing the ritual, his fingers burrowing through the silken, chestnut waves. In his mind he leaned forward, kissed her as gently as she'd kissed him earlier. Of her own volition she turned and fitted herself in his arms, pressing her slim body tightly against his.

Then the exploration began. In his imagination he roamed his hands down her back, cupped her backside, and brought her even closer, until he felt her softness entice his hardness. Through her nightdress her breasts teased his chest. He grazed his fingers across the generous flesh, felt her nipples grow taut. She threw back her head to bare her neck, and encouraged by her agonized moan, he kissed the creamy column.

Christ! Was it pleasure or pain that racked his body? Case wondered, cursing his wayward and untimely fantasy. She was no longer brushing her hair but was listening intently. Enlightenment came to him. He had moaned, not her. The brush fell from her hand and hit the floor as she moved toward the bureau. He heard the light fall of her bare feet and smelled the sweet fragrance of lavender. He sensed her coming closer, and again cursed his heightened awareness of Jasper's innocent daughter.

"Mr. O'Malley, are you awake?" she asked.

"Yes, Miss North, I have returned to the land of the living," he grumbled.

"I'm glad. Are you in pain?"

He did not need to look to know she stood close to the bed; the heat from her body warmed him. "Most excruciating pain."

"The doctor left medicine. Would you like some of it now?"

"A drink of water first, if you don't mind." He tensed. "If I'm able to swallow with these restricting binds." He watched her fill a glass.

"You have injured your ribs," she told him. "Can you lift your head?"

"Lifting a finger would require a miracle," Case muttered under his breath. "It appears I'm as helpless as an infant."

"A temporary inconvenience." Her mouth tilted up at the corners. "I'm sure you'll be fully recovered and back to your normal routine in no time at all."

The amusement in her voice annoyed him since she put him in an amorous mood he could do nothing about. It tempted him to test her amiable mood. "If you'd put your arm under my neck and assist me, I'd appreciate that drink now."

"Perhaps I should turn up the light first, so I can see better," she suggested.

"I'll find the glass if you place it close to my mouth."

She hesitated before finally agreeing.

"You *are* a merciful angel," Case said as her arm slid under his neck. Tendrils from her unbound hair tickled his neck and shoulder, sending a delectable shiver through his body. "It's so accommodating of you to help me this way."

As she aligned the glass with his lower lip, her eyes twinkled with mischief. "Drink quickly. Your head is *quite* heavy and strains my arm."

Case swallowed and choked, causing a pinching sensation in his side. He bit back a curse. "The binds are too tight."

Ignoring his complaint, she set the glass on the small table beside the bed. "The doctor knows best. Does your leg hurt much?"

"Like hell."

"Maybe if I put something soft under it," she suggested as she pulled a pillow from the bottom of the wardrobe and returned to stand at the foot of his bed. "Hold your breath, Mr. O'Malley. This may hurt, but I think it'll alleviate some of your discomfort."

"No ... don't ... goddammit!"

She fluffed the pillow under his leg, clicking her

tongue to reprimand his language. "Doesn't that feel better?"

It did, but Case swore he'd never admit it. "Have you ever broken *your* leg, Miss North?"

"Fortunately, no."

"If you ever do that again, I may strangle you."

"At the moment, I think not. Would you like your medicine now?"

"In a minute."

Aggravating Miss North may prove detrimental to my well-being, Case thought. The only weapon at his disposal was verbal threats. A damn lot of good they did. She seemed different. Certainly he no longer frightened her. But that was understandable. He was helpless. It was just like a woman to mother a man when he was unable to fight back.

"Would you open the window? It's stuffy."

Sounding truly aghast, she said, "Why, night air might be harmful to you in your weakened condition."

"Humor a dying man. Please."

"Very well," she returned, and shaking her head, she fulfilled his request. "Is there anything else I can do for you ... before you die?"

"Loosen this vise around my chest. How will I heal if I can't breathe?" he complained, annoyed that she found humor in his testy mood.

"If I do as you ask, I may cause you more harm."

"I relieve you of all responsibility."

"Perhaps the laudanum will assuage your suffering until the doctor comes in the morning."

"I'm completely lucid at the moment and capable of making my own decisions. I want this bandage loosened."

"If you insist. They are, after all, your ribs." She turned up the lamp, rounded the bed, and stood over him. "You'll have to sit up. Do you think it's possible?"

"Miss North!"

"What is it? Are you ill?"

"I'm incapacitated, not dead."

She looked bewildered. "What's your point?"

"You've turned up the lamp," he explained, striving to sound impersonal to spare her embarrassment. "You're wearing a nightgown. Need I say more?"

In a lightning-fast movement, she crossed her arms over her chest. It might have been better to pretend the light didn't make her gown transparent, but he'd felt obligated to enlighten her. Why, he didn't know. Maybe it was because she'd tended his wounds so tenderly earlier.

She walked proudly into her room and returned wearing her matronly flowered dressing gown. Her face looked utterly pale.

Case fought to hide his amusement. "Thank you for sparing my sensibilities."

Studiously avoiding his gaze, she said, "Thank you for bringing my state of undress to my attention. You were very considerate."

Case's laugh turned into a moan. "It was an act of self-protection." Her brow knitted with confusion, prompting him to explain, "My injuries aren't so extensive that they prevent me from feeling passion."

She held up a hand. "Please . . . say no more. I understand."

"I don't think you do, but I find your innocence refreshing."

"It's late. I suggest we loosen your bandage without further ado."

He grinned. "Any suggestions how we should go about it?"

"As quickly as possible." Allowing him no time to react, she dragged the sheet down to his waist and hesitating only a second, rested her hands on his shoulders. "When you're ready, I'll pull you forward."

His fingers snapped around her wrist as he met her gaze. "Sit beside me on the bed. There will be less chance you'll jerk me at the wrong angle."

"I hardly think sitting so close to you would be wise."

"Although I appreciate your confidence in my virility, let me assure you, I'm temporarily incapable of ravishment," he said as his thumb massaged her wrist.

"I'm not sure I believe you," she countered, fine lines of worry creasing her brow. "This is most irregular."

"There's no one here to see what transpires between us. Rest assured, your virtue is safe." Seeing her lips curve briefly, he added, "You're my only salvation. Would you have my death on your hands?"

She smiled fully now. "Remember, this was your insane idea." Cautiously she slid next to him. He felt the wild beating of her pulse under his thumb. "Are you ready?"

"Easy now. I'll move on my own. You just lend me support."

Case took as deep a breath as his ribs allowed, nodded, and released her wrist. He felt her fingers tighten on his shoulders. Cautiously he rose, gritting his teeth against the agony. After he sat upright, he exhaled and fell limp against her. He immediately regretted his stubborn refusal to wait until morning. Her hair smelled wonderful, and she felt soft and womanly. Damn!

Her mouth inches from his, she asked, "Are you steady? If I release you, will you remain sitting long enough for me to see to the binds?"

"I'll hold on to you."

"I don't think—"

She closed her eyes when his hands settled on her shoulders. Case sucked in a sharp breath. Even through the barrier of her gown, her skin gave off warmth.

"Search for the end and unwrap slowly," he advised, his request a hoarse whisper. "I'll tell you when you've gotten it loose enough."

She eased her hands down and slipped her arms under his. Her fingers touched the bandage. "I've found it." Gently she unwound the material. He felt her heartbeat quicken as the seconds passed. He sat still, barely able to think. She trembled. "Am I hurting you?"

"God no," Case said, gritting his teeth. "You have a light touch." He wondered how she'd react if he kissed her ear. Deciding she'd pull away too fast and cause him unbearable grief, he reconsidered. Finally he said, "That's fine. Tie it off."

Her hands fumbled with the bandage. "Your hands are shaking," he said.

"Yes, Mr. O'Malley, they are indeed."

Blood surged in his veins, but he managed an abbreviated laugh. "You're very much attracted to me, I believe, Miss North."

She went still. "If you stop breathing under my

ear, I might complete this endeavor, Mr. O'Malley."

"Don't make me laugh," he begged. "It hurts. If you stop caressing my back and sides, you may regain your train of thought."

"Is that what you think, that I'm— What are you doing? Mr. O'Malley, kissing my neck will not— Oh!"

"Tie the knot."

With a groan of frustration, she accomplished the deed and leaned away.

"Thank you. I feel much better now."

He stared at her slightly parted mouth and noticed she was inhaling short, irregular breaths. Her skin was lovely, creamy and umblemished by so much as a freckle. Her hair streamed down her back, tempting him to fulfill an earlier wish. He tangled his fingers in the silken mass.

"As a dying man, I have a last request."

"You're not dying."

"Oh, but I am. Dying of want. I want to kiss you."

"No, you mustn't. We're opposites and you—"

He brushed his mouth over hers, finding the brief, feather-soft contact oddly stimulating. He expected a protest, some resistance, but she offered none. Unable to help himself, he took another taste. No woman had ever tasted so sweet, or felt so right.

Unlike Rayne, the women with whom he normally associated knew the rules. They returned his advances with fierce, skilled abandon, not innocent awe.

When he finally broke away, he rested his forehead against hers. "You really shouldn't allow me to take such liberties."

Seconds passed before she answered. "You surprise me."

Her meaning registered immediately. It had been the first time he'd treated her with a tender regard. Her fingers skimmed over his skin below the bandage, sending a bolt of desire to his loins. Smiling, he rubbed his thumb over her mouth. "You'll be shocked unless you stop touching me."

"Have I hurt you?"

Carefully Case reclined against the pillow. He considered the consequences of correcting her ignorance and concluded it was necessary. "You're causing me hurt, but not the way you think. You've made me grow hard."

Her eyes were as wide as saucers as she leapt to her feet. Rayne may be uneducated in the ways of men and women, but she caught on fast. He felt compelled to further enlighten her.

"Do you want me to explain?"

"Positively not," she returned, turning a most becoming shade of crimson. "It wouldn't be decent."

"Forget decent for once in your life. Do you want your curiosity satisfied, or do you prefer to remain ignorant? You can't go through eternity a blushing virgin, you know. I'll be happy to tell you anything you want."

She cast a surreptitious glance at the sheet. He knew what she'd find—absolute proof of his desire for her. She seemed torn with indecision, her curiosity at war with her fear of appearing improper. Relieving her of the burden, he didn't take time to phrase his words delicately, saying simply,

"When a man feels passion for a woman, his member swells and becomes rigid."

She looked away so fast, he thought he heard her neck snap. "This is most embarrassing," she said, her voice cracking. "You shouldn't say such things to me."

"You want to know why, don't you?" Seeing her eyebrows shoot up, her lips roll together, Case continued. "Unless it gets hard, it can't go inside the woman."

Without moving her head, she stole another glimpse at the sheet. "In—side?"

"Between her legs." He watched bewilderment collide with shocked comprehension in her face. "It's called making love, and babies."

"Oh, so that's how—" Abruptly she averted her gaze. "My mother never—"

"Feel free to ask me anything. Your curiosity is only natural, contrary to what you've probably been taught."

"I couldn't possibly."

"Yes, I know. A woman's duty and all. Come on, Miss North. You traveled a long distance partly unchaperoned. That alone betrays your brave spirit. Who else are you going to ask? Jasper?"

A moment of stark distress crossed her features before she asked, "Does it hurt? It seems impossible considering the size of ... of ... From what I can tell, it looks too big."

Impressed by her stalwart acceptance of information that would have sent most gently bred women into a swoon, Case felt confident he'd made the right decision in speaking frankly with her. "It does hurt the woman a bit, but only the first time. After that it's a very pleasurable experience."

"Mr. O'Malley ... aren't *you* uncomfortable?"

Case laughed and grabbed his sides. "Yes, I am. In the future, I suggest you refrain from needlessly arousing me."

"I didn't ... on purpose. Oh, surely you don't think ... ?"

"I admire your grit," he admitted, flashing her a dazzling smile. "You are now armed with enough knowledge to be dangerous."

Twisting her fingers together, she observed, "It appears your pain has subsided."

He sensed her desperate desire to move on to another topic. "My ribs feel less confined and painful, but my leg hurts abominably."

"I'll get the laudanum."

"A small amount, Miss North. I've heard that too much may prove deadly."

She turned toward the bureau with a smile. "I haven't apologized for thinking you swindled my father. It was unfair and wrong of me. Can you ever forgive me?"

Remembering the infuriating incident, and his indignation, he withheld clemency, asking instead, "How did you learn the truth?"

"How I came to know isn't important. I hope you won't hold my behavior against me."

Deciding he'd find the source of her information soon enough, and that he, too, had behaved badly, he said, "I shouldn't have called you a liar. I was a boor."

"Indeed you were, but fortunately for you, I paid your insult little mind." A slow, evil grin slid over her mouth. "I'll get your medicine now. I'm *almost* certain I remember the correct amount Dr. Connell prescribed."

Struck by a painful spasm, Case flinched and tightened his grip on his sides.

Chapter 8

Rayne tossed and turned for hours. The thought of Case O'Malley sleeping in the next room made her skin prickle with gooseflesh. Listening now, as she had many times throughout the night, she heard his steady breathing. She slipped her legs over the side of the bed and sat up. She hadn't even remembered to braid her hair, and it would be a mass of tangles in the morning. Plus, she'd be a shrew if she didn't manage to rest.

She rose and donned her robe, not chancing another embarrassing encounter in just her nightdress. She carried a lighted lamp and tiptoed into his room, confident he'd succumbed to the drug. The cool night air that ruffled the curtains sent a chill down her spine. The stubborn man would probably develop a fever.

She closed the window, then paused by the bed, holding the lamp high. Shadows fell over his face. It was strange to see him unshaven with his hair mussed. He looked rather roguish, more like an outlaw. *A thief of hearts,* she thought lamentably.

A memory of the past night warmed her. She doubted she'd ever neglect to dress properly before visiting him again.

He could have had the decency to remain unconscious.

O'Malley may find her innocence refreshing, but she did not. She found it humiliating always to question the meaning behind his words and deeds. She didn't dare consider his explanation of lovemaking. Why couldn't he be a respectable, faithful man instead of a womanizing scoundrel?

In the future, she must take a firm stand in her dealings with him and not allow him to corrupt her further. It would take some doing on her part, but somehow she must remain unaffected and efficient. She set the lamp on the table and covered him with the heavy counterpane from the bottom of the bed. She tucked it snugly under his neck and tiptoed silently back to her room, where she slept fitfully until morning.

Case awoke with a start when a trickle of perspiration dripped into his eye. His earlier prediction had been right. Judging by the heavy counterpane covering him from neck to foot, Miss North *had* attempted to roast him alive. The closed window caught his attention next. Would she smother him, too?

She must have come into his room again during the night. How sweet. For some reason he thought of his coldhearted mother, who had never given him, her only child, the slightest affection. Certainly she wouldn't have deprived herself of sleep in order to care for him. Over the years, he'd learned not to care. Jasper's daughter, however, possessed a soft, sympathetic nature, which he longed to explore.

He must have bruised his brain in his fall, he

mused. Rayne might possess a tender side, but unless he planned to adopt the life of a blessed saint,
he wasn't likely to see much of that side!

Testing himself, Case rose slightly and tossed off
the heavy cover. Fire lashed his chest. His entire
body hurt, and his head pounded. As he eased
back to the pillow, he realized he had another,
more pressing problem. If he didn't relieve himself
very soon, he was going to be mighty embarrassed!

He called out several times, his voice rising in
volume, but no one came. Finally, with little recourse left, he grabbed hold of the chair next to his
bed and, grunting from the effort, lifted it high
enough to bang a leg on the floor. If this didn't
bring help, nothing would.

Moments later, the door swung open. Rayne
stood on the threshold, looking fresh and alluring.
But he hardly noticed. He was seconds away from
the most embarrassing moment of his life.

"Is something wrong?" Rayne asked, recovering
from her hasty sprint up the stairs. It appeared her
worry had been unjustified. O'Malley looked fine.
"Hung Lee and I were just downstairs. The way
you were beating on the floor, I thought an emergency had arisen."

"An emergency *has* arisen."

Rayne swept into the room. "What can I get
you?"

"Fetch Hung Lee and be quick about it."

She tapped her foot, determined to treat him
nicely despite his cranky behavior. "Hung Lee is
preparing your breakfast. He'll be up shortly. And
the sheriff arrived a few minutes ago. He wants to
ask you some questions."

"Miss North," he said succinctly, the sound coming from behind clenched teeth, "I need to relieve myself."

"Oh!" Rayne refused to blush. Kneeling, she reached under the bed and brought out an ornately decorated chamber pot. Holding it out, she trained her vision on the wall behind him. "I'll leave the room."

He grabbed the container, his eyes never leaving her face. "I need assistance, the kind of help you're incapable of giving. Either send up Hung Lee or suffer the consequences. And tell the damn sheriff he'll just have to wait."

Rayne backed away, acutely aware of the physical difference between women's and men's bodies. She tried to imagine how he planned to accomplish this function flat on his back, but however he decided to carry out the maneuver, she was sure she didn't want to watch. In the future she'd instruct either her father or Hung Lee to attend their patient before she entered the room.

O'Malley's laughter followed Rayne into the hall as she dashed down the stairs. A woman shouldn't have to deal with a man's personal functions, especially when doing so involved teaching her things she wasn't quite ready for! Already she'd learned the structure of a man's body, and how a man and woman joined together.

I'm not proper, she thought. A proper woman would never meet his gaze again. Instead, she felt beholden to O'Malley for giving her facts about which she'd always wondered.

"Mr. O'Malley will see you directly," she told the lawman waiting patiently downstairs. "It should only be a few minutes."

"I'll come back," the man returned. He pulled a pocket watch from his pants. "In an hour."

Rayne saw him out, then headed toward the back of the house, where she found Hung Lee in the kitchen. She dreaded the coming conversation.

"Hung Lee," she said, "please go help Mr. O'Malley."

"Hung Lee heap busy now, missy."

Rayne approached the table. "He needs a man to help him . . . help him . . . Go see. He'll explain."

"Hung Lee heap busy, missy. Go soon."

Her shoulders sagging, she rephrased her words. "You must go now. O'Malley is in *desperate* need."

"Go soon."

Her predicament seemed impossible. However, she would not, under any circumstances, resort to plain language to describe her patient's dilemma. "If you tarry any longer, you'll have to washee him *and* his bed."

"Ah," he replied, nodding.

Her embarrassment was so acute, she wanted to crawl into a corner. "While you're there, please help him shave." Seeing the man's bewildered expression, she rubbed her hand over her jaw. "Whiskers. Help *washee*, too."

"Hung Lee washee belly good."

Rayne rolled her eyes as she watched the Chinaman leave.

She finished the cooking and piled a silver tray high with O'Malley's breakfast. Her thoughts, however, roamed elsewhere. Dwelling on the knowledge as he had imparted to her, she imagined making love with him. He would be skilled, of course, as adept at loving as he was at engineering. He'd probably done it with many women. *Too many*, she concluded, her mood turning grim. He had even admitted that he enjoyed *sharing* his affections with several women.

The thought disheartened her. Making love should be special, and unless he changed his ways, he would never be the man for her.

While she waited, she finished eating her own breakfast and drank two cups of coffee. A half hour later, when she heard Hung Lee come down the stairs, she picked up the tray and detoured through the parlor, thus avoiding another taxing conversation with him.

As soon as she entered the bedroom, she noted O'Malley's mood had vastly improved during her absence.

Case watched Rayne approach, taking in every aspect of her manner and appearance. He admired her proud carriage. She held her spine as straight as a timber, and though the tray she carried looked heavy, she bore the weight with effortless grace. He cleared the small bedside table and hungrily sniffed the scents of coffee, bacon, and biscuits, all of which tempted him almost as much as the bewitching woman delivering them.

"What happened to Sheriff Monroe?" he asked.

"He left. He should be back in half an hour. I'm afraid your breakfast has gotten cold."

She spared him one cursory glance and didn't look at him again. His lips twitched. She had many reasons to be bashful, but he wondered which episode played in her mind now. "Hot or cold, I'll appreciate it. I'm easily pleased."

Although she averted her face slightly, he saw her mouth move, as if she were biting her tongue.

"Before I eat, I have a request, if you'd be so kind as to oblige me." Noting the almost imperceptible stiffening of her spine, he couldn't resist adding, "And you've been so very agreeable lately."

She shook open a neatly pressed napkin from the tray, and draped the cloth under his chin. He smelled the starch in the pristine white, fitted shirtwaist molding her full breasts and narrow waist. She straightened and smoothed her hands over her flaring brown skirt. Still looking elsewhere, she said, "Yes ... what is it?"

"My face stings," Case said. "Hung Lee lacks your gentle touch. I was hoping you'd put on some more of that salve the doctor left."

"How did you know ... ?" When she finally met his gaze, he gave her a coaxing smile. "You only have a few minor scrapes."

"Minor until Hung Lee removed a layer of skin with your father's dull razor."

She searched his face closely. "I'm sorry. You do require attention."

He watched her retrieve the medicine, her movements swift and efficient. Sunlight fell across her hair, bringing out its red highlights. To distract himself from the alluring sight, he said, "You're always apologizing to me. Why do you suppose that is?"

To his delight, she gave him a bright smile. "Mind your manners, Mr. O'Malley. After all, you are at my mercy, unable to leave your bed, hardly in a position to antagonize your sole caretaker."

"My very own angel of mercy," he said, lazily

appraising her. His angel seemed more at ease in his company today. He wasn't used to women countering his taunts.

"Your illness has forced us into a somewhat intimate setting," she said. "Rules are necessary."

"Rules?"

Her slender fingers touched her throat. He grinned. When he got through with Miss North, she'd bravely face down any man.

"I am not ill, merely broken up a bit. Still, I'm not a threat to your virtue."

She gave a snort of laughter and sat beside him. "Even bound, gagged, and unconscious, you, sir, are a danger to a woman's virtue. I will help you recover for as long as it's necessary, but I insist you abide by my terms."

Amused, Case realized her nearness was now making *him* uneasy. Her vivid hazel eyes gave off yellow sparks, luring him. "State your terms."

She cleared her throat. "Out of necessity, ours must remain a strictly platonic relationship."

Case envied her tongue when it darted over her lips, moistening them. Platonic relationship, hell. He should remind her that she had kissed and caressed *him* while she thought he was unaware.

"No touching, kissing, or what you're doing now," she continued.

"What am I doing now?"

"The way you're looking at me."

"How am I looking at you?" he asked, his tone low and seductive.

"Most indecently."

"Do you know what I'm thinking? What I wish I could do right now?"

Pressing a hand over her middle, she knitted together her finely arched brows.

"I'd dearly love to . . ." Seeing her jaw drop, the silent plea in her overly bright eyes, Case continued, ". . . eat my breakfast." He nearly laughed when her mouth clamped shut. "Please, treat my face quickly, before I die of starvation."

Without comment she smeared salve on his scrapes. "Gently, Miss North. There will be plenty of time after I've recovered."

Her lips curved up at the corners as she dipped her fingers into the smelly medicine. "Time for what?"

Case steadied his vision on the lumped mass on her fingertips, weighing the risk of continuing to taunt her. Feeling daring, he said, "To make love to you."

The barely perceptible narrowing of her eyes urged caution. He moved his hand up her arm. "You desire me. If you were honest, you'd admit it. You're trembling now. Undesirable womanizer or not, I wager I could seduce you with little effort."

She slapped the gob of salve on his nose and bolted to her feet. "You most certainly hold a high opinion of yourself."

Case grabbed the napkin and, wiping his nose, began to laugh, despite his pained ribs. He watched her lift the silver tray loaded with cold bacon, eggs, potatoes, and biscuits, and a pot of still-steaming coffee. Her blazing eyes told him she wanted to dump it over his head. He breathed easy only after she slid the tray over his legs. He should have known she'd resist the temptation to exact revenge in such a messy manner.

"Is there anything else I can get you?" she said smoothly.

Devilment lurked in his gaze. "Not unless a kiss is on the menu."

"You want a kiss?"

His earlier resolve faded. Perhaps he'd been too quick to form an opinion about her intent to retaliate.

"You've proven yourself a master of seduction." She leaned forward, whispering provocatively. "I'll give you one kiss. *One* only, mind you."

Case hesitated. Still, whatever she planned, his curiosity demanded satisfaction. Intending to question her uncharacteristic response, he opened his mouth.

And she stuffed a biscuit so far past his teeth, he nearly gagged. With a smug grin, she sailed out of the room.

Downstairs, Rayne wandered aimlessly, wishing for a chore to occupy her time. If she dared undertake a housecleaning task, Hung Lee would appear from nowhere. The Chinaman took his job seriously, eliminating any need for her help. She should be thankful that her father's prosperity allowed for a house servant, but she preferred to be of some use. At least Case O'Malley needed her.

Her thoughts shifted to her mother. Rayne's heart brimmed with sadness. Her mother's once delicate, soft hands were rough and callused from hard work, her reddish brown hair streaked with gray. At least the funds O'Malley had promised to send would allow her to escape her life of drudgery.

Rayne's mood brightened. Perhaps she'd find a

position in Virginia City. After Case recovered. She liked Virginia City, and her father still did need her help.

O'Malley's earlier accusation that she was a gold digger made her bristle. She had no designs on her father's wealth, or any man's, for that matter. She had her own plans, and they didn't include becoming a scoundrel's victim.

Instead, she hoped her stay in Virginia City would allow her a chance to discover her independence. First, however, she must see that her father truly mended his ways.

An incessant pounding from upstairs drew her from the parlor into the hall. She paused to listen. With a shake of her head she wondered how O'Malley would summon help if she took away the chair. He would mar the wood if he continued to ram the chair leg on the floor. Angry at being summoned in this churlish manner, Rayne slowly climbed the stairs.

She dawdled on the landing to study her reflection in a mirror, then leisurely tucked a stray strand of hair into the loose coil behind her head. The pounding stopped. She decided she'd tarried long enough to teach her cranky charge a lesson.

She'd just started down the hall when a string of vulgar oaths reached her ears. She hastened to the door but skidded to a halt when a deafening crash came from inside his room. Fearing he'd fallen from the bed, she darted into the room, her heart pounding in her chest. The remains of his breakfast were strewn on the floor. An ungodly mess. The beautiful silver tray had a large dent, the china had smashed into a thousand pieces, and coffee lay in puddles beneath the fragments.

His face as dark as a thundercloud, he cast her a withering glance.

"Mr. O'Malley, what have you done?"

"What have *I* done? Nothing save try to rest, which was impossible with a tray of dishes crushing my stomach."

Rayne stepped closer and looked at the littered floor, appalled.

"I rang, but you ignored my call," he informed her with a sardonic undertone.

She gracefully knelt and reached for the tray. She didn't know why, but she found his irascible mood endearing, bringing to mind a caged animal, a bear perhaps—an extremely attractive, very masculine bear of a man. "You didn't ring, sir. You beat the chair on the floor."

"So you heard me?"

"The entire Comstock heard you, Mr. O'Malley."

Feeling his hard gaze, she daintily lifted shards of porcelain. Apparently, her unruffled demeanor infuriated him further.

"You didn't come," he complained. "In fact, I thought I'd been left to die alone with my congealed breakfast rising from my stomach as my eternal marker."

Rayne bit her bottom lip to stifle another smile. She dropped a sliver of broken cup and heard it clink on the tray before she met his furious gaze. "I came."

"You took your own goddamn time about it," he said with a snarl, his eyes bulging.

"Actually, I did," she returned, continuing with her chore. *No man should have green eyes, especially a devil like Case O'Malley*, she thought. They smouldered, reminding her of a lush forest caught on fire. Her pulse pounded. "The next time you see fit to act in such a childish manner, perhaps I won't come at all."

"Childish manner? You regard being made to hold my breakfast for hours an inappropriate reason to want help?"

She gave him a patient look. "You threw your tray on the floor." His eyes bulged again, giving her pause. "Didn't you?"

"For your information, I did not throw the tray. Because I'd been neglected, I attempted to transfer it to the table with one hand. My aim wasn't exact, due to a severe pain in my side, and the blasted thing fell."

It wasn't the answer she had expected. Guilt held her silent. Wiping the liquid from the floor with the napkin, she awaited another outburst. When he remained silent, she offered, "What was I supposed to think?"

"You weren't supposed to think, Miss North, merely react. I needed your help and you failed me."

Balancing her burden, Rayne came to her feet. "Am I to be your obedient slave, then?"

A dark eyebrow winged up. His features relaxed into a crooked grin. "I'm sorry for my bad temper. It's damn humiliating to have to depend on someone else when I'd much rather see to my own needs."

Assuaged by his apology, she said, "I understand. I wouldn't want to be in your position, either."

"I believe I hear someone at the front door," he said, a violent shudder racking his body. "It may be the doctor."

"It's probably the sheriff. Are you ill?" She placed the tray on the floor outside the room, then returned and, peering at him, laid her hand on his brow. "You look rather peakish."

He closed his eyes.

She poked his arm with a finger. "Mr. O'Malley?"

Cracking open an eye, he flinched. "Is that you hovering over me, Miss North?"

"Yes, Mr. O'Malley. I thought you'd died on me."

"If I must die, I wish you'd hold my hand first."

He looked too ill to chastise, and his skin had felt hot when she'd touched it. "I do hear someone. I hope it's the doctor."

"Are you singing, Miss North?"

She leaned over him, drew up the counterpane, and tucked it under his neck. "I think you have a fever. And for your information, I don't sing. I croak like a frog."

"It must be the angels, then, come to take me," he said, his voice fading.

When she noticed the doctor standing in the doorway, Rayne motioned for him to enter. "Your patient has taken a turn for the worse. He hears angels."

"Angels?" With a wink at Rayne, the doctor dropped his small black bag on the chair. "I might have to bleed him."

"The hell you will, you quack!" O'Malley's eyes popped open. He threw her and the doctor a look that would have quelled a rattlesnake.

"Giving you trouble, is he?" the short, thin man asked Rayne.

"He has been very cross this morning."

"That right, Case? You're normally so mild-mannered."

Case devoutly considered the ceiling. And with a smile, Rayne strolled from the room.

Rayne twisted her fingers together while she waited at the bottom of the stairs. Despite Case's quick response when the doctor had threatened to bleed him, she feared her patient wasn't at all well. He had looked so drawn and pale. She wondered how he found the strength to make light of his injuries by playacting.

She frowned. Angels, indeed!

The physician finally came downstairs.

"Is he all right?" Rayne asked, worry in her voice.

"Coming along splendidly. He is, however, slightly feverish and will need constant watching. Send word if his temperature rises. I'll come as fast as possible."

"He isn't in danger of dying, is he?"

"Case?" The doctor gave a hoot of laughter. "Far from it. He has the strongest constitution of any man I've seen. Once the danger of this fever passes, I suspect you'll have your hands full."

Case O'Malley is a handful already, thought Rayne.

Chapter 9

O'Malley had been sleeping for two hours
when Hung Lee summoned Rayne.

A tall, attractive man was waiting inside the
front door. His curly brown hair contrasted with
his severe features, and his slightly crooked nose
appeared less prominent because of his thick,
darker brown mustache. But Rayne's attention focused on his leather vest, blue shirt, worn denim
pants, dusty black boots . . . and revolver strapped
to his thigh.

He looked hard and capable, a man who didn't
like to be crossed, exactly like the gunslingers
she'd read about in dime novels. She cleared her
throat to alert him to her presence, fearing he
would draw his gun at the slightest provocation.
Quickly she introduced herself.

"Name's Rogers, ma'am."

After wiping his palm on his pants, he clasped
her hand and gave it a mighty shake. Startled by
the power of his grip, Rayne hesitated before she
asked, "Are you a friend of Case O'Malley?"

"I owe him my life."

"He saved *your* life?" The thought amazed her
so much, she fell silent. She noted the intensity of

his deep blue eyes. "If I had to guess, I'd say you were the kind of man who would do the saving."

He grinned boldly. "Don't wear this Colt for show. I'm a guard for Wells Fargo. Case hired me to ride shotgun with him."

"And he saved your life?" she repeated, unable to imagine Case O'Malley performing such an amazing deed. "How did this happen?"

"Case pushed me off the wagon, outta the line of fire. That graze alongside his head was meant to go between my eyes. He's a hero, that's what he is." He glanced past her, down the hall. "Don't tell him I called him a hero, though."

"No, of course I won't." Stunned by the news that the man she knew to be a scoundrel had bravely risked his life to save another's, Rayne fell silent again.

"I want to make sure he's all right." He held out a telegram. "I also came to deliver this to you."

Rayne slipped the missive into a pocket of her skirt. "Thank you, Mr. Rogers. You may visit with O'Malley if he's awake."

Before Rogers could climb the stairs, someone else knocked on the door. Rayne admitted the sheriff, who motioned toward Rogers.

"Hold on just a minute," the lawman said. "I have three dead bodies to account for, and you're the man I want to question first."

"Anything to oblige, Sheriff."

"What happened on the Geiger Road? I have a fair idea, but I need your side, since you were the one responsible."

"It's simple, actually," Rogers explained. "O'Malley hires me to ride shotgun with him when I'm off duty and he thinks there might be trouble. Well, he guessed right this time. Those three bandits thought to make off with the load of ore they figured we were hauling, but I changed their minds."

The sheriff scratched his head. "How did Case get hurt?"

"They got off a round before I could react." Rogers looked a bit sheepish as his gaze met the lawman's. "O'Malley shoved me out of the line of fire and suffered a bullet for it."

"And that's when you shot the outlaws?"

"That's right," Rogers said. "It was them or me."

"Do you still want to speak with Mr. O'Malley, Sheriff?" Rayne asked.

"I have enough information for now. Unfortunately, things like this happen all too often in these parts. The Comstock sends out so much ore, it's too great a temptation for some. Tell Case I hope he mends soon and to stay the hell off ... Pardon my language, ma'am ... Tell him to let his hired men handle the dangerous stuff."

"I will," Rayne replied.

The sheriff stepped out the door, then hollered back to Rogers, "Next time try to leave one alive so maybe I can ask him some questions."

"Sure thing, Sheriff."

After the lawman left, Rayne gave Rogers directions to the correct room.

"I won't stay long," Rogers promised as he took the steps two at a time.

Rayne stood still, stunned by all she had learned in the past few minutes. Rogers must be very fast with his gun to have bested three outlaws at once. If he hadn't reacted so quickly, O'Malley might not have survived.

Anxious to read the telegram she guessed was from her mother, Rayne started down the hall when another knock sounded on the front door. She sighed in frustration.

The gentleman she admitted this time astonished her more than the dangerous-looking Rogers. Here was no gun-toting guard. He stood several inches over six feet and weighed no less than two hundred fifty pounds. Clad in an ankle-length black garment with long sleeves, a clerical collar, and buttons that descended from neck to hem, he appeared to be a man of the cloth. He removed his black hat with its round crown and wide brim, and smiled.

"Father Patrick Manogue," he announced, "of St. Mary's of the Mountains Catholic church."

Rayne introduced herself, wondering why the priest had come.

"Don't be worrying yourself," he said, jovially. "Case is a friend. I'll be offering him comfort, not the last rites."

"You've relieved my mind, Father. Mr. O'Malley has a visitor at the moment." She glanced above, wondering how long Rogers planned to stay. "Would you like a cup of tea?"

"Thank you, no. I'll wait."

"How do you know Case O'Malley?" she asked. His dark, closely spaced eyebrows gave her the idea that his eyes could penetrate clear through to her soul.

"Case is my most generous benefactor."

Rayne's mouth fell open. "Case O'Malley supports your church?"

"Case has put up the money to build St. Mary's

School for girls. It should be finished and open within six months. Case is a fine, generous man, Miss North. I hope my visit will offer him solace during his regretful misfortune."

Speechless, Rayne stared at the cleric. Case O'Malley funded a school?

Hearing voices out front, she glanced past the priest out the door to see three women in bright dresses headed down the walk.

"Father Manogue, I'll . . . . show you to Mr. O'Malley's room," she stuttered.

She scooted around the priest's massive body and led him up the stairs.

After she'd safely closeted Father Manogue in the room with O'Malley and Rogers, Rayne dashed back downstairs. She ushered the women inside and introduced herself. Her attention was drawn to the striking woman with red hair and blue eyes who gave her name as Kat. She was uncommonly beautiful, with a body any woman would envy.

Had O'Malley lain with Kat? Done the thing he'd told Rayne about?

"I hope you don't mind that we came," Kat said. "We were just so worried about Case, and Bessie said she'd met you and that you didn't act like some other high-thinking women we know. Did you really shake Bessie's hand right there on the street?"

Rayne nodded. She had been shunned by her mother's family and employer, and she would never purposely treat *anyone* that way.

"It's good of you to take care of Case," interjected Bessie Magovern. "He thinks about you a lot, Miss North."

Rayne couldn't help herself, she giggled. "I can well imagine his thoughts."

"He said you're a real lady. If ya want my opinion, he's right. Ya didn't slam the door in our faces like ya oughta have just now."

"I brung you these," said Annie, holding out a pot of geraniums.

Touched, Rayne accepted the gift. She liked these exuberant women in their bright, revealing dresses and painted faces. They seemed an affectionate lot, joined by a single mutual passion—Case O'Malley. The thought sent a dull pain to her heart.

"Ladies," Rayne said, "please come into the parlor for a cup of tea. Mr. O'Malley is occupied at the moment."

The women exchanged surprised glances at the generous request. Finally Bessie brushed off her skirt and stated, "Sure enough, honey. Come along, girls. We've been invited to tea."

Fifteen minutes later, Rayne accepted a tray from a disapproving Hung Lee. Conversation flowed, brisk and bawdy, her delicate ears filled with stories no proper woman should have heard. But instead of feeling embarrassment, Rayne was thoroughly enjoying this forbidden peek at a sinful but colorful world.

At the sound of footsteps on the stairs, she sprinted into the hallway and deftly escorted both Rogers and Father Manogue out.

Then she went to O'Malley's room.

His contented expression reminded her of a cat who had just lapped up a bowl of cream. Her eyes tearing from the smoke in the air, she immediately understood that one of his two visitors, probably Rogers, had given him a cigar. Rayne opened all three windows. "You have more guests, if you feel up to it."

He locked his hands behind his head. "And I was wondering how I'd fill the time until supper. Show them up, Miss North."

Rayne smoothed the wrinkles from the counterpane. "Aren't you curious who *they* are?"

"I'm sure you're dyin' to tell me."

She ignored his sarcastic tone. "Three women."

"Women?"

"Yes, Mr. O'Malley, women." She folded her arms at her waist. "We enjoyed an interesting conversation. I found Annie and Bessie fascinating, but Kat is definitely the prettiest."

She waited while he tried to control a severe coughing attack before she inquired, "Would you like me to show them in now? Mr. O'Malley? Is there an object lodged in your throat? Perhaps a glass of water will alleviate your affliction."

"You witch! You—"

"Why, you're coughing again. I do believe this sullied air is the cause of your distress. I'll summon your guests before you perish."

Rayne swallowed a laugh and walked out. When she escorted the women into the room, she noted that color had returned to Case's face. She wanted to escape. She didn't want to see him with them. While the women aroused her curiosity, and she liked them, they were, after all, his paramours.

"Don't go, sweetie," begged Bessie. "Make her stay, Case. She's treated us right fine. Asked us to tea."

"I don't think ... Oh, hell. Stay if you want."
His warm gaze briefly met Rayne's before he
turned to Bessie. "Asked you to tea, huh?"

With a sinking heart, Rayne watched Bessie lean
over O'Malley and fluff up his pillow. Annie held
his hand to her cheek while Kat waited at the foot
of the bed, eager to fulfill his every request.

Merciful heavens! He sported such an angelic
expression! It wasn't fair that a womanizer like
him could inspire such devotion in her, or any of
them.

Bessie finished fluffing the pillow and moved
away, and the redhead slithered close and offered
her lips. O'Malley looked abashed for a moment,
then gave her a quick peck. Evidently not satisfied, Kat placed her lips over his and kissed him
soundly.

Rayne didn't know whether to laugh or cry. Despite his obvious embarrassment, he clearly relished the attention. And the sight of the gorgeous
Kat kissing O'Malley drove a spike of jealousy
through Rayne's heart.

It was as clear as day that Rayne harbored some
feelings for him, Case decided, despite her calm
acceptance of his lady friends. *Not that it should
matter one way or the other*, he told himself. He had
no designs on Rayne, but he certainly admired her
for behaving graciously toward these women.

Not too long ago, he would've loved to have
three women pamper him. And he positively
wouldn't have had his mind elsewhere when a
beautiful, hot-blooded woman thrust her tongue
down his throat.

But as he disengaged himself from Kat's devouring mouth, he noticed the torment in Rayne's eyes, and felt guilty. He cursed the tightness in his chest and flopped an arm over his face. Maybe if they believed he felt ill, they'd all leave. He didn't want to purposely hurt Jasper's daughter.

"Case, honey, are you feeling poorly?" Kat asked, laying a hand over his brow.

"A mite, but I'll be good as new in no time." He captured her fingers and brought her hand to his mouth. "Thanks for coming, though."

"We'll visit another day," Annie said. "Come along, girls."

The women left, thanking Rayne on their way out.

Case sensed Rayne standing at the foot of the bed. He knew when she inched closer.

"O'Malley?"

"Death has not claimed me yet."

"You're not ill at all, are you?"

Case flung his arm away from his face. "I don't know," he admitted, though he felt extremely uncomfortable.

She crossed her arms over her chest. "You should have just allowed me to exit gracefully so you could have been alone with them."

Her eyes were flashing with anger. He loved to watch her come to life, for it sparked a similar reaction in him. No other woman had ever inflamed him so thoroughly. That she accomplished it fully clothed with a mere look or artless mannerism devastated him. He wondered if she could possibly be jealous.

"Your thinking is typically female," he accused. "May I remind you, I didn't invite them up here, you did? Did you think I was a saint?"

"Never that. Mrs. O'Flannigan told me about you, remember?"

"I regret what happened," he said quickly. "You shouldn't have been here when they visited me. I do, however, appreciate your kindness to my friends. I doubt most women would have treated them as you did."

"It isn't my business to know with whom you share your affections." Shrugging, she walked to the side window. "I like them."

"I didn't kiss Kat. She kissed me."

"It doesn't matter. Truly, it doesn't."

Her indifference angered him. That he cared, inflamed him further.

She left the window and came to stand directly opposite him, regarding him curiously. "If you feel strong enough, there are several questions I'd like you to answer."

"It'll be my pleasure."

"I spoke with Father Manogue. Is it true you've funded his school for girls?"

His eyebrows shot up, and Case immediately cursed his shocked reaction.

"Isn't that a rather benevolent deed for a devoted scoundrel?"

With a halfhearted smile, he replied, "He's a nice man. Why shouldn't I give him a little donation?" Rayne was definitely much too shrewd for her own good. What did she hope to gain by looking for his better qualities? "Considering my black soul, maybe I'll get a chance at the hereafter."

"Did you really save Rogers's life?"

Damn. Did no one hold their tongues anymore? "An accident. I leaned over to say something, and the bullet caught me instead."

In response to her skeptical look, Case gave her an indulgent smile. "Grant me a small amount of intelligence, my dear. Only a fool would risk his life needlessly."

"I do believe you're an expert at inventing fables. The trouble is, I don't know when to believe you and when to doubt you."

Case winced. Until now it had been relatively easy to guard his secret activities for the Union. Now close contact with Rayne might endanger his mission. She was too sharp. If he wasn't careful, before long she'd discover his plans.

"Save yourself the trouble," he advised. "Search for any virtue in me, and you'll end up disillusioned. Bridget O'Flannigan gave you an accurate accounting. I'm a lover of liquor, a devoted gambler, and a womanizer—nothing more. And if you fall in love with me, I'll treat you just like your father treated your mother."

"I will *not* fall in love with you." Her chin lifted. "I'm not a gambler, you see."

Looking as if she'd had a sudden thought, she delved into her pocket and brought out a piece of paper. After a quick reading, she clamped the missive tight against her heart, her lips trembling.

"Miss North? Have you had bad news?"

Tears welled in her eyes as she shook her head. "It's from my mother."

"Good God! Is she dying?"

"Mr. O'Malley." She choked back a sob. "You sent my mother ten thousand dollars!"

"Oh, for Chrissakes!" Case rolled his eyes. "Is that all?"

"All? You sent her *ten thousand* dollars."

Case peered intently at Rayne, cursing his stupid mistake. He shouldn't have given such a large amount. "I felt sorry for Jasper, that's all. I figured your mother would stop harrying him if I sent her enough money."

Snatching up an end of his bedsheet, she dabbed at her eyes. "Did you know my mother has worked as a housemaid ever since Papa left her? She saved nearly every cent so she could send me to the best schools and feed and clothe me. She often went without."

Case scowled. "I didn't know."

Damn Jasper. No wonder his daughter was so determined to make him fulfill his obligations. Case's spirits soared. He was thankful he'd wired such a large amount, after all. The woman deserved it and more.

"Thank you." She tugged more of the sheet to wipe her damp cheeks.

"Miss North! Slowly but surely, you're uncovering me."

To his amusement, she snapped the sheet back in place.

Capping a hand over his brow, Case moaned. His head felt as if someone were chipping away at it with a sharp pick. Fearing it might explode if he didn't lie down, he asked, "Would you kindly remove this extra pillow? My head is pounding."

She slid the telegram into her pocket, then did as he'd requested. "You should rest now. I fear you've had too much excitement today."

"You *will* wake me when it's time for supper?"

She grinned. "I trust it will deter you from thumping the floor with the chair?"

Although the effort pained him, he grinned back. "It might. I'm going to rest for a while. If the sheriff ever shows up, tell him to come back to-morrow."

"He came earlier and spoke with Mr. Rogers. He said he got the information he needed."

He closed his eyes and listened to her move about the room. His head drummed incessantly. When he heard her close the windows, he wanted to protest, but he couldn't find the energy. A shiver shook his body, and he thought he swore aloud.

He wasn't sure how much time passed. In the distance he heard the soft croon of Miss North's enchanting voice.

She did, indeed, sound like an angel.

"Did you bring all of his belongings?"

Jasper draped an armful of clothes haphazardly across the banister of the upstairs landing. "Now, Rayne, honey, there's no use in Case paying rent for a hotel room when he won't be staying there."

"He'll be well in no time at all. He won't thank you if he has no room to return to."

Jasper rifled through a sack and produced a rumpled nightshirt.

Shaking it, Rayne wrinkled her nose. "If all of his clothes are as unkempt as this, he'll be sure to complain."

"It wasn't easy bringing everything Case owns. I'm sure Hung Lee will make them look as good as new."

"I suppose you're right," Rayne agreed. She noticed her father's stooped shoulders. "He'll be proud of the way you've taken over the running of the mine."

Jasper puffed out his meager chest and smiled.

"I just hope he's on his feet soon. Never before appreciated the brains it takes to keep everything running smooth. I've barely had a chance to sit down."

Rayne rested a hand on her father's arm. "Hung Lee fixed *licee* and a peculiar, multicolored meat mixture and *tlee* vegetables." Grinning, she mimicked the Chinaman's speech. "I was much *flaid* to *askee* what's in it, but as usual, it's *heap* delicious."

Jasper chuckled as he headed for the stairs. "Heard Case received visitors today."

Rayne followed. "How? What did you hear?"

Jasper paused to glance over his shoulder at her. "Gossip gets around fast. It was mighty decent of you to welcome Annie, Bessie, and Kat." He started down the stairs. "I'd wager Case thought so, too."

Rayne wondered why O'Malley and her father felt the need to remark on her hospitality toward the women. Had they expected her to snub them? She entered O'Malley's room thinking that men were certainly hard to fathom at times. It struck her as strange that he hadn't thumped the floor, not once, demanding his dinner. After his lively afternoon, she had expected him to be ravenous.

He appeared to be sleeping soundly. Careful not to wake him, she selected items of clothing that had remained wrinkle-free during her father's heedless transport and filled the drawers of the bureau and wardrobe. Recognizing the black frock coat Case had worn when he'd met her in Carson City, she smoothed her hand over the lapels, admiring the fine tailoring The coat smelled like him, she thought, masculine and alluring.

Unable to resist the temptation, she slipped her

arms into the sleeves. She felt a lump in an inside pocket and dipped her fingers inside. The cold, hard revolver there gave her a start. She turned it cautiously, considering its size and shape, and quickly withdrew her hand.

She supposed, in a rough town, it was necessary for a person who frequented saloons to carry a gun.

The broad shoulders of the coat hung loosely on her. The sleeves fell inches past her hands. She tilted her head and inhaled the scent that clung to the garment, and a familiar warmth invaded her insides. She shook her head, reminding herself that Case O'Malley was not the right man for her.

She must remember. She must retain control of her fragile feelings where he was concerned. How easily she forgot, though, each time his green gaze moved over her. Already she was a different woman because of him, no longer as proper as when she had first arrived in Virginia City. Her movements were jerky as she shed the coat and stowed it in the wardrobe.

The same should be done with Case O'Malley, she thought. The scoundrel should be closeted away to protect unsuspecting, inexperienced women. But this same scoundrel performed deeds that touched her heart.

A vision of a canyon she'd seen during her journey to Virginia City popped into her mind. Beyond this canyon, called *Devils Gate*, lay the glorious Comstock Lode. Maybe, just maybe, if a woman could see past O'Malley's notorious activities and tunnel her way into his heart, she would be rewarded with such treasure as most women could only dream about.

Like the passage through Devil's Gate, the effort would be perilous. In the canyon, robbers lay hidden, ready to steal a traveler's worldly goods. Case O'Malley was a devil, and he might steal more than a woman's purse. He might steal her heart.

A whisper broke into her musings. She crossed to the bed and noticed his flushed face. Laying the back of her hand on his forehead, then his cheek, she affirmed her suspicion. He had taken a fever. She hoped it wasn't due to his injuries—an infection in his leg would be dangerous.

Quickly she summoned her father and sent him off in search of the doctor. Unsure what to do in the meantime, she considered her options. O'Malley's skin felt blisteringly hot. He was mumbling incoherent phrases. She often cooled herself during the summer by wiping a cool, wet rag over her neck and face. It seemed a logical solution to this situation as well.

Chapter 10

Case was sure he'd descended into an inferno. He hadn't felt this hot since the last time he'd gone into the sweltering bowels of the mine. Time and again, tremors quaked through his body, chilling him even as he burned with fever. Maybe Satan had finally claimed him. Then again, snatches of conversation he'd heard in the last few hours reminded him that he was still in his room. Sometime during the night the doctor had come and gone, as had Jasper. Now only Jasper's daughter remained. Without looking, Case sensed her presence.

His angel of mercy, the woman who had tended him in his moment of need.

He supposed Rayne felt gratitude for his kindness to her mother. Why else would she so diligently tend to him—a man of unsavory reputation who didn't know how to treat a decent woman? He was surprised to realize he wished her solicitude came from a tender regard instead of a sense of obligation. Surely, though, she had no designs on his wealth. In fact, he doubted the size of his purse would count for much with her. For some reason, it pleased him to think that.

Case's thoughts drifted to the past. His father

hadn't been rich, but he had done nicely enough, until an unwise business investment had left him nearly destitute. Then he'd scraped together enough to buy a farm, which he claimed would provide a more fulfilling life. Having grown up the son of a planter, he'd been able to draw on his experience and make a decent living for his wife and Case.

Case's mother, however, had come from a socially prominent family and didn't share her husband's love of the land. She saw his lack of interest in regaining his fortune as a betrayal, and never ceased harping about it. She became a bitter, loveless woman.

Thank God he'd escaped her, Case thought. At fourteen, he'd set out to make his own way. Remembering the tough time he'd had made him appreciate his recent prosperity all the more. It was a damn shame his father hadn't lived long enough to share his son's good fortune.

A warm, damp cloth was touched to his brow, startling Case. He opened his eyes. Even in the dim light he recognized the glint of concern in Rayne's gaze. Her breath whispered across his skin.

"You're finally awake," she said. "You had me worried."

Lines of fatigue marked her forehead, and dark smudges had appeared beneath her eyes. "Have you stayed at my side all night?" he asked.

"You had a high fever. It's nearly morning now."

He glanced at the cloth in her hand. "You've been bathing me, haven't you?"

She looked embarrassed and leaned away.

"It seems I owe you a debt of gratitude." He

reached out to touch her face but stopped when she flinched. "Pardon my blunder. I forgot your rules."

"It's for the best."

"I have no objection if you touch *me*." He watched a muscle twitch alongside her mouth and continued, "You were about to cool my skin. Please don't stop."

"I believe your fever has lowered now."

"But I want to know what I missed while I was unconscious. Besides, I still ache all over and my mouth feels like someone stuffed cotton down my throat." He grinned crookedly. "You didn't attempt to gag me again, did you?"

"No biscuits were available," she informed him, mischief dancing in her eyes. She filled a glass and held it to his lips. "Sip carefully. If you spill it, we'll be in a fine fix."

Case drank until his thirst was quenched and smiled. "I'll definitely have to compensate you."

"I put no price on my help. I would do the same for anyone in need."

"Yes, I suppose you would."

He studied her profile, admiring her bone structure, as she dampened the rag in a basin of water. Fine and delicate, her face was an artist's dream. He made a mental note to try his hand at sketching her. It would offer a far greater challenge than drawing timbers and pumping stations.

"If you can control your lusty nature, I'll bathe you once more before I retire."

"As you wish. I'll endeavor to behave in a gentlemanly manner."

He nearly laughed aloud when she dropped a towel over his nether region.

"Close your eyes, please."

Case obeyed, putting his complete trust in her. It was torture, though, a downright ecstatic torment, when she began to bathe him. Over his cheek, down his neck, across his shoulder, she swept the rag, her movements slow and sensuous. He swallowed a moan, determined to hide his response to the soothing sensations she brought to his burning flesh.

"How does that feel?"

"Wonderful. Don't stop."

She tended his other side, then returned and wiped his arm from shoulder to wrist. Case held his breath and bore the incredible agony as shivers of a different sort traveled through his limbs. He vowed he'd do the same to her one day, except she would be free to respond to the heady stimulation. He felt no pain now, except for the grumble in his empty stomach. Never had he felt so relaxed. Extending his other arm, he invited her to treat it in the same manner.

"You're enjoying this too much," she said. "Your expression is one of sheer pleasure."

"Indeed. You've cast a spell over me."

"Be sure you mention it to Dr. Connell. He seemed concerned that my remedy would impair your health."

"Did he? I'll set him straight the next time he calls."

"Let's hope you're alive tomorrow."

"I'm very much alive now," he returned before he could stop himself. Aware of her abrupt cessation of movement, he opened his eyes. "You haven't killed me," he amended. "You've saved me."

She reached for the towel. He seized her wrist. "Leave it," he warned.

Immediately she snatched back her hand and, averting her eyes, wiggled her other wrist free of his fingers.

Case controlled a grin. "You look tired. You needn't exhaust yourself on my account."

Slowly, pressing her palm over her lower back, she rose. "I am tired."

"Go get some sleep." The growling began again in his stomach, but he vowed he wouldn't bother her with a complaint. It was the least he could do to return her kindness. "I'll manage until morning."

By noon, however, Case didn't feel quite as charitable. Thanks to the combined efforts of Jasper and Hung Lee, he now wore a crisp, freshly laundered nightshirt, had seen to his morning functions, and eaten his morning meal, if one could possibly refer to a tasteless bowl of watery broth as food.

Although he felt a good deal better, his stomach growled a protest. The pain in his ribs had blessedly subsided, allowing him to sit upright without discomfort. After this accomplishment, unfortunately, he was left with nothing to do. He'd give a thousand gold pieces for a deck of cards, even more for a cigar. And the list of errands he'd given Jasper would keep him away for hours.

Case had left orders Rayne wasn't to be disturbed. She needed her sleep. Yet he kept glancing at the doorway, hoping she'd come through it. With a start, he realized he missed her. Fifteen more minutes passed before he heard sounds of movement in her room. The click of her door hinted that she was headed for the bathroom. Imagining her morning ablutions, he grew miserably warm.

It seemed she took unduly long to wash such a slim body . . . unless she had chosen to take a tub bath. The thought of her splashing about *naked* caused him to wiggle beneath the covers. Her legs would be long and slender, her tiny waist tapered perfectly, the skin of her abdomen white, her breasts voluptuous. He imagined them clearly, visible through lapping water.

Damn.

Case wiggled again, hoping to dispel his amorous daydream. He didn't know how long he could withstand this confinement. Already he wanted to smash his fist against a solid object. He couldn't even roll over for fear he'd jar his leg. If only he could leave this accursed bed, he'd dress and go to his office, where he might be able to bury himself in work. Maybe then he would be free of his absurd desire for her.

He laughed at the thought. It wasn't what he'd do at all. He would head for the room at the end of the hall, lift her from her bath, and kiss her senseless while he moved his hands over her luscious, dripping wet body.

Fanciful notions. Rayne would probably beat him senseless with the copper kettle—before she drowned him. She'd made it perfectly clear she wanted nothing to do with a philanderer like him. And even though there were plenty of available women in Virginia City, his for the asking, he wanted Jasper's daughter. He must be losing his mind.

He heard Rayne return to her room, followed by the creak of the wardrobe door, the clink of the brass bureau handle as it fell against the wood. She was dressing, probably slipping into her underthings right this second. He wondered if they were starched and stiff or soft and adorned with lace.

Maybe Bessie, Kat, or Annie would visit again, preferably with a bottle of imported brandy. Their lively company might divert his wayward yearnings. It was simple actually. He was bored. Any normal man would fall prey to sexual fantasies. A scoundrel like himself was especially vulnerable.

His stomach gave a loud, rumbling growl. Case folded his arms over the spot, determined to silently, graciously, wait until it suited Rayne to come to him. She would have no reason to fault his manners again.

With a backward glance at O'Malley's door, Rayne left her room. She should look in on him, but earlier she'd heard her father's and Hung Lee's voices, and she was confident that they'd seen to their patient's needs. So she went downstairs.

Caring for O'Malley wasn't truly any bother, she thought as she helped herself to a serving of the scrumptious noon meal the Chinaman had prepared. It was the constant close contact with such a persuasive, masculine man that had worn her nerves thin. The rascal had invaded her dreams again, tormenting her for hours, causing her to toss restlessly. For her own peace of mind, she decided to let her father and Hung Lee take on some of her nursing duties.

She had just finished eating when Hung Lee entered the dining room and handed her a distinctive calling card. Paul Devereau requested the favor of her company that afternoon. In the confusion surrounding O'Malley's mishap, she had forgotten Paul. His timing was excellent. She desperately needed time away from her irascible, disturbing patient.

She penned a response, asking Paul to return in an hour, then searched her mind for what to wear. Her wardrobe sadly lacked elegance, a quandary she had given little consideration until now. As she and her mother had done for most of their lives, she would simply have to make do. It was, after all, a person's inner worth that mattered.

She heard a thump, and crossed to the door to listen. Another, louder thump came, then another. Her mouth lifted in a smile as she leisurely climbed the stairs. O'Malley's bombardment of the floor increased, affirming his ire. She really must break him of the churlish habit.

Rayne went to her own room first, where she considered several outfits to wear for her coming engagement with Paul Devereau. Case O'Malley's Irish temper didn't frighten her, not one bit. She saw no reason for his impatience. And if he was strong enough to use such force on the floor, he had recovered enough to be left alone occasionally. Several minutes and several overheard expletives later, she entered his room.

Gripping his side and holding the chair poised ready for another attack, he had the grace to look embarrassed. He lowered the chair softly to the floor and laid one hand atop the other, drumming his fingers. She noted the obstinate set of his mouth.

"Good morning," she said with a bright smile.

He grunted. "The morning has long passed. It is midafternoon, Miss North."

She began to straighten his covers. "I'd hardly call one o'clock midafternoon."

He lifted his good leg and waggled it, purposely rumpling the counterpane. "Stop your infernal fussing. The state of my bed is not my immediate concern."

"It appears that all of your concerns are immediate," she responded sarcastically.

His attention lingered on the round collar of her white, pleated shirtwaist. "Have you eaten *your* lunch?" he asked nicely.

His friendly tone somewhat appeased her. He must regret his churlish behavior. "Yes, I have."

"Was it to your liking?"

"It was delicious, as usual. You were right. Hung Lee is an excellent cook."

"Do you know what I've eaten today, Miss North?"

The controlled tone of his voice warned of an underlying motive. He didn't regret his behavior and had been leading her into an ambush. "Your lunch wasn't satisfactory?" she asked.

"My lunch?" His mouth curled into a sneer. "If you refer to the watered-down broth I was served six hours ago—no, I didn't find it satisfactory!"

"Dr. Connell left instructions that you were to have chicken broth only until you regained your strength," she said.

"I do believe you're trying to starve me into a

weakened condition," he remarked, raking his eyes insolently over her.

She stiffened. "Judging from the power you exerted to pound the floor, and the energy it required to deliver the foul language I heard, your vigor has not suffered." She nodded. "In fact, you seem back to your normal, testy self."

Her bold counterattack seemed to take him by surprise. "Come closer, please," he said in a more amicable tone.

Rayne hesitated, questioning his sudden change of mood. "Closer?" She moved cautiously toward him. "I apologize for neglecting your lunch. If you feel well enough, I'll see that you get a substantial meal right away."

She noticed he wore a nightshirt. She had to admit, he looked rakishly handsome in it. The scrapes on his face were healing nicely, and he'd managed to get a respectable shave today. The bandage had been removed from his head, and his damp, dark hair had been slicked back.

"I tend to become grouchy when I haven't eaten," he said, his voice appropriately humble. "Will you forgive my rudeness?"

She considered his beguiling tone, the twinkle of amusement in his eyes—and wasn't deceived. "I haven't the time to humor you, sir. I'll be late for an appointment." She turned to leave.

He caught her hand and held her in place. "You shouldn't roam about town without an escort. It's too dangerous. When your father returns—"

"Thank you, but I already have a proper escort." She tugged on her hand, but he made no move to release her. "I must change clothes or I'll be late."

"Who is this escort? Has he been approved by Jasper?"

"Papa approved *you*. It was rather like closeting a lamb in a wolf's den."

He grinned, a devastating assault on her senses. "I've never before seen a lamb with claws. I don't believe you've suffered any harm by associating with a wolf like me."

"Kindly release my hand. I meant no insult, truly. You must admit, you are inclined to bearish behavior."

"This escort you mentioned. Has he a name?"

"Of course he has a name." His jaw looked taut, confirming her suspicions that he was merely pretending indifference. "Paul Devereau."

Anger flared briefly in his eyes. A second later, she wondered if she'd imagined his reaction. Coolly he studied her face. Could he be jealous? Her stomach churned at the thought. It seemed impossible for Case O'Malley to envy *any* man.

Rayne tugged on her hand once more, but his strong fingers held her firm. He had no right to choose her suitors. "You will cause me to be late for my engagement. Paul will think I intend to stand him up."

"That's precisely what you *will* do, my dear."

"You have no say in this matter," she retorted, irritated by his presumptuous manner. "Furthermore, Paul Devereau is cultured and courteous. In fact, if it weren't for him, I would still regard you as a swindler."

Her revelation had little impact on him. Gently he brought her hand to his mouth. Holding her surprised gaze, he folded her fingers over his and pressed his lips to her skin. Pleasurable sensations skipped up her arm.

"You are quite right. I am not your guardian and have no authority over you. I was only concerned for your welfare. One can only hope Devereau has not misrepresented himself."

"I assure you he has not. He told me all about that game of poker, and I believe him."

Giving her hand a pat, Case released her fingers. "There is nothing left to say. Your insight into a man's character appears to be amazingly accurate. You have correctly seen my own flaws and condemned me for them."

"I do not condemn you," she replied, aghast that he thought so harshly of her.

"Do you think it's appropriate for you to address Devereau by his given name?" He reached for the glass of water on the side table. "You haven't done so with me. Given our intimate circumstances, and the fact that you've known me longer, your continued formality betrays your lack of regard."

She watched him take several swallows from the glass. He was playing an insidious game with her. She was sure of it. Why else would he suddenly be concerned about what name she called him? "Our circumstances are not intimate. Were I to address you by your given name, it would suggest ... Let me assure you, I have no intention of allowing you to become ..."

"Your lover? Is that what you were about to say?"

Rayne allowed a moment to pass before she could continue. "I was about to say *more than a pa-*

tient. You know very well why it's important that we maintain an impersonal relationship."

He grinned. "You're thinking about your weakness for me. I understand. Perhaps it is better, then, if you don't call me Case."

Never had she met such a thoroughly conceited person.

"You will remember to have Hung Lee bring me some food before you leave to meet *Paul*, won't you?"

Rayne sighed and shook her head. Although tempted to continue their conversation, she would not put herself through the aggravation. Most likely he intended to rile her in the hope she'd transfer her agitation to Paul. "Certainly," she said. "Have a pleasant afternoon."

O'Malley sounded amiable enough, but the tightness around his mouth revealed his annoyance. Impossible man.

It was past dinnertime when Rayne returned home and from a side window watched Paul Devereau climb back into the buggy he had rented for their outing. Everything about the man impressed her. Certainly he knew how to charm a woman. His speech, manners, even the cut of his clothes, were elegant. Unlike O'Malley, Paul wasn't the least bit vain, and he had every reason to be. She hadn't missed the envious looks she'd received from several women when he'd escorted her through town.

Rayne laid her reticule and hat on a table and entered the parlor. She didn't want to see Case O'Malley yet, knowing he'd spoil the happiness she felt after her wonderful afternoon. She chose a wing chair next to a window and sat to enjoy a few minutes of privacy.

Looking up, she watched Hung Lee set a tray on a small, round table and pour tea into a dainty china cup. He held it out, inclining his head.

"Why, thank you, Mr. Lee."

"Missy want eat. Heap delicious."

"I have already dined." A sudden thought struck her. "Has Mr. O'Malley received his supper?"

The Chinaman nodded and slipped away. She found the peculiar little man fascinating. Unfortunately, due to their difficulty in communication, she couldn't question him. She would have liked to know more about him and his family.

Rayne settled back in the chair to savor the tea. Everything Hung Lee prepared was excellent. She felt so relaxed here in the parlor, she could almost forget her worry about her father, and her troublesome patient upstairs. At least she needn't be anxious about her mother's welfare again, thanks to O'Malley. She should show more patience with him. After all, he was incapacitated, which would try anyone's temper.

A sudden, deafening chorus of clangs jarred Rayne from her musings. She jumped to her feet. Tea sloshed over the rim of her cup and splashed down the front of her finest dress. Unsure from which direction the ungodly sound had come, she hurried into the hallway and listened. She had almost convinced herself she had dreamt the noise when it came again—from upstairs.

She looked up. A wire snaked along the ceiling

to a spot directly above her head. Attached to the end of the wire was a cowbell. She set the teacup still in her hands on the bottom step and covered her ears with her hands. Then she marched up the stairs . . . straight to Case O'Malley's room.

Chapter 11

About to give the braided cord that hung from the ceiling another tug, Case glanced at his accomplice.

Rogers motioned with his hand. "Try again. It'll wake the dead if you yank it hard enough. Want me to move this crate before I leave?"

"Slide it under the bed for now." Case pulled the rope once more and smiled when he heard the bell clang downstairs. As he thought of his precious stash of imported brandy, his smile widened.

Rogers had the crate of bottles under the bed and reached for his hat. "If you need anything else, give a holler."

"You might keep an eye on Jasper for me. Make sure he doesn't get into any card games and lose his ass while I'm laid up."

"Sure thing."

"You are most ungracious, Mr. O'Malley," Rayne said, stepping into the room. "Papa has been doing a wonderful job of managing your mine."

"So far, but I don't trust him not to gamble it away as soon as the sun sets." Case was grateful Rayne hadn't walked in seconds earlier and caught a glimpse of the brandy under the bed. He noticed her hurt expression. "I'm unable to come to your father's rescue right now."

She looked divine in a high-collared burgundy dress with long sleeves, despite the stain on the fitted bodice. Unlike her other clothes, this garment looked expensive, and it made her waist appear even smaller. Letting his gaze move upward in a slow exploration over her breasts to her face, he watched two dots of red color her cheeks. Her obvious embarrassment at his close scrutiny made him uncomfortable also.

"You remember Rogers, don't you?" Case gestured toward his friend. "He's remedied one of my problems."

"You have been very kind, and creative," Rayne said. "Mr. O'Malley has frequent demands. No longer will he have to pound the floor with a chair."

"Precisely," agreed Case.

She moved toward the connecting door. "Wherever did you find such a monstrous bell?"

"Case asked for the loudest—"

"A *capable* bell is what I requested," Case interjected, scowling at Rogers.

Before Rayne escaped to her room, he wanted to speak with her, but first, he had to get rid of his company. Rogers, it seemed, had other plans. He rounded the bed and faced her.

Executing an awkward bow, he told her, "It's been a pleasure to see you again, Miss North. You look ravishing today."

Rayne awarded him with a dazzling smile. "Thank you."

Twirling his hat on a finger, Rogers winked.

Case decided Rogers was purposely trying to exasperate him.

"You must come to visit again," Rayne said sweetly.

"I will." Holding her gaze, Rogers backed across the room to the doorway. "Very soon."

As soon as Rogers left, Rayne looked over at Case. He crossed his arms over his chest and returned her scrutiny.

"Are you in pain, Mr. O'Malley?"

He gave her his most seductive, lazy grin. "Come sit beside me. Tell me about your afternoon—what you did, what you saw."

"Why?"

"For all the obvious reasons. I'm trapped here in this room with nothing to stare at but four walls."

Her lips curled before she forced them into a straight line. "You could look at the ceiling. It's rather . . . nice."

Case slid the chair closer to the bed. "Entertain me, please."

"I'm afraid nothing I've seen or done today would interest you. From what I've discovered about you, your tastes are not as . . . simple as mine."

Never before had he suffered the pain of jealousy. That he should suffer the emotion because of Paul Devereau infuriated him. Rogers didn't worry him. Like himself, Rogers boasted a scandalous reputation. But if Devereau had laid a hand on Rayne, he'd throw him off a cliff.

Case strove to master his rage. Devereau had gained favor with her by distorting the events of their fateful card game—failing to reveal he had tried to cheat Jasper. But without proof, Case saw no advantage in blackening Devereau's name. Hopefully his own investigation into the man's character would provide enough ammunition to convince Rayne of the man's unsuitability. Still, her lack of insight annoyed him.

She sat on the chair he had indicated, folded her hands in her lap, and began to describe the sights she'd seen.

He hardly listened to her words. Her dress reminded him of rich, red wine, the shade perfect against her fair skin. Several tendrils of hair had escaped the coil at her nape and taunted him. Never had he seen a lovelier neck. The long, graceful column craved kisses—his kisses! He closed his eyes, seeing in his mind's eye an image of her in her nightdress.

"Mr. O'Malley, are you listening?"

Case roused himself. "I heard every word you said."

"Where did I leave off?"

"Sam Clemens was giving you a tour of the *Territorial Enterprise* office. I believe you were amazed at how much louder the blasting in the tunnels sounded there."

"Very good. You *were* listening."

He had always been able to keep track of more than one conversation at the same time. During card games, his ability to know everything that went on around him had given him an advantage over the others. She continued speaking, while he continued studying her. He loved the way her mouth moved, allowing him glimpses of her teeth. How sweetly she'd put her lips on his when she'd thought he was unconscious. The memory tormented him.

"You are definitely not listening now," Rayne accused.

"You saw the opera house," he said, his voice trailing away.

Rayne opened her mouth to comment, but the words lodged in her throat. Before she guessed his intent, her hairpins lay scattered on the floor and his fingers were slowly weaving through her coiled tresses.

"You have lovely hair," he said. "It's a shame to hide it."

He played with a curl. A luscious shiver skipped through Rayne's body. *Move away, out of his reach*, she told herself, but the message went unheeded.

"Please," she begged.

"Please?"

"Stop."

She inhaled and held the air in her lungs. If only she knew how to overcome the longing he awakened in her traitorous body. She felt as if a flame had been kindled in her limbs. Even when he angered her, the spark fired her blood.

"I've only let down your hair."

"You're touching . . ." The excitement in his eyes silenced her. He wanted her, wanted to kiss and hold her, maybe even make love to her. "Why are you doing this to me?"

"All you have to do is move. Why haven't you?"

"I honestly don't know."

"Yes, you do."

He urged her forward, until her lips were so close that their breath mingled. Of their own volition her hands crept over his cheeks. At that moment, she saw a vision of Kat kissing him. She closed her eyes. Unbidden, more images flew through her mind—Case in naked splendor on a bed with a harem of women all around, caressing him. Rayne lurched away, shaking her head to clear it.

"You are truly evil." How dare he give her that dumbfounded look? "I won't allow you to seduce me."

Sudden realization stunned her. If Case O'Malley weren't such a womanizer, she could love him.

"Mr. O'Malley," she said, pausing to clear her throat, "do you have any intention of changing your ways?"

He sat up straight. "Changing my ways?"

"Do you plan to be a womanizer for the rest of your life?"

Tilting his head, he squinted his eyes.

Rayne went to the window and gazed out at a distant, snowcapped mountain. The sun would vanish behind it soon. A chill raced down her spine. She felt like the sun, about to be doomed to darkness.

"Rayne."

It was the first time he'd called her by her Christian name.

"I'm content with my life as it is. Why would I want to change? You weren't thinking of trying to improve me, were you?"

Disappointment swamped her. His words had sounded so final. Why, then, was he devouring her with naked desire in his eyes? "I wouldn't dream of it. It would be rather like teaching a mule to dance."

A lofty grin lifted his mouth. "I dance very well."

"Of course you do," she shot back. "You are Satan in disguise."

"Is that supposed to be a compliment?"

"Take my words however you wish."

"You have a kind, generous heart, but unfortunately, you aren't a good judge of men."

"Clearly you want me to accept you as you are." She lowered her eyes, unable to hold his penetrating gaze.

"It wouldn't hurt you to unbend a little. We're attracted to each other, whether you want to admit it or not."

Was he asking her to become his paramour?

With Paul Devereau she could relax and enjoy herself. He didn't churn up her emotions or bring irreverent thoughts to her mind. When he touched her hand, wild yearnings didn't course through her body. He offered companionship, freedom to be herself without the need to guard her emotions. She knew what to expect from him.

Case O'Malley was the exact opposite. His contrary behavior confused her. Either he should be entirely corrupt, or totally good. If he were beyond redemption, he shouldn't have sent her mother such a preposterous amount of money. Most certainly he would never have contributed to Father Manogue's church. A devoted scoundrel would rob her father blind.

"You seem bothered. If I can be of any assistance, my time is yours."

Without turning, she said, "I'm bewildered. There are so many things I don't understand."

"What things?"

She glanced over her shoulder at him. "You confuse me."

"I'm a simple man with simple wants."

"You are *far* from simple. In fact, you mystify me."

Rayne walked over and stood at the foot of the bed, wrapping her fingers around the tall post. There was safety in distance, she decided.

"What do you want to know?"

From the skepticism in his voice, she sensed he'd tell her only what suited him. But perhaps she would be able to figure him out from his replies. "Why do you treat women with such casual regard?"

His eyebrows lifted in surprise. "Have you a complaint?"

She sighed. "You've answered with a question."

"I don't know what you're asking."

"Will you be truthful if I explain?"

"To the best of my ability," he said, shifting to sit more comfortably.

"You trifle with women's affections." She watched a wary expression settle over his face. Quickly, before she lost her courage, she asked, "Have you no conscience?"

"I never trifle. The women with whom I associate are well aware of my intentions. What, exactly, confuses you?"

Rayne steadied her vision on a button on his nightshirt. "You have so many women. How can you make love to them and then act as if you've done nothing more meaningful than share a . . . a cup of tea?"

"Should you be asking me such a personal question, Rayne?"

"We've discussed far more intimate matters, at least *you* have. Have I shocked you?"

"Frankly, yes. Would you ask the same of Paul?"

"Certainly not!" Rayne said. "It would be quite unseemly to pry into his private dealings."

"Well put. Dare I ask why, then, you can query me? Are my affairs not equally private?"

Rayne grew restless under his relentless gaze. This conversation wasn't going as she'd expected. "I am asking you because I know you will answer and not condemn me for my inquisitiveness."

"You *do* entertain me," he said, a thread of laughter in his voice.

Rayne stepped away from the bed, her hands dropping to her sides. "It is not my intention to entertain you. I just want to understand you."

"I'm not laughing at you. In fact, I find you delightful. Since you're so set upon knowing, I'll answer, although I doubt you'll understand. I don't think less of any woman I've been with. When I'm with a woman it is by mutual consent, and it has nothing to do with love. I have never been in love. There is a difference."

The truth hit her. If she dared love him, chances were she'd end up like her mother, alone with a broken heart, maybe even with an illegitimate child.

Case O'Malley had never loved a woman . . . and until he did, he would not change his ways.

"Perhaps, sir, one day you'll meet a woman for whom you'll want to give up your philandering."

Case's eyes grew very large as he reached for the glass on the bedside table. Apparently her comment had alarmed him.

While he gulped down the water, Rayne continued, "It's inevitable. You're so handsome, and you can be so charming when you want to be. Someday you'll meet a woman who'll mean more to you than any other. Then you will regret you have given so freely of yourself."

Case was speechless, and not entirely from Rayne's remarks. Gold and crimson light from the setting sun streamed in through the two side windows, casting her face in a warm glow. Her hair tumbled around her shoulders, bringing sultry images to his mind. She had spoken with such passion. Feelings the like of which he'd never before experienced overwhelmed him.

He wanted to silence her with his mouth, show her firsthand the passion of which he knew she was capable. She'd tremble from his caresses, melt against him, and instead of seeking to change him, she'd ignite in him another kind of change. She would surrender, be his—and he would be lost.

Lost in a hell of his own making. The thought sobered him. It was safer to anger her.

"Your efforts at reform would be better spent on your father," he said. "I have no intention of giving up any of my pleasures, especially the company of my female friends."

"Friends indeed!"

"You are unduly concerned for my welfare. Perhaps you should scrutinize Devereau as closely."

"Thus far, I've discovered no fault in Paul."

"That's obvious."

"What are you implying? Paul is cultured and mannered. *He* would never use women as playthings."

"Naturally not." This conversation was going

nowhere, Case decided. "Are you up to a challenge?"

"As I told you once already, I'm not a gambler. While you seem to relish defying convention, I do not."

"Have you *ever* done one daring, dangerous thing? Have you ever acted on sheer impulse?"

"I prefer to think before I act," Rayne replied.

"Oh, but you slapped me in my office. Considering my superior strength, it was a dangerous thing to do, and you did it without thinking first."

"There was no risk. Deep inside, I knew you would not strike a woman."

"You knew nothing of the sort."

"You are a gentleman. I've seen the good in you."

Rayne would never admit she possessed a weakness, Case decided. He remembered the day he'd followed her through town. She'd giggled over the antics of an organ grinder's monkey and secretly popped a piece of candy into her mouth. The images had been engraved into his mind.

"Besides, it was my duty to slap you," she said.

"So you admit you occasionally fall prey to impulsive acts."

"Is there a purpose to your questioning?"

Case shrugged. "I'm just trying to learn more about you. Chinks in your armor, you could say."

She frowned. "I'm not perfect. I certainly have my faults, just as you have yours."

"The difference is that I like *your* faults." Seeing her puzzled look, he continued, "You were wrong in believing I took advantage of Jasper, but you stood up for him. Admirably, I might add. Since my anger has cooled, I've come to cherish that slap. It took an abundance of inner fire to strike back. You look lovely standing there with your hair falling over your shoulders, the red glow of the setting sun on your face."

"I wonder how many women you've said *that* to."

He had no defense, Case realized. He had probably used the same phrase many times to charm women. Even he couldn't explain his inconsistent behavior. He wanted her to believe the worst of him, yet he had spoken aloud the things he admired about her. He must be losing his mind. Either that or the fever had caused him to take leave of his senses.

He wanted Rayne, but she asked too damn much. She was sweet, caring, and passionate—not at all like his mother, as he'd first thought. But Rayne was a woman who would possess a man.

If he allowed her to steal his heart, he might end up surrendering all he cherished for her. Even his soul.

Chapter 12

Rayne paused by her bedroom door the following morning and smoothed her hands over her hair. Shaking out the folds of her billowing skirt, she went to the bureau and gazed in the mirror. She had to admit, her severe hair style did little to enhance her features. Quickly she unpinned her tresses and brushed them over her shoulders. She tied a blue ribbon around the thick mass, then stood back. Her face looked softer, younger, and the ribbon matched her dress. The new style made her feel different.

Downstairs, she ate breakfast, wishing her father had not left so early so she could visit with him. She lingered over a cup of coffee. She wasn't anxious to face O'Malley yet. He would surely notice her hair and assume she'd altered it for his benefit.

A commotion in the front hall brought her out of her reverie. She hurried out to find her father struggling to carry several huge bundles up the stairs.

"Papa, what are you doing?"

Jasper froze. "I've only brought some more of Case's belongings."

Rayne eyed the bundles with misgiving. Her fa-

189

ther's unease made her suspicious. Although tempted to query him further, she decided against it. There were few places O'Malley could hide whatever goods he'd arranged for her father to smuggle into the house. She prayed her father had not procured spirits. Putting liquor within Case's reach would no doubt prove too great a temptation for him.

Just as Jasper disappeared around the corner upstairs, Bessie entered the open door, clutching a pot of red geraniums to her breast. "I hope Case's feelin' better today. Thought I'd cheer him up a bit, if you don't mind."

"I'm sure he'll be happy to see you."

Next came Rogers, who carried two wooden sticks with leather binding on the tops. Tipping his hat, he beamed a friendly smile at Rayne before loping up the steps. Rayne closed the front door, sure no more visitors would appear.

But a steady flow of people kept up all morning. Father Manogue came and went, as did Annie, and a strange woman who introduced herself as Julia Bulette. When Kat showed up, Rayne's control slipped. She headed for her room on the pretext of finding a handkerchief. The sound of Kat's bawdy laughter filtered through O'Malley's closed door, causing Rayne grave anguish. She didn't dare imagine what was going on inside.

Grabbing her reticule and hat, she left the house.

The streets of Virginia City were busy, as usual, and Rayne delighted in the boisterous goings-on. She wandered aimlessly down C Street, overhearing snatches of conversation from men grouped on corners and doorways. The topics were always the same—mining and the war raging in the East. She noticed some men in ragtag clothing and wondered if they were soldiers who had fled the conflict.

In front of one establishment, the sidewalk was completely blocked by people. Raised voices drew her closer and she glanced at the name on the building. It was the assayer's office. With little hope of breaking through the tight knot of men, she found her way into the midst of the boisterous crowd, ducked through and swept into the building.

Inside, everyone bustled around busily. Carefully she slipped toward the front, where a haggard little man with sparse gray hair worked within a barred cage. Bent over a scale, he measured out ore and dispensed coin to his customers, a ragtag lot all bearing the same expectant expressions on their craggy faces. They must be prospectors. Some were rewarded generously for their toil, while others were turned away with a mere pittance. Rayne became so engrossed in the proceedings that she lost track of the time.

Eventually the man inside the cage looked up and flexed his stooped shoulders. All his customers had been served and she was the only person left. The assayer removed his spectacles and began to wipe away smudges with the end of his apron.

"What can I do for you, young lady?" he asked.

"Nothing, sir," Rayne replied. "I was just watching. Your profession is exciting, isn't it?"

"I'm overworked, and that's the truth."

"Why don't you hire a helper?"

"Name's Pokinghorn," he said as he replaced his glasses and stared at her over the rim. "Jebediah Pokinghorn. I've tried to engage an assistant, but finding a man with an aptitude for figures hasn't been easy."

Rayne introduced herself, but her mind had already moved on to another thought. She wondered if she dared voice her idea. Mr. Pokinghorn would probably laugh and send her away. After a moment's deliberation, she bravely offered, "Perhaps you should hire a woman. If she possesses the skills you require, you may find your customers will behave in a more gentlemanly manner, instead of hollering and pushing."

He lowered his head to see her better, lines of concentration flitting across his brow. Several minutes passed before he said, "The position's yours, young lady, so long as you can count and have a good head on your shoulders."

Rayne sucked in a shocked breath. She hadn't truly believed he would give credence to her suggestion. "I'm not sure," she hedged. She wondered what her papa and O'Malley would say if she accepted employment. "I'll need time to think. How long do I have to make up my mind?"

"Been looking for help for a year. Don't make no difference to me. You want the position, just show up and it's yours."

She couldn't believe her good fortune. Of course, she couldn't accept the position immediately, not until Case fully recovered. She owed him that much. With confidence in her stride, she headed home. The opportunity that Pokinghorn had so kindly offered brought with it a sense of freedom. She no longer had to rely on anyone to support her.

The sun had set by the time Rayne entered the

house. She hadn't meant to be out so late. As she placed her hat and reticule on the hall table, she remembered she'd missed her evening meal. After she'd eaten she'd check to see how Case had weathered his eventful afternoon.

The click of a door above drew Rayne's attention. Sounds of gaiety filtered to her and she sped up the stairs, colliding with her father as he emerged from O'Malley's room. Jasper's eyes bugged open and he hastily slammed the door behind him.

"Case has company, but they should be leaving soon," he said.

"You look tired, Papa. Have you had your supper?"

"Yes, honey," he said, and quickly slipped into his room.

From the sounds of it, Case O'Malley was entertaining on a grand scale. She detected several men's voices, as well as two distinct female laughs.

The scoundrel was supposed to be recuperating from injuries, not hosting the social event of the season!

Rayne stood there, seething. Had he planned the afternoon purposely to prove he was a confirmed womanizer?

She knocked before she entered, unsure how she would be received. The three distinguished-looking gentlemen she saw upon entering were obviously business associates, or other wealthy mine owners. All three wore dark, tailor-made suits with matching vests. At the bottom of the bed three fashionable hats formed a line against the rail.

The air was rife with perfume, drink, and smoke, all of which threatened to gag her. Through the haze she noticed two women. One wore red, the other black. Other than that obvious difference, they seemed one and the same. Dark hair coiffed in bouncy curls, painted faces, daring décolletages showing off their voluptuous charms. Ostrich feathers adorned both the necklines and hems of their knee-length dresses.

Finally, Rayne allowed herself to look at Case. He appeared immensely pleased with himself. She cursed the impulse that had driven her to enter his room.

The smoke began to burn her eyes, causing them to tear. O'Malley introduced the men, but Rayne didn't pay attention. Instead she focused on the cigars they each held. Soon she would begin to sneeze and choke. She was barely able to disguise her relief when Case politely thanked the men for coming and they fled from the room.

Case's good-bye to the women was more expressive. "Ladies, thank you for a wonderful afternoon. You're like two shining stars on a dismal night."

Good heavens, Rayne thought as the giggling women followed the men into the hall. She waited until she heard the front door close. She didn't know what she would say to O'Malley, but she could not allow him to think she condoned his turning her father's home into a saloon.

He studied her silently. She grew warm under his scrutiny, and nervously touched her hair. There was something strange about him. She wished he would stop staring at her.

Case realized he had been holding his breath.

Slowly he expelled it. He had momentarily spared himself the onslaught of her accusations by unsettling her with a seductive glance. She responded as he expected, with nervousness ... and silence. He didn't want her to break the spell, to preach to him about his behavior, at least not now. In the lamplight, she looked lovely, the deep blue of her dress contrasting with the paler blue of the ribbon she had tied around her hair. Several strands had escaped their bind and trailed down one cheek. He watched her tuck the strands behind her ear.

He hadn't invited the three mining executives to call on him with the two dance-hall girls in tow, but he was glad they had come. He had thoroughly enjoyed himself. He had joined them in smoking cigars and drinking several bottles of brandy from the stash under his bed.

Rayne sniffed and gave a dainty cough. Case marveled that she'd held her tongue for so long. He prepared his defense, then dismissed it. If she subjected him to a tongue-lashing, he would take a different approach. She would not hold up long without a counterattack.

Then, contrary to his expectations, she turned her back on him and began to collect bottles from various spots in the room.

She held four bottles against her waist and reached out for the last, which he had set on the night table. Her expression was blank until she held the bottle up to the light and saw the half-finished Havana floating in an inch of liquor. Clicking her tongue, she headed for the window facing the rear of the house.

Her intention became clear to Case. Grinning, he watched her drain each bottle before she deposited it on the floor. No harm done there, he thought.

Then she threw open the wardrobe and searched it. When she came away empty-handed, the grim determination on her face gave him pause. Exactly what was she hoping to find? The answer came in a flash of truth so horrible, he would have leapt from his bed if he'd been able.

His brandy!

She stalked her prey. Confined to bed, he was helpless to stop her. Methodical in her hunt, she went through every drawer in the room and even peered behind the furniture.

Her search apparently completed, she came to stand over him. His smile was guileless. "Lost something, Miss North?"

"I know you've hidden spirits in this room."

"I haven't hidden anything." That was true enough, he thought. Rogers had performed the deed for him. "I am incapacitated."

"If you haven't a thought to your own well-being, you could at least think of my father. I saw him leave."

Case started. Jasper had had only two drinks. No harm in that, he mused.

"It would be prudent of you not to offer an excuse," she continued.

Case shrugged.

"As we are both aware, Papa is weak and needs to be encouraged to lead a sober life. Since he is your business partner, I had hoped you would join me in trying to help him." She released a heavy sigh. "I expected so much more from you, Mr. O'Malley."

She looked truly disappointed. A twinge of guilt

flickered in his heart. *Damn.* It made no difference to him what she thought of him.

He wondered why he had to keep reminding himself of that fact.

She lifted a corner of the counterpane, leaving the sheet over his legs. "There is one place I haven't checked. If you give me your word of honor that you haven't hidden liquor under your bed, I won't look."

This was too easy. There must be a catch. "Upon my honor, I did not hide liquor under my bed."

"Oh, Mr. O'Malley." She closed her eyes, her expression pained. "You have sunk lower than I believed possible."

Case was unprepared when Rayne tossed back the counterpane, dropped to her knees, and peeked under the bed frame. She pulled out the wooden crate.

"You said you'd accept my word," he reminded her with a grimace.

She gave him a reproachful look. "I made a statement, but I did not give *my* word."

"Rogers did the work, not me. I wasn't untruthful, at least not technically."

Disregarding his defense, she took three bottles from the crate and stood.

Case recognized sparks of uncommon wrath in her eyes. "That is my property."

"It *was* your property," she said as she headed for the window. Carefully she set the bottles on the window ledge. "I have just confiscated it!"

Case bolted straight up in bed.

She pried open one of her captured prizes and held it outside. Tipping it slightly, she watched a stream of amber liquid trickle out.

"Rayne! You're spilling it." Case eased his feet over the side of the bed and cursed the broken leg that kept him from crossing the room. He watched in horror as she tipped the bottle further. "That's imported brandy you're wasting, you witch!"

Dropping the empty container on the floor, she reached for another. "Call me any names you wish. We both know the identity of the guilty person."

Threats would serve no purpose, Case realized. Rogers had brought him a pair of crutches, but he hadn't tried walking on them yet. Without practice, he'd probably fall on his ass. But maybe he could make his point another way.

"You censure me while your own actions condemn you," he said, immediately getting her attention.

She paused long enough to peer at him over her shoulder.

"What a righteous little hypocrite you are," he added.

She swung around, as if ready to throw the bottle. It occurred to him that she looked magnificent when enraged, brimming with fire. A bolt of desire shook his control. How different she looked from the shy girl he'd met in Carson City. He loved the change, even if he deplored her actions.

"Very well. I'll allow you a moment to offer an explanation. Make it convincing."

"You've condemned every amusement I enjoy without ever once experiencing them for yourself. In all fairness, you should allow me a chance to correct your ignorance. I'll make you a deal. Sample that brandy. If you still think it's Satan's own brew, you have my permission to confiscate the entire lot."

She looked a bit shocked by his suggestion.

"Come on, it wouldn't kill you to unbend a little. Prove to me and yourself that you aren't totally unreasonable. Judge from experience, not from some righteous sense of duty."

"Very well, I'll show you how wrong you are."

She handed him a bottle and watched in dismay as he poured a generous amount in the glass on his night table. His eyes brimmed with challenge and confidence.

Squaring her shoulders, she picked up the glass and met his eyes. At that moment, he liked her tremendously.

"Sip it, Rayne. Don't gulp it down."

"I know how to take a drink."

He grinned. She was by far the most obstinate woman he'd ever met. And the most fascinating. He wondered when he'd begun to admire her.

She lifted the glass and sniffed. Then, aiming a superior look at him, she allowed a minute drop to flow onto her tongue. With a lavish flourish she contorted her facial features and professed, "It is, as I suspected, unworthy of consumption. Are you satisfied?"

"No, I am not satisfied. I doubt you swallowed even a drop."

Closing her eyes, she took a breath, tipped the glass, and downed the contents.

"You didn't listen," he reproached her, regretting his dare. She looked stricken, dizzy, swaying on her feet. "I said *sip*. Are you all right? Open your eyes."

Rayne forced herself to obey. Through her watery vision, O'Malley's features looked distorted. She had thought to bluff and had lost. Her only recourse had been to swallow the liquor. It had scorched a path down her throat, into her chest. Instant heat had welled in her stomach and shot to her limbs. A rush of warmth tore through her.

Suddenly her knees seemed to be melting. She stumbled. Only strict determination allowed her to maintain her balance.

"I think you had better sit."

Rayne wasn't sure whether he had made the suggestion, or her mind had sent the order. The next thing she knew, she felt the softness of a mattress beneath her, and a firm grip on her wrist. Had he grabbed her and forced her to sit? In any case, she was grateful. The glass was no longer in her hand. Where had that gone? Through a haze she spotted it on the table.

"You drank too much. Relax and you'll feel better in a few minutes."

The command came from behind her. She recognized concern in the masculine voice. Strong fingers began to massage her neck, then trail down her back. The sensuous touch sent shivers of delight along her nerve endings. "Where did you . . . did . . . you import it from?"

"France," he answered as he leaned forward. "A costly endeavor, I might add."

"It may serve some medicinal purpose."

"Yes," he agreed with a laugh, "it does. Do I take it you've changed your mind?"

His hand drifted down her side and lingered on her waist. Rational thought deserted her. "It must be sinful."

"What? The way you're feeling now?"

"I haven't eaten. Do you suppose it made a difference?"

"It would explain your extreme reaction."

"I don't believe I can stand. Where have my legs gone, Case?"

"You'll find them soon," he said with amusement. "Do you want me to ring my bell and have Hung Lee bring up your supper?"

"I couldn't possibly eat now." Briskly Rayne fanned her face with her hand. "I promise I won't throw out your sinful potion if you give me your word you will imbibe only for medicinal purposes, and you will not share with Papa." She turned her head very slowly, so as not to cause additional dizziness, and smiled. "Can I trust you?"

He laid a hand over his heart. "You have my word. For your information, I had no intention of sharing with your father."

She became lost in his devastating smile.

"You are truly concerned for my welfare, aren't you, Rayne?"

She nodded, confused by his sudden insight.

"I'm honored you think I'm worth the bother."

Touched by his admission, Rayne grazed her fingers over his cheek. He had the intelligence and means to be everything she could ever expect to find in a man. *Yes, he was worth the bother*, she thought.

She was falling in love with Case O'Malley— devoted scoundrel, irreverent thief of hearts.

And she didn't care—at least not now with his mouth so close, his breath warm on her skin, and his firm hands capturing her shoulders. It was she who pressed her lips to his, she who sought to demonstrate what could be his.

She could love him as he'd never before been loved.

Oh God. His kiss was a wonder, melting her body and soul. The brandy had warmed her all over, but not like this.

Not like *this!*

Surely he was a serpent. A flame of desire twisted around and through her, and the world faded away. There was only him, the feel of his tongue as it slipped past her lips and mated with hers in an intimate dance. She wanted to share with him the awe she felt. Concentrating, she copied his sinuous moves. He took her somewhere outside her body, to a paradise where pleasure ruled. His groan, deep in his throat, was her reward. His arms tightly embraced her. And his kiss, which had been powerful before, deepened into a sensual possession that left her weak and breathless.

Never before had Case experienced euphoria of this sort, especially not from merely kissing a woman, and he had kissed many over the course of his life. Emotion never played a role in any of his intimate relations. He had convinced himself he liked it that way.

He should have listened to his own advice concerning innocent women. The feelings Rayne had aroused in him the first time he'd kissed her had been an indisputable warning. Now it was too late. Now he was physically and emotionally unable to heed his own advice. Worse, at the moment he didn't give a damn.

Her lips moved over his with the skill of a sorceress. She learned fast, and she reacted instinctively. The woman inside the proper lady was

warm and exciting, a siren who stirred his blood
and drove him insane. He wanted her in a way he
hadn't wanted a woman before. He wanted to
make love to her, tender, passionate love, a joining
of mind and spirit as well as bodies.

Fire leapt to life in his body, a desire so keen, it
jolted his mind. Even through his nightshirt he felt
the heat of her body. His arousal throbbed unmer-
cifully, demanding release. He couldn't remember
suffering such a fierce reaction to a woman before.
Used to satisfying his needs whenever the mood
struck him, he didn't find it easy to govern his lust
now. Their moment of sweet discovery would
soon be lost if he didn't dominate the passion
threatening to become his master.

Abruptly he pulled away.

Chapter 13

Rayne's eyes remained closed. Although Case had stopped kissing her, his proximity continued to fill her mind with erotic images. An unbearable ache throbbed between her legs, and her breasts felt tender. A pang of sorrow had struck her when he'd pulled away, and she felt it keenly still. Blood thundered in her head, making her feel as if she'd been tossed into a stormy sea.

She regretted neither her wanton response to him, nor her bold initiation of their kiss. She only regretted that it had ended so soon.

"Rayne."

His voice sounded husky in her ear. She loved the sound of her name on his lips, the sensuous way he drew it out.

"Rayne, open your eyes. Look at me."

The effects of the liquor had faded, but the heady sensations remained with her. Case O'Malley had proved to be as potent as imported French brandy. A slow, sensuous smile lifted her mouth as she finally looked at him. Gazing into the mesmerizing green depths of his eyes, she felt a delicious heat flow through her again.

"You are causing me unbearable agony, sweetheart. If you continue to look at me like that, I can't promise your virtue won't suffer."

Rayne gave her head a shake, sure she had imagined his words. Something drastic had changed between them, and she wished she knew how it had come about. "My virtue was compromised the first instant I gazed into your green eyes, Mr. . . . Case."

"When you sober up, you'll feel remorse over your behavior," he said, grazing his thumb over her still swollen lips. "You'll admonish yourself."

Rayne tilted her head, relishing the tingles of pleasure on her neck as he released the ribbon holding her hair. "I am well aware of what I'm doing."

"Consorting with Satan?"

His fingers tangled in her hair. Her breath caught in her throat when he trailed hot kisses down her exposed neck. Hands on his chest, she tilted her head farther back to allow him easier access.

He gently gripped her shoulders and held her away. "Before I lose control and touch you in ways you'll hate me for later, you had best go downstairs and eat your supper."

Rayne stood slowly. It was understandable if she, or any woman, was driven to a state of insensibility by him, but she failed to see how an inexperienced woman like herself could inflame Case O'Malley beyond reason. Confused and hurt by his sudden withdrawal, she said, "I should eat now before it gets too late and Hung Lee is gone for the night."

Allowing him no time to reply, Rayne ran from the room.

* * *

In the morning, after a restless night, Case was in a nasty mood. His caustic manner made Jasper raise his eyebrows. Case hadn't meant to vent his frustration on the older man—in fact, he was appreciating him more every day. Jasper was trying hard to make up to his daughter for the past, and minding the mine as well.

"I was heading for the office," Jasper said, turning his hat with shaky fingers. "Figured I'd see if there was anything I can get you."

"There are a few more items I could use. I've made a list." Case held out a piece of paper on which he had scribbled several instructions. "The last two are the most important. Take care of them first off."

Jasper glanced at the list and pulled a face.

Case nearly grinned. "Also, I want you to go to the bank and open an account for Rayne. Tell Harvey you have my permission to deposit five hundred dollars. Don't tell Rayne the money came from me, though. She's to think it's a gift from you so she can buy new clothes, or anything else she needs."

"Sure, Case. If that's what you want." Jasper fell silent, considering Case. "You haven't taken up with my Rayne, have you?"

Case raked his fingers through his hair, hesitant to answer. "You haven't learned anything at all about Rayne, have you? She wouldn't take up with the likes of me."

"So the wind blows that way."

"What the hell are you implying now?"

Jasper backed toward the door. "You know what I mean." And shaking his head, he donned his dented bowler hat and walked out without elaborating.

Jasper's accusation hit home. He had trusted Case not to dishonor his daughter, yet Case had nearly compromised her last night. For too long he had indulged his desires—and he desired Rayne. He could no longer trust himself to behave honorably.

He was headed down *his* own path of destruction.

In her room, Rayne stepped away from the connecting door. She hadn't meant to eavesdrop on her father's conversation with Case, but she hadn't been able to keep herself from doing it either.

She appreciated Case's generosity, but she could not in good conscience accept money from him, even if he chose to disguise it as a gift from her father.

The rest of their talk confused her. Papa had referred to the wind, but he had spoken so low, she hadn't understood his meaning. With a shrug, she went downstairs. Hung Lee's cooking was not only excellent, but he also made coffee strong enough to rouse the dead. Rayne found the hearty brew just what she needed on this particular morning. Although she had expected to toss restlessly all night after her amorous encounter with Case, she had fallen into a deep sleep that had left her groggy.

She whispered his name, marveling at how easily it slipped from her tongue. Case. While she ate her breakfast, her thoughts again returned to the ardent moments they'd shared the evening before, particularly her own lustful behavior. *It isn't safe to kiss him*, she thought, especially when she didn't have the experience necessary to know how to construe his words or conduct. He had enjoyed their intimacy as much as she, but he had withdrawn afterward.

Had he thought her too forward? No. Case O'Malley would never think that.

There was only one possible conclusion: He had pulled away to protect her sensibilities. If only he knew how she regretted his honorable act. She had been completely under his spell at that moment, and would have done whatever he wanted, no matter the consequences.

And that's why he was dangerous.

When he touched her she forgot everything else—that he was a womanizer, and that he pledged never to change. She was falling in love with him, but she didn't love him completely yet—at least she felt sure she didn't, though she feared it was inevitable. As long as he kept company with other women, no matter how likable she found them, a part of her heart would remain locked.

After breakfast, Rayne whiled away the morning by writing a letter to her mother. Twice she heard the bell clang in the hall, but since Hung Lee hurried to attend to the needs of her handsome, disturbing patient, she remained in the dining room. Only when she heard someone at the front door did she set aside her letter.

The delivery of a dozen yellow rosebuds in an exquisite vase and a small package piqued her interest. Flowers were an unusual present to send a man, even to Case O'Malley. The package rattled when she shook it, and she knew curiosity would drive her crazy, so she decided to chance a visit to Case's room after all.

At the sound of footsteps on the stairs, Case gazed longingly at the cigar he had been about to light. He didn't mind temporarily limiting his consumption of liquor, but smoking was a pleasure he wasn't sure he could deny himself. His shoulders drooping, he passed the cigar under his nose and inhaled deeply, then quickly returned the Havana to the box he had hidden between the mattress and the headboard.

Rayne would leave the house eventually. Rather than offend her, he would wait her out. It was a small concession; she had taken care of him in his hour of need, and he owed her a debt of gratitude.

Case's eyes lit with pleasure when Rayne entered his room. The small package tucked under her arm, and the flowers in her hands, confirmed that Jasper had not failed him. He often bought presents for women, but never before had it given him such joy.

"Someone has sent you gifts," he said smugly. "Why do you look so surprised?"

"They were delivered for *you*."

"I'm sure you're mistaken," Case returned, hiding his amusement. "Is there a card?"

"I haven't looked."

He watched her lay the package on the bed while she searched inside the vase. He found it endearing that she seemed more interested in the buds than the much more costly item contained in the small box. She found the card and read it to herself.

"What does it say? Has another of my female

admirers favored me with a small token of her devotion?" he asked with a devilish grin.

Rayne pressed the card to her chest with a look of rapture and disbelief. "They're for me. But it doesn't say who they're from." She sniffed the fragrant buds and smiled. "Oh, he shouldn't have."

Case's eyebrows shot up. This was a turn of events he hadn't expected. Exactly *who* did she think had gone to such expense? Surely not Devereau!

"Oh, I wonder what's in the box. This is so exciting. No one has ever sent me presents before."

"Obviously."

She set the vase on the bureau and picked up the package. His moment of pleasure ruined by his jealous thoughts, Case held his temper in check. The subtle tremor in her hands as she tore open the paper and lifted the lid added to his fury. If Paul Devereau were here at the moment, Case knew he'd eagerly break both his legs.

Rayne gasped. Her mouth gaping open, she held up the diamond necklace Case had described to Jasper. He would have to reward his partner; he had been worried Jasper would buy the wrong one.

"Do you like it?"

"My goodness, *yes!*"

"Would you try it on for me?"

Obviously stunned by his words, she did not respond. Case crossed his arms over his chest. Her thoughts became evident to him, angering him anew. "Yes, the gifts are from me. Who else do you think holds you in such high regard—Devereau?"

Aghast, Rayne froze. She had committed an unpardonable offense, and Case's furious expression only drove the guilt deeper into her heart. How could she have been so blind, so ignorant of his generosity?

"I do apologize. I never dreamed—"

Silenced by the menacing slant of his dark brows, Rayne dropped her gaze. The brilliant, elegant necklace must have cost a fortune. She should have known. Only Case O'Malley could spend his money on frivolous trinkets.

But this *trinket* was dazzling.

She had to admit, he had excellent taste. The most refined gentleman could not have chosen better. In fact, the quality of the necklace compared favorably with the accoutrements of her father's house. She blinked, startled by the thought she had stumbled upon. Early on, she'd dismissed the idea that he might have selected the furnishings. Apparently there were more areas in which Case O'Malley excelled than she'd thought.

She looked up, directly into his angry gaze. "I wrongly presumed Paul sent the gifts because, as you cannot dispute, you are unable to leave this room. What I fail to see is why my innocent assumption has provoked your temper."

"For your information, I am able to arrange anything, even confined to this damnable lumpy bed!"

Rayne bit her lip, warding off a smile. "There are no lumps in your bed. I believe it was recently purchased."

"Then my bones have become grossly misaligned from having to lie in one position!" He wiggled his backside.

Flicking her vision over his long, well-proportioned body, Rayne swallowed. There was nothing misaligned on Case O'Malley, not even a hair. Perhaps if he weren't so wondrously put together, he wouldn't present such a problem. But though she found his looks striking, there was some quality within him that challenged her. This irascible, charming rogue had forever changed her, and her life.

"Your generosity overwhelms me, but I'm sorry I can't accept so personal a gift from a man."

"You seemed prepared to accept it from Devereau. In fact, if my eyes didn't deceive me, you looked ready to pounce on it."

She did not want Case to know that, while she found Paul attractive and cultured, he did not spark a fire in her blood the way Case did. If he guessed the truth, he'd become even more insufferable.

"I have no intention of allowing you to provoke me." She moved toward him, reluctantly holding out the box, yet wishing she could keep his gift. "I sincerely appreciate your thoughtfulness, but propriety demands I return this."

"I suppose you must also reject the flowers," Case remarked.

The sarcasm in his voice amused Rayne. It was unfathomable that her action could cause him to feel slighted. Since he wouldn't reach out and accept the box, she explained, "My mother and I had little after my father left us, not even a house in which to live. We shared a small room off the kitchen in the home of my mother's employer. I suppose I place a different value on priceless objects than you do."

"All the more reason for you to accept, and all the more reason why I insist you do so. I want you to have something of beauty. I appreciate the kindness you've shown me, and I want to repay you."

"But I don't expect payment. I want nothing from you."

Case's mouth tightened.

"Clearly you have a need to put a price on my kindness. You can't buy me, Mr. O'Malley. You can't buy my affection, either."

Her words appalled Case. She was a damn stubborn fool! Her intractable stand made him more determined than ever. No longer did he consider the necklace recompense for her care. He *wanted* her to have it.

By all that was holy, she would accept it!

With a feigned look of defeat, Case held out his hand. Like an innocent lamb, she fell into his trap. When she came near enough, he took the box and laid it aside, and before she could suspect his intention, he snatched her wrist and tugged her forward, throwing her off balance and into his waiting arms. Hoping his ribs would withstand the impact, he rolled onto his side.

Pinned to his bed, her eyes wide with shock, she caught her breath. He grinned, confident he had the upper hand.

She met his assured gaze. "I suppose you have a reason for this maneuver?" she asked, amusement evident in her sparkling eyes.

"You're a constant surprise. I expected a furious outburst. Do you delight in twisting my every word and action to suit yourself?"

"Indeed. Especially when you behave outrageously."

"Why aren't you struggling?"

"What purpose would it serve? You are obviously stronger. You can't do me actual harm because I will scream and Hung Lee will come to my rescue. And you are injured. If I feel the need, I can gain my freedom in an instant with an accurate strike at your side."

"I find this position to my liking," Case admitted, subdued by her unerring logic. "Until you decide to wound me, scream, or whatever else your crafty mind comes up with, you are an infinitely softer cushion for my bruised bones." He felt her tremble, felt the rapid beat of the pulse at the base of her throat, giving away her excitement.

"Won't you explain your motives?" she asked.

"Very well. Please accept my gifts. I want you to have the necklace. There is no obligation attached to it, you know. Won't you relent and change your mind? Make me happy. Please."

"I'll accept the flowers, but I cannot take the necklace."

"You are an unusual woman."

Rayne lay very still. "Neither can I accept money from you, even if you offer it through my father."

"He told you?"

"I overheard your conversation. I must say, you have a devious mind."

He moved slightly, his face coming closer to hers. She stared at his mouth and wondered if she wanted him to kiss her again.

"You could use a new wardrobe. It matters little whose money pays for it. Jasper and I share the wealth we get from the mine."

"It matters to me," she stammered. "My clothes suit me just fine."

"Well, they don't suit me. You resemble a church mouse."

She looked crushed. Case was immediately sorry for his unthinking remark.

"You've twisted my words again," Case said with an exasperated sigh. "It was not my intention to insult you. I meant your father can afford to buy you the finest now, and you should take advantage of the opportunity. What good is money if you can't enjoy it? You've admitted your mother and you had little. Let us make up for it."

A long moment of silence passed before she conceded, "All right, I will purchase new clothes. But only if they are paid for with Papa's money, not yours."

"Now, that's more like it."

Case considered his captive's face. She looked sweet and desirable. Her sense of humor, her giving nature, and the wild passion he had discovered in her all appealed to him. He wanted to embrace her, feel her surrender to the same desire that pulsed in his body. He needed to exercise caution, though. She wasn't used to a man's flowery words and physical needs.

Rayne's expression changed to one of puzzlement. "I was deep in thought," he explained. "Did you think I'd had a relapse?"

She shook her head.

"Are you curious about my thoughts?"

Again she shook her head.

"I was considering kissing you again."

"I don't think you should."

"Why?"

"It's dangerous. We're so unalike. There's no hope we will ever come to terms."

"Men are different from women," he pointed out. "Difference of opinion makes life interesting." He leaned closer, grazing his fingers across her shoulder. "*You* intrigue me."

"Is that a reason to kiss me?" she asked breathlessly.

"Must I have a reason?"

His fingers caressed her neck and a soft moan escaped her. Cradling her chin, he angled his head.

"Don't . . . please."

Bewildered by her fickle behavior, Case retreated. He turned on his back, allowing her a moment to leave the bed. When she made no move to do so, he said, "Unless I'm mistaken, you kissed me yesterday. Passionately, I might add. Would you mind telling me why you have reservations about doing so now?"

"No good can come of it."

"I see your point." He remembered the ineffectual lectures he'd given himself about staying clear of innocents like Rayne. "I thoroughly enjoyed our kiss. Apparently the same cannot be said for you."

She leaned on her elbow and laid her hand on his chest. "Oh, but you're so wrong. I liked it *too* much."

Flabbergasted, but moved that she'd admit it to him, Case regarded her affectionately.

"You're a dangerous man. You only trifle with me because you're bored and unable to . . . to spend time with your other women friends."

If he had an ounce of sense, he'd agree with her. Knowing he'd later condemn himself for his insane need to answer truthfully, he admitted, "Don't make a wager about that. You'd lose."

He felt the slight shake of her hand against his chest; her eyes were large with amazement. Although she remained silent, he guessed the question foremost on her mind.

"I don't know what I'm feeling, but it sure as hell isn't boredom," he said. "You are an exceptional woman. If you cherish that precious virtue you so painstakingly guard, you're right to fear me. I can't seem to heed my own advice concerning you. Hell, I change my mind from minute to minute."

"What are you saying?"

"Only that I want you in the way a man wants a woman, but I want more than that, too. It's not just your body I'd lay claim to, but your heart and soul as well."

His words shocked her. Her partly open mouth, the dazed look on her face as she regarded him, gave away her thoughts. Hell, he might as well say it all so she couldn't later accuse him of misleading her.

"If you're as wise as I think you are, you'll take the advice of a seasoned rogue, because whether you believe me or not, I do have your best interests at heart."

He captured her hand, turned it over, and pressed his lips to her palm. "Run as far and as fast as you can, my dear. You were right. I *am* dangerous to a decent woman. Leave Virginia City now. If you choose to stay, one of these nights you'll share my bed."

Chapter 14

O ver the next two weeks, Case made satisfactory progress in his recovery, though he kept one of his accomplishments to himself: He'd mastered walking with the aid of the crutches Rogers had brought him. It was a matter of pride, but deep down, he knew the actual reason for his secrecy. If anyone guessed the ease with which he'd learned to navigate, there would be no reason for him to remain with Jasper and his daughter.

Determined to reside in the comfort of his own house, he was forced to resort to subterfuge. If he was loath to remove himself from Rayne's care, it was his affair. So he contented himself with taking his exercise, such as it was, when no one was home to see him. Dressing had also become a daily ritual, even if he'd had to slit several pant legs. His ribs had blessedly ceased bothering him.

He felt almost whole again.

Case propped the crutches against the bureau and hopped the short distance to his desk, which Rogers and two accomplices had brought from the mine office. This arrangement allowed him to handle business from his room. He sorted through his papers, but was unable to concentrate. Despite his best efforts to discipline his thoughts, they always drifted to Jasper's daughter.

To his consternation, Rayne had clearly taken his warning to heart, avoiding contact with him. He had seen little of her, especially in the afternoons, and some evenings. He suspected she'd been seeing Devereau, but he hadn't questioned her. Without proof to condemn Devereau, it would be futile to broach the subject. Any day now he should receive word from Sacramento, if his contact proved reliable.

Cooped up in his bedroom, he had also been unable to meet with John, the miner who passed along information whenever Case needed it. John would eventually get word when the Union expected the next shipment of gold, since the last had been necessarily postponed because of Case's injury. Unless a plan was agreed upon, though, the miner would be helpless to make the contact.

Again Case thought of Rayne. He trusted her. He could not, in good conscience, place her in any danger, so he didn't dare reveal his undercover activities. Also, he must remember how easily he fell prey to her allure.

Good Lord! What was happening to him?

Case sighed. Sliding his drawings in front of him, he idled away the time by sketching. Until Rayne offered him encouragement, he'd continue to hold himself in check. The decision was hers. If she made the first move, he would then follow her lead . . . and take them both to paradise.

Rayne allowed her companion to help her alight from the rented buggy onto a wide, flat ledge. From this vantage point high atop the hill, the view was spectacular. But the winding, narrow road all the way up had terrified her. Paul Devereau's expert handling of the horses had finally stilled her fears, and she had thus far enjoyed their outing.

He spread a blanket out on a smooth area of rock. A twinkle of mischief danced in his light brown eyes as he executed a dashing bow. "M'lady's seat awaits."

It was easy to like Paul, even if he acted a bit too whimsical at times. His pleasant company over the last two weeks had helped her keep a promise she'd made to herself—not to dwell on Case O'Malley and the hopeless longing she felt for him.

"Thank you, kind sir," she responded. She claimed a place to one side of the blanket, tucked her skirt around her legs, and motioned for him to follow suit, which he did. "I'm unused to such chivalrous behavior."

"If O'Malley has dared to compromise you, I shall have no choice but to call him out."

Shocked, Rayne stared at him. "That isn't what I meant at all. It was a jest."

Devereau removed his smart bowler, set it on the ground between them, and smoothed his hands over his hair. "Has he treated you with the respect due a lady?"

"He has. O'Malley is far from the wastrel I first thought. He has many fine qualities."

"Nevertheless," Paul said, looking away, "having him reside in the same house is bound to cause tongues to wag. Is he not yet well enough to leave your father's residence?"

"I wouldn't presume to suggest such a thing. It

would be difficult for him to move around, especially in a city built into the side of a mountain. Some of the streets are dangerously precipitous, even for a person with the use of both legs. It's best that he remain with us for the present."

"O'Malley is lucky to have such a softhearted caretaker."

"Look," Rayne said, anxious to change the subject. "The lake far off in the distance. The sun is hitting it just so, and the water looks like it's on fire."

"Magnificent. It's the only thing exceptional about this godforsaken territory. From high up one can see for miles and miles and never really see it all."

A gust of wind came from nowhere and sent the blanket flapping against Rayne's back. Devereau's hat danced along his leg, onto the bare ground, stopping an inch from the cliff's edge. Muttering a curse, he rose to his knees and crawled forward.

Rayne tried to catch hold of his foot. "Paul! The ground may be unstable there. It's only a hat."

A smaller gust of wind caught the bowler, carrying it out of sight. Determined to retrieve his property despite her advice, he inched cautiously forward. Bracing his hands on what he judged to be sound rock, he leaned out to peer over the edge.

Worried, Rayne held her breath. She dared not speak for fear she'd cause him to move suddenly and lose his balance.

"Good riddance to the thing," he yelled into the wind. Retracing his movements, he turned around, sat back on his heels, and dusted off his hands.

"Paul Devereau! You could have fallen. Don't ever frighten me like that again."

In her mind she saw the distinguished Paul Devereau on his knees in the dirt, his gentlemanly backside up in the air. Suddenly she knew she was going to laugh—and embarrass them both. Quickly she drew open her reticule, snatched out her hankie, and slapped it over her nose and mouth.

"My dear," he cried in alarm, "you mustn't shed tears on my account. I'm fine."

His words added to Rayne's distress, her impending laughter at war with her guilt. How *could* she find amusement in a situation that might have resulted in his death?

"I'm relieved you were spared from harm," she managed to say. She dabbed at her eyes, then balled the hankie in her hand. "The wind has turned cold. Perhaps we should be on our way."

Another powerful gust tore her own hat from her head and plucked out several hairpins. Her bonnet smacked against Paul's face. Quick as a flash, he captured her hat and handed it to her. Rayne averted her gaze and pretended she hadn't noticed his chagrined expression.

The wind died down as suddenly as it had arisen. By mutual agreement they both rose. Paul shook out the blanket, then reached for her hand. Rayne was anxious to call an end to their afternoon, before another disaster struck, and turned toward the buggy. But Paul halted her.

"Paul?"

"My dear, I've wanted to take you in my arms and kiss you since we first met, but I knew you would regard me as impertinent. May I do so now?"

Merciful heavens. What am I to do now? If she refused him, she would hurt his feelings. If she agreed, he would think she regarded him in a romantic way. While she looked on him with fondness, as a friend, she didn't want to mislead him. She gazed up into his warm, brown eyes, then at his darker mustache. At least he had the courtesy to ask permission. Case had kissed her the first time without warning. The memory decided the matter. Tilting her head, she offered her lips.

It was over in seconds, a fleeting touch of his mouth to hers. Either she had been taught what to expect from Satan's own servant, or Devereau hadn't learned the fine points of the act. Case's tongue would have mated with hers, and he would have left her weak and quivery. She hadn't felt even a twinge of that with Paul. Maybe he had thought to spare her sensibilities. In all fairness, she owed him a chance to outshine Case.

"You may do it again if you wish," she said.

Encouraged, he curled his arm around her waist and drew her closer. He kissed her more passionately this time, his mouth moving over hers with purpose. She decided he knew the intricacies well enough. Relieved, she waited for the weakness, the heat, the flutters in her stomach. When nothing happened, frustration filled her.

With regret, she slipped out of his embrace. This fine gentleman did not spark a flame in her. It wasn't fair! Why, of all the men in the world, had fated decreed that Case O'Malley should be the one to put a torch to her insides? She was irrevocably drawn to a man who possessed no conscience regarding women.

He was going to steal her heart, and there wasn't a thing she could do to prevent it.

Back at the house, Rayne peeked into Case's room. Finding him asleep, she felt it safe to enter. His desk was strewn with newspapers, which told her he'd spent his afternoon catching up on the war and events in Virginia City. She wondered how she located anything among the disorder. Although tempted to tidy up, she restrained herself; he wouldn't thank her if she misplaced something of importance.

The edge of a large, heavier paper protruding from under a stack of documents caught her eye. It looked like a drawing. Probably of timbers for his mine, she thought, and none of her business. Nonetheless, curiosity got the better of her and, using one finger, she casually nudged an edge aside. This revealed little more, however, frustrating her. Too curious to allow the opportunity to pass, Rayne whisked the drawing from beneath the other papers.

Dumbstruck, she stared for a long time at a detailed sketch of herself.

His talent surprised her. He had captured her likeness with amazing accuracy. Her pose and the style of her dress stole her breath.

Was this how he saw her?

In his sketch her head was tilted back, her hair flowing freely about her shoulders. Her dreamy expression was surely one he had witnessed, but she wondered when. Was this how she looked to him when he touched her?

Her gaze moved lower, to the dress. Never had she worn such a scandalous gown. The décolletage dipped disgracefully low, revealing an indecent amount of her breasts. The bold neckline showed her bare shoulders, and around her throat, the diamond necklace he had given her endowed her with a scandalous worldliness.

A flush crept over her face. The rogue certainly had a vivid imagination.

Then again, the dress was suspiciously similar to an evening gown she had recently purchased. In fact, it could be an exact replica. She laid aside the sketch and slipped into her room to study the actual garment, which the dressmaker had practically insisted she purchase.

"It just so happens this dress is your exact size and will suit you perfectly," the woman had said. "Every woman should have an evening dress to wear to the opera in case a handsome gentleman invites her."

Thinking back on the woman's words now, Rayne began to wonder if Case could have specifically asked the seamstress to make up the gown, knowing that Rayne would visit the shop soon afterward and assuming she could be coerced into purchasing the garment.

In fact, the more Rayne considered the possibility, the more sure she was that that's exactly what had happened. And the angrier she became. She forced herself to remain calm. After all, nothing Case O'Malley did should shock her anymore.

She must return the drawing to its rightful place before he discovered she'd found it. As she passed the bed, she paused, enticed by his sprawled body. He lay on his back, his head resting on his arm.

His white shirt, open at the neck, revealed a dark, curly patch of hair. His black trousers molded his slim hips and muscular thighs. It was a shame he'd needed to slit one of the pant legs. The garment looked costly.

Given time, and the pull he had upon her, it was perhaps inevitable that she'd eventually succumb to his devastating charm. If she had an ounce of sense, she would take his advice and leave Virginia City now, before her unseemly desire for him brought her to the same end as her mother.

But Case wasn't weak like her father, she told herself. He possessed an inner strength and goodness that he preferred to disguise.

Rayne hadn't moved or uttered a sound to give away her presence, yet when she pulled herself from her musings, she found Case observing her through slitted eyelids. She wondered if he was fully awake and remembered that she hadn't returned his drawing to the bottom of the stack of documents. Slowly she retreated several steps and, slipping her arm behind her, felt around for the drawing, moved it underneath, and started to flee from the room.

Abruptly Case shot up in the bed, bringing her to a halt.

"Leaving so soon? Another engagement, perhaps?"

His sarcastic tone gave her a turn. Bewildered, she moved closer and watched him swing his good leg over the side of the bed, brushing her skirt. His mussed hair stood out in several places, a dark lock falling over his brow. His disheveled appearance added to his potent appeal, keeping Rayne silent.

"Did you find Paul charming this afternoon? Since you know few men in Virginia City, I presume it was Devereau who sent you home looking as if you'd spent the past hours locked in a passionate embrace."

Rayne touched her unbound hair. She hadn't given a thought to her appearance and realized how untidy she must look.

"What? No protest?"

"It was windy," she admitted, wondering why she felt the need to answer to him.

Judging from the cynical twist of his lips, she knew her explanation had fallen on deaf ears. "If you are implying anything untoward happened between Paul and me, you are sadly mistaken."

"So you blame your state of undress on the wind?"

"My state of—" Rayne checked her bodice, at the precise spot where Case was staring. "Why, I've lost a button. I can't imagine how that happened."

"It seems your imagination isn't as colorful as mine."

Is he jealous? She watched in fascination as he fingered a fold in her skirt. A wicked temptation drove her to say, "On second thought, it would have been impossible for the wind to steal a button. It must have happened when Paul kissed me."

Case moved faster than she would have imagined possible. One instant she was standing, the next she was sprawled out on top of him. Bracing her hands on either side of his head, she shoved her upper body away from him.

"You push a man too far," he said with a growl.

His arm around her waist manacled them together. *When did he recover so much of his strength?* she wondered. His other hand brushed her cheek, trailed down her neck. She couldn't think when she was so close to him. She could only react. Her pulse raced.

"Meet that pompous pantywaist again and I'll strangle you. If you want to be kissed so badly, I'll be happy to oblige you."

She opened her mouth, intending to censure him, but swallowed the words when she realized he had unfastened the remaining buttons on her bodice. He touched his tongue to the cleavage above her corset. Rayne's gasp sounded loud in the quiet room, almost as loud as the ragged moan that followed. Although coherent thought escaped her, she thought she heard him grumble something about decent women and their stiff-boned trappings.

His arm no longer bound her to him; there was no need. Propped on her elbows, she dug her fingers into his hair. Under her petticoats, his hands swept over her legs in an insidious exploration, sending shivers up her spine. Cupping her backside, he moved his mouth to her throat.

His voice sounded husky as he whispered against her skin, "Why, Rayne, you *do* have lace on your drawers."

"Oh!"

Rayne would never be sure whether her exclamation was prompted by his outrageous comment, or by the fact that at that moment he wiggled apart her legs and suddenly, distinctly, she felt the rigid length of him pressing against her most private place. A tremor shook her from

the intimate contact. He felt so good, so hot, so unyielding. She should be shocked, but she wasn't. If
the room burned down around them, she would
not be able to utter a protest. Her corset grew too
tight, limiting her air. He rose against her, groaning. She looked into the smokey green depths of
his eyes and surrendered to fate.

He seemed to know the exact instant when she
yielded to her yearnings. He grinned, a wicked,
knowing grin that sent her blood roiling through
her veins. Gripping his face, she planted her
mouth over his, and took control of their kiss,
slowly tantalizing him until it was he who trembled. She felt him ease his hands under her pantalets and caress her bare skin. In response, she
moaned softly, deep in her throat.

He rolled slightly, onto his side, taking her with
him and possessing her with his kiss. He delved
his tongue into her mouth while he grazed his
hand over her flat stomach. She gripped his shoulders, shivering all over, wanting him never to stop
touching her.

She was lost.

Nothing in the world existed except Case
O'Malley and the wondrous feelings he aroused.
His fingers skimmed across her stomach, then
drifted lower. Rayne jerked in shock. No one had
ever touched her there before.

Only Case O'Malley would dare.

Only *he* could reduce her resolve to a throbbing
ache that left her mindless and hungry for something beyond her comprehension. The ache built
to a raging need. Unable even to return his kiss,
she threw her arms around his broad shoulders

and buried her face in his neck, as her body convulsed in an exquisite release.

"Ohhh . . . Malley."

Dazed by the splendor he'd brought her, she couldn't say more. His hand clamped around her waist; his lips caressed her ear, adding to her torment.

"Did you like that?" he whispered as he dug his fingers through her hair.

She nodded.

"I want to do more, love you completely, but now is not the time. It's daylight. The bedroom door is open."

Rayne went still. She hadn't considered the danger of their situation. Anyone could have walked in on them.

"I've never lost control so completely before," he said, his voice a hoarse whisper.

Rayne lifted her head and touched her lips to his. "You know exactly the right thing to say."

"You're wrong. This is different."

"Yes, it is," she returned as she brushed a lock of hair from his brow. "You—"

Rayne's head turned in the direction of the door, her eyes large and dismayed.

Voices in the hall below floated up to them. Case bolted up, bringing her with him. He pulled down her petticoats and skirt and pushed her to the edge of the mattress. "Go. Quickly!"

Clutching her bodice together, Rayne stood on shaky legs, noticing at once the thick bulge in Case's pants, there for all the world to see. The sound of a man's boots on the stairs fired her into action. She snatched the counterpane and yanked it up to cover his midsection, but his howl of pain jolted her. She jumped away, realizing that she had forgotten about his injured leg and had jarred it.

His eyes shut tightly, Case gritted his teeth.

The man in the hall had neared the landing. Rayne scooted through the connecting door into her room and breathed a sigh of relief. Through the wall she heard Case greet Father Manogue.

Dear God!

Father Manogue had nearly caught them together.

She leaned against the closed door, trying to compose herself; her heart continued to beat erratically. Excitement of this nature was foreign to her, but she had to admit she found it exhilarating.

Remembering how Case had stroked her, she grew hot all over again. She would have to change her clothes and fix her hair before she went downstairs. Humming softly, thoughts of her father's devastating, beguiling partner filling her head, she set about dressing.

A half hour later, Rayne heard a knock on her hallway bedroom door. Before she could answer she watched a folded paper slip through the crack underneath the door. She hurried to read the message.

Her heart hammering, she looked at Case's bold script. The missive took her by surprise: He requested the honor of her presence for dinner at precisely seven o'clock.

Dress for an evening at the opera, with a very distinguished gentleman of impeccable taste and refinement.

Impeccable taste and refinement indeed! Notorious scoundrel with seduction on his mind was more like it!

Nevertheless, his request surprised and delighted her. He may be confined to this house, but he'd found a way to pretend otherwise. She knew he wanted her to wear the green gown he'd so scandalously drawn. Tingles of anticipation flitted over her skin. She longed to wear the dress, longed to feel as seductive as she looked in his drawing. *Just for tonight*, she told herself.

But she knew this would be a night she would remember forever.

Chapter 15

At precisely seven o'clock Rayne left her room and headed for Case's. The anticipation had been unbearable. The sounds of preparation she'd heard during the past hour alone had frayed her nerves. There had been bumps, clinks, and scrapes, plus muffled voices to taunt her and tantalizing aromas to torture her nervous stomach. She knocked, unwilling to spoil his plans for an evening full of surprises. A series of thuds behind his door added to her curiosity. Then she was face-to-face with him.

Astonished, she stared at him with wide eyes. "You're walking."

"How very gracious of you to call it that."

He looked magnificent in a dignified black coat and pants with a red, patterned vest that contrasted with his immaculate white shirt. A black tie was fashionably knotted around his neck. On his lapel, his diamond cluster pin added the final dashing touch.

Bracing his large frame on a crutch, he balanced on one foot. She'd forgotten what it was like to look up at him. In bed, he had seemed smaller, more vulnerable. Not now. He looked imposing, rakishly handsome. Taking her hand, he pressed his lips to the spot above her knuckles as his green eyes devoured her.

The warmth of his gaze sent a trail of fire down to her toes. She remembered the first time she'd met him in Carson City. He had kissed her hand in the same manner. At that time she'd found his attentions forward, shocking. Now she prayed he would continue.

He coaxed her into the room. "Please be seated. Everything's ready."

Rayne couldn't believe her eyes. The heavy burgundy draperies had been drawn closed and his bed moved several feet so that a small table could be placed in the space between the bed and the door to her room. An exquisite tablecloth trimmed with dainty lace adorned the elegantly set table. Two candles, supported in intricately designed silver holders, gave off a flickering light. A bottle of champagne lay in a bucket of chipped ice.

"I'd assist you with your chair, but as you can see, I'm easily unbalanced."

She sat and arranged her billowing skirt. "Don't trouble yourself. It's more important that you remain on your feet."

Case retrieved his other crutch, thumped around the table, and seated himself. "Just today, I tried putting weight on my foot. I can support myself for several seconds, but anything longer is impractical."

"A wise conclusion," she muttered, unable to tear her gaze from him. She felt giddy with excitement.

"Wisdom didn't enter into my conclusion at all. Pain decided the matter."

Melting under his ardent gaze, Rayne considered the scrumptious feast set before her ... and grew nauseous. There was no way she was going to be able to eat tonight.

Case felt equally uncomfortable. He'd hoped but hadn't dared believe that Rayne would wear the gown he'd ordered from the dressmaker. It was difficult to conceal his pleasure knowing that Rayne had not only purchased the gown, but had also worn it to please him this evening.

She looked delectable, the tops of her creamy white bosom bare for his scrutiny. Only three things kept her from perfection. She wore her hair knotted at her nape, the gown was not draped low enough on her shoulders, and the diamond necklace was missing. Case pulled the necklace from his inside pocket and hobbled behind her.

"What are you doing?" she asked anxiously. "You know you shouldn't put weight on your foot."

He pressed her shoulders gently, allowing his fingers to linger on her warm skin. "Relax. If you'll indulge a fantasy of mine, I'll be eternally grateful."

He felt a tremor pass through her slim body. Taking advantage of her disquiet, he draped the necklace around her neck and fastened it. His hands returned to her shoulders, and slowly, seductively, he slid the gown down, over her arms.

"Case," she whispered.

"You're trembling. Are you cold?"

"I'm quite warm, as you very well know." She drew in a shaky breath. "Please, sit down."

At the moment food was the last thing on Case's mind. He'd rather feast on her, roam his lips along the alluring neckline of the emerald green velvet dress molding Rayne's womanly curves. He had dreamt of her wearing this gown, dreamt of removing it, easing it lower and lower until—

Damn.

His intention to show her that he could treat her like a lady would soon fly out the window if he didn't slow down. He skimmed his knuckle over her cheek and sat down. She fingered the necklace, uncertainty evident on her face.

"Wear it tonight," he pleaded, "for my pleasure, and yours. You should always wear diamonds. They make your eyes sparkle."

"For tonight, then."

He motioned toward the food, urging her to join him.

She covertly watched him while she pretended interest in a serving of veal. "How can you eat at a time like this?" she asked.

"Do I make you nervous?" he asked with a smile. "We're not exactly strangers, you know." Catching her staring at him, he raised a dark eyebrow. "No appetite yet? Would you care for champagne instead?"

He didn't wait for a reply. Expertly he popped open the bottle and poured liberal amounts for them both. Holding up his glass, he said, "To the most beautiful woman ever to share my table."

Her hands betrayed her nervousness, shaking when she reached for her own crystal glass. Her toast, however, shook his composure.

"To the most accomplished womanizer ever to share mine."

Case smiled as he swallowed the tart wine.

Aiming an impish grin at him, she followed his example.

"If you don't put food in your stomach, Rayne, your knees will go weak again." He gazed pointedly at her. "Remember what happened the last time?"

"Surely a little won't do any harm."

He gave her a skeptical look.

"I trust you won't take advantage of my infirmity if I imbibe too freely." She sipped from her glass, studying him provocatively over the rim. "I've never drunk champagne before. It tickles my nose."

He motioned toward her bone china plate. "Oblige me, if you will. Let it not be said that Case O'Malley took advantage of an intoxicated woman. I want you with your senses about you."

Rayne's heart leapt at his declaration. Was it his intention to make love to her tonight?

Did she want him to?

His eyes wandered to her neckline again. His hot, hungry gaze seared her skin. Never in her life had she exposed so much of herself to a man. She'd worn the dress for him because she wanted to please him, because . . . because she loved him.

"You appear upset," he remarked, leaning forward.

"No," she said quickly. "It's just . . ."

"Just what? Don't you like your dinner?"

"It looks delicious, truly."

"What, then? Is it something I've done? Please tell me so I can apologize for my transgression."

"You haven't transgressed . . . Case. Your behavior tonight has been above reproach."

He drummed a finger on the table. "Have I made you uneasy?"

"I'm not *uneasy*."

"Your hands are shaking."

"They are not," she lied smoothly. She gulped a swallow of champagne. "It's your imagination. Perhaps you injured your head more than Dr. Connell thought."

"You may be right." His grin was shameless. "I haven't been right in the head since I met you."

"On the contrary, you have benefited greatly from knowing me. Just think of the vices you've already given up."

Clearing his throat, he regarded her through narrowed eyes. "Precisely which vices do you mean?"

"Women, for one," she replied without thinking.

He leaned forward again. "Now that you mention it, I have noticed a marked decline in visits from my friends."

Rayne pretended interest in her food and picked up a silver fork. "They might have grown bored, since you've been unable to . . . What I mean is—"

"I know what you mean."

Refusing to meet his gaze, Rayne fidgeted.

"I see your hand in this. Did you discourage my female visitors? Is that why they haven't come to see me lately?"

"Yes," she admitted in a low voice.

"I didn't quite hear you. Would you mind repeating that?"

Rayne laid aside her fork and looked up. "Yes! I *did*."

"I hope you didn't insult them."

"I could never behave so ungraciously." Wilting

under his penetrating stare, she confessed, "I suppose I owe you an apology. It wasn't my place to
interfere in your life. I'll send word, tell them
you're well enough to receive visitors."

"You needn't apologize. I know your motives
were pure."

Pure, indeed, she mused. She'd wanted him all to
herself. The truth was hard to admit.

"To be honest, I haven't minded all that much,"
he said.

"You're being kind. You liked their company before."

"If it will make you feel better to know the
truth, I'll give it to you. I would like them to visit
me, but only as friends."

Rayne's heart leapt to her throat.

"I thought you'd catch on faster," he said, holding out his hand. "Come here."

She slipped her fingers in his as he guided her
to his side of the table. He pushed back his chair
and, careful not to crush her dress, drew her onto
his lap. Unsure what to do with her hands, she
rested them on his shoulders. Flickering candle-
light danced over his handsome features,
emphasizing the devilish glint in his eyes. An intoxicating scent sent fevered messages to her
brain. It was a sinful fragrance, almost as sinful as
he looked.

She'd never taken notice of how long his lashes
were, how thickly they fringed his green eyes.

Cupping her face, he grazed his thumb over her
lips. "You have such a tempting mouth."

Trembling from his gentle stroking, Rayne drew
in a faltering breath. "Please," she stammered.

A chuckle came from deep in his throat as he

plucked the pins from her hair. "When you kissed Devereau, did your knees go weak? Did blood rush to your face? Did you feel *anything* at all?"

His fingers burrowed in to her hair, loosening the coil. He arranged her hair to fall over her shoulders. A delicious shiver skipped along her spine. "It's impolite of you to ask such a question."

"Just as I thought. He left you unmoved."

"If you say so."

"I know so. I'm the only man who can make you hot."

"You conceited oaf," she whispered, but her words lacked conviction.

"At least I'm honest. I didn't want this to happen, either. I thought all proper ladies were coldhearted by nature."

Rayne's stomach convulsed. "Perhaps you were right."

He nibbled a path along the curve of her jaw, then brushed his lips over hers. "If I still thought so, I wouldn't be doing what I'm doing."

"What exactly *are* you doing?" *Besides setting fire to my insides. Besides causing gooseflesh to rise up all over my body.*

"Aren't you woman enough to know?"

"I've amassed quite an education because of you," she conceded.

"Not nearly enough," he said, laving the underside of her ear.

She moaned and his lips slid down her neck, moving lower until they skimmed over the rise of flesh skirting the edge of her gown. She felt like butter melting over a blazing fire. "You're seducing me."

"Am I?" His breath was hot against her skin. He lifted his head. "You haven't answered."

She brushed an errant lock of hair from his brow. "Why don't you want your women friends to visit you?"

"You honestly don't know, do you?"

Rayne shook her head. She wanted to believe he felt something more than desire for her.

She felt the gown slip farther down her arms. Demonstrating the know-how of a man proficient in the removal of a woman's clothes, he made easy work of releasing the front fastenings of her corset. She wanted to gasp, but her throat had grown thick. She should push him away, before it was too late.

She found him considering her camisole. "Mr. O'Malley, I do wish you would—"

"Case."

"Case, I wish you'd—"

"Make love to me," he finished for her.

Yes, yes, she wanted to say.

"Say it."

He pressed his lips into the valley between her breasts. Pushing aside her clothing, he slipped his hands inside, filling them with her soft flesh. She heard a whimper and sincerely prayed it hadn't come from her.

"Tell me that you want me," he whispered against her skin. He detoured upward and thoroughly possessed her mouth. "Tell me that you want me to love you, and that you won't regret it later."

Intoxicated from his ardent attention, Rayne slowly opened her eyes. His hands still covered her breasts, disorienting and thrilling her. Yes, she wanted him. She would never regret it, no matter what her fate. She nodded.

"I hope you know what you're doing," he said, "because I sure as hell don't. I haven't changed. Will you accept me, knowing all my flaws?"

"I . . . I can't think with your hands there— please."

Chuckling, he dropped his arms to his sides.

Composing herself somewhat, Rayne laid her hand on his cheek. He seemed reluctant to seduce her. There could only be one reason for his chivalrous reserve. She wondered how she could have been so stupid. "You steal my breath," she told him.

"I'll steal your virtue unless you come to your senses and leave me."

"Will you steal my heart, too?"

"Are you offering it?"

"With reservation."

He sighed. "Which of my vices must I forfeit?"

She lowered her eyes and concentrated on the cluster pin on his lapel. "Women. I couldn't love you if I thought you'd continue to share yourself with them."

"Demanding little shrew, aren't you?"

The amusement and warmth in his voice brought up Rayne's head. His eyes smoldered with desire, making heat course through her body.

"I'll give up the women. You have my word."

Rayne smiled as she began to unknot his tie. Removing his stiff collar, she grazed her nails over his neck.

He cleared his throat. "The cigars are another matter. You can't expect a man to live like a monk." He looked down, watched her unfasten his waistcoat, then work on the buttons of his shirt. His voice dropped lower, showing signs of strain. "And the gambling. It's an honest pastime, one I enjoy."

Spreading his shirt wide, she let her fingers drift over the tight curls on his chest.

"You've become mighty bold, Miss North, to undress a man in such a shameful fashion."

She gave him a chiding glance as her hands traveled over his ribs. This daring woman couldn't be her, she thought, but his enjoyment gave her the courage to continue.

"You haven't said a word." He captured her wrists and held them between their bodies. "You can only torment a man so far."

"Since you seem prepared to ramble on, I thought I'd respond in a more obvious manner." She leaned forward and pressed her cheek against his. "You may steal my heart, Case, provided you cherish it."

"I'll cherish much more than your heart. There's still time to change your mind."

"It's too late," she said against his lips.

He kissed her deeply, releasing her hands to bind her more tightly against him. A ringing sounded in her ears, and she tingled all over. When he finally drew back, she sagged against him, panting.

"Do you want me to put out the candles?" he asked.

"Is it supposed to be dark?" His silence prompted her to search his eyes. "Did I say something wrong?"

"I'm just surprised you'd want to make love the first time with light in the room. It's your choice."

She hadn't considered the consequences of her suggestion. Struck by a sudden attack of bashfulness, she said, "Dark."

"Why don't we make ourselves more comfortable, then. You lock the door and I'll make my way towards the bed."

Holding up her drooping gown, Rayne rose and went to fulfill his request. "Do you always talk so long before you make love to a woman?"

He blew out the candles, leaving behind the scent of melted wax. She heard the thump of his crutch, then the creak of the bed.

"I've never wasted time talking before."

Rayne slipped out of her shoes and stockings in the dark before she followed the husky timbre of his voice. She stopped near him. "I can't see you at all now."

She heard the rustle of his clothes, a low curse when his pants didn't come off easily over his splint. His tug on her skirt pulled her closer, until she stood between his legs. Deftly he swept her gown down to her feet, then the four petticoats. He chuckled as he sent her corset flying, then sighed with satisfaction when he met only her underclothes.

A quivery sensation threatened to buckle Rayne's knees. She fervently wished she'd drunk more champagne. She felt the heat of his hand as he captured her fingers and coaxed her forward. Gently he scooted backward on the bed, taking her with him, until she lay stretched out on top of him.

It was a shock to feel his bare, hot body through the thin barrier of her camisole. Rayne let out a shaky breath, trembling all over.

"Rest easy."

"I'm not nervous," she fibbed. "I just . . . I wanted you to know that."

"When did you realize you loved me?" he asked as he worked her camisole up from between their bodies and flung it toward the bottom of the bed.

Chagrined that her feelings were so obvious, she kept silent.

Flattening his hands against her back, he held her to him. She registered the tantalizing feel of her soft breasts crushed against his hard chest. He moaned and slipped her pantalets down, over her hips.

"You're here in my bed, unclothed, love. I've just taken off your drawers. That tells me a lot." He rolled her onto her side and nibbled on her shoulder as he caressed her hip. "You fell in love with me right away, didn't you? You might as well confess. I'll have the truth from you before the night's through."

"It was a slow, agonizing process," she admitted, her voice breaking. It was hard to concentrate this close to him, which was probably the scoundrel's intention. "The few redeeming qualities you possess, you certainly do keep hidden."

The heat of his bare skin pressed along the length of her side caused warmth to invade her insides. Was he purposely trying to drive her insane?

"Ummm. You smell good—lavender."

"Ummm. You smell even better. Do we have to keep talking?" she asked, wanting to concentrate on the delightful sensations coursing through her.

"I was only trying to ease your jittery nerves."

"I'm not jittery."

"Not *now*, you're not."

He moved, covering her body with his. His fingers tangled in her hair as he pressed his lips to her forehead, cheeks, the tip of her nose, and finally her mouth. His hands, however, were her undoing. They skimmed over every inch of her fevered skin, leaving delicious tingles in their wake. She'd known Case O'Malley would be a wonderful lover, but she hadn't guessed he possessed the power to devastate her.

The man was truly a devil.

She found it impossible to deal with so many feelings at once. She felt drugged. His hands moved with purpose, lower, coming to rest on her hips. Then, before she guessed his intention, he cupped her backside and lifted her, easing himself between her legs.

Her mouth fell open.

Taking advantage of the opportunity, he deepened his kiss. He began an erotic rhythm with his tongue, the rigid length of him pressed intimately against her. As close as they were, she wanted more. She wanted to be part of him, to love him with every breath of her body. If only she could move.

But she didn't have to. He did.

His lips left her mouth, roamed down her neck. Her nipples grew taut as he teased first one, then the other with his lips and teeth. It was a torment she hadn't known existed, a sensuality so keen, it ignited a throbbing below. Without considering the result of her action, she threw her legs over his, seeking to move against his hard, hot manhood. The ragged moan torn from his throat told her he'd found the contact as marvelous as she. She was grateful he had told her what to expect.

"You're driving me insane," he said in a raspy voice.

Rayne couldn't speak. Instead, she repeated the movement, this time grazing her nails along his sides and back. She wanted to touch him all over, to torture him in the same manner that he was torturing her. She loved the feel of him, smooth skin over hard muscle. His lips seared her neck. Determined to do the same, she changed position so that she was free to scorch a similar path across his shoulder, to the base of his throat. She felt his hips thrust against her soft center.

"Case!"

"I'm trying to go slow. I've never made love to a—"

"Lady," she interjected.

"Yes."

She had an aching desire to be possessed body and soul by this man. Instinct drove her. She wiggled her hips, seeking closer contact. His response was immediate, excruciating, a grinding motion that sent her reeling.

"You're a wicked woman, Rayne."

She found his mouth and, throwing her arms around his shoulders, kissed him with a fierceness that startled him and amazed her. Gripping her bottom tightly, he entered her. She didn't care that he hurt her.

Mere words could never express the wonder of it. Case's concise description hadn't prepared her for the actual experience. He was imbedded deep within her, his movements deliberate, achingly precise, leading her to question the command he exercised over his passion. His kiss had subsided to a leisurely rhythm.

An unendurable tension began deep within her, confusing and thrilling her, making her cling to him and duplicate the rocking motion of his hips. Each time he withdrew from her, she followed, so that he never quite achieved his goal. But his control wasn't as great as she thought. His mouth left hers. The low string of endearments muttered against her lips gave testimony to his frustration. She sucked in a breath at the exact moment when his gentle rocking changed.

Chapter 16

Making love to Rayne was sweet hell, Case thought as he surrendered to the full force of his desire. No mortal man could be expected to hold back when faced with such a fiery temptress. He had tasted her desire before, but he hadn't guessed the true depth of her passion.

He was being consumed by a raging fire, laid to waste by touches made all the more powerful because they were given innocently. There was no wanton skill involved in the light caress of Rayne's hands. She moved with hesitant curiosity and eagerness. The combination drove him wild.

Burying his face against her neck, he thrust quick and deep, driven by her moans of pleasure. He existed in a state of divine torment until he felt her body stiffen and her nails dig into the tender skin above his waist. He sought his own thunderous release. Violent spasms ripped through him in a climax so complete, he thought he might die.

She grazed her hands down his back while her lips played over his throat. She was as breathless as he. He sought to regain his senses. Unfortunately, Rayne wiggled the right way at the wrong moment. Reflexively his hips pressed down into her sweet, hot body. She instinctively clenched her muscles, enfolding him tighter.

"Good Lord, woman, have you no mercy?"

Instantly she went still, holding herself rigid.

He kissed her cheek, then her lips, smiling at her in the dark. "I didn't mean you should turn to stone."

"Do you think I'm ... wicked?" she asked in a small voice.

"Thoroughly wicked."

"Oh."

Her distress confused him. Did Rayne believe she'd disappointed him? He'd meant his words as a compliment, but she'd sounded hurt. "When I said you were wicked, I was only teasing. A man likes a woman to holler and dig her nails in his back. Is that what you wanted to know?"

Resting her hands on his cheeks, she brushed her lips over his chin. "Yes."

"I told you before you could ask me anything."

"I wasn't sure ... I was afraid I wasn't normal. I thought ladies shouldn't like ... you know."

"And did you like it?"

"Actually, I did. Very much. Are you sure I'm not wanton? I've heard decent women don't carry on so, that they ... they ..."

"Lie like sticks beneath their men?"

She gasped. "It's true?"

Try as he might, Case couldn't hold back a grin. "I haven't any notion of how a decent woman acts, but if you're an example, then I sure as hell have no complaints."

He rolled to his side and brushed his hand along her shoulder and arm. Encouraged by the shiver that shook her, he nibbled a path from her neck, straight down her chest. He smiled when she sucked in a ragged breath. With a fingertip, he drew a circle around a taut nipple.

"If you reacted this way with just any man, then I guess you'd be wanton. Since I'm the only man who can claim that honor, I'd say you just have a passionate nature."

Rayne captured his wayward hand and held it firmly between their bodies. Case broke into a full-throated laugh.

Rayne laughed, too. "I think you're impossibly pleased with yourself, Case O'Malley."

"Well now, I do enjoy a reputation as a capable lover. With a little encouragement, I might be persuaded to show you just *how* capable I can be."

"Conceited rogue." She remained silent for a moment before she asked, "Can we really make love again so soon?"

"I do adore a greedy woman."

"After the weeks you've spent confined to this room, you'd probably appreciate *any* willing woman in your bed."

Case pulled back. He'd played as fair as he could with Rayne; he had even allowed her a chance to walk away from him.

"Case O'Malley! Surely you know I wasn't serious," she said as she splayed her fingers on his chest and leaned over him.

Damn. Case released a frustrated sigh.

"I'm sorry, Case. I didn't think you'd take offense." She stroked his chest, seducing him again with an innocent touch. "So," she asked softly, "when can we do it again?"

Insatiable little witch, Case thought. "Soon. And we'll light a candle. When I make love to you again, I want to look at the woman warming my bed."

"That sounds rather like a challenge," she countered, her voice brimming with amusement. "Unfortunately, I didn't eat my dinner and suddenly I'm hungry. Perhaps later."

With a menacing growl, Case caught her waist and slid her atop him. He hooked his hands behind her knees and adjusted her so she straddled his hips. "I'm hungry, too, but not for food."

Rayne's eyes grew wide at what her new position implied. "Surely you can't mean for me to. . . ?"

"But I do. Make love to me, sweetheart."

"But I can't—Oh!"

Case laughed and moaned simultaneously. He found the blistering reality of Rayne impaling herself on him such an exquisite torture, he congratulated himself for his brazen decision to rapidly advance her education. This arrangement suited him better. He didn't have to worry about bumping his leg and he was free to roam his hands over Rayne's velvety skin, to rub his thumbs over her breasts and feel her nipples grow taut. He reveled in hearing the whimpers of delight she was too guileless to hide.

After some guidance from him, she moved of her own accord, adopting a provocative rhythm that set his senses reeling. She trembled, moaned, and rode him with an inborn knowledge that jolted him. Case groaned aloud as he dragged Rayne down against him. He devoured her mouth, his tongue snaking past her lips to duplicate the erotic motion of her hips. He had stumbled upon a sorceress intent on draining him of his life's blood.

And he meant to cherish every explosive second.

Rayne didn't know where she'd found the audacity to behave so boldly. Another man would most likely condemn her for her unbridled enjoyment, but not Case O'Malley. He relished her frenzy, the uncontrollable fever that had gripped her from the instant he'd thrust deep inside her. Her breathing sounded harsh to her own ears. Blinding pleasure spiraled throughout her body. Above all, she wanted to gratify him, to demonstrate the love she felt for him, to give him all he wanted and more.

He kissed her shamelessly, with an insatiable appetite that engendered a like hunger in her. She hadn't known a man could kiss like that, as though he were devouring her alive.

No, she wasn't wanton. Case O'Malley was the reason for her immodest responses.

Suddenly he tore his mouth from hers, an agonized growl coming from deep in his throat. For a split second she feared she'd done something wrong. Then he swore softly, gripped her hips with his large, hot hands, and led her into a series of reckless movements destined to bring their heated joining to a crescendo.

He seemed to swell inside her, driving her to the verge of insanity. She threw back her head and sank her teeth into her bottom lip. Savage tremors wracked her as bright lights exploded behind her eyes.

Rayne collapsed atop Case, gasping for air. She felt his heavy, fiery breath against her cheek, the dampness of his hair against her forehead. She'd never be the same now, because of him, because of the oneness she felt with this devil of a man. She'd treasure the memory of this night forever. Only one thing marred the moment. Only one thing hindered her happiness.

He hadn't told her he loved her.

She knew he cared for her. He had hinted as much earlier. But she wanted it all. She loved him with every ounce of passion within her, but she had no assurance that he felt the same.

A playful slap on her bottom, and a nip on her ear, brought Rayne from her musings.

"It appears my opinion of ladies was completely wrong. You, my dear, bring a new meaning to the word *proper*. You're an excellent student, Rayne. Excellent indeed. You mastered the *proper* way to love a man with little coaching."

He pulled up the sheet and gently changed positions so that she lay nestled in his arms. He felt hard and warm against her, a sturdy rock of flesh and muscle. She cherished the moment, disheartened by the thought of going to her own cold bed, alone.

Rayne shut her eyes and curled closer to him, looping her arm over his middle. No fragrance on earth compared with his masculine scent. The hair on his chest tickled her cheek, and the steady beat of his heart lulled her. If she could suspend a precious moment in time, it would be this one. She had never felt so sheltered, so content.

Sunlight peeked from behind the edges of the heavy drapes, forming a dazzling line across the wall and the headboard. Rayne blinked, for a moment unsure of her whereabouts. Reality came in a sudden rush of heated memories that brought a flush of embarrassment to her cheeks. She turned to the man sprawled at her side and studied him as he slept.

She loved him. Heaven help her, she had come to love everything about him.

Although greatly tempted to awaken him with a kiss, she dared not. She must leave Case's room immediately, before Hung Lee or her father found them together. Glancing around, Rayne sighed. Her clothes were strewn about, far enough out of her reach to present an embarrassing problem if Case were to awaken prematurely. Despite their passion, she felt bashful about him seeing her naked.

Carefully holding her breath, she eased out of his arms and from the bed. Shivering in the cool morning air, she tiptoed to the wardrobe and cracked open the door far enough to grab Case's dark blue dressing gown. She slipped into its welcoming, overly large folds. The garment trailed behind her as she gathered up her clothes, but she managed not to trip on the hem. With both arms full, she used her foot to slide a chair out of the path leading to her room.

A sleepy-sounding grunt came from behind her. "Come back to bed."

Rayne turned and stepped closer to him. Good Lord, the devil was even more handsome with his hair tousled and a shadow of beard darkening his face. A cocky grin on his face, he looked exactly like a rogue who had spent the night making love to a woman.

Rayne's cheeks suddenly felt hot. She knew they

must be bright red. She cursed the reaction and wished she could pretend sophistication instead. Making the best of the awkward moment, she said, "I think it would be best if I returned to my own room."

Case's grin grew even wider. His eyes narrowed with amusement as he caught hold of the robe and tugged her near. His hands disappeared into the front opening, his fingers drifting up her thigh.

Rayne closed her eyes in an attempt to hide the thrilling tingles shooting through her body at his touch. "It's a shame I fell asleep," he said. "I was waiting for morning so I could see you."

The meaning of his words deepened Rayne's distress. "You have no shame!"

"None whatsoever. On second thought, it might be more fun to save something special for next time." He plowed the fingers of his other hand through his hair, then over his beard stubble. "You aren't sorry, are you?"

Tightening her grip on her clothes, Rayne raised her chin. "No. Are you?"

"I only regret I'll have to look Jasper in the eye and pretend I haven't ruined his daughter."

Seeing Case's frown, Rayne said, "I made a decision, and I don't see why you should feel responsible. I wouldn't change what happened, no matter what."

His fingers grazed back down her thigh and he squeezed her knee. "Neither would I. I never thought it could be so . . ." He fell silent, a troubled look on his face. "I think you should leave me and get dressed now, while you have the chance."

He was right, of course. She should see to her

morning ablutions. But the thought of his unsaid words puzzled her. Curiosity gnawed at her, but she made a mental vow not to prompt him into finishing that sentence.

And he didn't.

During the following days, Case received a steady stream of visitors, mostly business acquaintances. Taking his cue, Rayne behaved coolly in his presence, pretending he was a patient and nothing more. Although she knew he had her best interests in mind, she couldn't help wishing things were different. If he loved her, he should want to openly claim her. Since he seemed to prefer to keep their relationship secret, she tried to be patient.

She consoled herself with the thought that he hadn't accepted his feelings yet. Perhaps he needed time to get used to the drastic change in his life. One didn't transform from a notorious scoundrel into a paragon of virtue overnight.

Only in the evenings did she dare let down her guard. The nights were filled with splendor, stolen hours of passionate discovery—long, torrid hours during which she gloried in his tender lovemaking.

Rayne went upstairs and stood in the hall outside Case's room. She pressed cool fingers against her warm cheeks to banish the fevered memories. Case had taken to leaving his door open until dinner. It was his way of guarding her good name. For that she loved him even more.

Voices drifted to her from his room. Hung Lee had told her Case had received a call from a businessman earlier, but Rayne had assumed the man had gone.

Then she heard Case say, "And you, my dear, are quite welcome to accompany your uncle any time you wish. Having a beautiful woman present has made tedious business more interesting indeed."

"Oh, Mr. O'Malley, you say the sweetest things."

"Come, Iris," said the man, "before he completely turns your head. Thanks for the drawings, Case. Get better soon. I heard several complaints from the female population that their evenings are boring without you around."

"Uncle Richard, really. You make Mr. O'Malley sound simply awful."

"And well you should remember that, young lady. But don't mind me. Case sure doesn't. I'm just envious."

As the man and his niece left Case's room, Rayne smiled at them. He nodded and escorted the young woman down the stairs. Rayne's smile slipped the moment they were out of sight. Poor Iris was bone-thin and plain, but that hadn't prevented Case from flirting with her.

Case O'Malley was a natural-born charmer. Rayne's heart ached. She must have lost her mind to hope he would ask her to marry him. Why should he settle for her when every woman who got near him melted?

Rayne reminded herself that she'd known all this from the beginning, yet still she'd fallen in love with him.

Calmly she entered his room and crossed to where he sat at his desk, scribbling on a large drawing. Absorbed in his work, he seemed not to

have noticed her arrival. She peered over his
shoulder, watching him add a set of timbers to an
elaborate skeleton that comprised the labyrinth of
tunnels under the city.

She resisted the temptation to run her fingers
through his hair. She found it even more difficult
not to kiss his neck, or brush her hand over his
smooth cheek. Downstairs, in the foyer, a clock
chimed. A gust of wind rattled a window. Rayne
sighed softly. She grinned as he returned his pen
to the inkwell on his desk.

"I didn't mean to disturb your work."

He captured her wrist and led her around his
chair and onto his lap. A devilish grin split his
face, sending delightful tingles along Rayne's
spine; his green eyes twinkled with wicked promise.

His gaze settled on her mouth. Rayne felt as
though her breath were trapped in her throat. It
was the middle of the afternoon, but she could not
help herself. She leaned forward and offered her
lips.

Case's growl of frustration gratified her. He, too,
felt the undercurrent of tension passing between
them. He kissed her playfully, nibbling her lips,
slanting his mouth over hers first one way, then
another. His hands slid up her back and settled behind her shoulder blades. It was sweet torment, as
if he only meant to give her a taste and nothing
more.

This time, *she* growled with frustration. In response, he laughed and yielded. She would never
know how or where he'd learned to turn a kiss
into an act of devastation, but she didn't care. He
knew and that was enough. She felt her body wilt,

like ice melting under a blazing sun. He devoured her, his tongue performing a fiery dance with hers, making her blood run hot through her veins. Her head felt as if it spun round and round . . .

He broke away without warning, leaving Rayne dazed and breathless. She saw the pulse pounding in his throat, his green eyes glazed with desire. Color rode high on his cheeks as he sucked in a ragged breath.

"Tonight we'll finish what we started."

She smiled wickedly at him.

"Witch," he said, guiding her hand over his stomach, down under the folds of her skirt. "How am I supposed to keep my thoughts on mine tunnels when your hot little mouth has left me with this?"

Through his trousers, Rayne felt the hard ridge fill the palm of her hand. She had wanted to touch him intimately, but she hadn't yet found the courage. Now he held her hand over his pulsing manhood, and it was broad daylight. Flaming images filled her mind, robbing her of breath once again. As if the same images had occurred to him, too, he abruptly lifted her from his lap and mumbled an irreverent litany that would have shocked the most degenerate villain.

He shoved his fingers through his hair as he turned away. "I'm expecting Rogers any minute. Please, if you have an ounce of mercy, open a damn window and then go downstairs."

An amused smile slid across Rayne's mouth. After she adjusted the curtains so the cool air blew straight at Case's desk and rustled his papers, she headed for the door.

She paused on the upper landing. It wasn't Rogers who stood below in the front hall but a strange man who twisted a soiled slouch hat in his hands. He glanced around nervously. Rayne wondered why Hung Lee hadn't announced the man's arrival.

She greeted the man and introduced herself, fervently hoping the effects of her last moments with Case weren't obvious. Her lips still tingled and she still felt unusually warm all over.

"John Bidwell," he said with a nod. "I . . . Is O'Malley able to see me?"

Watching him continue to abuse his hat, Rayne privately questioned the man's reasons for wanting to see Case. She quickly scrutinized the fellow, noting his blue woolen shirt, dark baggy trousers, and heavy, dusty boots. His clean-shaven face looked freshly scrubbed, his brown, thinning hair was slicked neatly back, but his fingernails were encrusted with dirt. His attire and wan appearance convinced her he was a miner.

"Of course Mr. O'Malley can see you. I'm sorry you were left waiting in the hall."

Rayne led the way up stairs.

"No apology needed," Bidwell said as he followed her. "The Chinaman went up. He said O'Malley was presently occupied."

A flush surged up Rayne's neck and washed over her face. It took all her control to say calmly, "Mr. O'Malley has been working on a drawing of mine tunnels all morning."

Mine tunnels indeed, she thought, as she indicated the correct doorway. Case's tongue had probably been tunneling down her throat when Hung Lee saw them! She wanted to crawl into a corner and die.

"I won't be a moment," the miner told her before he gave her another nod and disappeared into Case's room.

Rayne intended to go to her own room to repair any damage done to her hair by Case's torrid embrace when she heard his voice. His urgent tone halted her steps.

"John! Good God, man, shut the door!"

The reason for the miner's visit was none of her business, Rayne told herself, and she was about to walk away when a slip of paper on the floor caught her attention. Bidwell must have dropped it. Surely it was her moral obligation to rescue what might be an important document and see it returned to its owner.

Case's door was shut firmly. He spoke in a lower voice, and she fought to resist the temptation to listen.

Alone in the hall, she bent down and picked up the slip of paper. As she did, Case's booming voice commanded, "Don't just stand there! Find it before someone else does!"

Rayne froze.

The door swung open and Rayne stood face-to-face with the anxious miner. Holding out her hand, she said, "I believe you dropped this, Mr. Bidwell."

"I did. Thank you, Miss North."

Although only an instant passed before Bidwell disappeared back into the room, Rayne managed to read two words in the middle of a sentence.

Her heart began to pound. Her palms grew damp.

The words she'd read were enough to defeat all her reservations about eavesdropping on Case's personal affairs. The words raised questions for which she must find answers.

What possible involvement could Case O'Malley have with *Union gold?*

Chapter 17

"You know you shouldn't put anything in writing," Case said as he waved a match under the incriminating paper and watched it turn to ashes. "I presume you have a good reason."

"I hadn't heard from you. Time ran out," John Bidwell said.

Case glanced past the miner's shoulder. "Check to make sure no one's in the hall or the next room. We've come this far without a leak. Let's not get sloppy now." While the man did as he'd asked, Case hobbled back to his desk. "Make sure Miss North went downstairs."

"I'm sure she didn't read anything. There wasn't time."

Case turned his chair sideways and sat down. "It's Miss North I'm particularly worried about. There's safety in ignorance." Seeing the speculation brewing in the miner's eyes, Case added, "Rayne is Jasper's daughter and therefore my concern."

Bidwell propped his hip on a corner of the desk. "The shipment has to go out tomorrow to reach Sacramento before the wagon train sets out for New York."

"Tomorrow!" Case plowed his fingers through

his hair. "I see why you took the risk and came in person. There's only one thing I can do now."

The miner's eyes narrowed. "You aren't thinking of driving the wagon yourself after what happened, are you? Those southern sympathizers might make a connection."

Case grinned. "Damn right I'm driving the wagon. But this time I have a better idea. I don't plan to get shot again. Look between the mattress and the headboard and bring me the box."

Shaking his head, Bidwell did as he was told. He smiled when Case plucked out two cigars and handed him one.

"Now I'll be able to think straight." Case passed the fine Havana under his nose, inhaling deeply. "There's no reason why anyone should guess I'm supplying gold to the Union. I'm just one of many mine owners transporting gold bullion. Even if the southerners check the dates of the shipments, they won't necessarily connect them to me. Who's to say for sure what my final destination is? For all they know, it could be one of my regular shipments to San Francisco."

"I hope you're right." ·

Case struck a match and held the flame for his companion before lighting his own cigar. Speaking from inside a cloud of smoke, he outlined his plan. "There will be two wagons. One with heavily armed guards."

"But that'll attract notice," Bidwell protested. "Is attention what you want?"

"Precisely. If I figure right, no one will suspect the gold will be in the unprotected wagon I'll be driving. It would be damn stupid of any mine owner to haul bullion, be it his own or the government's, without armed guards."

"Sounds risky. It seems too obvious."

"My thoughts exactly. It is too obvious. That's why it'll work."

Bidwell stood and donned his hat. "I think you ought to have at least one guard."

"I'll take along a driver, but he won't be visibly armed." Case shifted through the clutter on his desk and laid out two pieces of paper. After he'd scribbled simple instructions on both, he handed them to John. "Give one to Jasper. The other has the directions for the loading of the ore. No need to worry, though. There's nothing written here to incriminate either of us. We'll leave at dawn. Don't contact me again unless it's a life-or-death situation."

"Have you figured out how you'll leave the house? What about Miss North?"

"I'll slip her some laudanum after dinner. She should sleep well into the morning."

The miner shifted his cigar from one hand to the other and squeezed Case's shoulder. "Good luck. For God's sake, be careful and arm yourself."

"A little fresh air will do me a world of good," Case remarked nonchalantly.

Bidwell shook his head again. "So long as it's not your last breath of it."

Case waited until the man had left before he allowed his feigned good humor to fade. *Tomorrow.* The short notice was unexpected, but he had no choice in the matter. Thank goodness he'd sent a message to Rogers that morning, requesting his presence for another reason. There wasn't time for caution. He must rely on his gut instinct; Rogers was proficient and loyal.

He hoped Rogers's sympathies were with the Union.

Case's thoughts turned to Rayne. He glanced at the bureau, where the bottle of laudanum had remained these past weeks. Somehow he must drug her and see that she fell asleep in her own bed. The evening sure was going to be interesting.

Rayne pushed herself up from her crouched position and moved away from the wall, where she had spent the past minutes hidden by the width of the bureau. There hadn't been time to hurry downstairs, merely to duck out of sight. To her relief, when the miner had looked into her room, he hadn't walked in far enough to spot her. And in his hurry to speak with Case, the man had left the door ajar, allowing her to listen to their conversation.

Her immediate concern was to escape before Case discovered her presence. She tiptoed out to the hall and reached belowstairs in time to admit Rogers. After a brief greeting, she went in search of Hung Lee and a cup of tea to soothe her nerves.

Once again, Case O'Malley had surprised her, but surprise was too mild a word to describe the emotion that had churned in her breast when she'd discovered he was working secretly for the North. It was more like shock. She wondered what else she would find out about him.

Having been brought up in Chicago, she sided with the Union. Earlier, for several agonizing minutes, she had thought Case might be planning to steal Union gold. She'd been immensely relieved to find out otherwise.

The rogue's entire existence was a contradiction.

This latest facet of his character so amazed her, she felt light-headed. If she hadn't misunderstood, he was going to risk his life again by driving a wagon filled with ore. An image of Case being carried into the house on a stretcher, broken and bruised, formed so vividly in her mind that she nearly stumbled.

"Rayne, honey, where are your thoughts?"

She looked up from her plate and saw her father's concerned expression. "I'm sorry. Guess I was daydreaming."

"About Case?"

Rayne laid down her fork and reached for a glass of water. "Don't worry, Papa."

"I can't help it, honey. You know I think highly of Case, but I know him better than anyone else does."

"You think he'll break my heart like you did Mama's?" The misery on his face made her instantly regret her rash words. Then again, maybe it was time to speak of the way Jasper had treated Rayne and her mother. "Papa, tell me why you left. Didn't you love us anymore?"

Jasper stared down at the table. "I always loved you both. I just couldn't help myself."

"Why? I need to know. Papa, you owe me that much."

"I guess I do. Nothing went right from the beginning," he said. "Your grandparents hated me, thought I was good for nothing, and I proved them right. They cut your mother off when she married me. Never even spoke to her again. At first I honestly tried, but I didn't have it in me to make a decent living."

"Mama didn't need money to make her happy."

"I know. But there were other things. Rayne, I can't help myself. I like to go out to saloons. Never did like stayin' in every night."

"You're better now, Papa. I've seen it."

"The wantin's still there. Guess some men just crave the excitement, the lure of the poker games, and . . . She'll never forgive me after so long."

Rayne reached over and touched his hand. "You might ask her. If she believes you're sincere, I think she'll forgive you. Mama has always had a kind heart."

"That's the one thing I never forgot about her."

Rayne pushed away her plate and sighed. She wasn't hungry, and her thoughts kept returning to Case.

"You thinkin' about Case?" Jasper asked.

"Yes. Is it so obvious?"

"Women are always drawn to him."

Rayne smiled. "I guess he was very spoiled as a child, particularly by his mother."

"You're wrong about that. Far as I know, she never showed him an ounce of love."

"Case told you that?"

"Not intentionally, I think. He had a few too many one night and it slipped out. Better not tell him I told you. He's mighty proud about some things."

"Of course I won't." Rayne stored away the bit of information. Her own mother's love made up for whatever she lacked in her life.

After dinner, Rayne went to Case's room, still carrying in her mind the vision of him broken and bleeding. He was going to die; she just knew it. No man could be lucky enough to survive two attacks.

Well, Case O'Malley could just think again. She wasn't about to sleep peacefully in her bed while he went out and got himself killed. His own mother might not have loved him, but *she* did.

He looked obscenely innocent sitting on the side of the bed. Rayne noticed two glasses of liquor on the small table, but she kept her gaze on Case, pretending ignorance. She had dressed with care in a midnight blue dress with black piping. The skirt belled out over numerous petticoats, emphasizing her narrow waist. White lace adorned the bodice, the round neckline, and formed small cuffs at her wrists. Her hair fell over her shoulders in what she hoped was a seductive manner.

"You look lovely," he said, his eyes drifting appreciatively over her before returning to her face. "Far too lovely to spend the evening cooped in this room with the likes of me."

"I'd rather be here with you than in the fanciest ballroom with anyone else."

He raised a dark eyebrow.

"Well, it's true," she said. "Do you doubt me?"

"No."

She sighed and sat beside him. She folded her hands in her lap and chewed on her bottom lip. Outsmarting Case O'Malley wasn't going to be as easy as she'd thought. But she had to; he had become essential to her.

"I thought you'd join me in a drink." He

reached for the two glasses and held one out to her. "Purely medicinal, my dear."

Panic seized her. She wondered which glass held the drug. She hadn't figured he'd make his move so fast. Her eyes flashed to his face but collided with a smile so devastating that heat slid through her veins. *Dear Lord.* All he had to do was smile at her and her blood turned to hot syrup. If she didn't master her weakness for him, all would be lost.

"I don't care for any just now," she managed to say.

He closed his eyes for a second, his smile changing into a wry grin.

She watched him swallow the liquid from the other glass, feeling a measure of success. If he drank enough, it might be possible to trick him into taking the laudanum himself. "Do you want a refill?" she asked sweetly.

He set both glasses on the table while his wicked green gaze plundered her senses. "I'd rather devour you."

As tempting as the idea might be, she couldn't allow him to seduce her from her goal. Somehow she had to make sure he slept soundly. Otherwise he'd hear her when she crept into his room later to borrow his pocket pistol. And he had to remain asleep while she slipped off to take his place in the morning.

It was a flawless plan, she thought, pleased with herself. What man would attack a wagon driven by a lady?

Rayne modestly lowered her eyes. "I'm feeling rather peakish tonight," she said, deliberately making her voice sound frail. She touched her cheek and shivered. "I do hope I'm not taking a cold."

Case laid a hand on her brow. "You don't seem to have a fever. I'll ring for Hung Lee and have him bring you something hot. That and a good night's sleep should cure what ails you."

Rayne left the bed and backed away. "Yes, tea would be nice. Have him bring it to my room. I suddenly feel as if I should lie down."

"Do you want me to send for the doctor? Hung Lee could call on him on his way home. He'll be leaving soon, though, so you have to decide now."

"Please don't bother. I'm sure a good night's sleep is all I need."

She waited while Case tugged on the rope, summoning Hung Lee, then she eased toward the door of her room.

"I'll miss having your warmth beside me tonight," he whispered as he swung his legs onto the mattress. He stretched out with his hands folded behind his head. "Be sure to call if the tea doesn't make you feel better."

"I will."

A cup of tea wasn't what she wanted at all. Case looked unbearably appealing lying there on the bed, his white shirt gaping open. She'd much rather join him. She'd much rather run her fingers through the curls on his chest, following the line of dark hair until it disappeared beneath his pants. But making love with him wouldn't prevent him from risking his life in the morning.

Ignoring the heat that sprang to life low in her abdomen, Rayne tore her gaze from Case. "If I can't sleep, maybe I will come back and have a drink with you."

Not allowing him time to respond, she escaped into her room, where she paced the floor until Hung Lee finally brought her a pot of tea. Lifting the lid, she sniffed the steaming brew. It smelled like tea with no additives, but Rayne knew better. After she disposed of the tea, she donned her nightgown and climbed into bed. She couldn't chance falling asleep, but she had to look as if she'd tried.

She wasn't about to fall prey to Case's scheme. She had one of her own to pull off.

At midnight Rayne felt sure it was safe to sneak into Case's room. Cracking open the adjoining door, she held up a candle and breathed a sigh of relief. His eyes were closed. She heard the steady sound of his breathing. She intended to snatch his derringer from the wardrobe, but first she must tend to another chore.

She crept cautiously toward the small table, grabbed the still full glass containing the laudanum, and emptied it out the window. Then she re-filled the other glass and set it aside. Uncapping the brandy bottle on the bureau, she saw that it contained more than enough for her purpose. Quickly she poured the drug into the bottle, then blew out the candle. After she stole his gun and hid it in her room, she planned to crawl into bed with him. Once he was awake, she'd trick him into drinking the drug, even if it meant seducing him as well.

Rayne sighed. Clandestine activities certainly took a toll on a person's nerves.

Searching through his wardrobe seemed to take hours instead of minutes. Finally she located the right coat. She felt the cold steel of the small gun in the palm of her hand. The sudden creak of a floorboard behind her brought her heart to her throat with such violence, she jumped back. The gun fell from her hand and thudded on the wardrobe's floor.

She stood deathly still, afraid to move, afraid to breathe. It wasn't Case a few feet from her. He would have called out. And he wasn't able to move about without the aid of his crutches.

Someone else was in the room.

Her heart hammered against her ribs. Her stomach felt as if she'd swallowed a lead ball. She wanted to scream, or run. She did neither, sensing it would be a costly mistake. Praying it was only her imagination, she strained to hear any sound that would give away an intruder.

Deep, uneven breathing rasped from behind her. Icy fingers of fear clawed up her spine, and dizziness swept through her. Her knees buckled as she unwillingly sucked in a breath. She thought she saw the silhouette of a man's body, his arms reaching out to touch her. Terrified, she spun around, and collided with a solid object.

All of her senses came to life in a rush of fear. The smell of whiskey mingled with body sweat assaulted her. The man's roughly woven shirt chafed her cheek, and his belt buckle jabbed her hip. Her arms flailed in a desperate effort to push him away.

A beefy arm clamped around her neck, locking her to him. Rayne planted her hands on his chest and shoved as hard as she could. He staggered and went down, his viselike hold pulling her with him. She heard his head hit the floor.

"What the hell!"

Case's exclamation spurred Rayne to action. She pounded her fists on the body of the groaning hulk beneath her, and his arm eased from around her neck. She threw herself into a roll, landing on the hard floor. She had gained her freedom, at least temporarily. With a curse and a pained grunt, the man groped for her. His fingers clawed at her ankle.

Rayne released a bloodcurdling scream.

She scrambled backward, but his hand found her in the dark. He seized her wrist with such brutal strength, her scream turned into a yelp of pain. Rayne kicked futilely. Her assailant had slithered so close, she smelled his foul breath. In a matter of seconds she would be completely at his mercy. Guided by instinct, she utilized the only weapon at her disposal.

She sank her teeth in his hand.

A savage howl filled the room. She was free, but braced herself for another attack. Then she heard animal-like growls and strange thumping noises— the sounds of fists making contact with flesh.

Rayne crawled around the corner of the bed and grasped blindly until she felt cold porcelain. She scrambled to her feet and whipped around, her hands held high over her head.

Case was in no condition to fight an intruder. Under the circumstances, there was only one thing she could do to help him. Praying her aim was true and she hit the right man, she slammed down the ornate chamber pot.

"Christ!"

Rayne slapped a hand over her mouth. She had expected the pot to shatter, but there had been only an ominous thump. And, to her horror, that voice belonged to Case.

Before she could move, the intruder ran into the hall and pounded down the stairs. Rayne dropped the chamber pot and heard it crack as it hit the floor. Fingers touched her arm, the shock making her blood run cold. She opened her mouth to scream, but the sound died in her throat.

She recognized the hand on her wrist and willingly tumbled against a broad, strong chest, relishing the warmth and safety of Case's embrace.

With a cry of relief, she flung her arms around him and flattened her face against his bare chest. The impact threw him off balance, but he leaned back to steady himself.

"It's all right. He's gone."

Never had Case's deep voice sounded more welcome or comforting. A tremor shook her, savage in its intensity.

"Rest easy now. He won't be back any time soon," Case whispered.

"How can you be sure?"

Digging his fingers into her hair, he kissed the top of her head. "Because if you didn't splinter his head, the poor bastard's going to have a lump the size of a goose egg. What *did* you hit him with?"

"The . . . the container you keep under the bed."

"Ah." He threw back his head and laughed. "A fine choice of weaponry, my dear, suitable to the occasion."

How could he find amusement in the situation? Rayne trembled again. "What did he want?"

Case shifted his weight and murmured offhandedly, "Probably a robber. I don't think he figured on locking horns with a ferocious wildcat, though."

"I was terrified."

"I know." He hugged her tightly for a long moment, then with his arm around her waist, he moved toward the bed and together they dropped to the mattress. "I couldn't bear to think of you hurt."

"Do you think I should check on Papa?"

"If Jasper slept through all *that* racket, there's no way you'll wake him."

"Just the same, I believe I'll look in on him to make sure."

Rayne slipped from the bed and returned within minutes to reclaim her spot. "You were right. He's snoring so loud, I doubt dynamite would disturb him."

"That's a comforting thought. I could've been murdered in my sleep and he wouldn't even know."

"You have me, Case."

Half sitting, half lying, Rayne pulled back. Her hand slid over Case's ribs and came to rest on his bare abdomen. She felt his stomach suck in as he drew in a breath. It thrilled her to realize she could so easily stir his passions. Until this second she hadn't given any thought to what he wore. Tempted to investigate, she swept her fingers over his hip, then down his thigh.

"Case O'Malley, you're not wearing a stitch of clothes."

"I sleep naked," he confessed, his voice amused. He caught her hand and brought it back to his waist. "I *was* sleeping before you and your zealous friend started tussling on my floor."

"How can you make light of what happened? He was an awful man. He might have killed you."

"Or you." He gripped her upper arms and brought both of them to a sitting position. "When I think of what could have happened . . ."

Riddled with guilt, Rayne kept silent. She had come into his room to steal his derringer and to drug him.

"What? No defense?"

She didn't answer. She felt around on the small table for some matchsticks. Finding the lamp, she struck the match and lit the wick. Then, holding her breath, she turned to look at him. She desperately wanted him to hold her in his arms again, but she dreaded the consequences if he did.

Gently he shook her. "You should have screamed sooner."

"I was afraid he'd hurt you."

His hands fell away. Anger radiated from him, his strained silence stretching Rayne's nerves taut.

"Contrary to what you may think, I'm perfectly capable of protecting you and defending myself."

"I didn't mean . . ."

"You did. Considering the way you've had to look after me the past weeks, I suppose it's only natural for you to think of me as weak, but let me assure you, I don't need a woman to fight my battles!"

Rayne instantly saw the error she'd made, a grievous error indeed, judging by his testy mood. In her concern for his welfare, she had trampled his pride. *Men and their precious pride,* she thought morosely as she struggled to find words to soothe him.

"You saved me," she reminded him. "Your memory may be lax, but mine is not. That monster was about to overpower me when you grabbed him."

That seemed to appease him, and aiming an insolent grin at her, he slanted one eyebrow sheepishly upward. "I concede the point. Together, we foiled the enemy. It appears we make an excellent team, Rayne. I don't know about you, but I sure could use a drink."

He nodded at the bureau, giving her a pleading look.

Rayne set the brandy on the small table beside him. Forgetting her plan, she allowed her eyes to roam over his magnificent body; her gaze lingered on his well-formed shoulders and arms. Unable to resist, she trailed her fingers over his shoulder as he started to reach for the bottle. An agonized groan came from his throat.

She noticed he held his eyes tightly closed. She glanced down at his legs and gave in to the desire to stroke him again. She loved to feel the heat of his body under her hand. Laying her palm on his thigh, she caressed his hair-roughened skin while she pressed her lips to the muscle that bulged in his upper arm.

His reaction stunned her. He jerked suddenly, almost as if she had used a searing branding iron on his leg. Muttering under his breath, he snatched up the bottle of brandy, and before she realized his intention, he'd gulped down the entire contents. To his credit, or as a result of his wicked indulgences, he drank it like water instead of potent spirits. Rayne didn't know whether she should be impressed or shocked. Any normal man would have at least coughed.

Then, like lightning, it hit her that the bottle had contained laudanum, enough to put him to sleep for the entire night and into tomorrow. She prayed that those would be the only consequences.

"Shut the door. Lock it, too."

His tone sounded husky, provocative. Offering no objection, Rayne hurried to do his bidding. Case O'Malley was just stubborn enough to resist the effects of the drug until he decided it suited him to surrender.

"Come here."

Rayne timidly approached him, wondering if he had tasted the laudanum and knew of her treachery. When she stood a few inches from him, she saw the answer in his glowing green eyes.

He wanted her.

His hands settled on her waist, nearly spanning its circumference, but it was his gaze that fueled the fire inside her. Drawing her forward, he pressed his face between her breasts. She felt the heat of his breath through the layer of material separating his mouth from her skin. Suddenly her prim nightgown no longer provided a safe barrier. Liquid heat ignited in her belly, spreading like wildfire to her very core.

Rayne laid her hands on Case's shoulders and used her thumbs to massage his neck. His hands traveled down the backs of her legs, making shivers skip over her skin. Tipping back her head, she submitted to the luscious torture.

When she least expected it, his hands began a sensual exploration under her gown, all the way to her hips.

Rayne moaned, no longer able to bear the exquisite pleasure. Wherever he touched, he left his mark.

He cupped her breasts, his voice so deep and seductive that her legs trembled. "I want to see you."

Until now, they'd always made love in the dark.

She had dreaded this moment, but now that it had finally arrived, her modesty vanished. She released the tiny buttons down the front of her nightgown. She knew by the slight curve to his lips that he noticed her hands shook.

"It's all right. I'll do it for you." He swept the gown over Rayne's head and flung it away, then stretched out fully on the bed. "There's no reason to be embarrassed."

Struck by the magnificent sight of him lying naked before her, Rayne bit her lip. Case looked like a god, a perfectly sculpted work of art. She had always been too thin, never voluptuous as some women were. She suddenly felt unequal to him. A man as handsome as Case O'Malley deserved a stunning woman—like Kat.

His hand ran up her thigh, brushed over her stomach. "You're even more beautiful than I'd imagined. I should have lit a candle before this."

He thought she was beautiful, and his smile confirmed the truth of his words. Her skin tingled and felt hot under his hand.

His eyes drifted shut for a second. Rayne realized the drug was taking effect, making him drowsy. But he recovered quickly.

"See for yourself what the sight of you is doin' to me."

The challenge in his voice and eyes taunted her. She accepted his dare and saw the bold proof of his desire springing proudly from a nest of dark curls.

"Touch me," he said. "I want you to."

Rayne hesitated only a second. She circled her fingers around him.

He laughed and grunted, then he seized her wrist. "You drive me mad when you touch me."

She fell on top of him and began to kiss his face, delirious with a longing to have him inside her. His fingers tangled in her hair as his mouth slanted over hers. His kiss melted her very soul. Gradually, though, the intensity of his kiss dwindled.

She leaned back and peered into his slitted eyes.

"Witch," he cursed. "You put laudanum in the brandy."

"I'm sorry. I had to."

He shook his head, a murderous light in his eyes. "You don't . . . know what . . . you've done!"

"Oh, yes, I do. I've probably saved your life. You won't be getting shot tomorrow driving a wagon, not if I can help it."

"Damn." With the last of his strength, he reached out, but his arms fell back against the bed. "You . . . you'll pay dearly . . . for . . ."

"I have no doubt that you'll be angry for a little while, Case O'Malley, but at least you'll be alive."

Gently she brushed his hair off his brow, pulled the covers up to his neck, and kissed him. She waited until he slipped into a deep sleep before she returned to her room, hoping she'd done right, knowing she'd had no choice.

No matter what the future brought, Case would always be the only man in her heart. He had laid a claim on her soul. She would do anything in her power to keep him from gambling away his life—even if it meant risking her own.

Chapter 18

Case was furious.

It was already morning and it had taken two hours and four cups of Hung Lee's strong coffee before he could even focus his eyes. His head felt as though a miner wielding a sharp pick were chipping at it, and setting off occasional explosions as a bonus. Adding to his misery, his jaw smarted and the knuckles of his right hand felt stiff, thanks to the man who'd stolen into his room last night. He hoped Rayne *had* cracked the dumb bastard's skull.

Standing at the window, leaning heavily on his crutches, Case scowled. He hadn't meant to sleep at all last night, merely to rest for a few hours. Instead, Rayne had deftly tricked him and left him unconscious. When he'd finally recovered enough to demand an explanation, Hung Lee had informed him that she'd gone out—with Rogers, of all people. Rogers should be riding shotgun over the shipment of Union gold with *him*.

It was too late now to worry about that *minor* detail. God only knew what had happened to the precious shipment. Rayne had a lot of explaining to do, if he didn't strangle her lovely neck first. He remembered the final minutes before he'd passed out last night.

He could think of only one reason why she had drugged him. Contrary to Bidwell's belief, Rayne had read enough of the note to discover their plans. But it didn't atone for her crime. Weighed against his own safety, the welfare of his country came first. Rayne had not only ruined his plans, but also endangered his mission and herself.

And probably saved his life with her meddling.

The thought came unbidden, momentarily lightening his burden. No woman had ever loved him enough to want to protect him from himself. And, although he hated to admit it, it had been clever of Rayne to put the laudanum in the brandy bottle. She constantly surprised him. However, she had gone too far when she had jeopardized his work for the Union, regardless of her good intention.

Unless she was a spy.

No, that was ridiculous! Case shook his head and instantly regretted the careless move. Pain splintered from his temples to the base of his spine. Maybe it was the pain that made him suspect Rayne. Jasper's naive daughter didn't have a treacherous bone in her body.

Or did she?

Remembering the day he'd realized she'd been snooping in his papers, Case frowned. Could Rayne have secrets of her own to hide? Was she a southern sympathizer? As much as he hated giving credence to the thought, he knew he must. Had he foolishly fallen in with *her* scheme to discover his undercover work and sabotage the shipments?

At the time it had looked as if only his drawing

had been touched, but it might have been a ploy to conceal her real incentive—searching his papers for a clue to his involvement with the Union.

Confusion and anger sent blood roiling through his veins. His head throbbed anew. He threw open the large window and breathed in, praying the crisp air would bring him a measure of relief. He needed his wits about him if he was to discover the truth before the day ended.

It was midday by the time Case heard sounds of activity below. He gripped his crutches and thumped across the room into the hall. He wouldn't wait a moment longer to interrogate Rayne. When he reached the landing, however, he changed his mind.

Rayne wasn't alone.

Case told himself to control his temper. Early on, he'd decided Rayne needed a keeper, but the man standing at her side was hardly his choice. Rogers exuded danger and looked ruggedly handsome—just the sort of man some women found attractive. Rogers was a useful man when it came to the Cause, but he wasn't to be trusted with a decent woman, especially not one as inexperienced as Rayne. His Rayne.

Case bit his tongue and scowled at them. He watched Rayne lean close and speak in a low voice. When she laid her hand on Rogers's arm, the intimate gesture fed Case's imagination. His intention to master his temper went unheeded as rage rendered him incapable of speech. He recognized the emotion seething in him as jealousy, but knowing the cause of his wrath did little to soothe him.

When he saw Rogers pat Rayne's gloved hand, deep furrows of irritation plowed across Case's brow. He clenched his jaw, nailing both of them with a murderous glare.

Rayne looked up at him just then. Her beautiful hazel eyes widened with shock and another indefinable emotion. Guilt? Fear? Instantly she lowered her eyes and bit her bottom lip. Further provoking Case's wrath, Rogers squeezed her shoulder and whispered in her ear. Rayne strode briskly from the room.

"Coward," Case muttered.

Rogers advanced up the stairs. A mocking grin split his face as he stepped in front of Case. They were of the same height, an equal match, but Rogers wore his gun belt and carried a shotgun under his arm. Weapons or no weapons, Case could have cheerfully taken Rogers apart with his bare hands.

"I want an explanation," Case snarled. "Now!"

Rogers shifted his weight to one foot, adopting an insolent stance. "You won't like it."

"Tell me something I don't already know."

"How 'bout we go into your room." Rogers sauntered down the hall. "You'll be grateful for the privacy."

The crutches punished the polished wood floor as Case beat a path to his room. Finding Rogers leaning against the bureau, Case balanced himself and kicked the door shut.

"You'd better sit down," Rogers said. "You look a little pale."

Case fell onto the chair at his desk. "You'd look damned pale, too, if you'd been fed enough laudanum to down a buffalo."

"Laudanum? I thought you'd had a relapse."

"Our dear Miss North told you that?"

A hint of color crept up Rogers's neck. "When I came to get you this morning, she said you weren't up to driving a wagon."

"She should know. She drugged me."

His color deepening, Rogers said defensively, "I didn't take her word. I came up here and saw for myself."

Case drummed his fingers on a spot free of papers on his desk. "And? What else did Rayne say?"

"Only that you wanted her to drive the wagon in your place."

Pounding a fist on the wood, Case muttered under his breath. His voice sounding more like a growl, he demanded, "Do you think I'm an idiot or just an unfeeling jackass? Did you really believe I'd send a woman, my own partner's daughter, into such danger?"

"Well, not at first, but Miss North was very convincing." He moved away from the bureau. "Eventually she told me it had been her idea to go in your place. She was right, you know. You have her to thank that everything worked out."

"Tell me you didn't actually allow Rayne to drive the wagon!"

"I handled the team. She just rode with me."

"Christ!"

So much for his suspicion that Rayne was a southern spy, Case thought. But the little fool was too brave for her own good. The idea of her riding the wagon through a perilous mountain pass made his stomach churn. If she had been injured or killed, he never would have forgiven himself.

God, he hadn't realized the true depth of his

feelings until now. The troublesome minx had wormed her way into his heart, and there wasn't a damned thing he could do about it.

"I want to know exactly what happened from start to finish," Case said, his tone deceptively calm. "Beginning with why you agreed to this asinine scheme."

Rogers cleared his throat. "I *agreed* because the idea of a lady decked out in her finest dress riding a wagon sounded real smart to me. I was a bit dubious, but as it turned out, I was right to play along with her. In the end, she proved that. Even the lowest of men respect a lady and will hesitate to shoot at one."

"It was devil's luck and you damn well know it!"

"Maybe. Maybe not. You gotta admit she looks real fine in that crimson dress. She was a sight, her cheeks all pink with excitement. No one would have thought we were carrying gold."

Case grunted, his mouth pinching into a grimace. He didn't need Rogers to tell him how ravishing Rayne looked.

"She was scared out of her wits, but she didn't show it. Don't think anyone but me realized she was shaking like a leaf. That's one brave little lady."

Despite his anger, Case felt a genuine pride for Rayne's courage. "I ought to break your goddamn neck, and hers, too."

"You could try. I wouldn't recommend taking me on until you're done healing. You know I can be trusted. I delivered your woman back safe and sound. You can thank me by doubling my pay."

"I'm already paying you too damn much," Case

retorted, a muscle ticking in his cheek. "I'll thank you by not breaking your blasted neck."

A smirk played over Rogers's mouth as he retrieved the shotgun. He settled it firmly under his arm while he searched Case's face.

A paralyzing thought entered Case's mind. "What if someone recognized her?"

"Give me some credit O'Malley. I took care of that."

"How?"

"I had her pull that bonnet of hers down over her brow. I also made her wait to be picked up a safe distance from the mine. She was just a lady out for a ride. No one recognized her as Jasper's daughter. I'd bet my life on it."

Feeling a vein throb in his neck, and his face mottle with rage, Case balled his hands into tight fists. "If I find out you're wrong, I'm going to personally see that you die a slow, agonizing death, Rogers."

"I don't know why you're so riled. Things went just like you planned. The southerners went after the other wagon. I'd like to have been there to see their faces when they found out they only got rock."

"Was anyone hurt?"

"The guards did just like you said and surrendered without a fight."

"Thank God for that at least," Case said tersely.

"You better make up your mind what you're going to do about Miss North since she's on to your work for the Union. She's clouding your thinking. Marry her and cart her off someplace safe, or else make sure no one suspects how much she means to you. Someone might get the idea of using her to get to you."

Case's forehead creased with worry. Rogers needn't have bothered to tell him what he already knew. He'd tried to keep some distance from Rayne, but it had been impossible to hide his desire for her. Still, he doubted she guessed how deep into his soul she had burrowed.

Rayne knew from the start he wasn't the marrying kind. He'd made it absolutely clear. But he also knew Rayne hoped he'd change his mind. It was in her eyes every time he kissed her. She was the sort who'd risk everything for the man she loved, and now, because of him, her life might be in the same danger that he confronted daily.

What the hell am I going to do now?

"Guess I'll be leaving," Rogers said, "unless you got another job."

Case stared at him, needing a moment to adjust his thoughts. "There is one more thing you can take care of for me. Double pay, if you're interested."

"Double pay, huh?"

"Last night a man paid me a social call, only it wasn't so social. I want you to find him. He should be easy to spot." Case rubbed his sore knuckles. "Just look for anyone sporting bruises and a very large lump on his head." Grinning, he added, "He might even have gone away with a few teeth marks."

"You bit him?"

"I had a little help from Miss North. She also hit him over the head with the chamber pot."

"Miss North is a handy woman to have at your back." Rogers headed for the door. "I'll see what I can find out. I admit, I'm looking forward to meeting this luckless fellow. Any other orders?"

"Tell Miss North I want a word with her."

Rogers grinned. With a mock salute, he disappeared into the hall.

It wasn't quite five minutes before Case heard Rayne coming up the stairs. Considering her eventful night and morning, and her reluctance to face him, he'd prepared himself for a longer wait.

She entered his room and locked the door behind her. Case remembered Rogers's words. She did look *real fine*. More than fine. The burgundy color brought out lights in her hazel eyes and complemented her fair skin. The full skirt accentuated her tiny waist, the petticoats beneath rustling when she moved. The sensual sound brought erotic images to his mind. His groin tightened.

Damn. Rogers had been right about that, too. Rayne did more than cloud his thinking—she possessed his mind and body whenever she came near him. At that moment he didn't know whether he wanted to strangle her or kiss her.

"Did you want to speak with me?" she asked, folding her hands primly at her waist.

She didn't look one bit sorry for her actions, Case thought grimly. In fact, she appeared triumphant as her eyes met his.

"I trust you enjoyed your *outing* with Rogers?"

"It went very well, as I'm sure he must have told you."

"He told me a lot of things. Now I'd like to hear your version. I'm especially interested in knowing why an obviously intelligent woman would behave with such foolish disregard for her own wellbeing!"

"Rogers didn't think I was foolish," she countered in a silky smooth tone. "Indeed, he praised my courage."

"Rogers is a jackass. And if he cared one iota for your safety, he would never have allowed you on that wagon."

"I hardly think you need to resort to foul language," Rayne reprimanded softly, eyes downcast.

"You are the most exasperating, infuriating female I've ever met! And for your information, Rogers is a gunslinger who hires out for the right price. The only reason he's still alive is because he's faster, smarter, and more experienced than anyone he's come up against." Case narrowed his eyes, pinning her with a lethal look. "He is not, however, qualified to judge a person's courage. Courage does not merely consist of blindly facing overwhelming odds. Luck was on your side, and luck can be a very fickle partner."

Rayne lifted her chin indignantly. "I took a calculated risk, and I had Rogers beside me. What's more, if it meant saving you from certain death, I'd do it again."

"What?"

"I said, I'd do it again." She stared off, past him, her eyes growing moist. "I owe you an apology for putting laudanum in the brandy, but I'm not sorry for trying to protect you. You are still too weak to be putting yourself in that kind of danger, no matter how noble the cause."

Both touched and angered by her speech, Case rose to his feet. "You'll be the death of me yet. What you did was—"

"Oh, please don't say any more," she cried as she ran toward him and threw her arms around his neck. "I knew you'd be angry, and you are, but you're also safe. Going in your place may not have been one of my wiser decisions, but I did it for you."

His arms went around her, binding her against his chest. He buried his face in her hair. Breathing in its heavenly scent, he felt his resolve weaken. She felt so right in his arms, soft and warm. He stroked her hair, murmuring, "Promise me you won't meddle in my affairs again."

"I can't." She leaned back and gazed up at his face. She touched his jaw and winced. "You have a bruise where that man hit you."

"I'm sure he has a few also."

"I don't care about him, only you."

"Then give me your promise."

She shook her head. "I can't."

"I thought you might be a southern spy, you know."

Rayne laughed, amusement sparkling in her eyes. "Me? A spy?"

"Until I spoke with Rogers." He pulled her close against him again, needing her warmth, hating himself for wanting her so much and for his inability to make her see reason. "I want your promise, Rayne. I'll have it before you leave this room. You don't know how stubborn I can be."

She rested her cheek on his chest, sighing. "I do know how stubborn you are, Case, but I can't make that promise, at least not until you do the same."

"You ask the impossible. I committed myself long before I met you, and I can't back out now. Helping the Union is a cause I strongly believe in, Rayne. Ask me to give up anything else."

Her arms went around his middle, hugging him so tightly, he found it difficult to breathe. Or maybe it was her nearness that choked off his supply of air.

"I've become fond of your flaws. Can't you accept mine?" she said.

"I won't be mollycoddled by a woman," he stated flatly, irritated. Her will was as unyielding as his own, yet somehow he had to make her understand. "You will not interfere in my work again, and that's not a request. It's an order. This isn't a game I'm playing. Lives hang in the balance. Yours will not be one of them!"

Case felt Rayne stiffen. He wasn't saying it right. "You mean more to me than anyone. Can you understand that? Someone could have recognized you! Now, I'll either have your promise, or I'll take matters into my own hands. One way or the other, I'll see you safely out of harm's way."

Rayne stood perfectly still. Gripping her arms, he held her away from him. "If I have to bind and gag you each time a shipment goes out, I will. And if you think my conscience will trouble me, rest assured, it won't."

"Did you really mean what you said before?"

"Which part didn't you understand?"

She gazed up at him. "The part about me meaning more to you than anyone."

"Of course I meant it. I love you, dammit."

A misty look came into her eyes, and he cursed his loose tongue. He knew what that look meant, what she wanted him to say next.

Marry me.

It was the one thing he wasn't prepared to say, especially while his commitment to the Union placed his life in danger. Besides, it was up to him to protect *her*, and he couldn't protect her if anyone knew how much she meant to him. Rogers had been right about that too.

Brushing his lips across hers, he spoke in a whisper against her mouth. "No lady in her right mind would hook up with a no-good scoundrel like me."

She placed her hands on his cheeks and kissed him. "I have a weakness for this particular scoundrel."

"Rayne," he said, determined to make his point before the heat building in his body overrode his determination, "I feel obligated to speak bluntly."

She pressed her soft curves against him, while her tongue danced wickedly, sensuously, over his neck. The tightening in his groin became painful as desire and longing lanced through him.

"I have . . . no . . . intention of marr— of forgetting . . . you owe me a promise."

Although he had gotten out the words, they hadn't sounded as sincere as he intended. Rational thought escaped him, his wayward body responding to her wiles. Her mouth slipped from his throat to his chin, then upward. His skin felt scorched, as if he were trapped fifteen hundred feet down in the steaming core of a mine tunnel.

He swept her into his arms. "I'm glad you locked the door." Dismissing the pain in his leg, he headed toward the bed. "I'm just unprincipled enough to take everything you have to give and offer nothing in return. I'll have your promise if I have to make love to you all day and night."

Unceremoniously he tossed her onto the center of the mattress. He relished her gasp of amazement, and the attractive sight of her skirts riding up to reveal shapely legs. His gaze never left hers as he divested himself of his shirt and began unbuttoning his trousers.

Through love-clouded eyes, she propped herself on her elbows to watch his hands, her silent perusal increasing his passion.

It was her words, however, that left him trembling.

"You're very sure of yourself, sir, to claim victory before you've even begun an assault."

He grinned wickedly. Allowing his trousers to drop, he fell forward and pinned her to his bed. "I have a most persuasive weapon, my dear."

Chapter 19

It was nearly noon before Rayne completed her ablutions the following morning. Try as she might, she couldn't summon up much energy. Small wonder, she thought. Thanks to Case, she hadn't gotten much sleep.

His most persuasive weapon indeed, she mused, remembering his final words before he'd loved her to distraction. The man's entire body should be termed a weapon. She had surrendered unconditionally, promising not to interfere in his undercover work, or to speak of it to anyone, particularly her father. Also, she must remember not to wear the burgundy dress in public ever again. Case's list of orders seemed endless, but she loved the way he gave them.

It had been so hard to leave the warm haven of Case's arms, especially after he'd confessed his feelings. She would have given her promise anyway. She'd give anything to prevent further risk to him.

Case O'Malley loved her.

Rayne hugged herself, savoring the happiness that surged in her heart. She gazed longingly at the connecting door, tempted to return to his room and entice him into repeating the splendor they'd shared only hours earlier. But it would be a foolish risk. Their involvement must be kept a secret in case she was identified as the woman who rode the wagon. Thank goodness they hadn't encountered anyone, but Rogers had taken special pains to protect her. At the time she hadn't cared about the danger to herself, only that Case was safe.

When Rayne finally left her room, she heard muttering down the hall. She went to investigate and found Jasper struggling with his tie.

"Let me fix it for you, Papa."

"Damn thing wants to bunch up," Jasper grumbled.

After she'd fashioned a respectable-looking knot, Rayne stared with exasperation at his drab brown coat. No one would ever accuse her father of dressing flamboyantly, she thought affectionately. Smoothing her hands over the rumpled lapels, she buttoned the coat high on his chest, as was the style.

Jasper patted Rayne's hand. "You're a good girl to fuss over me. I know I'm a disappointment to you."

"You need guidance, that's all."

He looked at her solemnly. "Sometimes a body hasn't got it in him to change."

"If Case can mend his wicked ways, you can, too."

Jasper arched a shaggy, gray brow. "So . . . you think you have Case wearing a halo? Don't be fooled, honey. Case is a good friend, and I think the world of him, but he's not about to turn suddenly into a monk."

A slow, pleased smile touched Rayne's lips. "I

certainly hope not. He wouldn't be the man I . . . I know him to be."

Jasper grasped Rayne's hand and squeezed it gently. "You haven't gone and fallen in love with Case, have you?"

A faint flush tinted her cheeks as she remembered the first time she saw Case standing across the street in Carson City. He'd looked so dashing with his hat cocked at a rakish angle, the diamond pin flashing in the sun. He'd put every other man in town to shame. Then he'd smiled and walked toward her . . .

Seeing no reason to lie to her father, she said, "It took a while to discover the good things about him, but I guess I always knew that deep inside, he wasn't what he first seemed."

Jasper released Rayne's hand. "Does he know?"

"Yes," she said shyly, unsure of her father's reaction to the startling news.

"Has he made you an offer?"

Rayne dropped her gaze, regretting her impulsive confession. She hadn't expected her father to quiz her so thoroughly, though his concern pleased her after the many years of neglect. "Case hasn't proposed marriage, if that's what you mean. He does love me, though. He said so."

Jasper shook his head, his shoulders hunched. "He won't propose. Case ain't the sort to settle down. Why, most of the women he's . . . he's acquainted with would sell their souls to be the one to tame him. Of course Case cares some for you. It's only natural, seeing as how you took such good care of him, but don't hope for more."

Rayne lifted her chin. "I know all about his past. So long as he's faithful to me, it doesn't matter."

"Rayne, honey, Case has a roving eye, and a way with women. He told me himself he likes his life the way it is. You probably took something he said the wrong way."

The sympathy she read in his eyes brought a wave of doubt spiraling through her. If anyone knew Case, her father did. She fought her uncertainty. Jasper didn't know Case as intimately as she did.

"He said he loves me, and I believe him. He also swore he wouldn't see other women. If I've learned nothing else about Case O'Malley, I know he wouldn't go back on his word."

"You're right about that. Case's word is as good as gold. I just never figured on this happening. Case hasn't shown any interest in decent women before."

Case kept secrets from Jasper, Rayne thought, which could account for part of her father's reluctance to believe Case truly loved her.

Jasper regarded her with burning intensity. "He hasn't—"

"Papa . . . please!"

Thank heavens she'd cut him off before he'd managed to ask her *that* fateful question.

Jasper's features hardened for a moment, then softened again.

His mind was easy enough to read, Rayne thought. For a moment, a very brief moment, he'd entertained the notion of demanding Case declare his intentions. Thank goodness he'd decided against it.

She crossed over to the bureau and, with comb in hand, slicked down her father's hair and teased his mustache into curls on the ends. "You mustn't trouble yourself on my account. I have all the patience in the world. In time, Case will do the right thing. He's never let *you* down, has he?"

Jasper gave Rayne a relieved smile. "I've always been able to depend on Case."

Her arm looped through his, she walked with him out the door. "Well, then, the matter's settled."

Rayne saw her father off to work, then she whiled away time writing a letter to her mother. Later, ignoring Hung Lee's chiding look, she set about dusting the contents of the front room. She heard the Chinaman admit visitors but paid them no mind. Case's steady stream of business associates and friends had become a commonplace occurrence. Besides, if a gentleman brought along another niece, she preferred not to know about it.

When dinnertime arrived, she found she'd worked up quite an appetite. The thought of eating alone, however, held no appeal. Glancing up at the dining room ceiling, she wondered when, if ever, Case's guests would leave. Judging by Hung Lee's behavior, he, too, thought the guests had overstayed their welcome. For the third time, he shuffled from the dining room in his slipper shoes, his pigtail swinging behind him. Folding his arms on his stomach, he tucked his hands into the large sleeves of his outer garment and listened intently at the bottom of the stairs before he shuffled back to her side.

Rayne laid her napkin on the table and rose. "Perhaps if I go up, they will take the hint. What do you think, Mr. Lee?"

The Chinaman bent low in a bow. "Missy North one smart cookie."

"I'll ring Mr. O'Malley's bell to let you know if I'm successful." She hid a grin. "You may bring my meal as well."

Hung Lee smiled widely. *Merciful heavens*, Rayne thought as she hurried into the hall. Until this minute she'd forgotten Hung Lee had seen Case kiss her. She must remember to tell Case. She doubted the Chinaman would mention the incident to anyone, but they must guard against the possibility.

She halted at the top of the stairs. Case had taken to leaving his door open during the day, but it was closed now. Could he be discussing his undercover work for the Union? Or, worse, planning another dangerous shipment of gold?

Rayne pressed her hand over her stomach, seeking to stem her rising fear. Now that he'd made her promise not to interfere, he wouldn't hesitate to endanger his own life. Well, she hadn't come to meddle in his business. Her mission was innocent, merely to inform him his dinner was ready.

Abruptly she opened the door and swept into the room. Three startled pairs of eyes flew to her face, but only Case's narrowed as her mouth dropped open.

Oh, how could he?

Propped against two pillows, Case reclined on his bed with his two companions, Bessie and Annie, cuddled against him. He had an arm around each of them. Bessie's hand rested on his chest, while Annie's lay suggestively high on his thigh.

Case, whom she might have expected to be embarrassed, grinned. "Why, Miss North, to what do we owe this pleasant interruption?"

Rayne managed a smile. "I hate to disturb you,

but Hung Lee has your dinner waiting." She whirled around intending to flee.

"One moment, Miss North."

Rayne didn't know why she obeyed his demand, but she did. She faced him reluctantly.

"Ladies, thank you for coming. It has been an enjoyable afternoon," he told Bessie and Annie.

He gently prodded the women from his bed and, an arm still possessively around each of them, limped with them to the door. He said his farewells quickly and sent the women on their way with a kiss to each of their cheeks.

Remembering her manners, Rayne stepped into the hall and called, "You'll both come another day, won't you?"

"Sure, honey," hollered Bessie. "We can't let Case get lonely now, can we?"

Case pulled Rayne back into his room. "I know what you're thinking, Rayne, but you're dead wrong."

She slipped out of his hands and skittered away. "Don't touch me."

He reached for her again and nearly lost his balance.

"Keep putting weight on your leg, Case, and you'll end up crippled for life."

"I don't give a damn about my leg." His lips thinned with annoyance. "Am I going to have to explain my every word and deed from now on?"

Rayne glanced at the bed, then back to Case. "What I saw when I came in was—"

"What you saw was a friendly visit."

Rayne crossed her arms over her chest, releasing an exasperated sigh.

"I'm not normally in the habit of defending myself, Rayne, as you should have discovered when you thought I'd cheated Jasper."

She had hoped that awful incident had been buried and forgotten long ago. She had been dreadfully wrong about Case then, but romping in bed with two women was an entirely different matter.

He limped the few steps toward her. "I'm going to make an exception this one time." Tipping up her chin with a finger, he studied her face for a long, tension-filled moment. "It's important for everyone to think I haven't changed. Once Bessie and Annie spread word around town how they spent the afternoon, no one will possibly suspect there's anything between you and me."

"I understand completely," Rayne said, her tone clipped despite her best intention to sound sincere. The vision of Case with the two women continued to flash across her mind, causing an ache in her heart. "I suppose next you'll expect me to believe you hated every minute of it."

He gave her a rueful grin. "You'd never believe me if I said I did."

"Oh! How can you act as if nothing happened when I saw—"

In a lightning-fast movement, he dragged her against him. "My patience is wearing thin, Rayne."

She pushed against his chest but found his hold too hard to break. Despite her anger, heat sprang to life in her traitorous body. Delicious shivers rippled down her spine. He was an unconscionable rogue, but she still wanted him.

Muttering a curse, he held her away and pinned her with his steadfast gaze. "I admit I enjoyed myself for a while. You would, too, if you'd been holed up in this room as long as I have. But let me point out a few things to you. One, Bessie and Annie are an excellent source of the hottest gossip in town. Two, they are still my friends. Three, conversation was all I wanted or got from them."

"Case, I—"

"I haven't finished," he snapped. "Since you're forcing me to explain something you should already understand, you'll hear me out. Nothing happened, Rayne. In fact, the last two hours were pure hell. In case you haven't noticed, Hung Lee has not brought my dinner. I was expecting you hours ago. You certainly took your own sweet time before you barged into my room. I couldn't very well come right out and ask them to leave without hurting their feelings, could I?"

"I'm sorry, Case. I should have trusted you."

"Yes, you should have, especially since I was dying to do this the entire time."

He pulled her against him and she went willingly. His arms encircled her with the strength of steel, and his mouth ravaged her lips. When he finally broke off his kiss, she was breathless and warm all over.

"Ring for Hung Lee," she said, a noticeable quiver in her voice.

Placing hot kisses under her ear and down her neck, he groaned. "I could be persuaded to make a meal of *you*."

A tremor shook her as she went limp in his arms. In a deep, low voice, he said, "But right now I have need of nourishment to sustain me. Tonight I intend to convince you that I want no other woman in my bed."

He kissed her thoroughly. Blood sang through her veins, and the room swam around her. He needed no persuasion, after all; true to his words, he was devouring her, creating a hunger so keen, she knew where it would take them.

Breaking away, she heaved a breath. "Hung Lee."

He gave her a puzzled look. "What about him?"

It was a moment before her mind functioned enough to say, "He saw you kiss me the other day. I thought you should know."

He grinned and stroked a finger over her cheek. "You were right to tell me, but there's no need for concern. I pay him enough to guarantee his silence."

He leaned forward, but she laid her fingers over his mouth. "No more, please, not right now. Hung Lee's waiting for me to ring so he can bring up our dinners."

"You're right, of course. We shouldn't press our luck." He crossed the room, gave the rope a hard tug, and fell onto his chair. "I think our illustrious Chinaman deserves to be excused early tonight."

"You're so generous, sir."

"You will see exactly how generous in a very short while."

Paul Devereau called the following afternoon. Rayne was startled to see him. She hadn't spared him a moment's thought, which she considered extremely rude in view of his kindness to her. But things were different now.

She liked Paul, though his presence presented a quandary for which she had no answer. It wasn't fair to lead him on, yet she couldn't tell him she loved Case. Having no other choice, she asked him to stay for tea. She entertained him in the front room, hoping all the while Case wouldn't find out about her caller, which wasn't impossible since Case had a steady stream of his own visitors including Kat.

"Are you feeling well?" Paul asked.

Embarrassed that her attention had once again wandered, Rayne flushed. "I beg your pardon?"

"You seem distracted. Please tell me if this is an inconvenient time for you."

"You are very perceptive, Paul," Rayne replied, relieved to be given an excuse to cut short his visit. "I am feeling a bit tired today. Perhaps another time?"

Devereau waited until she stood before he came to his feet. He reached for his hat. "You have only to send me word."

There was no way to let him down without hurting his feelings. "I shall look forward to seeing you soon."

She saw him out, then breathed a sigh of relief. Paul was a problem that, sooner or later, she'd have to deal with. Unfortunately, she lacked experience in handling suitors and hadn't the slightest idea what to say to him. She couldn't very well tell Paul she shared Case O'Malley's bed. If only her mother were here to advise her.

She tried to dismiss Case from her mind. There were other problems she needed to attend to, like her laundry. She could never accept the idea of a man handling her unmentionables, and had refused to allow Hung Lee to do her washing. She supposed it was silly of her to refuse his services, but she had always done for herself in the past.

Deciding the chore would help occupy her, she headed upstairs to collect her things.

Rayne paused on the landing and smiled when she noticed that Case's door stood open. She took a step toward her room. She had no intention of eavesdropping on Case's private dealings again. Yet despite her best intentions, their conversation drifted into the hall.

God, he hated to see a woman cry.

Sitting beside Kat on his bed, Case dug in the pocket of his pants and fished out his handkerchief. He pressed it into her hand and waited while she dabbed at her eyes. He had never seen her like this before. What could have happened to throw Kat into such a state of despair? He'd known her for a long time and always thought her able to handle anything life threw her way. It must be something terrible for Kat to carry on so.

"Wipe your nose and tell me what's wrong," he said gruffly, wishing she'd quit crying. He'd rather face ten gunslingers than one woman with tears in her eyes. "Otherwise, I can't help you."

"Jack said I'd have to leave. You know how he is, Case, strutting around like he's somethin' special when everyone knows all he owns is a whorehouse."

"That can't be all of it, Kat. I've never seen you so torn up." Putting his arm around her shoulders, he gave her a gentle squeeze. "What's the real reason? You wouldn't have come to me if you didn't think I could help, so spit it out."

Kat balled Case's handkerchief in her hand, her knuckles white with strain. "You're the only one I *can* turn to, Case, the only one who'd understand and tell me what to do."

He leaned forward and cupped her chin. Her normally beautiful blue eyes were now red and puffy from crying. "I can fix just about anything, but even I haven't developed the ability to read minds."

Giving him a faint smile, she sniffed.

"Well? Nothing's that bad. Just say it. I guarantee you'll feel better."

A bitter laugh escaped her before she sniffed again and swiped at her eyes. "All right, Case. I'm having a baby. Think you can fix that?"

His hands fell away from her as though he'd been burned. He didn't know what he expected, but a baby hadn't entered his mind. Women like Kat knew how to prevent such things, or so he'd been led to believe. His eyes widened. Why had she come to him?

Gripping her shoulders, he turned her to face him. "Is it mine?"

"No," she whispered softly.

Case hadn't realized he had been holding his breath until it burst from his lungs. "Are you sure?"

"I'm very sure, Case." She hung her head, fresh tears slipping down her cheeks. Her voice was a barely audible whisper as she admitted, "I wish it were yours."

Guilt washed over him. He had been thinking only of himself and what a baby would have done to his life, instead of considering Kat. She needed him, had no one else to turn to. He couldn't let her down. He wrapped his arms around her and drew her against his chest. "Everything will be fine. Leave it to me."

She clutched at his shirt, sobbing freely now.

"There, Kat. It may be a blessing in disguise, you know, a way to change your life for the better."

"How?"

"Well, you told me once you'd always been alone, never had any family. Now you will. You'll have someone to love. Someone who'll love you in return."

She glanced up at him, a ray of hope sparkling in her eyes before her features settled into a mask of despair. "The whole town knows what I am, Case. What kind of life do I have to give a kid? He'll be the bastard son of a whore."

He gave her a gentle shake. "No, he won't. He'll be the son of a very loving mother. You're going to leave Virginia City and head east to a small town where no one knows you or your past. With a ring on your finger and a convincing story of the gallant soldier who gave his life fighting for the North, you'll be the poor grieving widow."

"Who'd believe it?"

"Who wouldn't? Make up a name and stick to it."

"How will I live? I've kept a little, but not enough to last long." She dropped her gaze and stared at his shirt. "I don't know nothing but whoring, Case."

"You'll have plenty of money to live on. I'll see to it."

"You're too good to me, Case. You always were, but I can't let you do that."

"Nonsense. What else am I going to do with all

the wealth I've gained from the mine? If I can't help a friend in need, I wouldn't be worth much, would I?"

Case left the bed, went to his desk, and scribbled out directions on a piece of paper. "Take this to Harvey at the bank. He'll see that you have enough to get you out of town. Wire me when you decide where you want to live. I'll set up an account for you and the baby. It's the least I can do after all the good times we shared."

Kat wept profusely, hiccuping loudly.

Case returned to her side and shoved the paper into her hand. "If Harvey gives you any trouble, let me know and I'll go myself. Kat? Could you stop crying now? Nothing drives me crazier than a teary-eyed woman."

Kat burst out laughing and had to hiccup again. "You're the best, Case. You know I'll never be able to repay you?"

"There's no need. Just let me know from time to time how you and the kid are doing. Maybe it'll be a boy. You'd like that, wouldn't you?"

"Yeah. I never thought I'd get the chance to have a baby of my own." She held his hand to her cheek. "I can't thank you enough for all you're doin' for me. I always knew I could count on you. You were never like all them others, wantin' a good time but never givin' a hoot about any of the girls."

Case wiggled his hand free, embarrassed by her display of gratitude. He wasn't helping her in order to gain praise. Immensely uncomfortable, he said, "Hell." He lifted her to her feet. "You run along now. And whatever you do, don't let it get out why you've leaving town. As far as anyone else is concerned, you're tired of Virginia City and need a change. Don't say where you're going, either."

"I won't say anything, Case."

"Good. Things *will* work out for the best, Kat. Trust me."

Standing on her toes, Kat took Case by surprise. Circling his neck with her hands, she pulled him down and kissed him. Knowing it might be the last time he saw her, he crushed her against him. When she released him, he saw that a spark of contentment had replaced the sadness in her eyes.

"I'm gonna miss you," she said. "Sure you don't wanna come along? Marry me, maybe?"

"Me? It's not in my nature to settle down. You're better off without another burden. You know a man like me could never be happy tied to one woman."

She gave him a playful slap and moved away. "Of that, I'm sure. You'll never be anything but a rogue, but you're a good-hearted one."

Laughing, Case circled his arm around her waist to escort her out. "Don't forget to let me know how you and the baby make out, now. Promise? You know I—" The rest of Case's words died in his throat.

Rayne stood in the doorway, as pale as a ghost.

Chapter 20

❦

She held herself as rigid as one of the timbers in his mine, but it was the deathly pale cast of Rayne's skin that drew Case's attention. He thought she was ill until he met her gaze. The hazel eyes that normally looked at him with devotion or passion now held pain.

Kat left him, walking past Rayne into the hall.

Rayne remained as if bolted to the floor. A moment passed, then two. The sound of Kat's steps faded away. The front door closed, leaving the house silent. Too silent. At that moment Case knew how it would feel to be locked in a tomb.

Case leaned against the bedpost. "You were listening at my door again, weren't you, Rayne?"

"Not intentionally."

He gave her a puzzled look. "Something's bothering you. What is it?"

"I know I'm not sophisticated like your other women."

Case shoved his fingers through his hair. "Other women? Exactly how many females are in this *harem* you think I have?"

Her lips pressed together into a line.

Case muttered a curse. "I don't imagine you'd

believe me if I said I was merely helping a friend?"

"If you said so, I'd believe you. What kind of help?"

Case withdrew a cigar from his pocket and slowly, deliberately, lit it. Through a cloud of smoke, he looked at Rayne.

"I heard some of your conversation, but not all," she murmured, blinking back tears.

Case stepped toward her and, before she could prevent him, he put a hand beneath her chin and tilted her head up. "You could trust me just a little, you know."

"I want to. I do."

Case clamped his mouth shut and watched her take a deep, unsteady breath. She bit her bottom lip before she said softly, "Why did you kiss her?"

"Ah, I understand now. I was saying good-bye. Kat's leaving town and I might not ever see her again."

"Oh. Case, Kat's baby isn't . . . ?"

Their gazes met and held before Case strode to the window and looked out.

"It isn't, is it? For a moment I thought—"

"It's all right. Considering the life I've led, it was a natural conclusion. I thought the same thing until Kat said someone else is the father."

"Case, I swore to myself that I wouldn't press you, but I feel I must. We can't go on this way."

Case lifted a brow. An uneasy feeling settled in his gut. He turned slowly to face her.

"I can't continue to live in the same house with you, as your paramour."

"And?"

"Heavens, this is the hardest thing I've ever had to say."

"Well, don't say it then."

"I have to." She twisted her fingers together. "I need to know if you ... what your intentions are. Am I to be just a casual dalliance, or is there to be something more between us?"

"Such as marriage?"

"Yes."

"I suppose if I don't marry you, you'll move out of my— your father's house?"

She gave a horrified gasp. He had caught himself before he'd said *my house*, but he knew she'd made the connection. *Damn.* He wanted to walk the few steps and take her into his arms, but he held himself back.

"I should have guessed the truth myself," she said. "The furnishings give you away." She paused a moment, her head lowering. "I guess I just wanted to believe you and Papa hadn't lied to me."

"Don't hold it against Jasper. He only wanted to impress you and put you up in style."

"I know."

"Rayne, sweetheart, I never lied to you. I'm just not ready to be tied down. Maybe when the war is over I'll see things differently."

"Yes, you told me." She lifted her head and stared at him. "Silly me, I thought I could change your mind. I hoped you'd come to love me so much that you wouldn't be able to live without me."

Frustrated, Case stubbed out his cigar. "I do love you, very much. It's not your fault. It's something in me. I don't have a high opinion of marriage, for one thing. My parents were miserable. My mother always harped at my father because she felt he wasn't a good enough provider. When he wouldn't give her the satisfaction of fighting back, she shifted her wrath to me. I stood it as long as I could, then I left. I was fourteen."

"I'm sorry, Case, but I'm not her."

"No, you're nothing like her. You're sweet and loving, and you wouldn't care if I didn't have a dime."

"You don't want to give up your freedom. Is that why, Case?"

"I thought you understood, that I made myself perfectly clear."

Rayne sucked in an unsteady breath. "You did. It's my fault entirely. I thought I could live however you wanted, if only I had you. But . . . but I can't."

"Someone will come for my things," he said. "I'll move back to the hotel tonight."

Her shoulders tensed. "How will it look if you move out of your own home?" She walked toward her room, her shoulders drooping. "It's only right that I be the one to leave."

"Like hell you will. It isn't safe for you anywhere else."

She hesitated at the door. "Please don't try to stop me, Case. And please, don't hold my decision against my father. Will you continue to let him live here? I won't worry about him if I know he has you to look after him."

"Of course Jasper can stay. Rayne, I don't want you to leave. Why don't you wait awhile longer? We can talk about it. You know I can be persuasive. Give me an opportunity to bring you around to my way of thinking."

She laughed, but it came out a sorrowful sound. "If I don't leave now, that's exactly what *will* happen."

He stepped forward, intending to take her in his arms, to make her see how foolish she was behaving. But she held up a hand, stopping him.

"No, I can't allow you to touch me. I won't let you seduce me all over again, Case."

"A kiss good-bye is harmless enough."

"Devastation is a more apt description."

Case stared at the ceiling for a moment, his heart heavy, searching for a way to convince Rayne. When he looked back, she was gone.

Rayne thought the pain would grow easier with time, but after two weeks, she was still devastated. Case had warned her, and she hadn't listened. She had given him her love of her own free will, but she hadn't known it would hurt this much; as if her heart had withered to the size of a pea.

She had tried to turn him into the sort of man she wanted, but she'd failed. After a week of missing him, she had nearly given in and gone back. Then she'd seen him riding in a carriage on C Street. Luckily, he hadn't noticed her, but that was understandable. He had been too interested in the woman at his side, a woman Rayne had never seen before.

If only she could stop thinking of him.

She should have gone home to her mother, but she couldn't bring herself to leave the Nevada Territory. At least here she was near Case, and she'd come to like Virginia City. It was exciting, brimming with life. If she couldn't have Case, at least she could discover her independence instead.

Mr. Pokinghorn had kindly honored his word and given her a position in his office, weighing ore and distributing coin. She had found gainful employment and a respectable place of residence, a room at the International Hotel.

Now, though, she wished she hadn't persuaded her father to remain in Case's house. She missed him. He had tried to deceive her about the house, but for her own benefit. She had gambled on Case and lost, but she knew Case would take care of her father.

Paul Devereau had proved a godsend. Whenever able, he acted as her protector, even escorting her to and from work. He treated her with respect, asking for nothing except friendship in return. That suited Rayne just fine. If she couldn't have Case O'Malley, she wanted no romantic involvement in her life.

She pinned on her hat, tucked her reticule under her arm, and left her hotel room. It was her day off. She vowed she wouldn't waste it by pining over Case.

When she stepped outside, she noticed a marked decline in the number of vehicles on the main thoroughfare. An exceptionally strong gust of wind tore down the street. Chills raced up her legs. Due to Virginia City's high altitude, sudden blasts of air were commonplace.

She glanced down Union Street, past the slag heaps of the mines and the multitude of stacks that spewed smoke into the sky. Beyond was a spectacular view of mountains surrounded by desert and the barrier of the snowy Sierras.

She strolled down the sidewalk, past the Virginia City bank, the hotels, gambling palaces, and Fuller's meat market. In front of the Klapstock and Harris store, a portly man wrapped in a buffalo robe tipped his hat. She found him a strange sight with his brown checkered pantaloons stuffed into scuffed boots, gray whiskers trailing to his waist, and a revolver slung from his belt.

She smiled and moved on, but her smile died when she glanced into the window of Miller's Drug Emporium and saw the reflection of a man in a long-tailed black frock coat. Only one person she knew dressed in such a manner. Only one man she knew wore his hat tilted at a rakish angle. Rayne lowered her eyes, pretending interest in the large gold-mounted decanters of red, blue, and green on display in the window.

She waited three long, torturous minutes, expecting at any second to feel a hand on her shoulder. When nothing happened, she risked another look. Her shoulders sagged in defeat. Not only had Case remained in the same spot, he met her gaze in the glass. *Merciful heavens. Is there no escaping the man?*

Case O'Malley could just stand there forever. One look into his sensuous green eyes and she knew she'd lose her last shred of self-control.

And he only wanted her to warm his bed.

She still loved him, wanted him, needed him. She could so easily agree to anything just to be with him. Oh, dear God, how could she even conceive of such a thought? Truly she was her mother's daughter—doomed to a life of misery because she loved the wrong man.

The wind came again, blowing out of the west.

Stronger now, the gust swept down the street, shaking windows and rattling doors. It plucked her hat from her head and whisked it out of sight. Rayne refused to move. Not for anything as inconsequential as a hat would she brave a confrontation with Case O'Malley. She immediately regretted her decision. This was no ordinary wind, and the rising intensity of the storm frightened her.

The violent blasts were unlike any force of nature she'd ever encountered. A horse screamed and reared up, catapulting a wagon and throwing the driver a startling five feet into the air. Then the street vanished in an immense, swirling dust cloud. She heard an ominous creaking, like metal being ripped through wood. A board was sucked off the front wall of the store she stood in front of and hurtled through the air until it slammed into a nearby post.

Within seconds, the striped awning above Rayne groaned, ripped, and thumped to the walk, missing her by inches. End over end, it somersaulted down the street. The large cask that had stood beside the awning post toppled and rolled toward Rayne's legs. Her heart hammered as breath rushed from her lungs.

She whirled away, smack into the fury of the blustering squall. The merciless wind bore her down the walk with such impetus, she felt as if she were being driven by a locomotive.

Suddenly, strong arms clamped around her waist and scooped her up. She grabbed on to Case O'Malley. Burying her face against his shoulder, she grasped his coat, clinging to him in desperation.

"Washoe zephyr," he shouted above the din. "We have to get off the street."

Rayne didn't care what crazy name they gave this mighty wind that had roared up so swiftly. She hoped she never encountered it again. Even Case's sturdy frame was no match for the vicious Washoe zephyr. He staggered several times before he managed to travel two feet.

The pins were snatched from Rayne's hair. Strands whipped around her face. Remarkably, her reticule remained tucked under her arm. Case wrenched away the bag and jammed it between their bodies. Her skirts flapped wildly. Putting the brunt of the wind at his back, Case forced his way across the remaining sidewalk. At the exact second that a huge section of severed tin roofing soared toward them, he threw his weight against a door. The wood splintered under the brutal impact, but the hinges surrendered first. The floor came up to meet them.

Case's body acted like a cushion as they fell into the building. Rayne lay sideways across him. Hearing a low curse, she started to rise, but he slipped one arm free and stayed her by gripping her shoulder.

"Don't . . . move . . . yet."

Rayne twisted slightly and saw the pain etched on his face. "Are you hurt?"

"Not sure." He grunted as he wiggled his other arm from under her legs. "Your hip is . . . Whatever you do, don't press down any harder when you get up."

His meaning registered immediately. Her hip was located directly over a very private area . . . and they weren't alone. She glanced up and saw the proprietor of the store rush from behind a long counter, his hands raised. A loud roar came from outside. Startled, Rayne followed the man's distraught gaze to the large front window.

"Stay back, Hingle," Case ordered as he forced Rayne's head against his chest and used his arms to shield her.

The sound of shattering glass preceded a boom so horrendous that the floor rocked. Rayne began to shake uncontrollably. Shards of glass rained over her and Case. Icy fingers of fear skipped up her spine. She was afraid to see the results of the crash, afraid she'd find Case cut, bleeding, or even dead. Slowly, cautiously, she lifted her head and heard a tinkling sound.

She sucked in a horrified gasp. Splinters covered Case's face, some sticking from his hair. "Don't open your eyes," she said.

With shaky hands she picked the larger slivers off of him and pitched them to the side. She heard Hingle mumble under his breath as he scurried away. When he returned, he carried a broom and a soft rag. He handed her the rag, mumbling all the while, and proceeded to sweep clean the area around them.

It was tedious work, but Rayne didn't care. She didn't even care that she pricked her fingers many times and blood tricked from small cuts. She thought only of Case. She prayed the smudges of red on his handsome face came from her, not from injuries of his own. When no more large pieces of glass remained, she gently brushed the rag over his skin, until she was satisfied she'd removed all but minute shavings.

"Hold still," she told him. "I'll be done in just a

second." She took a deep breath and blew small puffs of air over his face. "Try opening your eyes now."

Case's lids gradually slit open and Rayne smiled with relief. She'd always admired the color of Case's eyes, but somehow they glittered a deeper shade of green than she remembered.

"Zephyr's done gone," remarked Hingle. "I'll fetch Doc Connell if you want. That hand looks mighty bad."

"It's nothing," Rayne said.

"I think he means mine," Case said. Gingerly he raised his arms and held them out. "I'd appreciate it, Mr. Hingle, if you'd help Miss North. Be careful. I imagine she has plenty of glass in her hair."

Hingle stepped forward. Rayne gratefully accepted his assistance, permitting him to pull her to her feet. Just as Case had figured, splinters of all shapes and sizes showered over his legs and the floor as she rose. She shivered when she thought of what could have happened to either of them. Hearing a strange noise behind her, she looked back and noticed Case gritting his teeth. Her eyes widened in dismay when she saw the jagged cut on the back of his hand.

"You ... Why didn't ... Oh!" She gestured for Hingle to go around Case. "We'll lift you before we send for the doctor."

A look of stubborn defiance settling on his face, Case managed to sit without assistance. "I don't need any doctor. There are probably worse injuries he should be tending to."

"At least let us help you up," Rayne said.

Although he allowed Rayne and Mr. Hingle to help him up, Case scowled with annoyance. He glared down at his injury, and wrapped his hand-kerchief over the wound. "All I need is something to use for a bandage, and whiskey if you have it." He aimed a mocking smile at Rayne. "Purely medicinal, of course."

Memories flooded back, both pleasurable and painful, Case's rejection the most painful of all. Her lips trembled as she retreated a step. For the first time she noticed the fragrant tobacco smell of the store. Out of the corner of her eye she saw the wooden Indian she'd admired earlier, now lying on its side through the window it had smashed. Amazingly, the sun was shining outside. The door stood at an angle, dangling from one hinge. Beyond that, the section of tin roof lay in the exact spot where she had stood earlier.

Case had saved her life.

If he hadn't picked her up and protected her, the roofing would have struck her. If his body hadn't shielded her, she'd probably have been badly cut by glass. Her gaze shifted to his face. Devilment danced in his eyes. He knew she'd just realized what he'd done. Then his mouth lifted in a sardonic smile. Warmth spread through her.

Mr. Hingle's return was a welcome relief. Rayne took the liquor bottle, strips of cloth, and a cigar box from him, and moved close to Case. "I wish you'd let us summon Dr. Connell," she said with a catch in her voice.

Case took the bottle from her and extended his hand.

Hingle stared at the crimson handkerchief and walked unsteadily to the back of the store.

Case rolled his eyes. "You can wrap it for me."

"I have no medical training. I think you need a few stitches."

"Don't go squeamish on me now, Rayne."

"I'm not squeamish. I'm afraid you'll bleed to death. I wouldn't know where to begin."

Amazing her, he barely winced as he uncovered his hand and doused the wound with whiskey. She knew pride kept him from showing his discomfort. As much as she wanted to hate him for not wanting her, a tender feeling washed over her. More than anything, she yearned to soothe away his hurt, to show him how much she admired his bravery in saving her during the Washoe zephyr.

"I believe you were right," he said with a sour expression. "It needs a few stitches." His expression slid into a cynical grin. "You're the perfect choice for this job. Who else would take such pleasure in sticking me with a pointed object."

Lifting open the lid of the cigar box, Rayne fished through the assortment of sewing materials. She settled on a small but exceedingly sharp needle. "Indeed, Mr. O'Malley. I should like nothing better."

He lifted a brow. "I believe you would."

His probing gaze made Rayne uncomfortable. Her fingers shook as she forced thread through the tiny hole in the needle and laid the sewing implements on a nearby chair. She left briefly to seek out Mr. Hingle's washroom and returned to find Case considering the cigars displayed behind the glass case.

An unbearable ache throbbed in her heart. Even with smudges of blood and dirt on his face, his hair mussed and falling over his brow, he had never looked more handsome to her. He was bleeding all over poor Mr. Hingle's counter, but he seemed more interested in selecting a cigar than in stanching the flow. Giving herself a shake, she grabbed part of the bandage material and pressed it against his wound.

"Finally," he said. "I was beginning to think you'd decided to take a bath." He tilted his head and slowly, insolently, raked his eyes over her. "I regret that's one pleasure you never allowed me to do for you. I guarantee you would have enjoyed having me soap every inch of your luscious body. Then I would have joined you, sat you on my lap, and buried myself so deep inside you . . . Well, I'm sure you can visualize the rest."

On wobbly legs she retrieved needle and thread and, forcing the heated image from her thoughts, prepared to tend to his injury. She would not allow him to paint intimate portraits of them together in the hope of coaxing her back to his bed.

He stood very close, his hot breath fanning her neck, both dismaying and thrilling her. Silently praying she wouldn't hurt him, she uncovered his hand and cleaned the area around the wound. She had to force herself to concentrate on the task. Touching him, even in a remedial way, brought out her feelings of tenderness for him, reminding her of the weeks of care she'd given him. More than anything she wished she could go back in time. Perhaps if she hadn't asked him that fateful question about whether he would ever marry her, she'd still be able to hope.

More foolishness, she told herself. She had no choice but to accept reality.

She closed the cut swiftly with four precise stitches. It was a pity she couldn't mend herself as easily, she mused, but it would take more than a thread and needle to repair the rent in her heart.

Surveying her handiwork, Case grunted his approval. "Fine work, Rayne. Now, if you'll wrap it with the same efficient haste, I'll see you home and be about my business. I'm late for an important appointment."

Jarred by his cold words, Rayne fumbled with the strips of cloth. She trembled as she wound the material around his hand and tied off the ends. As she cleaned up the counter, she replied, "You needn't concern yourself on my account. I am perfectly capable of seeing myself home."

"As you wish." He withdrew a fine leather pouch from inside his coat and left a stack of shiny fifty-dollar gold pieces on the display case. "Tell Hingle I'm sorry I made a shambles of his door."

Rayne's eyes widened in response to Case's generosity. "That's entirely too much for a mere door."

"I wouldn't want it said that Case O'Malley doesn't pay for his blunders, be they intentional or not."

Before she could react, he caught her wrist and surveyed the tiny cuts on her fingers. Leisurely, he pressed his lips to her upturned palm. Rayne's breath hissed through her lips, her knees buckling from the familiar contact.

After a cursory glance at the back room, he inclined his head and whispered, "One of these nights, I'm going to prove to you we belong together."

Chapter 21

"**W**hat have you found out?" Case skidded his chair closer to the table and refilled his companion's glass. "Good news, I hope. I've had one hell of a day so far."

"I think you'll be pleased. I have more than you wanted."

Case surveyed the interior of the seedy saloon he'd chosen as a meeting place. Satisfied that they were alone and unnoticeable in the dim corner, he returned his attention to his contact. No one would take Tom Randolph for anything other than a down-and-out prospector. With his bristly beard and mop of woolly brown hair, he looked more like a tumbleweed than a seasoned Union spy.

"The gold is safe in the Union Treasury in Sacramento," Randolph said. "Thanks to your plan, we caught Virginia City's Confederate ringleader."

Case grinned. "Where is he now?"

"Suffice it to say, he's safely tucked away until this bloody conflict ends." After a furtive glance around, Randolph lowered his voice. "Word is, he's already been replaced."

"Who?" Case demanded.

"I'm getting to that, but first I wanted to congratulate you on getting out the last shipment.

Brilliant plan of yours, dressing that soiled dove up like a lady and sending her with the guard. Those sympathizers played right into our hands. You oughta get a medal."

Case gripped his glass in a choking hold. "It wasn't a pretense. She *is* a lady. And for your information, it wasn't *my* idea to send her, so they can keep their blasted medal. What else do you know?"

Randolph leaned forward. "The woman you've been seen round town with is connected to the new ringleader."

To protect Rayne, he'd made it a point to be seen with several women recently. "Which one?"

"Hair like wheat. Generously endowed."

"Cecile Bowman," Case said, nodding. "I thought she was a might inquisitive."

"She's a beauty, but watch your back." Randolph grinned lewdly. "Or should I suggest you guard your most prized possession?"

Case drummed his fingers on the scarred table. "Thanks for the advice, but I know how to handle Cecile. How else do you think I've gotten so close to her in such a short time?"

"Damn if you don't get the fun jobs, O'Malley."

Case's lips thinned with annoyance at the man's comment. "That's all it is, Randolph. A job."

"This Bowman woman is rumored to be a real wildcat between the sheets. We suspect she's managed to drain quite a few secrets from her fortunate victims. Make sure you don't get too involved with her."

"Believe me, I'm in no danger. Women like her no longer interest me."

"Since when?"

Unbidden, Rayne's image invaded his thoughts. He downed the whiskey in his glass, in an attempt to push Jasper's bewitching daughter from his mind. "I'll handle Cecile," he snapped. "You just do your part. Who's this ringleader friend of hers?"

"Fellow named Devereau."

"*Paul* Devereau?"

Randolph nodded. "We did some checking on him, like you asked a while back. Not only was he *in* Sacramento, but he was there at the exact moment an attempt was made to waylay the Overland Stage on its trip east. That alone puts him under suspicion. Do you think he's their new man?"

"He could very well be." Case mulled over the information for several minutes. "Miss Bowman may prove useful. I'll feed her word of a shipment going out a week from today, and we'll see what happens. You take care of the rest. If we're lucky, maybe we can capture the whole bunch."

They came to their feet and shook hands. "You know," Randolph said, "if this works out, it could put an end to the southerners' cause, at least here. The city has always been mostly pro-Union, and the number of sympathizers has already dwindled."

"My thoughts exactly."

Case waited until Randolph left the saloon, then he slipped out the rear door. His mood dipped. He'd grown tired of this kind of life. Drinking, gambling, even his women friends, had lost their appeal. He set a brisk pace home, anxious to get the evening over with. A twinge of pain in his hand brought his thoughts back to Rayne. She'd played hell with his mind for the last two weeks. His patience was nearly exhausted.

Remembering how she'd painstakingly removed the splinters of glass from his face, and the gentle way she'd tended his hand, he smiled. Rayne still cared about him. God, but he missed her. Perhaps a little friendly persuasion was in order.

He frowned. First, another chore awaited him, one not nearly so agreeable.

Attired in an expertly tailored black evening suit, Case strolled from a restaurant on C Street with Cecile Bowman cleaving to his arm. The three hours he'd spent plying her with the finest champagne and food had been tedious, but he anticipated a profitable return. A tipsy woman should prove easy to manipulate, or so he hoped. He'd never tried to outsmart a female Confederate spy before.

"Case, darlin', where are you takin' me?"

Her perfume overpowered him as she leaned against his shoulder, gazing up at him with naked desire in her blue eyes. Her bountiful breasts swelled from the precipitous neckline of a ravishing red silk gown. She was a beauty, all right, blatantly forward and seductive as hell.

He smiled down at her. "To your room. Does that meet with your approval?"

"I thought you'd never ask."

He steered her past a group of men milling on a corner. "I haven't asked you anything yet. What makes you think I will?"

Cecile's lips parted in surprise. "I've heard all about you, darlin', so don't play coy with me."

Case's mouth twisted into a wry grin. "What have you heard?"

Tugging on his lapel, she pulled him closer and whispered a ribald description of his anatomy.

Case arched a brow, his lips twitching with amusement. "A gross exaggeration, I assure you."

Cecile giggled, drawing attention from a group of people passing by.

A matronly woman stared openly at them. Case touched the brim of his hat, winked, and watched her turn beet red. Cecile tightened her grip and laid her head against his arm with a provocative sigh. Case quickened his pace, disturbed by the stares they were receiving. His reaction surprised even himself. It should be Rayne clinging to his arm, Rayne looking up at him with invitation, Rayne—

Damn.

It *was* Rayne. She stood directly in front of him, blocking his path, her hand pressed over her mouth. She seemed as shocked as he was by their accidental, untimely meeting. She regarded him warmly at first, her gaze roaming over his face as if she meant to memorize every feature. The world around him evaporated, and only they existed. He wanted to crush her in an embrace and kiss her senseless, make love to her until she surrendered not just her body, but her very being. But, of course, he couldn't do any such thing.

A sharp tug on his sleeve broke the spell.

"Darlin', I'm gettin' restless."

Case ignored Cecile and faced Rayne. "Good evening, Miss North."

Hurt glittered in Rayne's eyes, but she lifted her chin to a challenging angle. "Good evening, Mr.

O'Malley." She glanced for a second at Cecile, then pulled her skirt close to her side and swept past him.

Furious with Rayne, angry at himself, and annoyed with Cecile, Case walked on, dragging the woman at his side with him. He waited until he was a safe distance away before he looked over his shoulder and saw Rayne meet Paul Devereau. Cold rage raced through his veins.

Jasper had mentioned that Rayne had been seeing Devereau, but Case hadn't considered it a cause for worry. Until this moment. Until he'd seen them together, he'd trusted her judgment. Rayne wasn't the sort to jump into another man's bed. After what Randolph had told him, though, he could no longer allow Rayne to associate with Devereau. There was no telling what devious scheme the man had in mind, possibly wooing Rayne to get at Jasper's wealth.

His own circumstances would change after tomorrow, Case recklessly decided. And he didn't give a damn if what he planned put his life in greater danger.

It was late when Case returned home. Rogers waited at the end of the sidewalk.

"I found your man."

"Took you long enough," Case said.

"He was laying low," Rogers replied with a laugh. "I didn't know you packed such a wallop, O'Malley. You broke his damn jaw."

"Pity it wasn't his neck."

"Well, at least you made certain he'd keep his mouth shut."

"But I presume you found the means to persuade him to talk."

"I have ways. He was hired by a tall man with light brown hair and a mustache, with polished manners. You were right. The orders were to murder you in your sleep."

Rogers's words startled Case. There weren't many well-mannered men around Virginia City who fit that description, but he knew one. He hadn't thought Devereau would go so far. He considered the implications for a moment. If Devereau's man had succeeded . . .

"Contact me tomorrow and I'll see you get paid. I might have another job for you in a week, so keep in touch."

The clock chimed twice as Case stepped inside the house. He slammed the door so hard behind him, several objects rattled on the adjacent wall. He didn't care if they all broke. The past hours had been sheer torture, even if everything had gone according to plan. Catching a whiff of perfume off his coat, he scowled. He smelled like a French whore!

Thanks to the time he'd spent with Cecile Bowman, he knew how it felt to be mauled by a she-cat in heat. Nevertheless, her tempestuous enthusiasm had worked to his advantage in more ways than one. With her head fuzzy from drink, she'd had to concentrate all her efforts on seducing him. He had resisted, at least until she had boldly shoved her hand over the front of his pants. By that point, it hadn't mattered. He had already slipped her enough information to bait the trap. The whole episode left him with a sour taste in his mouth.

He climbed the stairs and spotted Jasper standing in his doorway, scratching his head. The old man wore a knee-length nightshirt, and his hair stuck out. Noticing his partner's spindly legs and ghostly white feet, Case forgot his irritation and grinned.

"I heard the door bang," Jasper said.

"Everything's all right. Go back to sleep."

Case went into his room and lit the lamp, Jasper trailing behind him. "I thought I told you to go to bed."

Wrinkling his nose, Jasper yawned. "What's that stink?"

Case sighed in exasperation. "Me, you fool."

A strange expression passed over Jasper's face before he asked, "You seein' women again, Case?"

Case stiffened and met the older man's eyes without flinching. "No, dammit!"

Jasper seemed to shrink inside his nightshirt, stabbing Case with guilt. He shouldn't have spoken so harshly. In a more amicable tone, he said, "Sorry."

"That's all right, Case."

"I shouldn't blame you. My reputation speaks for itself."

Jasper toddled across the room but stopped in the doorway. "Maybe Rayne would come back if *you* asked her. She won't listen to me."

His eyes darkening, Case tore off his coat and tossed it on the bed. "If I thought it would be that easy, I would have already asked her."

Jasper coughed. "You could propose. The way you've been actin' lately ... well, maybe it's time you settled down."

"Mind your own business."

"Rayne *is* my business. I didn't want to say this, Case, but I don't like how you've treated my girl. I trusted you not to hurt her." Jasper backed up a step when Case glared at him. "I know I have no place lecturing you after the way I treated Rayne and Mary, but I know that, like me, you'll live to regret your actions."

Case's gaze softened.

"A good woman is hard to find, specially one who can love a man like you and me," Jasper went on. "But I won't say anything more. I've got no right."

"You've got every right. Go back to bed and don't worry. Things will work out."

Jasper's words disturbed Case. He had warned Rayne, and she'd decided on her own to become involved with him. He felt a twinge of guilt. He could not deny that he *had* used all his charm on an inexperienced woman. *Damn.* He didn't need this. He had enough to worry about at present.

Case decided he needed to warn Rayne to stay away from Devereau, but he didn't want to frighten her. He threw open a drawer, and the diamond necklace he'd given her sparkled brilliantly, reminding him of the way her eyes glittered when he kissed or touched her. His reaction to the memory was swift and violent, a rush of blood to every nerve in his body, leaving him aroused and aching.

Muttering a curse, he stalked to the wardrobe and seized a fresh coat.

Rayne pushed aside the window curtain and stared at the full moon. She felt lost. She had come to Virginia City with such high hopes, only to find herself alone and desolate. A tear slipped down her cheek as she remembered the anguish she'd suffered when she'd seen Case earlier.

She had been so happy to see him that for an instant she hadn't noticed the woman clinging to him, a woman even more beautiful than Kat. Every time she dared hope he might change his mind and propose, fate threw her into his path—a path teeming with voluptuous females!

His good looks and flirtatious manner may have drawn her to him initially, but it was the wonderful traits she'd discovered in him, his compassion, his generosity, his tenderness, that made her love him. If women didn't flock to him like flies to honey, maybe she'd stand a chance.

She must put him out of her mind, try to get some sleep, she decided. She enjoyed her work at the assay office, and she didn't want to jeopardize it by showing up looking as if she'd spent the night shedding tears over a man. Fresh remorse coursed through her. No matter how hard she tried to deny the truth, it returned to torment her.

She loved Case O'Malley, loved him so deeply, she couldn't stop thinking about him, or wanting him, or—

She heard a click, then another. She froze, biting her bottom lip so hard, she tasted blood. Listening intently, shivering uncontrollably, she heard heavy breathing. When a floorboard creaked, her heart lunged to her throat. Reflexively she whipped around and collided with the large, rock-hard body of a man. She parted her lips to scream, but a hand clamped over her mouth.

"Be still, Rayne. It's me, Case."

Relieved, and angry, she pounded her fists on

his chest. The second he removed his hand from her mouth, she sank her teeth into the tender area between his thumb and index finger. He released her and let out a string of foul oaths. She lit a lamp and as she set the glass top back on the base, she shot her intruder a scathing look. "You terrified me! What do you mean by sneaking into my room?"

"I thought you'd be asleep." He gazed at her with devilment in his green eyes. "Had you *been* sleeping, it wouldn't have been necessary to grab you."

Rayne planted her hands on her hips. "Case O'Malley, you have some nerve. How dare you creep in here in the middle of the night after spending the evening with that woman? And don't deny it, either. You reek of her scent."

Case sniffed his shirt. "Damn. I thought only my coat stunk."

The pulse at the base of Rayne's throat beat wildly. "You think you can shed your women like you shed your coat?"

"I've never groveled before a woman before, and I don't intend to start now."

"No one asked you to grovel, Case."

"Like hell you haven't." A cynical smile played over his mouth. "I don't want you to see Devereau again."

Her chin came up. "I will see whomever I please. You most certainly do."

He tore off his coat and threw it on a chair. His tie followed. "That's precisely what I thought you'd say."

Seeing the lustful gleam in his eyes, Rayne

inched backward. "What do you think you're doing?"

"What does it look like?"

Anger burgeoned into blistering fury. "How did you get into my room? Are you an expert at breaking locks, too?"

His hand dipped into the pocket of his pants. Grinning smugly, he held up a key. "This is my room."

"It is not!"

Slowly, his eyes roaming over her, he opened the buttons on his shirt. Rayne's breath caught in her throat. Inch by seductive inch, his chest came into view.

"I personally arranged for you to have this room. I never gave it up. I have a habit of holding on to things, especially if there's a chance I may need them again."

"Why, you pompous, arrogant ... scoundrel! I suppose you regard me as one of the *things* you may fall back on if the mood strikes you?"

In a tone laced with sarcasm, he said, "I'd hoped this time apart had made you see reason."

She couldn't speak. She couldn't even breathe. Not while his hands moved to the waist of his trousers. Fire raced through her veins, pooling low in her belly. Against her will, the sight of him shedding his pants threw her emotions into turmoil. He stood naked before her, unabashed, resplendent.

She had seen Case without clothes before, but not on his feet, completely, utterly aroused. Her entire body burned, and she realized her hand shook. He was magnificent, his chest, his shoul-

ders, his arms, every aspect of him a tribute to the
God who had created him.

"You have no shame," she said weakly, embarrassed by her own rising desire.

He grinned. "None whatsoever."

He strode toward her, smoldering passion in his
gaze. He had never looked at her like this, like an
untamed, unconquerable animal stalking his prey.
The heat in her body flamed out of control. She
closed her eyes, hoping to regain her senses. But it
was no use. She hadn't the power to fight him, or
the love she bore him. He touched her cheek,
brushed his fingers down her neck.

"You're trembling," he said. "You want me as
much as I want you. Tell me."

She shook her head, praying her denial would
make it so. Startled by a ripping sound, she
snapped her eyes open. Case's fingers tore at her
nightgown. "Stop it!" she cried, slapping at his
hands.

"I'll buy you another. Hell, I'll buy you a dozen.
I never liked this thing anyway." He paused to admire his handiwork, adding in a husky whisper, "I
prefer you as you are."

She stepped back and bumped into the bed. "I
won't allow you to do this. You can't just take any
woman you want. I have feelings. I'm not one of
your precious cigars. You can't pluck me from a
display case and light me at your whim!"

Unperturbed by her speech, he closed the distance between them in one long stride. "Can I still
light a flame in you, Rayne?"

No power on earth could save her. God help
her, even if escape were possible, she wouldn't
want it. Knowing he was unconscionable, still she

loved him. Knowing she was his only when he chose, still she wanted him. Knowing her pain would be even greater tomorrow, still she longed for his touch.

Chapter 22

"I swore I wouldn't do this," Case murmured, pulling Rayne into his arms, "but it's time to stop playing games. You belong to me, Rayne."

Her breath caught in her throat. The rational part of her mind told her to protest, but his lips grazed her neck, settling under her ear while his fingers tangled in her hair, and she forgot everything. A delightful shiver skipped along her spine. He felt so warm and solid against her, she had to force herself not to press tighter to him.

Holding her head, he covered her lips. He plundered her senses, his tongue snaking inside her mouth and mating with it in a fiery dance that put flame to her insides. Time ceased to exist as he ravaged her lips. The only thing she wanted in the whole world was to surrender to him.

Case lifted his head, inhaling deeply. "Feel what you do to me, Rayne." He caught her wrist and drew it down between their bodies.

Rayne gasped when he held her hand over him, guiding it back and forth over his silky, throbbing length. Instinct told her what he wanted. Cradling his manhood in her fingers, she explored, teased, and stroked him until, with a tortured moan, he began to explore her body. Rayne bit her tongue to keep from crying out when his palms skimmed over her thighs, hips, and sides, leaving her skin tingling. He caressed her breasts while he buried his face against her shoulder and placed a searing kiss there. Her pulse pounded, her mind reeled, her whole being aching for more of his touches.

"For two long weeks I've dreamt of this moment," he said, his voice a harsh rasp.

He eased her gently onto the bed and lowered his body over hers. Feeling him hot and rigid between her thighs, Rayne closed her eyes and flung her arms around his shoulders. Nothing mattered, nothing but Case. She didn't care what tomorrow might bring. She didn't care about the other women in his life. She loved him and he was with her, and that was all that mattered to her at this moment.

"Do you still doubt my feelings, Rayne? I'll prove how much I love you. Only you."

She didn't want to listen. Unwilling to hope again for something she couldn't have, she remained silent.

He shifted slightly and bore down with his hips. A bolt of fire tore through her, igniting her desire. She moaned softly, hooked her legs over his, and rose up against him.

His mouth swooped over hers and his kiss burned with savage intensity. Suddenly he pulled back. "Too fast," he whispered as he slid lower. "I want to love you slowly, all night if that's what it takes."

She wasn't paying attention to his words. It was the husky sound of his voice that intoxicated her. His hands traced a sensual path over her hips and thighs, his mouth teasing her nipples into taut nubs. Blood pounded through her veins. She squirmed beneath him, driven by the fiery sensations exploding through her. She clutched at his shoulders, wanting more, wanting all of him inside her.

Instead, his lips grazed down along her middle, pausing in their sensual advance to scorch a path across her stomach. A tumultuous tremor rocked Rayne. She quivered as he trailed kisses down the inside of one thigh, then up the inside of the other. She could no longer bear the exquisite agony. A low, tortured moan escaped her.

She felt his fiery breath at the juncture of her legs. Realizing his intent, suddenly turning shy, she reached for him. "No, please."

He laughed softly and placed featherlight kisses all the way to her neck. His mouth brushed hers, his fingers stroking her thighs before they eased inside her. She gasped and dug her nails into his shoulders, quivering as her desire burst into a blazing inferno. Slipping his hands under her bottom, he lifted her slightly.

Rayne didn't think; she reacted. She rubbed against his hardness, felt a tremor pass through him, and knew he'd been restraining himself. Taking matters into her own hands, she gripped his backside and arched up against him.

"Dammit, Rayne, I wanted to go slow ..."

His words trailed away as he entered her and began to move, vigorous at first, then subsiding into a gentle, pulse-pounding rhythm that drove her wild. She writhed beneath him, contracting her muscles. With a groan, he lifted her hips higher and plunged deep and hard, shattering her

senses in a blazing climax. Rayne's breath lodged
in her lungs as wave after glorious wave of ecstasy
washed over her.

He ceased moving, but she felt his heart beating
furiously in his chest, and his rigid length hard inside her still. She opened her eyes and found him
watching her. She couldn't decipher his emotions
as tiny creases formed at the corners of his eyes
and his lips curved into a lopsided grin.

It must be sinful to love a man as much as she
loved Case, she thought. She plowed her fingers
through his hair and gazed at him with all her
love. He gritted his teeth for an instant, shutting
his eyes. He lunged three times, climaxed explo-
sively inside her, then collapsed on her chest.

Relishing the feel of his body, she wished secretly that they would never leave this bed. Her
arms around his neck, she savored the moment,
the heat and strength of his body flattened against
hers, the erotic feel of the hair on his heaving chest
teasing her tender breasts.

He leaned to the side, startling her.

"Don't go," she begged.

He brushed his lips across hers and rolled off
the bed. "I won't. I'm just going to put out the
lamp."

He returned and, pulling the covers over them
both, nestled beside her.

"Case, I—"

"I didn't come to talk."

"Why did you come?"

"Because I couldn't stay away."

Rayne lay awake long after she heard his steady,
even breathing. Finally she, too, fell into a deep
sleep, only to be awakened by sweet kisses and

gentle touches. He made love to her again, this time with such excruciating tenderness that tears welled in her eyes.

Afterwards they lay spent in each other's embrace. "You need me, Rayne, as much as I need you. Come home with me, and we'll forget all this nonsense."

She pulled away. "Is that what you think? It's not nonsense, Case, to want to be your wife instead of your paramour."

"You're much more than that." His lips grazed her neck. "You're the only woman I've ever loved."

She stiffened. "I thought you'd had a change of heart, but nothing's changed."

He pulled away. "Dammit, Rayne, I never made any promises."

"I know you didn't. It's just that . . . Case, I can't let this happen again."

She heard him mutter under his breath.

"You can stay until morning, but you're not welcome here again." She took a deep breath, hoping her pain didn't slip into her voice. "Promise me you'll honor my wishes."

The bed dipped. She heard the rustle of clothes as he dressed. Tears welled in her eyes as she tried to still the temptation to tell him she'd accept him on any terms.

He stood over her, his heavy breathing sounding angry, then abruptly he bent low and kissed her thoroughly, his mouth slanting over hers in a last attempt to change her mind. It almost killed her to keep her arms at her sides instead of wrapping them around his neck.

His lips slid to her ear. "The only promise I'll

make is not to give up until you realize you belong with me."

He left, closing the door quietly behind him.

Clutching the pillow he'd lain on, Rayne cursed the weakness she felt when she was near Case. He had been trying to show her with his body how deeply he loved her. No man, not even a skilled womanizer like Case O'Malley, could make such tender love to a woman unless he cared.

So why didn't he want to marry her?

She came to a decision then. Somehow she would just have to convince him he couldn't bear to live without her.

The following day a large package was delivered to Rayne's door. Inside she found a dozen exquisite nightgowns in various shades. The last was of a sheer black, diaphanous material, trimmed with delicate lace. A note was pinned to the neckline. Her fingers trembled as she unfolded it and read the handwritten lines.

I prefer the black. Think of me when you wear it, and remember that I never break a promise.

Your Devoted Scoundrel

Devoted scoundrel, indeed!

Hugging the sheer nightgown to her chest, she grinned. Devil was more like it. He had said anything was to be had in Virginia City, but she hadn't guessed even Case O'Malley could procure intimate apparel on such short notice. But considering his many women friends, she realized that it probably wasn't that difficult for him.

* * *

On her way to work several mornings later, Rayne ran into Samuel Clemens, the harried reporter for Virginia City's *Territorial Enterprise*, who escorted her across the congested main thoroughfare. She liked Clemens; his friendly manner perked up her mood. They conversed for several minutes before Rayne gathered enough courage to ask the question foremost on her mind.

"I hear Mr. O'Malley has fully recovered from his accident. Have you seen him lately?"

Walking with her to the door of the assayer's office, Clemens responded, "It would hardly be an exaggeration to say the entire town has taken note of his prodigious reformation."

Rayne could barely believe her ears. "He's changed?"

"I must say, he has me wondrously fascinated. He's changed from a hard-drinking rogue into a distinguished, respectable citizen."

Surely it couldn't be true, Rayne mused. She wondered what had motivated Case to do such a thing. Had she played a part in his reformation?

After saying good-bye to Mr. Clemens, Rayne entered the assayer's office. Paul Devereau was waiting inside. They exchanged greetings, and she drew him aside. Calling upon every ounce of her courage, she gently told him she could no longer see him.

His mouth thinned into a tight line before he said tersely, "I suppose O'Malley has had something to do with your decision. He's been against me from the beginning. Be warned, Miss North. He changes women more often than his clothes!"

Stunned by Devereau's sudden attack, Rayne

watched him stalk out the door. She had meant to let him down without hurting him. His quick surge of temper and impetuous departure left her feeling uneasy. With a heavy heart, she began her morning's work. When she chanced to glance up from her weighing device, Case stood just inside the door, staring at her.

Rayne's throat constricted. If appearances gave a true indication of a person's character, Clemens had been right. Case's whole demeanor seemed different, as well as his attire. His dark gray coat and trousers were of the finest cut, and his stylish hat sat square on his head, not tilted at its usual rakish angle. Instead of his customary bright, patterned red waistcoat, he now wore somber gray. She searched for the diamond cluster pin and found it absent, too. Flamboyant Case O'Malley now resembled a prosperous, distinguished gentleman.

Unless it was a guise.

As her first customer collected his coin and left, Rayne couldn't tear her gaze away from Case. His cynical expression confused and troubled her. *Had he seen Paul leave just now?* She lowered her eyes.

She heard him cross the room and knew he stood in front of the half-barred counter.

"I see you've taken on an assistant, Jeb," Case said. "Judging by the quiet, orderly line I saw when I came in, you were wise to hire a lady. This particular lady is *very* competent in anything she undertakes. You would do well to raise her salary."

"Miss North has worked out splendidly, indeed," Jebediah Pokinghorn stated. "I'll consider your suggestion."

Embarrassed, Rayne excused herself and disappeared into the back room, where she braced her back against a wall. Her distress didn't stem entirely from their praise. Sensual memories from last night assaulted her as she recalled Case's heated gaze raking over her. When she returned to her desk, to her relief and sorrow, she discovered Case had left.

The next day dawned crisp and clear. Case hoped it was a good omen. After a visit to the sheriff's office, he joined Rogers and a posse of twenty men at the base of a canyon near Gold Hill, where they had arranged to intercept the shipment of gold Case had sent out several hours earlier. The southerners should have had enough time to steal the wagon by now. Clamping a cigar between his teeth, Case settled his gun belt more comfortably on his hips.

Rogers looked at him, raising an eyebrow.

Case ignored him. Just because he chose not to wear a sidearm around town didn't mean he wasn't a crack shot. He had never seen any reason to publicly announce his proficiency.

The sheriff motioned with his arm. The men assumed their places on either side of the canyon, behind huge piles of rock. The minutes stretched endlessly, grating on Case's nerves. He wanted this job over and done with. He was almost convinced something had gone wrong when he heard the wagon approaching. He spit out his cigar and crouched behind the nearest rock. Beside him, Rogers propped a rifle on a flat ledge; Case followed suit with his own Colt .44.

Within minutes, the clamor of thundering

horses' hooves and wagon wheels scraping the hard-packed trail grew unbearably loud. Eight masked men charged at breakneck speed through the rough opening of the canyon, ahead of the wagon. When the robbers reached the midway point, the sheriff gave a shrill whistle. The trap was set.

Surprised and outnumbered, the southern sympathizers put up only a token resistance before they surrendered. Case didn't wait for an invitation. After a brief perusal of the scene in front of him, he vaulted from behind the rock and dragged one of the masked riders from his horse. He snatched off the mask and stepped back with a wry grin.

"Well, well," Case said as he relieved Paul Devereau of his weapons. "We've caught a prize worth more than gold."

Coming up beside him, Rogers used the end of his rifle to poke Devereau in the belly. "Take a look in his saddlebags, boss. I think this Confederate ain't as loyal to the South as he wants them to believe." He cocked an eyebrow at Case. "Thought you were sending out rock instead of ore, though. What happened?"

"I had a change of heart at the last moment." Lifting the leather flap, he peeked inside the saddlebags and grinned when he saw it bulged with gold bullion. He turned to their captive. "You'll have a lot of explaining to do, Devereau, when they get you to Sacramento. The Union doesn't take kindly to having its gold stolen for personal causes."

"By all rights, you should be dead, O'Malley,"

Devereau shot back. "If you hadn't gotten in my way, I would've had it all."

Case grabbed Devereau's shirt and yanked him close. "Sorry to disappoint you, but your plan to murder me failed. I'm very much alive. There's one thing you can tell me, though. You were only using Rayne to get to Jasper's money, weren't you?"

Devereau jerked himself free and aimed Case a murderous glare. "I would've succeeded, too, if you'd kept out of it. If that idiot I hired hadn't failed, I would've married the naive little bitch and been a rich man. But as God is my witness, I'll get even one day, O'Malley."

Very slowly, Case took a cigar from his pocket. Narrowing his eyes on Devereau, he scraped a match on his pants and lit the Havana. He blew a cloud of smoke into the man's face, his voice deceptively calm. "You have just insulted the woman I love. That was your final mistake."

Case pulled back his fist and cracked it against Devereau's jaw.

Several deputies rushed forward, dragged the unconscious Devereau from the ground, and took him and his accomplices away. Case plucked another cigar from his breast pocket and handed it to Rogers.

"We made a good haul," Rogers said as he bit off the end. "You sure pack a wallop, O'Malley. If you hadn't done that, though, I would've had to do it for you."

"Thanks, but I don't need you to defend Rayne's honor."

"If you love her so damn much, why don't you marry her and be done with it?"

"I don't recall asking for your goddamn opinion."

"You didn't," Rogers said as he held a match under the cigar. "There's no charge for my advice. Anyone can see she's got you hooked."

Case stewed in silence. He couldn't argue with the truth.

"You got any more jobs for me?"

Case grinned. "Only one, but you'll have to collect your pay from the government. Find the woman named Cecile Bowman and turn her in. I think we can prove now that she's a very crafty Confederate spy. The Union probably wants her bad enough to make it worth your while. Play your cards right and she might make you a very lucrative counteroffer."

"Thanks for the tip. Say, you don't think Devereau would really try to get even?"

"We've seen the last of him around these parts. The bars of his jail cell will most likely rust before he sees the light of day again." Idly Case watched Rogers stuff his shotgun in the sheath on his saddle. "He's got you worried, does he?"

The gunslinger tensed, then swung around. "You're the only man with enough guts to make such an asinine insinuation. You're damn lucky I like you."

Case smiled. "Or what? You'd gun me down?"

Shaking his head, Rogers swung up onto his horse. "Hell, no. Who else would keep me supplied with decent cigars?" He rode off, laughing.

Case dawdled until the posse and Rogers left before he slipped back to town and headed home to clean up. He had another task to do.

But first he had to meet the noon stage.

* * *

Rayne took a deep breath before she knocked on O'Malley's door. The summons she had received earlier had sounded urgent. She silently prayed no harm had befallen her father. She could think of no other reason why Case would send for her, stressing it was imperative that she come immediately. Expecting Hung Lee to admit her, Rayne blinked in surprise when Case himself answered the door.

She flicked her eyes over him, trying not to notice how unbearably handsome he was, determined to hide the emotions that roiled through her at his nearness. She swept past him. "Where's Papa? Has something happened to him?"

Case laughed and closed the door behind her. "Something has happened, yes. I sincerely hope good will come of it, and that you'll forgive me for acting presumptuously."

Rayne gripped her reticule tighter, and met his penetrating green gaze. "Spit it out, Case."

"I have a surprise for you, Rayne." He motioned toward the front room, smiling warmly. "See for yourself."

Unease filled her as she walked slowly to the closed doors. She didn't like surprises, especially when the perpetrator grinned devilishly and seemed inordinately pleased with himself. She opened the doors.

Her mother and father stood in the middle of the room, *kissing*.

"Mama!" Rayne broke into a run and flung her arms around the petite woman. "What are you doing in Virginia City?"

Holding her daughter away, Mary North replied, "Mr. O'Malley sent for me and wired me the money to come. He's a very generous and kind man, Rayne."

Her eyes moist, Rayne looked over her shoulder at Case. She had witnessed his generosity and compassion before, but this latest deed staggered her. "He is most kind indeed. Why, he never mentioned a word about asking you here."

Case shrugged. "It was nothing. Come along, Jasper. It's time we went to the mine. I'm sure Rayne and Mary have a lot of catching up to do."

Jasper dropped a quick kiss on her mother's cheek before he said to Rayne, "Your mother has forgiven me, though it's more than I deserve."

"Oh, Papa. This is wonderful news."

"She's agreed to stay and see if we can make a go of it." Jasper shuffled his feet, a flush creeping up his neck. "I gave her my word I wouldn't fail her again." He embraced Rayne, whispering, "Have you made any headway in taming Case?"

Rayne shook her head.

"He'll come around. I know it."

Jasper followed Case from the room. Rayne took her mother's arm and led her to the settee by the window, where she noticed tea had been set out on a lovely silver tray. She held her mother's hand, patting it affectionately. "I can't believe you actually came."

"Mostly I missed you. I believe your father is sincere in trying to mend his ways. Oh, Rayne, I'm so happy."

Rayne's eyes opened wide.

"Your Mr. O'Malley is quite the handsomest man I've ever seen. From the way he looks at you,

I know he's madly in love with you. Do you feel the same for him, dear?"

Rayne sucked in her breath and said softly, "I love him something fierce, Mama."

"Well, then, my fondest wish has been granted. He's certainly a gentleman, and rich, too."

"It's not his wealth I love, Mama, but the man himself."

"I'm pleased to hear it. He seems quite exceptional to me."

"I don't understand him, though."

Mary leaned forward, touching Rayne's cheek. "You just tell me what's troubling you and I'll try to make it right."

"If only you could." Encouraged by her mother's sympathetic smile, Rayne told her everything that had happened, leaving out the intimate details. "What would you do?" she asked when she'd finished.

"Quite simply, I'd wrap my arms around him and never let go. You'll not find a man like him again, Rayne. I got the impression that he's ready to settle down."

"What makes you say that?"

"Oh, I don't know. A look in his eyes, I suppose. Give him the time he needs."

"I love him so much."

"He has offered to sell me and Jasper this house if I remain in Virginia City," Mary said, giving Rayne's arm a squeeze.

Dumbstruck, Rayne kept silent for several seconds before she could ask, "Did Case say where he planned to live?"

Mary smiled and pointed out the front window. "I believe he mentioned A Street. He said there's an even better house to be had, a mansion, I believe, and that he'd be a fool to pass up the opportunity."

Case O'Malley was no fool; of that, Rayne was certain. His actions were, however, peculiar. He had built this house and furnished it beautifully. She didn't dare give credence to the thought that was forming in her mind.

As she read the latest edition of the *Territorial Enterprise* that evening, Rayne's hands shook. According to Samuel Clemens's account, hijackers had attempted to steal gold meant for the Union. Paul Devereau had not only been apprehended as their ringleader, but additional charges of attempted murder were being held against him as well. And the town seemed satisfied that the small cache of southern sympathizers had been routed.

The news devastated Rayne. She had thought Paul an honorable, impoverished southern gentleman. She would never condemn him if he had stolen the gold for the southern cause, which he always boasted about. But the article stated that all along he had intended to line his own pockets, not help the South.

Although Case's name wasn't mentioned, she knew without a doubt that he had been involved in the entrapment of the hijackers.

He was a hero.

The next night, after she returned to her room from the assayer's office, a boy delivered a yellow rose to her door. Although she found no note, she knew the flower had come from Case.

In the days that followed, other presents began to arrive, all lavishly extravagant. She returned the diamond bracelets and pins, keeping only the flowers. Then, on the fifth night, a note finally came, an invitation to attend the opera, along with the same diamond necklace he'd given her earlier.

Rayne penned an acceptance to his invitation and hurried to dress. She donned the green dress Case had sketched her wearing, the one she'd worn the first night they'd made love.

He knocked on her door before she'd managed to hook the necklace. Her fingers trembled. She wet her dry lips, smoothed her hair, and took a deep breath before she swung open the door. The sight of him in evening attire made her senses reel.

"Come in," she managed to say.

"That wouldn't be proper, Rayne, considering you have no chaperone."

"Since when has propriety bothered *you*, Case O'Malley?"

He arched a dark eyebrow, his mouth lifting on one side. "Perhaps you haven't noticed, but I've abandoned my former ways."

She touched a finger to the black satin binding on his lapel. "You can dress a wolf in lamb's wool, but underneath is there not still a wolf?"

He grinned. "Even wolves can be trusted on occasion, my dear. That is, if you believe in them enough. Do you, Rayne?"

"Come inside and I'll tell you." Her eyes twinkled with challenge as she stepped back to let him pass.

Case shut the door behind him. He had a look in his eyes that said he would accept any challenge she might throw his way.

She handed him the necklace. "I need help with this, sir, if you would be so obliging."

His fingers felt both cool and hot on her skin as he hooked the clasp. It was the same every time he touched her; shivers of pleasure danced over her skin. Then his lips touched the back of her neck and Rayne held her breath. Wildfire swept through her.

He slipped her gown off one shoulder, and placed a searing, passionate kiss against her bare skin. "I love you."

Rayne tilted her head and gazed up at him. "I never doubted that."

He turned her in his arms. "I've done a lot of thinking. I can't lose you."

Cupping his face in her hands, she sighed. "I suppose I have to accept that there will always be some woman pining for you."

"And I suppose there will always be a Paul Devereau wanting to steal you away from me."

"You tried to warn me about him. I see it now. It's still hard to believe I was so wrong about him."

"Maybe next time you'll listen to me," he said, kissing her brow.

Rayne lowered her eyes to his waistcoat. "I love you, Case. Must we go to some silly opera? We could stay here instead."

"And have it said that I spent the night in a hotel room with the woman I plan to marry? Never."

Her eyes met his. "What did you say?"

"You heard me. I'm asking you to marry me. That is, if you'll have me?"

She wrapped her arms around his neck, press-

ing her lips against his throat. "Yes. A thousand
times, yes!"

"A very wise decision, my dear. I am considered
to be an extraordinarily good catch."

Rayne giggled and nipped his ear with her
teeth. "Lucky for you I have a weakness for conceited rogues."

"You've returned all of my gifts, Rayne, except
for the flowers." Case dug in his pocket, then held
his closed hand in front of her face. "Will you refuse this, also?"

He opened his hand to reveal a ring set in gold
with seven emeralds surrounding a dazzling diamond.

Rayne gasped, her heart brimming with love as
he slipped the ring on her finger. "Good heavens.
How did you ever find such a wondrous—"

"I have my ways. I am not only a good catch,
but also very, very rich." Case laughed and
brushed his lips over hers. "I gather this is one gift
you'll accept?"

Rayne wiggled her fingers and smiled. "Yes."
Grazing her nails along his finely chiseled jaw, she
said, "Thank you for bringing my mother here.
You've made her and my father very happy. And
me, too."

"I hope things work out for them."

"It will. I'm sure of it. Which reminds me, Case.
Why did you agree to sell your house?"

Crushing her in his arms, he smiled. "Because I
want my wife to live in a grand mansion with all
the nabobs, where she can look down over the city
knowing her husband places her above anything
else life has to offer."

As his head lowered and his mouth closed over hers, Rayne whispered, "Case O'Malley, you're more precious to me than all the gold and silver in the Comstock."

Epilogue

Virginia City, Summer 1864

The christening of Briana Christine O'Malley sparked much interest in Virginia City. Invitations were limited to friends of the family, but guests and curious onlookers filled St. Mary's of the Mountain Catholic Church to capacity. An hour after the ceremony, a large crowd still lingered outside the church.

Standing beside her husband, Rayne peeked at the delicate silver watch Case had recently given her. They were expecting a few guests to come to their house afterward for refreshments, but if they dallied any longer, she and Case would not be there to greet them. She should have expected that someone would demand Case's attention.

She looked up at him and sighed. Case was in his element, surrounded by well-wishing friends, charming them all, especially the women. In some ways her handsome rascal of a husband hadn't changed. He still flirted with every female he met. And now there was a special girl in his life—their six-week-old daughter. Cradled in his arms, swaddled in a white lace blanket crocheted by her grandmother, Briana O'Malley was already as popular as her proud father.

Briana also had Case's dark hair, and her eyes looked as if they would turn green. She was her father's child, all right; not even out of the cradle and already she had enchanted everyone. Case rarely let her out of his sight. If Rayne didn't take her husband in hand soon, their little girl would be spoiled rotten before she said her first word.

Rayne cleared her throat and tapped Case's arm. "May I take my daughter now?" When he leaned down to hand over the baby, she whispered, "If you are finished showing off, and can tear yourself away from your admirers, I think we need to go home to see to our guests."

Flashing her a devastating grin, he whispered back, "Your obedient servant, Mrs. O'Malley. After they leave, however, I have every intention of—"

Rayne deliberately stepped on Case's booted foot to shut him up.

He chuckled, then announced, "Ladies, I regret we must take our daughter home. The air remains a bit cool for her delicate age."

"Such a considerate man," remarked a matronly woman.

"It's plain to see you're quite the doting father," said another. "Little Briana will be the queen of the Comstock one day."

Case stood straighter, basking in their compliments. "It's kind of you to say so, Mrs. Weems, but I believe your position is safe until then."

Mrs. Weems blushed and waved a bejeweled hand at him. "Case O'Malley, marriage hasn't changed you one iota. You're still the most charming man in these parts."

Shaking her head, Rayne watched Father Patrick Manogue, Jasper, and Mary push their way through the crowd. Her father looked so dignified in his gray, striped coat and dark pants. Her mother's appearance had drastically changed, too. Never before did she remember her mother's eyes sparkling as they did now. Jasper's reformation, attentiveness, and good fortune had relieved her of the burden she'd endured for so long. Her loving heart had forgiven her wayward husband, and they seemed to be as in love now as when they first met.

Mary reached them first. "Your father and I are going to the house to see that Hung Lee has everything in order."

"Thank you, Mama. It appears we will be a few minutes more."

Her mother gave her a sympathetic smile, then allowed her husband to lead her down the street.

The priest eyed the gathering. "If all you good people were to attend mass every Sunday with such enthusiasm, the house of the Lord would be filled to capacity, instead of half-empty."

The gentlemen in the group took charge of their women and quickly steered them down the walk. Father Manogue frowned at their retreating backs.

Case patted him on the shoulder, his eyes brimming with amusement. "They probably thought you intended to go into one of your tediously long sermons, Patrick."

Rayne slipped her arm through the priest's before he could respond. "Come along, Father. Pay him no mind."

Father Manogue made cooing sounds to Briana

as he escorted Rayne to the coach and four Case had ordered specially for the occasion.

Case held Briana as Rayne slid inside the coach, then motioned for the cleric to sit beside her. Seeing Case's scowl, she hid a grin and said, "Pardon Case's manners, Father. He's entirely too possessive and probably thinks you will foul the child by breathing on her."

"Rayne . . ." Case warned.

"Oh, do take a seat, Case. We are already late," she gently reprimanded.

The priest ran a finger inside his collar and clicked his tongue. "I must say, you two are an unorthodox couple."

They were, indeed, Rayne thought. She finally managed to steal her own daughter away from Case for a few minutes; she fussed with Briana's tiny crocheted hat and grazed a finger over her soft cheek. Of all the gifts Case had given her, Briana was the most precious.

She had never thought she would be so happy. She loved her husband to distraction, and relished taunting him. Remembering the time he'd spent under her care, confined to bed, made her smile. Case was still prone to bearish behavior whenever he wasn't happy with a situation, but soothing him always led to other things, usually making love. Unfortunately, that had not been the case for the past three months, but he hadn't complained. Tonight, however, she planned to make up for lost time. Her virile husband would be loved until he had no strength left.

Several hours later, when only a few guests remained, Rayne fed Briana and then left her in her mother's charge. With a warm feeling, Rayne watched Mary and Jasper whisk off to put the baby to sleep. Her father, to her astonishment, had kept his promise and not stumbled. He no longer stayed out all night or came home drunk and stinking of whiskey and perfume. Of course, her mother had a hand in his success. She'd come to realize, Mary said, that a woman couldn't expect to hold a man on a leash. Jasper frequently visited saloons and watched the card games, but he never gambled and only drank on special occasions.

Rayne saw the last of their friends out, then went to Case's study. She stood outside his door. It was his room of sinful excess, as he called it, and women were strictly forbidden. Since it was usually rife with cigar smoke, she didn't mind this restriction. The only vice she'd asked him to forgo was women. Although he continued to charm every female in sight, and he probably always would, she knew he was faithful to her. Case O'Malley always honored his word.

Rayne walked in to find Case talking with Bessie Magovern and Johnny Harkins. "Bess and Johnny are leaving town." Case paused to grin broadly. "Getting hitched."

Rayne was not entirely surprised by this news and congratulated them warmly. Their glowing faces told her they were in love.

Bessie handed her bulging reticule to Johnny, then hugged Rayne. "We'll miss both of ya."

"Where are you going?" Rayne asked.

"Don't know yet. Been tryin' to get enough money together to leave for some time. Case . . ." Tears flooded her eyes, forcing her to snatch a hankie from Johnny's pocket. "Case is so sweet to help us."

Case came from behind his desk and, with an arm around each of his friends, saw them into the hall. "It's nothing. Besides, what are friends for? Now, you be sure to let me know where you settle and how you're doing. Okay?"

Rayne listened to the farewells. Case was entirely too free with his wealth, she thought with a smile. The incorrigible scoundrel had probably set them up for life! It was only one of many reasons why she adored him.

Despite his generosity, though, he was a shrewd businessman. He still sent bullion to the Union, but he wisely realized that the Comstock's precious ore would not last forever. While some miners continued to haul out gold and silver as fast as possible, the O'Malley-North Mine had cut production to prolong the inevitable. Also, Case had begun to invest in various ventures in San Francisco in order to secure their future.

A warm caress at her neck startled her; strong arms banded around her waist. Rayne settled against Case's broad chest with a sigh.

"We're finally alone," he said, his voice husky. "I thought they'd never leave. Where's my daughter?"

"Sleeping."

"Has she been fed?"

"Yes, darling, she has."

"Good." His hands drifted up her sides and slid over her breasts. "I've been waiting all day—hell, for three months—to have some time alone with you."

Rayne laughed. "I planned to surprise you with the news that it's okay for us to resume marital relations, but you seem to know that already. I

should have known you would have been count-
ing the days." Shivers of pleasure skipped over
her from the pressure of his hands. "You are a
lusty man, Case O'Malley. How did you know it
was all right to— Oh! My goodness, you *are* impa-
tient. Do you think it's decent to have your hand
under my dress at this early hour?"

"I locked the door," he said. Slowly he turned
her in his arms and faced her. "As for the other, I
asked Dr. Connell."

"You didn't! Heavens, how will I ever look him
in the eye again?"

Case laughed and pulled her against him. "Oh,
I think the good doctor knows what mischief we
do between the sheets."

"Surely the man has no inkling of how demanding a husband you are."

Nibbling her neck, he cupped her bottom, drawing her closer. Suddenly he lifted his head and met
her gaze. "Dr. Connell was right, wasn't he? You
are healed enough? If not, I can wait awhile
longer."

She couldn't help but giggle when she saw his
strained expression. Judging by the hard bulge
pressing against her stomach, he'd just told a lie.
"I'm fine, Case. The doctor said I'm fit as a fiddle,
and I am. Lord Almighty! I thought he was referring to my health when all along he meant *that*."

Case reached into his coat and withdrew a box
with a dainty yellow bow. "I have a little something for you to thank you for my daughter. I
saved it until today."

"Case O'Malley, you shouldn't have."

"Of course I should. I love you very much, you
know."

Rayne tore open the ribbon and peeked inside the box. With a lump in her throat she fingered a diamond brooch that boasted two brilliant emeralds.

"The diamonds represent you, Rayne."

"And the emeralds? What do they signify?"

"My eyes are green, my dear wife, in case you hadn't noticed. It means that I'll have eyes only for you, from now until eternity."

Speechless, Rayne held Case's gift against her heart. After a moment, she dipped her hand into a pocket in her dove gray gown. Before he could guess her intention, she pinned an extravagant diamond cluster pin on his lapel.

"What the devil?" he said, tilting his head to examine the pin.

"I ordered it special." Her arms crept around his neck, her lips sliding sensually up his throat. "You, my darling, will always be a bit of a rogue. It's only fitting that you look like one."

True to his reputation, Rayne found he'd skillfully opened her gown to her waist without her noticing. She sucked in her breath and held it as he bared first one, then both of her shoulders. Pressing his lips to her skin, he asked, "How long do you think Briana will sleep?"

He didn't wait for an answer. Instead Case swept her dress to the floor. Passion flared in his green gaze. He tore off his coat, tossed it across the room, then worked feverishly on the buttons of his shirt.

"You are a wicked man even to consider making love here, at this hour, with my parents just upstairs."

"Indeed," he muttered. His shirt joined the coat.

"What we don't finish now, we'll finish later. Quite thoroughly, I might add."

The deep tone of his voice sent a wave of desire coursing through her. She explored his bare chest with her hands. She watched him open the waist of his pants. His gaze locked with hers for a moment, stilling the movement of his fingers. She swore she saw flashes of fire in the green depths of his eyes when she finally said, "Can you hurry just a bit?"

Crushing her in his embrace, Case let his laughter mingle with his potent kiss, making her head reel. She felt an enormous explosion rock through her. Or was it deep in the earth? Right now she could not care if the ground gave way. When Case held her in his arms and kissed her, he took her to heaven.

Avon Romances—
the best in exceptional authors and unforgettable novels!

MONTANA ANGEL   **Kathleen Harrington**
77059-8/ $4.50 US/ $5.50 Can

EMBRACE THE WILD DAWN   **Selina MacPherson**
77251-5/ $4.50 US/ $5.50 Can

VIKING'S PRIZE   **Tanya Anne Crosby**
77457-7/ $4.50 US/ $5.50 Can

THE LADY AND THE OUTLAW   **Katherine Compton**
77454-2/ $4.50 US/ $5.50 Can

KENTUCKY BRIDE   **Hannah Howell**
77183-7/ $4.50 US/ $5.50 Can

HIGHLAND JEWEL   **Lois Greiman**
77443-7/ $4.50 US/ $5.50 Can

TENDER IS THE TOUCH   **Ana Leigh**
77350-3/ $4.50 US/ $5.50 Can

PROMISE ME HEAVEN   **Connie Brockway**
77550-6/ $4.50 US/ $5.50 Can

A GENTLE TAMING   **Adrienne Day**
77411-9/ $4.50 US/ $5.50 Can

SCANDALOUS   **Sonia Simone**
77496-8/ $4.50 US/ $5.50 Can